EVA GARCÍA SÁENZ

THE SILENCE OF THE WHITE CITY

Eva García Sáenz de Urturi was born in Vitoria and
has been living in Alicante since she was fifteen years
old. She published her first novel, *La saga de los longe-
vos* (*The Immortal Collection*), in 2012, and it became
a sales phenomenon in Spain, Latin America, the
United States, and the United Kingdom. She is also
the author of *Los hijos de Adán* (*The Sons of Adam*)
and the historical novel *Pasaje a Tahití* (*Passage to
Tahiti*). In 2016 she published the first installment
of the White City Trilogy, titled *El silencio de la ciudad blanca* (*The Silence of the White City*), followed by
Los ritos del agua (*The Water Rituals*) and *Los señores
del tiempo* (*The Lords of Time*). She is married and has
two children.

ALSO BY EVA GARCÍA SÁENZ

The White City Trilogy
The Water Rituals
The Lords of Time

The Ancient Family Saga
The Immortal Collection
The Sons of Adam

Other Novels
Passage to Tahiti

THE SILENCE OF THE WHITE CITY

THE
SILENCE
OF THE
WHITE
CITY

EVA GARCÍA SÁENZ

Translated from the Spanish
by Nick Caistor

VINTAGE BOOKS
A Division of Penguin Random House LLC
New York

TETON COUNTY LIBRARY
JACKSON, WYOMING

A VINTAGE CRIME/BLACK LIZARD ORIGINAL, JULY 2020

Translation copyright © 2020 by Penguin Random House LLC

All rights reserved. Published in the United States
by Vintage Books, a division of Penguin Random House LLC, New York,
and distributed in Canada by Penguin Random House Limited, Toronto.
Originally published in Spain as *El silencio de la ciudad blanca* by
Editorial Planeta S.A., Barcelona, in 2016,
and subsequently in the United States by Vintage Español,
a division of Penguin Random House LLC, New York, in 2019.
Copyright © 2016 by Eva García Sáenz de Urturi.

Vintage is a registered trademark and Vintage Crime/Black Lizard and
colophon are trademarks of Penguin Random House LLC.

This is a work of fiction. Names, characters, places,
and incidents either are the product of the author's imagination or
are used fictitiously. Any resemblance to actual persons, living or dead,
events, or locales is entirely coincidental.

Library of Congress Cataloging-in-Publication Data
Name: García Saénz, Eva, 1972– author.
Title: The silence of the white city / Eva García Saénz ;
translated from the Spanish by Nick Caistor.
Description: New York : Vintage Crime/Black Lizard, 2020.
Identifiers: LCCN 2019058952 (print) | LCCN 2019058953 (ebook)
Classification: LCC PQ6707.A7325 S5413 2020 (print) |
LCC PQ6707.A7325 (ebook) | DDC 863/.7—dc23
LC record available at https://lccn.loc.gov/2019058952

Vintage Crime/Black Lizard Trade Paperback ISBN: 978-1-9848-9859-3
eBook ISBN: 978-1-9848-9860-9

Map illustrations © Gradual Maps
Book design by Elizabeth A. D. Eno

www.vintagebooks.com

Printed in the United States of America
10 9 8 7 6 5 4 3 2 1

TETON COUNTY LIBRARY
JACKSON, WYOMING

To my grandfather. For any number of reasons.

[The] world needs bad men. We keep the other bad men from the door.

—RUST COHLE, *True Detective*

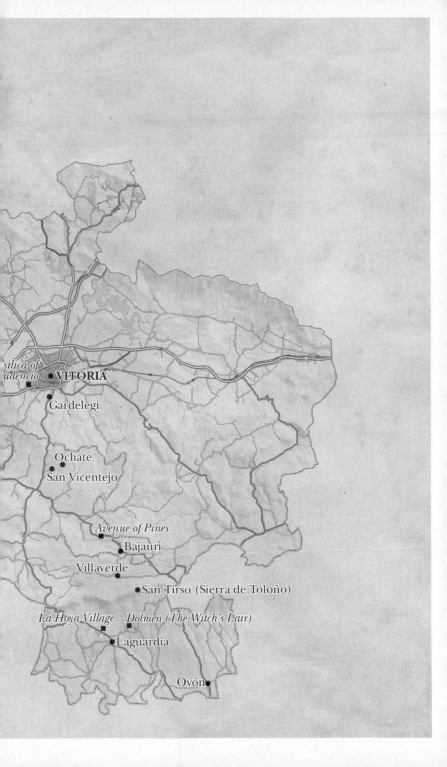

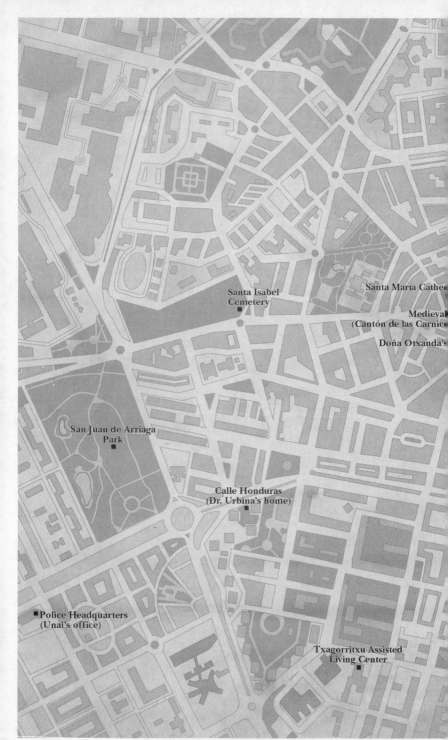

Santa Isabel
Cemetery

Santa María Cathe

Medieval
(Cantón de las Carnice

Doña Otxanda's

San Juan de Arriaga
Park

Calle Honduras
(Dr. Urbina's home)

Police Headquarters
(Unai's office)

Txagorritxu Assisted
Living Center

Villa Suso Palace

Casa del
Cordón
(~ría, 24)

Plaza del Machete

The Arquillos

Calle San Prudencio

Calle Dato, 1
(Tasio's home)

El Caminante
Statue

Triumph
~ria

Calle Dato, 2
(Ignacio's home)

~ntón de
Soledad

General Álava, 2
(Blanca's Apartment)

Niche of the
~rgen Blanca
(San Miguel
~gel Church)

Florida Park

Plaza de la
~gen Blanca, 2
~Unai's home)

New Cathedral
(María Inmaculada Cathedral)

Paseo de la Senda

Armory Museum

Palacio de Justicia

Monte de la Tortilla ∎

Prado Park

Duende Underpass

THE SILENCE OF THE WHITE CITY

PROLOGUE

VITORIA
AUGUST 2016

The TV crews were obsessed with hounding my oldest friends in the *cuadrilla*. They needed a headline and were convinced those closest to me could supply it. From the moment the news broke that the killer had shot me, reporters chased them all over Vitoria: from then on, nobody got any peace.

Posted on their doorsteps at the crack of dawn. They lingered at Saburdi's on Calle Dato for a few quiet tapas in the evening. At the time, no one felt like talking, and the unrelenting media presence didn't help.

"We're sorry about what happened to Inspector Ayala. Are you going to the demonstration this afternoon?" one reporter asked, brandishing a newspaper with the story splashed across the front page. A large photograph competed with the headline.

The big, dark-haired guy trying unsuccessfully to hide his face from the cameras in the image was me, a few days before the shooting.

My female friends lowered their eyes; my male ones turned their backs to the cameras.

"We're in shock," Jota finally blurted out, draining his glass of red wine. "Life isn't fair; it's not fair."

Maybe he thought the journalists would be satisfied with that and stop harassing them, but just at that moment they spotted Germán, my brother. He was impossible to miss: only four feet tall, his dwarfism made him obvious to everyone. Germán tried to escape to the restrooms. The reporter, a veteran with a thousand scoops under his belt, alerted the cameramen as soon as he spotted him.

"That's his brother. After him!"

My brother turned around before he slammed the door in the man's face, and that gesture appeared on all the national TV channels that night.

"Go to hell" was all he said. He wasn't angry or offended. Simply exhausted.

I know everyone in Vitoria was stunned by the fact that I had been shot in the head, and if thinking hadn't been a physical impossibility just then, it would have moved me to tears.

A policeman never expects to close a case by becoming the final victim of a serial killer who has plunged his city into a state of terror, but life has sly ways of playing tricks on you.

So . . . yes, things didn't turn out too well for me. As I say, I ended up with a bullet in my brain. But maybe I should start by telling the story of what, at first, became known as the "double crime of the dolmen" and, in the end, turned out to be a massacre carefully planned for many years by a criminal mind boasting an IQ far higher than those who were trying to stop him.

When the person killing one victim after another is a damned genius, you can only hope your number doesn't pop out of the golden lottery drum for the little orphan to sing out in his quavering voice.

1

THE OLD CATHEDRAL

Sunday, July 24

I was enjoying the best Spanish tortilla in the world, the egg still runny and the potatoes cooked but firm, when I took the call that changed my life. For the worse, I should add.

It was the eve of El Día de Santiago, and in Vitoria we were celebrating El Día de la Blusa, an homage to the youngsters who enlivened the early-August celebrations by wearing traditional smocks. The bar where I was trying to finish my tasty snack was so crowded and noisy that when I realized my cell phone was vibrating in my shirt pocket, I had to go out into Calle del Prado.

"What's wrong, Estíbaliz?"

My partner didn't usually bother me on my days off, and El Día de la Blusa and the evening before were too sacred for anyone to even think about going to work. The entire city was in a state of commotion.

At first, the noise of the brass bands and the flood of people following them prevented my hearing what Estíbaliz was trying to say.

"Unai, you have to come to the Old Cathedral," she insisted.

Her tone of voice, and the undercurrent of urgency and bewilderment, struck me as odd. Estíbaliz has more guts than me, and that's saying something.

I understood immediately that something serious must have happened.

Trying to get away from the ever-present racket that was engulfing the city, I walked automatically toward La Florida Park so that our conversation could be at least minimally productive.

"What happened?" I asked, trying to shake off the effects of the last glass of Rioja.

"You won't believe it. It's exactly the same as twenty years ago."

"What are you talking about, Estí? I'm not at my sharpest today."

"Some archaeologists from the company restoring the cathedral found two naked corpses in the crypt. A boy and a girl, with their hands resting on each other's cheek. You remember that, don't you? Come right now, Unai. This is serious, very serious." She told me where to find her and ended the call.

It can't be, I thought.

It can't be.

I didn't even say good-bye to my friends in the *cuadrilla.* They were going to stay in Sagartoki's, in the midst of that flood of humans. It was unlikely any of them would even pay attention to their phone if I called to say that El Día de la Blusa was over for me.

With my colleague's words echoing in my brain, I headed for the Plaza de la Virgen Blanca. I passed my own doorway and went up Calle de la Correría, one of the oldest streets in the medieval heart of the city.

It was a bad choice. Like everywhere else in the city center that day, it was packed. La Malquerida and the other bars lining the Old City were crammed with locals. It took me more than fifteen minutes to reach La Burullería Square, at the rear of the cathedral, where I'd agreed to meet Estíbaliz.

In the fifteenth century, the square had been the market of the *burulleros,* or weavers, who made the city one of the main trading arteries in northern Spain, and it had retained their name. As I walked across the cobblestones, the bronze statue of Ken Follett seemed to watch me go by, as if the writer had anticipated the dark web of intrigue being spun around us.

Estíbaliz Ruiz de Gauna, my colleague and fellow inspector in the Criminal Investigation Unit, was waiting in the square, making a thousand phone calls, darting back and forth like a lizard. Her red hair framed her face. At five feet two inches tall, she just met the height requirement to join the force. Had Estí been any shorter, Vitoria would have lost one of its finest, most tenacious detectives.

We were both damned good at solving cases, although we weren't quite as good at playing by the rules. We had received more than one warning for disobedience, and so we'd learned to cover ourselves. As for following orders, we were working on it.

We were working on it.

I turned a blind eye to some of the addictions that still slipped into Estí's life. She looked the other way when I disobeyed my superiors and investigated on my own.

My specialty was criminal profiling, so I was usually called in when we had a case involving a serial killer or rapist—any delinquent who reoffended. If there were more than three events with a cooling-off period between them, I was your man.

Estíbaliz specialized in victimology, that great forgotten science. Why *that* person, and not someone else? She was also better than anyone at using the police databases, like the one that compiled the treads of every imaginable vehicle, or SoleMate, a guide to the footprints left by all the international makes and brands of shoes and sneakers.

As soon as she saw me, she hung up her cell phone and looked at me, distraught.

"What's inside the cathedral?" I asked.

"You'd better see for yourself," she whispered, as if the heavens—or perhaps hell—could hear us, who knew? "Super-intendent Medina himself called me. They want a profiling expert like you, and they've called me in to examine the victims. You'll soon see why. I want you to tell me your first impression. The crime-scene techs are already here, and so are the pathologist and the judge. Let's go in via Cuchi."

Calle Cuchillería was one of the ancient streets where the guilds had been established in the Middle Ages. Vitoria could boast an indelible record of our ancestors' trades: La Herrería for black-smiths, La Zapatería for shoemakers, La Correría for ropemakers, La Pintorería for the dyers' guild. Despite the passage of centuries, the city's medieval core was still intact.

Oddly enough, from Calle Cuchillería you could enter the cathedral through what looked like the doorway to an ordinary dwelling.

There were already two uniforms guarding the heavy wooden door at Number 85. They saluted and let us in.

"I've questioned the two archaeologists who found them," my colleague said. "They came today to try to make some headway with their work: the Santa María Cathedral Foundation is pressur-ing them to finish the crypt and the vault this year. They left us the keys. As you can see, the lock is intact. It hasn't been forced."

"They came to work on the eve of El Día de Santiago? Isn't that slightly . . . unusual for people from Vitoria?"

"I didn't notice anything strange about their reactions, Unai." Estí shook her head. "They were shocked, or rather horrified. Hor-ror like that isn't faked."

All right, I thought. I trusted Estíbaliz's judgment the way the back wheel of a bicycle trusts the front wheel. That's how we functioned; that's how we pedaled along.

We went in through the restored porch. My colleague closed the door behind us, and the noise of the festivities finally faded.

Until that moment, the news that two dead bodies had been found hadn't really hit me; it had been too much at odds with the joyful, carefree atmosphere all around. But in that cloistered silence, with the archaeologists' lamps dimly lighting the wooden staircase down to the crypt, it all seemed more plausible. And not exactly welcome.

"Here, put on a helmet." Estíbaliz handed me one of the white helmets bearing the foundation's logo that every tourist visiting the cathedral was obliged to wear. "With your height, you're bound to bump your head."

"I'll be fine without it," I said, busy peering around the room.

"It's mandatory," she insisted, holding out the white monstrosity to me again and brushing the edge of my hand with her fingertips.

This game we played had one very clear rule: So far and no further. In fact, there was a complementary one: Don't ask; that's far enough. I figured that two years without going any further constituted a status quo, an established code of conduct, and Estíbaliz and I got along very well. It was also true that she was busy with her wedding preparations, and I had been widowed for several— Well, that doesn't matter.

"You're going soft," I muttered, but took the plastic helmet.

We climbed the curving staircase, leaving behind the models of the village of Gasteiz, the first settlement that had become the foundation of the city. Estíbaliz had to stop once more to find the right key to the door that would take us to the inner area of the Old Cathedral, one of our city's symbols. It had been restored and patched up more often than my childhood bike. A sign reading OPEN greeted us on the right.

I knew all my region's emblems. They had been stored in my

memory ever since the double crime of the dolmen had thrown the people of Vitoria into a panic twenty years and four months earlier.

The dolmen, known as the Witch's Lair; the Celtic village at La Hoya; the Roman salt pans at Añana; the medieval wall—those were the sites a serial killer had chosen that put Vitoria and the province of Álava on the world news map. And the morbid fascination created by his macabre staging of the murders had led to the establishment of tourist trails throughout the region.

I was almost twenty when it happened; my obsession with the killings became the main reason I joined the police. I followed the investigation day after day, with an anxiety that only a single-minded young person could understand. I analyzed what little appeared in *El Diario Alavés* and thought: *I can do better. They're being stupid. They're forgetting the most important thing: the* why. Although I wasn't even twenty, I thought I was smarter than the police. How naive that seems now.

Soon afterward, the truth hit me in the face harder than a boxer's fist. I was stunned, just like all of Spain. No one expected Tasio Ortiz de Zárate to be guilty. I wouldn't have cared if it had been anyone else: my neighbor, a Poor Clare nun, the baker, the mayor. I wouldn't have cared.

But not Tasio, our local hero who was more than an idol: he was a role model, a TV archaeologist who starred in a show that won record ratings each season, the author of books of history and mythology that sold out in weeks. Tasio was the most charismatic, entrancing character that Vitoria had produced in decades. Intelligent and, in the unanimous view of Vitoria's women, very attractive. And duplicated.

Yes, duplicated.

We had two to choose from. Tasio had a monozygotic twin, and they were identical down to the way they cut their fingernails. Indistinguishable. An optimist like him, from a good family, cheerful, full of fun, cultured, well-mannered. At the age of twenty-four, the brothers had Vitoria at their feet and a future that was generally expected to be beyond stellar, stratospheric.

His twin, Ignacio, leaned toward the law. He became a policeman in the tough ETA years and was the most honest man we'd ever had in the force. Nobody ever imagined things would end up the way they did between them. Everything, and I mean *everything,* was too sordid and cruel.

Ignacio uncovered irrefutable proof that his twin was the most wanted and, later, most studied serial killer since Spain had returned to democracy. Ignacio arrested Tasio, even though until that moment they had been as inseparable as conjoined twins. Ignacio became the man of the year, a hero worthy of our respect, the person brave enough to face the consequences and do what few of us would have ever done: hand over his own flesh and blood to a life behind bars.

As I stood in the cathedral, my reverie led to a disturbing thought: Our two local newspapers—*El Diario Alavés* and its bitter rival, *El Correo Vitoriano*—never ceased reminding their readers that Tasio Ortiz de Zárate would be leaving prison soon, released on parole after twenty years. And at that very moment, the city with the lowest crime rate in the north of Spain was adding two corpses to its ghastly scoreboard.

I shook my head, as if that could clear the phantoms from my brain. I forced myself not to draw conclusions until later and to focus on what we had in front of us.

When we entered the recently restored crypt, I had to duck because the ceiling was so low. The space still smelled of recently sawn wood. I stepped cautiously across the polished gray flagstones, so perfectly rectangular they could only have been made in the twenty-first century by a machine. It seemed a shame to get them dirty. Two thick columns in front of us did their best to support the heavy weight of the centuries: the original foundations of the old, buckling cathedral.

When I saw the two lifeless bodies lying there, I felt the need to retch rise from the pit of my stomach, but I resisted.

I resisted.

The crime techs in their white plastic suits and overshoes had been examining the area for some time. They had brought in lamps to shed some light in the dark crypt, and it seemed they had finished photographing the scene. Estíbaliz asked for a sketch, studied it closely for a while, then passed it to me.

"Tell me they're not twenty years old, Estíbaliz," I begged her.

Any other age, but not twenty.

The previous serial killer had stopped at fifteen-year-olds: four naked couples, female and male, each affectionately laying the palm of one hand on the other's cheek in an incongruously gentle gesture. Nobody had ever been able to explain this placement, especially since it was reported that none of the victims knew each other. They all had double-barreled names that originated in the Álava region: López de Armentia, Fernández de Retana, Ruiz de Arcaute, García de Vicuña, Martínez de Guereñu . . .

On the dolmen known as the Witch's Lair, near the village of Elvillar, the lifeless bodies of two newborn babies had been discovered. Shortly afterward, in the remains of the Celtic-Iberian settlement of La Hoya de Laguardia, a boy and a girl aged five were found, their hands comforting each other, their gazes lost in the heavens.

In the Valle Salado at Añana, a prosperous salt pan dating to the time of the Romans, the bodies of a boy and a girl aged ten were found. By the time the crimes reached the city of Vitoria and two dead fifteen-year-olds had appeared close to the gate in the medieval wall, the population was in such a state of psychosis that we twenty-year-olds stayed at home all the time, playing cards with our grandparents. No one dared go out in the streets if they weren't in a big group. It was as if the ages of the victims were progressing according to the chronology of our region's history. It was all very archaeological, very Tasio.

Eventually he was caught. Inspector Ignacio Ortiz de Zárate ordered the arrest of Tasio Ortiz de Zárate, Spain's most famous and well-loved archaeologist. He was put on trial, convicted of the premeditated murder of eight children, and sent to prison.

The grim harvest of young people in Vitoria ceased.

My partner's voice brought me back to the present.

The pathologist, Doctor Guevara, a slender fifty-year-old woman with smooth pink cheeks, was whispering to Judge Olano, a stocky, elderly man with broad shoulders and short legs. One of his feet was pointing to the exit as he listened, as if he couldn't wait to race out of there. We decided not to approach them; they looked as though they didn't want to be disturbed.

"They still haven't been identified," Estíbaliz said in a low voice. "We're matching their descriptions with reports of missing people. Both the male and the female appear to be about twenty years old. Are you thinking what I'm thinking, Kraken?"

She sometimes called me by my adolescent nickname. It was a token of trust that had grown between us.

"It's impossible," I muttered between clenched teeth.

"But it is happening."

"We can't be sure of that," I insisted.

She fell silent.

"We still can't be sure," I repeated, as much to convince myself as anything else. "Let's concentrate on what we have in front of us. Later we can calmly discuss our conclusions in my office, okay?"

"Agreed. What do you see?"

I approached the two bodies, knelt beside them, and whispered my plea:

This is where your hunt ends and mine begins.

"Three *eguzkilores,* flowers of the sun," I said eventually, "laid next to their heads and feet. I can't grasp their meaning in this context yet."

In Basque culture, the *eguzkilore* was an ancient protective symbol hung on the doors of rural homes to prevent witches and demons from entering. Except, in this case, they hadn't worked.

"No, I don't understand what they're doing here, either," said Estíbaliz, crouching beside me. "I'll continue with the victims: Caucasian female and male, both aged twenty or thereabouts. Lying on their backs, naked, on the cathedral floor. No indications of wounds, blows, or any other form of violence. But look: they both have a small pinprick on the side of their neck. An injection. They've both been injected with something."

"We'll have to wait for the toxicology reports," I said. "We'll need to send samples to the forensic lab in Bilbao, to see if they find any drugs or psychotropic substances. Anything else?"

"One hand of each victim is lying on the other's cheek. The pathologist will establish the time of death, but rigor mortis hasn't set in, so I assume they've only been dead a few hours. I'm going to ask the techs to preserve the hands in paper bags. It doesn't look as if they defended themselves, but you never know."

"Come closer," I said. "Do you smell something? It's quite faint, but I'd say there's an odor of gasoline."

"You have a good sense of smell. I hadn't noticed it," she said after sniffing the bodies closely. "We still have to establish the cause of death. Do you think they've been poisoned, as in the earlier cases? Maybe they were forced to swallow gasoline?"

I took a close look at the young woman's face before replying. It was frozen in a rictus of pain. She had suffered as she'd died, and so had the young man. I looked at his hair, recently trimmed on the sides. The forelock was still prominent, stiff from what looked to be expensive hair gel. He had clearly taken care of himself; he was well groomed. She had also been attractive. Her eyebrows were plucked, no blemishes or acne. She belonged to the generation that grew up frequenting beauty parlors.

Little rich kids, I thought. *Just like before.* But then I realized the mistake we were making.

"Estíbaliz," I said, "we have to reset and start again. We're not examining the crime scene with open minds; we've immediately started comparing it to the other scenes. First we need to look at this one in a vacuum. We can compare later."

"But I think that's exactly what the killer or killers want. The staging is identical to the earlier crimes. If you're asking me about the victims, Kraken, I'd say they follow the series from twenty years ago."

"Yes, but there are differences. I don't think they were poisoned. The kind of poison used in the past never appeared in the press. I don't think they died from swallowing gasoline, either. The smell would be much stronger, it would have taken much more of the liquid, and there's no sign of chemical burns. It's as though they had only been in contact with one or two drops."

I bent over the young man's face. It was odd the way his mouth was closed with the lips pressed slightly inward, as if he had been biting them.

I had an idea, so I examined the young woman's face as well.

"They both had tape over their mouths, and it was ripped off. Look."

The rectangular mark from the adhesive tape stuck over their lips had left the skin slightly flushed.

It felt as though the Old Cathedral was staring down at us in horror. Then I thought I heard something.

A faint, annoying buzz.

I signaled for Estíbaliz to be quiet and brought my ear to within an inch of the man's face. What on Earth was that sound?

I closed my eyes and focused on it, on its strangeness, trying to discover where the slight buzzing was loudest. I almost brushed against the tip of the victim's nose, and then I moved down across the orbicularis oris muscle to his lips.

"Do you have a pen?"

My partner took one out of her back pocket, a quizzical look on her face.

I used the tip of the pen to prize open the corner of the victim's mouth. Suddenly, an enraged bee flew out. I fell over backward.

"Shit, a bee!" I yelled from the ground.

Everyone turned to stare at us. The techs looked reprovingly at me for having fallen over so close to the center of the crime scene.

Estíbaliz reacted quickly and tried to catch the bee, but it flew over our heads toward the covered remains of the model of the ancient village. In just a few seconds, it was out of reach.

"We should catch it," said Estíbaliz, watching it escape. "If it is connected to the murder, it could be crucial for the investigation."

"Catch it, in a church that measures ninety-six meters from apse to door? Don't look at me like that," I said when I saw the face she was making. "Whenever a friend comes to visit Vitoria, I bring them for a guided tour of the cathedral."

With a sigh, Estíbaliz turned her attention back to the bodies.

"All right, let's forget the bee for now. Can you discern whether there was a sexual motive?"

"No," I said, approaching the bodies again. "As far as I can tell, the vagina is still intact. We can ask the pathologist. I think she's finished with the judge." In fact, the two were walking toward us.

"Your Honor," said Estíbaliz, pushing up her hair under her helmet.

"Good evening, if you'll pardon the expression," said Olano. "My secretary will leave the visual inspection report for you to sign. I've had enough, especially on a holiday."

"You're right there," I muttered.

The judge walked quickly out of the crypt, leaving us with the pathologist.

"Did you find any biological residue?" I asked.

"We've examined the bodies and sprayed the surrounding area with luminol," she said. "There's no trace of blood. We've also searched for semen, but we didn't find any. We'll have to wait for the autopsy results; they'll be more precise. I'm afraid this is going to be complicated. Do you need anything else, inspectors?"

"No, doctor. Not at the moment," said Estíbaliz by way of good-bye. When the pathologist left, she turned to me: "Well, Unai, what's your read on the staging?"

"They're naked, so there's a definite sexual aspect. By placing their hands in that odd gesture, the killer seems to be suggesting that they are a couple, although I think that was done postmortem, when the killer brought them here and lined up the bodies facing . . ."

Taking my cell phone from my pocket, I opened an app that served as a compass. Bending down again, I took my time until I was sure.

"They're pointing to where the sun rises at the winter solstice," I told her.

"Meaning? I'm not a wild soul who communes with Mother Earth on weekends like you."

"I don't align with any telluric forces. I simply go back to the village to help my grandfather with his farm. If you had a ninety-four-year-old grandfather determined never to retire, you'd do the same. But to answer your question, the bodies are facing northwest."

Like the first double crime at the dolmen, I thought nervously. That much had come out in the press.

But I didn't say it.

I didn't want to appear to contradict myself, and I didn't want Estíbaliz to realize that, despite my attempts to isolate this crime in my mind, I, too, was comparing it to our adolescent terror. She was probably doing the same thing.

The fact was, something was vibrating inside me. I couldn't help thinking that I was breathing the same air the murderer had. That only a few hours earlier, some asshole with an undiagnosed psychopathic illness had stood on the same spot. I peered at the air trapped inside the cathedral as if he had left visible traces in the void. His movements flashed through my mind. How he must have transported the bodies, then placed them in the crypt without leaving any sign. I knew that he was meticulous and that he had done this before.

This display was not his first.

I could picture his face. Could the answer be so simple and yet impossible, a riddle that was solved before it had even been posed?

Estíbaliz was watching, waiting for me to emerge from the mental spirals I occasionally got lost in. She knew me well, and she respected my silences and rituals.

Finally, I straightened up. We looked at each other, and I realized we were ten years older than the pair of detectives who had entered the cathedral only half an hour before.

"All right, Unai, what does your profiler's brain tell you?"

"This person is an organized killer. It's not a random choice. Yet I could swear he didn't know his victims. He turned them into objects. And there's an absolute control of the scene. But what concerns me most is the disconcerting lack of any clues. That coincides with the profile: the murderer has an almost pathological awareness, and that's very worrying."

"What else?" she pressed me. She knew that I hadn't finished, that I was thinking out loud. We often did that; it allowed our thoughts to flow more freely.

"The victims' eyes are wide-open, which means the killer felt no compunction or pity. That's a psychopathic trait."

"Any mixed traits?"

"No, there's not a single trait that would indicate a disorganized killer. Do you know how uncommon that is? Disorganized murderers usually leave behind a scene marked by brutal, explosive violence. There are attacks to the face, or the victims are disfigured. Blows with improvised instruments like sticks or stones. This is different. This guy isn't psychotic; he's more of a psychopath or a sociopath. He's meticulous, he plans ahead, and he doesn't suffer from mental illness, which means that, fortunately for us, he is fully responsible for his acts. What troubles me is the kind of weapon he used, if that's what it is. Bees? That's a fetishistic weapon."

"Objects that normally are not weapons but that have a special meaning for the killer," said Estíbaliz, pondering aloud.

"That's my fear," I said. "We need to check what poison the murderer used twenty years ago. We'll have to ask for the old files when we get back to headquarters. And if we accept that these murders are a continuation of the series of four crimes in 1996, we're talking about a cooling-off period of two decades. When we talk about 'organized serial killers,' the longer the gap, the calmer the psychopath's personality, but statistically we're usually talking about weeks or months. Do you have any idea what it would mean if we're facing someone who can wait twenty years?"

"That's for you to say, Unai. And say it out loud. Because the whole of Vitoria is going to be asking that question in a few hours, as soon as it starts trending all over Spain, and we have to be prepared to answer when the press is on our backs."

I sighed.

"All right. I'll ask the obvious questions. We'll see where that takes us."

"Go on, then."

An idea settled on my left shoulder, like a black butterfly. I knew it with absolute certainty: if I'd had a crystal ball, if I'd known I was going to be put in charge of this case, I would never have become a homicide detective.

It was as clear and undeniable as that.

I would have stayed in Villaverde, sowing wheat with my grandfather.

Because I didn't want to have to face it. Not this. Any other case. For years I had been preparing myself mentally, and until now things had gone well for me. Good statistics, cases solved in a reasonable time frame, congratulations and pats on the back from my superiors. But not this, not with Tasio Ortiz de Zárate involved.

But I had to put it into words, to make it real. I couldn't leave it buzzing annoyingly above our heads.

"All right," I said, giving in, "I'll say it out loud: How on Earth has Tasio committed two more murders with the same signature as the killings that happened twenty years ago, when at this very moment he's locked up in Zaballa? Can a person, however devilish they are, be in two places at the same time?"

2

THE ARQUILLOS

EL DÍA DE SANTIAGO
MONDAY, JULY 25

I was fascinated by the strange symmetry of events. A pair of victims, with ages ending in zero or five . . . a murderer and a policeman identical in all aspects . . . the crimes stopping when Tasio was sent to prison and starting again just as he was about to leave for the first time . . .

I must confess, I didn't sleep that night.

I gave up and got out of bed at six o'clock. Partly because, under my wooden balcony on the Plaza de la Virgen Blanca, people were still celebrating El Día de la Blusa as if there were no tomorrow. And partly because my day looked as if it was going to be complicated: I would have to struggle with the press and listen to instructions from Superintendent Medina. It was going to be a long day stuck at the station, and I needed to get some fresh air to face it.

I put on my running shoes and trotted down the stairs to the doorway separating me from the heart of Vitoria. A couple of years earlier I had found an apartment in the center of the city that I could rent for a good price. A friend who worked at Perales, Vitoria's leading real estate agency, owed me a favor after I expedited a restraining order on an ex-boyfriend who was harassing her. A real asshole.

Begoña was more than grateful. She knew I was looking for a

place to live after what had happened to Paula and the children, so she offered me a bargain on a place before she put the announcement in her firm's window. A newly renovated one-bedroom apartment. Very elderly neighbors, good as gold but deaf as doorknobs. The best views possible for a third-floor apartment, but no elevator. Just for me, no room to share it with anybody else. In other words, perfect.

I raced out onto the street, bumping into waves of people finally making their way home. It almost looked like a procession. They were running out of things to say, and most of them were walking along wearily, some zigzagging into Calle Zapatería, keys in hand.

Escaping from the crowds, I headed for less busy streets. I went down through the square to Calle de la Diputación, continued along Siervas de Jesús, and ran around the entire medieval quarter. Half an hour later I was coming back over Cuesta de San Francisco a second time, feeling fresher and more awake. I turned down along Arquillos—and there she was, the mysterious runner I had been encountering every morning for the past week. The only other person crazy or motivated enough to go running this early.

She never went down narrow alleyways. She kept out of the shadows, seeming to connect the dots between streetlamps, and always ran down the center of the streets. She wore a whistle around her neck. A cautious person. More than that, someone aware of danger. Either she had been attacked, or she was afraid of an attack. And yet, she went out running before dawn every day of the week.

I slowed down when I reached the end of the arcades: I didn't want her to think I was following her. I didn't want to scare her. I wasn't pursuing her, even though this woman, who always wore her dark hair in a long braid under an incongruous baseball cap, intrigued me more than I cared to admit. I turned my attention to a huge poster advertising a musical version of *Moby-Dick* at the Teatro Principal.

Call me Ishmael, I thought, recalling the opening lines of the novel. *Some years ago—never mind how long precisely—having little or no money in my purse, and nothing particular to interest me on shore, I thought I would sail about a little and see the watery part of the world. It is a way I have of driving off the spleen, and regulating the circulation.*

To my surprise, she was the one who broke the ice and snapped me out of my daydream. When she reached the esplanade outside San Miguel Arcángel Church, she stopped by the bronze statue of the Celedón holding his umbrella and raised her leg onto the railing to stretch.

I ran past, politely pretending not to notice her, but she raised her head.

"Aren't you joining the celebrations today?" She laughed, her infectious energy stopping me in my tracks. "Either you're not or you like running too much."

If you only knew, I said to myself.

"Neither, I'm afraid," I said, not wanting to get too involved. "Or maybe both."

I had never seen her close-up. Her thin face had a friendly expression in the streetlamp's feeble glow. It was impossible to make out the color of her eyes, but she was quite tall, with very pale skin. Pleasant, desirable. All that, and yet there was something distant.

"What about you?" I asked, standing a few feet away. "Do you like being different?"

"Perhaps this is the only moment all day that I have to myself."

Either you have family duties or a stressful job. Possibly morning and evening. A lot of overtime, a responsible position, I deduced, but I kept these conclusions to myself.

"I'm glad ours is not a species in danger of extinction," I said. She smiled and came over to me.

"My name is . . . Blanca."

A two-second pause and a quick glance at the Virgen Blanca's niche on the wall opposite us. Too long to tell somebody what your real name is.

Why are you lying?

"What about you?" she asked.

Call me Ishmael.

"Ishmael."

"Ishmael, I see. Well, pleased to meet you, Ishmael. If you're crazy enough to keep running at this time of the morning, I imagine we'll see each other again," said Blanca before running off down the steps.

I stood by the Celedón, watching her go past my doorway and head for La Florida Park.

Two hours later I was pedaling to my office in the Lakua neighborhood, where our new police headquarters was situated in an impressive concrete building. I chained my bike to a rail in the parking lot, took a deep breath, and went in.

What would the day hold for me? What would I be turning over in my mind that night as I tried to go to sleep?

Focus on whatever comes up today, and everything will be fine, I tried to persuade myself, but I didn't believe it.

I climbed the stairs to the second floor. Sitting at my computer, I began to gather all the information we had and to organize my ideas. Then Superintendent Medina knocked twice on the door and came in, grim-faced. The superintendent, a man with thick black eyebrows and a bushy white beard, could be either harsh or understanding, depending on the day.

"Good morning, Inspector Ayala. Have you read this morning's newspapers?"

"I haven't had a chance, sir. Has the war started already?"

"I'm afraid it has." He sighed and tossed me a copy of *El Diario*

Alavés. "Someone leaked the news about the discovery of the bodies in the Old Cathedral. They put out a special edition yesterday evening."

"A newspaper edition that late?" I said, puzzled. "Nobody ever publishes extra editions like that anymore. As far as I know, anything that doesn't get into the morning edition is updated online."

"Exactly. That gives you an idea of how closely *El Diario Alavés* intends to follow this case. It's no surprise. No one on the streets of Vitoria after midnight was talking about anything else. I've already fielded calls from a dozen radio stations and several national television channels. They all want to know what's going on, and they want more details. Come into my office; Inspector Gauna is waiting for us. Deputy Superintendent Díaz de Salvatierra is joining the force today. She's the one you'll be reporting to. Naturally we were all hoping her first day would be calmer, but news is news, as journalists say. Follow me, won't you?"

I agreed, glancing quickly at the newspaper headline: TWO YOUNG ADULTS FOUND DEAD IN THE OLD CATHEDRAL.

I sighed in relief. The headline was simply descriptive, and the tone was surprisingly neutral. It was nothing like the rivaling headlines we'd seen twenty years earlier, when *El Diario Alavés* and *El Correo Vitoriano*'s competition was at its peak.

I must admit I was quite curious about the new deputy superintendent as I walked into the wood-paneled office. New appointments were always guarded like state secrets; there was no point trying to find out about them beforehand. Our superiors kept quiet, and usually no one knew who would be coming in, because they were frequently transferred from other police stations. Estíbaliz was waiting in uniform at the huge conference table. I gazed at the new deputy superintendent and, for a second, didn't know how to react.

"Deputy Superintendent Alba Díaz de Salvatierra, this is Inspector Unai López de Ayala."

Standing in front of me, extending her hand, was an elegant woman in a two-piece suit. She was pretending this was the first time we had met, even though we both knew it wasn't. Because this was the same woman I had met early that morning. The woman who had called herself Blanca.

"Deputy Superintendent," I said as neutrally as I could. "Welcome to Vitoria. I hope you'll enjoy working with us."

She stared at me a fraction of a second longer than required, smiled for her audience, and shook my hand for the second time in less than five hours.

"A pleasure to meet you, Inspector Ayala. I'm afraid we're going to have to hold our first briefing right away."

"Inspector Gauna," said Medina, "do you already have the crime-scene report?"

"I do," said Estíbaliz, getting up and handing out three copies. "I'll summarize: The killer or killers have not left a single fingerprint or palm print. CSU tried every process they could think of. There are no footprints, either. The victims had only been dead a couple of hours when they were deposited in the cathedral crypt. There are no signs of sexual abuse, or of resistance. What we can say, even before the autopsy results come in later today, is that the probable cause of death was asphyxia caused by repeated bee stings in their throats."

"Bees?" said the deputy superintendent. "How did they get there?"

"Inspector Ayala and I found signs that both victims had adhesive tape stuck across their mouths. I think the killer stuffed several bees into their mouths and then taped them up. There was an odor of gasoline around the victims' faces. That kind of smell infuriates bees. It seems as if the killer wanted the bees to sting his victims in the throat so that the swelling in their mucous membranes would block their windpipes and cause death by asphyxiation. To accomplish this, he had to block their nostrils as well. I'm afraid it must have been a very painful death."

I was watching the deputy superintendent out of the corner of my eye. When she heard that, she clenched her teeth.

"What do we know about their identities?" she asked, brushing a lock of hair from her face.

"I wanted to mention that. We're matching their descriptions to recent missing person reports in Vitoria and the province. Until yesterday evening, there were no reported disappearances, but last night's headlines are having an effect. We can expect calls to increase throughout the morning, but they should ease by evening."

"I don't get it."

"Putting it simply, ma'am," Estíbaliz replied, "parents read in last night's special edition that a young man and a young woman were found dead in the Old Cathedral. Last night was the eve of El Día de la Blusa. A lot of twenty-year-olds haven't returned from the celebrations yet. Now it's eleven a.m. Parents have grown hysterical, calling their children's cell phones and getting no response. It's normal for young people to switch off their phones at night or to simply not reply. Then they tell their parents there was no coverage or that their battery died. The Calle Olaguíbel station house is overflowing with desperate parents who can't locate their children. Our emergency services are struggling to cope. When I last checked, five minutes ago, we had logged almost three hundred calls. We can't officially process them, though, until twenty-four hours have passed without the person appearing. Most of the callers read the news this morning and are worried because their children haven't come home yet. As the day goes on, the kids will return and many of the parents won't bother calling us again to let us know. They'll simply be so relieved they'll want to forget the whole thing as quickly as possible."

"Which gives the killer or killers a precious few hours," I said,

thinking out loud. "It's no coincidence he killed them on the evening before El Día de la Blusa. I think that's precisely what he
wanted: to stay a step ahead of us, and to create this atmosphere of
collective psychosis in the wake of the celebrations."

"First impressions?" asked Deputy Superintendent Díaz de
Salvatierra.

"They're very small," I blurted out.

"What's that?"

"The two victims. Both are very small. And they're not heavily
built."

"So where does that get us? Why do you bring that up, Ayala?"

"Because we always assume the killer is a man. But for the
moment I wouldn't rule out the possibility that it could be a woman,
at least a tall, fairly strong one. I could see her killing them one after
the other. Up until now, the victims have been babies, or children
aged five, ten, and fifteen years old. If we're right, the latest ones are
twenty-year-olds. Not very tall or strongly built. It's equally possible for the killer to be a man or a woman. If the murders continue,
it'll be interesting to see the size and build of the next victims."

"The next victims," the deputy superintendent repeated. "Are
you so sure there'll be more?"

"Oh, please! We have to stop pretending this is an isolated
crime," I said, rising to my feet. "That's handing the killer an advantage. We must accept that these latest murders are directly related
to the ones that took place twenty years ago. They've started again,
and they'll continue. I recommend we warn all twenty-five-year-
olds in the city with double-barreled names from the Álava region.
We can't possibly protect five thousand young people, but we can
give them advice to help them stay safe. We can tell them not to
go out alone, to make sure they're always with someone when they
come back at night. Not to stand on their own in doorways; not
to go out to the countryside by themselves on the weekends. We

have no idea where the killer captures and keeps the victims before killing them. We simply have to try to make it more difficult for him or her."

DSU Salvatierra stood in front of me, her arms crossed. "We're not going to do that."

"What do you mean?" I asked, unable to believe my ears.

"We're not going to alarm people further," she said, shaking her head so coolly it exasperated me. "If we announce those self-protection measures, the whole city will be plunged into panic, and that will only make it harder for us to do our jobs. I don't want the situation to become chaotic."

"It already is chaotic, that's what the murderer wants. Are you telling me, ma'am, that your aim right now, at this very moment, isn't to prevent the very likely murder of two twenty-five-year-olds?"

That was what we had to do, what the whole thing was about: to hunt down the murderer before he, or she, struck again.

That was what it was about.

But when I looked at the other three, there was a strange look in their eyes, as if I had gone too far and shouted at them. Maybe I had, I don't remember.

At that moment Pancorbo, one of our longest-serving inspectors, came in, scratching the rebellious strands of hair on his round, polished head.

He whispered in the superintendent's ear and gave us all a worried look, then disappeared as stealthily as he had arrived.

Superintendent Medina pinched the top of his nose between his bushy eyebrows and closed his eyes for a second.

"Are your computers on?" he asked.

Not following, Estíbaliz and I shrugged.

"Yes, of course," she said.

"Well then, get back to your offices right now, leave the intranet, and shut down your computers. And turn off the Internet connections on your cell phones as well. The station's systems are being hacked."

I ran back to my office and closed the document in which I had been writing my first impressions of the Old Cathedral case. I was about to shut my e-mail when I saw a new, unopened message that made my blood freeze: sent by *Fromjail*.

I know I have specific orders from my superior not to open any new messages. I know it's incredibly risky. I know . . .

I opened it. The message was short, but it left me frozen in my seat, stunned.

> Kraken: Together you and I could form a team to hunt down the murderer. Come and visit me today. This is urgent, and you know it. He's going to continue.
>
> With all due respect for your investigative methods.
>
> Tasio

3

ZABALLA PRISON

Monday, July 25

Kraken! How did Tasio Ortiz de Zárate know my childhood nickname? How had someone who had been behind bars for twenty years found out about me and sent me an e-mail when he didn't have access to the Internet? Was it really him, or was this a trap?

I hurried to Estíbaliz's office and closed the door.

"You're going to have to cover for me, and lie if you need to," I blurted out.

"Yet again," she said, playing with her ponytail.

Estíbaliz never failed me. She was as trustworthy and reliable as the engine in an old Cuban Cadillac.

"I'm going to Zaballa to talk to the warden. I think Tasio Ortiz de Zárate has been in contact with me. It could be an impostor, but even if it is, I need to meet him. I want to start to build a profile of the murderer. If Tasio is the puppet master, there are certain things he won't be able to hide. Obviously our bosses are not as eager to solve these crimes as we are, so we won't tell them. Officially, I'll be with you all morning taking statements from everyone who had access to the Old Cathedral: the clergy, the janitors, the cleaners, the archaeologists, and the tour guides. I found out this morning that the maintenance company is Alfredo Ruiz and Company. Talk

to the manager. Get him to give you the contact information for
everyone who has keys to the cathedral. I'll see you at three o'clock
sharp at Toloño's to have lunch and share info."

I took a white patrol car out of the police impound and headed
for the N-1 highway and the Álava penitentiary, the huge prison
where Tasio had been transferred when the old jail at Nanclares de
la Oca was closed.

Tasio had had twenty years behind bars to remake his life, to
reinvent himself. He was no longer an archaeologist and didn't
plan on returning to that profession. Now he claimed he was a
criminologist; he wrote scripts for procedurals. The news that he
had sold a screenplay for six figures to HBO had brought his name
back into Spanish headlines. Of course, that was much more lucra-
tive than working for the Álava Regional Council.

Shortly afterward, once Tasio was again enjoying the media
fame he obviously loved, a mysterious Twitter account with a
strange username had appeared: @scripttipsfromjail.

What was particularly striking was that the profile photo
showed Tasio at his best, shortly before he was arrested: dark blond
hair, rectangular face, and a broad, white-toothed smile that oozed
confidence. An attractive man, a winner.

The account header was the Vitoria skyline with the four spires
of its tallest churches: the Old Cathedral, San Vicente, San Miguel,
and San Pedro. An iconic image that was found everywhere, even
on bumper stickers.

The account's bio was also disturbing: "I'm just a scriptwriter
living in the underbelly of reality. True serial addict, fake serial
killer. Tasio Ortiz de Zárate."

He gave advice: "The viewer has to love to hate your protagonist." "The best way to produce dramatic irony is to show that the
viewer knows more than the protagonist in the first act." Or "When
you are creating your protagonist, bear in mind that villains don't

know they're villains. They're characters who go to bed at night with a clear conscience, convinced they're doing the right thing."

The account had more than half a million followers, and of course whoever was sending the messages claimed to be Tasio, although no one knew how he managed to send tweets from prison.

The world was divided with regard to Tasio: in general, Vitoria loathed him, but the rest of the planet—including a new generation that had not witnessed the horror of the four double crimes and was fascinated by the myth of the serial killer who sold his scripts for millions—idolized him for every snippet of wisdom he posted on the web.

As I approached the vast parking lot in front of the prison, I found myself nervously drumming my fingers on the steering wheel.

Don't be so ridiculous; you're an adult now.

I parked and then reviewed the list of recommendations we had been given at the Arkaute Academy on how to deal with this kind of manipulative, egomaniacal personality.

I showed my badge to the man at the gate, an ordinary-looking guy with a round face and close-set eyes. I had no intention of meeting with the warden to tell her what had happened, but I shouldn't have worried—when he saw my name, the guard looked down at his list and told me:

"Go to the visitors' wing. Tasio Ortiz de Zárate is expecting you in Room Three."

I nodded, hiding my surprise, and walked over to the block he had indicated.

I went down a green hallway and entered the room but immediately realized I must have made a mistake. The only people I could see on the far side of the double-paned security window were a bored guard sitting by the door and an inmate who looked like a habitual drug user sitting on a black plastic chair. A skeleton staring into space, lost in his thoughts as he waited for a relative's visit. He held a lit cigarette.

I turned around and grabbed the doorknob, ready to leave. Then I heard bony knuckles tapping on the glass. Puzzled, I turned back around. The prisoner pointed for me to pick up the telephone on the stainless-steel counter and sit in an empty chair identical to his.

"What do you want, drugs?" I said, even though I knew he wouldn't be able to hear me through the thick glass. I approached the chair and, still standing, picked up the phone.

"Kraken," whispered a deep, slurred voice that drilled into my brain and burst into my memory like a bullet.

I turned into a statue. I forgot to breathe while Tasio raised his eyes and fixed them on mine.

I had difficulty matching the image I had of the handsome, all-conquering man of the past with this human wreck. By now Tasio was over forty-five, but the person sitting across from me looked much older. To say he had aged badly would have been far too kind, because this Tasio looked like a poor imitation of some inmate from a particularly bad American prison. He was now a bony junkie with unkempt gray hair that had been gathered into a ponytail. He had an upside-down U-shaped mustache straight out of the seventies that looked so out of place it was ugly and comical at the same time.

No, I'm lying. It was disturbing.

He wasn't in good shape. He looked as though he'd spent twenty years on smack or something worse.

What's life done to you, Tasio?

That was my first thought.

For some reason I don't understand, I blurted out the words, just like that. Like someone incapable of hiding his feelings, like a drunk or a child.

"What's life done to you?" I heard myself say, as if hypnotized.

I flinched when I realized what I had done, but it was too late. What a way to start.

"That's what we're going to try to fix, Kraken. What life has done to me." He was talking slowly, deliberately, in a cavernous voice that seared my eardrums.

I thought his drawl must be the result of heroin. It occurred to me, then, that his voice, much deeper than what I remembered, could also have been a by-product of twenty years of heavy smoking.

As if to confirm my theory, Tasio took a long drag on a cigarette, then calmly blew out the smoke. He toyed with a small pack on the counter beside him. Another unopened one lay beside it. And two ashtrays. Two.

He motioned for me to sit down, and for a moment our reflections were superimposed on the security glass like a double hologram.

"All right," I said with a sigh. I sat reluctantly. "Let's get straight to the point. Why did you bring me here?"

"I'm very worried," he said after what seemed like an eternity. "I'll be out on parole in a couple of weeks. If these crimes continue, the murderer will find a way to incriminate me again."

"Incriminate you? You're in prison. How on Earth could anybody incriminate you?"

"Don't pretend. You already think I'm pulling the strings, just like everyone else in Vitoria. That's why I got in touch with you. If I help you catch him, Vitoria will accept me again."

"Accept you?" I echoed incredulously. "After you killed eight children? Do you have any idea how ridiculous you sound?"

Tasio looked at me with vacant eyes. He took his time, as if it were barely worth answering me.

"I'm not going to bother to try to convince you I didn't commit those eight murders. I know that, in your eyes, I'm already guilty.

The same goes for the rest of humanity. For the first few years I tried as hard as I could to persuade people of the opposite. I hired the best defense I could afford for the trial, but it wasn't enough. Afterward, when the sentence was confirmed and I was sent to Nanclares, put with the other inmates and the prison wardens—all of you were convinced I was guilty. It was difficult to accept there was nothing I could do, that nobody cared about the truth. The facts were that there was a convicted man in prison and the murders had stopped. But I was obsessed: I needed to understand what had happened to make people go from asking for my autograph to hating me in the space of a few hours. I took a course in criminology. I studied profiles and processes and all the cases about serial killers I could find. I developed a taste for the few police films I could get here in prison. Then I became addicted to thrillers. I began to understand that reality and fiction were twins, that one fed off the other. In every story there's the introduction, the development, and the denouement. A protagonist, an opposing force, allies, enemies, evidence, and a mentor. What am I talking about, Kraken? Fiction or reality?"

"That's why you became a screenwriter—"

"I discovered I was good at uncovering the structure of stories. It's like the scaffolding on a building. After that, you just have to make it look beautiful, don't you? The thing is I'll be out on parole in less than two weeks, and this isn't looking good for me. I want us to help each other."

"And how do you plan to help me? Are you going to solve this new crime from prison?"

"I have an advantage you don't believe in yet. I know I'm not the puppet master, and I know I wasn't the killer twenty years ago. That means I can concentrate on discovering who it could have been. You, on the other hand, think I'm guilty of committing the first series of murders, so now you're going to have to investigate my friends to rule out the possibility that they're involved with the recent killings. That will take you precious time that you can be sure the killer will use to his advantage."

All right, Tasio. Let's play your game and see where it leads us, I thought.

"Let's just suppose that, against all odds, I believe you," I said. "It wasn't you. You were framed, as you insisted in your initial statement."

"Yes," he said, then waved his cigarette in the air for me to continue.

"Tell me, do you think yesterday's murders are the work of the same person?"

"I haven't seen the photos. You could bring them."

"Don't push it, Tasio," I warned him.

"All right." He leaned back in his chair. "Let's see. I'll put on my archaeologist hat. The first murders represented the history of Álava: the dolmen of the Witch's Lair dates back to the Chalcolithic Age, five thousand years ago. The babies were newborn, as if they represented the first age of man. Do you see the parallels?"

Was he having fun? Was his mind really that twisted?

"Yes, Tasio, I've had twenty years to see them—and so has the entire country."

"So then you know what came next. The Celtic-Iberian village at La Hoya, from around 1200 BC. Five-year-old victims. The Valle Salado, the first century BC. Ten-year-old children. The medieval wall, the eleventh century. A fifteen-year-old girl and a boy the same age."

As he said this, I detected a slight painful twitch at the corner of his mouth. He raised the cigarette to conceal it. It also hadn't escaped my notice that he had changed the generic "children" to "a fifteen-year-old girl." Could there be something personal in that last crime? I'd have to dig deeply into those files.

"So what can we expect, Tasio? Do you know? Have you brought me here to illuminate me?"

Ignoring my last question, he leaned his head against the glass.

"The time frame for yesterday's murders, if you found them in the Old Cathedral, corresponds to the twelfth century. The crimes are moving forward. What you can expect now is that the next murders will be set among the icons of our history from the Middle Ages: the Casa de los Anda, the streets of the guilds—the Pinto, the Cuchi, and the former Jewry. Possibly the Casa del Cordón. The victims will be twenty-five years old. Then it will be Renaissance Vitoria. Watch out for the palaces: Bendaña, Montehermoso, Villa Suso. Oh, there are so many. What are you going to do, put patrols on all the streets?"

I had to laugh at his outrageous suggestion.

"Do you really think I'm going to share that kind of information with you? That would be like giving you a wish list. Free rein to kill at your leisure in unguarded spots."

"You're still refusing to see that I'm offering to help you. I can be valuable. I'm one of the few people who know all the details of the previous crimes, because the trial focused on them. And I'm probably the person most likely to have information on everyone you'll investigate during your inquiries. You don't realize it, but soon you'll be back in this room begging me for what I'm offering you right now."

"Okay," I said, raising my hand to stop him. "Again, let's just suppose I believe you. Give me something I don't know as a token of your good intentions."

"Something you don't know. I have no idea what you don't know, Kraken. For God's sake, have the guts to ask me straight out."

"Okay, fine. What was the cause of death in the first murders?"

"Yew."

"Yew?" I asked, uncomprehending.

"Yes, yew poisoning." He shrugged. "In pre-Roman times, people used it to commit suicide. There's evidence that the Celts used yew as poison three thousand years before Christ. In this region, it's one of those secrets that are never mentioned out loud, but the older generation living in the villages knows it. The bark, the leaves, everything in the yew tree is poisonous other than the aril of the berry. For the Celts, it was a sacred tree. They believed it was immortal because it lived so long. Even when Christianity reached these shores, yew trees were planted next to churches and cemeteries. The old beliefs persisted. Right through to our time."

For a moment, I thought I saw a flash of the Tasio I had admired in my youth: the popular figure who loved his work, the man who knew everything about our history and offered it to us in small, informative packages.

"That sounds archaeological."

"That's what the judge said," Tasio replied, crushing his cigarette in one of the ashtrays. "At the trial we were made to watch one of the first shows I recorded for Basque television, back before the ratings went through the roof. In it I was talking about yew. I explained at great length that fifty grams of boiled yew leaves would be enough to poison a child or a small adult. Now do you see why I'm convinced the murderer had investigated me before he began his crimes and why he carried them out in the way he did? To incriminate me. The same was true of the *eguzkilore*. In those days, I saw the flower as a talisman for my personal protection and wore it whenever I felt it was necessary. I used to wear silver *eguzkilore* bracelets and pendants. There was one hanging in my office, which was seen by millions of viewers over the course of my show. Do you want me to go on?"

We eyeballed each other. I didn't answer. Twenty years ear-

lier, the press hadn't mentioned the *eguzkilores*. Tasio didn't seem
to want to skip any details, but last night's special edition of the
newspaper hadn't mentioned that we had found three of the same
plant by the bodies, either.

"No . . . you don't believe me," he muttered. "How could you?
That would make you the only person in two decades."

With that, he lit another cigarette, gazing at it as if it were
made of gold. It took him a second to remember I was there.

"So if you asked me what the cause of death was back then and
you didn't know it was yew, that means the killer has changed his
modus operandi?"

Be careful, Unai.

"I'm not going to share that information with you."

He assumed that meant yes.

"That changes a lot. What the devil is he after now?" Tasio
wondered, talking to himself. "It would have been easier to copy
the crimes, carry them out exactly as he did in the past. Why
change now?"

Tasio was thinking out loud, his eyes following the shapes the
smoke traced as if I didn't exist. That made the situation even more
unnerving. It was like peering through a hole in the wall, watching
a madman rave.

"Do we have a deal?" he asked suddenly, turning back toward me.

"What kind of deal, Tasio?"

"I help you when you get stuck, tell you all the details of the
old cases. In exchange, you keep me up to date on the new ones.
I want to help you solve this before the murderer strikes again."

At least that's something we agree on, I had to admit.

"First, I want you to explain how you know my nickname, how
you managed to send me an e-mail, how you've opened a Twitter
account, and how you hacked into our police computers this morning. Tell me, who on the outside is doing all this for you?"

"Do you think I'm stupid?" he said, smiling to show gray, nicotine-stained teeth.

"You must be a little stupid if you've spent twenty years in the slammer despite being innocent, don't you think?"

At this he grew apoplectic. He jumped up and crushed the lit cigarette against the security glass, the burning tip level with my eye. He wasn't used to having anyone insult him.

"I'm getting out of here!" he roared, the tendons bulging in his neck. "I'm getting out of here, or you'll be leaving the jail in a box."

For a moment, my mind went blank. I was taken aback by this fit of rage in my former hero. Then I stood slowly to leave, while a guard, alarmed at the shouting, opened the door on Tasio's side. Before he relinquished the telephone, Tasio met my gaze, chin trembling.

I made a mental note of his weak points: arrogance, uncontrollable fits of anger, a crazy, unrealistic wish to clear his name in Vitoria. I would need to remember them all when I had to put pressure on him.

Above all, though, the most important thing for me as a profiler, and the reason I had wanted to talk to him face-to-face, was to ascertain whether his profile fit the crime committed in the Old Cathedral. And a fit of rage over something this trivial didn't correspond in the slightest to the profile of the highly organized, psychopathic murderer we were now facing. Tasio's extremely violent reaction was more like that of a disorganized killer, a psychotic.

"Don't try me. Don't think for even a second that you can threaten me. Be very careful, Tasio," I warned him, and I marched out of the room.

For one fleeting moment as I looked at him, I had the impression that Tasio was desperate. That beneath the mask of an inmate perfectly adapted to life in prison was a terrified man who had disguised himself for twenty years in order to survive.

4

VILLA SUSO PALACE

He had followed her down several streets in the snowbound Old Quarter, surprised to see her while on his way home from attending a medical emergency. Why was this elegant woman walking alone at dawn during a blizzard that had paralyzed the entire city?

Blanca Díaz de Antoñana, engaged to the prominent industrialist Javier Ortiz de Zárate, owner of the Ferrerías Alavesas steelworks, was struggling along the narrow pathway that had been cleared by municipal workers.

His clinician's eye told him something was wrong. He'd noticed that the young woman had a slight limp, and he wondered why she hadn't come in to have it examined.

An icy blast stung his cheeks as he passed Cantón de Santa Ana, and he turned up the collar of his new wool overcoat. He had recently been appointed to the Vitoria Clinic and had spent a large part of his salary on clothes that would be suitable for a doctor in a good position. His wife, Emilia, had protested. She was keen on saving money to enroll their two sons at the College of the Sacred Heart. However, Emilia understood little about his job or his new life in the city. She was unable to grasp that the only way for him to be considered more than a country doctor was to mingle with the city's most influential men, to act like their equal by adopting their gestures and clothes. If only he could also adopt their sophisticated wives and girlfriends.

Like Blanca.

He had to conceal his excitement whenever she came into his clinic. After all, he was first her doctor, and only after that was he a man. Even so, he always took a five-minute break before seeing his next patient after the beautiful, gracious, elegant Blanca left his exam room. His nurse, an experienced older woman who could anticipate his instructions with a mere glance, had understood from the start. She was his silent, discreet accomplice.

He wished he had come to work there sooner; he wished he and Blanca had met when he had still been a free man. Perhaps at a nightclub like El Elefante Blanco, or at the Hotel Canciller Ayala, which opened its doors on Sunday afternoons to a throng of eligible young men strutting awkwardly, trying to impress the dolled-up women at the far end of the room, who stood in protective circles, pretending to look demure.

Blanca headed purposefully along Calle Santa María, apparently ignoring the pain in her ankle. She seemed to walk without fear of slipping on the thin layer of ice that had formed beneath the hardened snow.

Álvaro quickened his pace, worried he might lose sight of her. He kept his eyes on the slender young woman's blond hair until she did something strange.

She stopped abruptly at the top of the staircase next to the Villa Suso Palace: a flight of fifty or more steps leading down three levels to the Plaza de Machete below.

He crept up on Blanca noiselessly, unsure of what she was doing. The snow on the steps of San Bartolomé had been cleared, heaped in piles as high as the old iron handrails on either side.

She turned slowly, eyes closed, and raised her arms in the shape of a cross. And yet she no longer looked like an angel. Her face was bruised, one eye swollen shut, her lip split, and there was dried blood on her neck.

He rushed to intervene, just as Blanca let herself fall backward like a rag doll. At the last second, he grabbed her wrist and they plunged together. They rolled down several steps in an embrace until he managed to use his body as a brake and they came to a halt.

Blanca was confused. Shouldn't death be more violent? Shouldn't it hurt more?

She ventured to open her good eye and was startled by the closeness of this vaguely familiar face. She recognized him by his red hair and his kindly expression. A courteous man with a timid manner.

"Doctor Urbina?" she cried, shocked. "What on Earth are you doing?"

"Trying to stop you from falling to your death. What possessed you, woman? Whatever possessed you?" he shouted, voice quaking.

Calm down, Álvaro. Don't let her see your nerves. Calm down, he scolded himself.

They got to their feet, embarrassed by this inappropriate contact between doctor and patient. Instinctively they glanced around, but dawn had just broken, and everyone who lived at this end of the city was still asleep.

"Did someone assault you? Were you robbed or attacked? Did someone . . . violate you? You must come with me to the clinic straightaway," he insisted.

"That's out of the question!" Blanca retorted, clutching his arm.

A few seconds later, the truth dawned on Álvaro Urbina, and he looked at her, aghast.

"This wasn't a random assault, was it? Someone you know did this to you."

Blanca looked away, intending to keep quiet as she always did. But she was still shaken from her failed attempt to end it all, and perhaps for that reason she said more than she should have.

"You know my fiancé. Who would listen to me? They'd say I was to blame, and it's partially true, because he had no idea about my reputation." Blanca started back up the steps, aware of the time. She was talking more to herself than to the doctor, but her nerves had gotten the better of her, and she couldn't stop.

Álvaro followed a few paces behind, keeping an eye on her limp.

"What reputation are you talking about, Blanca?"

"Don't you know? Well, I suppose I'd rather tell you than have you hear about it from someone else," she replied, coming to a halt.

Why not? she thought, still distraught. Doctor Urbina seemed like a good man, and as a gynecologist he must have heard all kinds of stories in his clinic.

"I'm guilty of a youthful mistake. I flirted with a village boy during the fiesta at Salvatierra. He asked me to accompany him to his farmhouse on the edge of the village. There was a north wind that day, and he wanted to fetch his coat. Like a fool, I agreed. I waited outside for him, and nothing inappropriate happened. But someone saw us return together and claimed they had seen us come out of the barn. The rumor spread, and my father, my family, everyone heard about it. No one believed me when I said we had just been walking. Deep down, whether the story was true or not didn't matter to them. Actually, I think that maybe they did believe me, but they didn't care about my innocence. What mattered was the fuss that it caused, and that my family and I were branded. Going into a hay barn with a boy is the worst mistake an unmarried girl can make in a village like that. My father was furious and banned me from going to dances. I wasn't even allowed out during Las Fiestas de la Virgen Blanca. The villagers started to make fun of me, calling *me* 'la Virgen Blanca.' Since then, a question mark has hung over my virginity.

"When Javier started courting me, I assumed he already knew about the story, but I thought he genuinely liked me and didn't care about the gossip, so I never mentioned it. But he didn't know, until a month ago. He asked what this Virgen Blanca story meant. He said it was too late to break off our engagement, that the invitations had already been sent out to his business associates, and that the scandal of canceling the wedding would be even more damaging to the company's and his family's reputations. Then he flew into a rage, and the beatings started. Before that, he was charming. Not exactly affectionate, but certainly attentive and polite. Once I realized he didn't know, I couldn't tell him; he would never want to marry me. In my heart, I wish he would just go ahead and end our engagement. Even if it means I'll never get married—"

Álvaro Urbina had heard enough.

"You're terrified," he said.

"I'm just afraid he'll get angry about something and start hitting me again."

"Don't marry him!" Álvaro blurted out despite himself. Then he blushed to the roots of his hair. He wasn't usually this outspoken, but his disgust had been rising since she told him about la Virgen Blanca.

"If I lose my good name, I'm nothing. I'll end up an old maid. And I have no profession. Although I was good at school and liked studying, the nuns insisted that learning to sew and embroider would be more useful. This isn't the life I was hoping for," Blanca said. She was pouring out her heart to him, perhaps because she hadn't had a confidante for so long, not since all her friends deserted her after the fiesta at Salvatierra.

"Who has such a life?" said Álvaro, looking at her gravely.

"You mean you don't, either, Doctor Urbina?"

He turned up the collar of his coat again. He was shivering from the cold, but he wouldn't have left that deserted street for all the world, not while Blanca Díaz de Antoñana stood beside him, hanging on his every word.

"I've achieved more than my parents could have imagined, even in their wildest dreams. I escaped a life of poverty and ignorance, tending cattle and laboring in the fields. But, like everyone else, I'm a slave to the choices I made in the rashness of youth. I've known my wife since we were born. We were close in age, playmates—there weren't many children in the village. I suppose I thought it was fated. When I came to Vitoria at fourteen to study at the seminary, people already assumed we were a couple," he said, raising his head and gazing at the imposing building where he had spent much of his youth. "We exchanged letters, but when I decided to accompany Father Luis Mari to the missions, Emilia's father grew impatient. I knew nothing of the outside world and assumed I would finish my vocational training and return to a low-paid job in Vitoria. However, after helping with a couple of emergency childbirths, I discovered my calling as a doctor. Father Mari thought my talents would be wasted in a factory, so the priests paid for my education. My parents were so proud of me, and Emilia's father was over the moon: a son-in-law who was a doctor and would take his daughter to Vitoria. He couldn't have asked for more."

"So you married Emilia out of duty?"

Álvaro gritted his teeth and looked away. He had come back from Ecuador an adult, a man, but Emilia remained semi-illiterate. She was cheerful enough, but she had few manners and was too loud, too spontaneous. But that's who she'd always been; she hadn't changed. And if he'd jilted her, she would never have found another husband.

"As far as the people in the village were concerned," he said at last, "Emilia had always been my girlfriend; no other suitor would have wanted to be second-best. I'm afraid our customs are hard on women. I couldn't bring myself to act like a scoundrel and abandon her. It wasn't Emilia's fault that I had seen more of the world and become more sophisticated."

"You're a man of conscience."

If you only knew me, Álvaro thought but didn't say.

"Don't make me into a saint, Blanca. I'm guilty of plenty of wicked thoughts and sins of omission."

"But not of deeds," she said.

"But not of deeds."

"I think that's more important."

"No, what's more important in this region is not just being moral but also appearing moral. Julius Caesar said that about his wife, Pompeia Sila, remember? 'It's not enough for Caesar's wife merely to be honest; she must also appear to be so.'"

His words were a stinging reminder to Blanca of her own reality. She remembered the reason she was there, and her confession to Doctor Urbina. She had doubtless said too much. How could she have been so naive, yet again?

"Doctor, please don't repeat anything you have seen or heard today. You mustn't tell a soul. I'm protected by patient confidentiality that you are duty bound to respect," she added rather sharply. She seemed almost angry, though more with herself than with the doctor.

Álvaro drew back, offended.

"You don't need to worry. I won't say anything, nor will I make your life more difficult than it already is. But please let me help you."

"You can't help me. It's my problem. Please don't interfere. Forget this ever happened, and don't mention it the next time I visit your clinic."

"Let me be your friend," he ventured at last. "Someone you can confide in, feel at ease with, someone who can help you. I'll treat you at the clinic. I promise to be discreet."

"Friends? Who are married to other people? You don't know this city very well, do you? The gossip would ruin me *and* your career. No, doctor, I can't have that." Blanca shook her head. "Please don't tell anyone what you saw."

With that she left, head lowered, turning into Cantón de las Pulmonías as the doctor, shivering with cold and rage, watched her go.

Álvaro Urbina had taken his wife and sons to see the life-size Nativity scene in La Florida Park. He had been restless for the past few days. Blanca hadn't been to the clinic, and almost a month had passed since the incident on the steps next to the Villa Suso Palace. He was worried about her: Had that brute of a fiancé laid his hands on her again?

He prolonged the outing with Emilia and the children, bought them a packet of roast chestnuts from a kiosk shaped like a black railway carriage, and after eating some skewers at El Dólar, headed toward Calle Dato. It was the time of day when the members of El Círculo Vitoriano left the luxury of the city's most exclusive club after having coffee and lounging in full view behind its enormous windows.

Emilia, a plump, dark-haired woman with rosy cheeks, prattled on about whether to buy pork or lamb for Christmas. She couldn't decide. Álvaro nodded absentmindedly, gazing at the couples coming out of that world of gold-and-crimson draperies, a universe as yet inaccessible to him but which he hoped to conquer soon.

He stiffened slightly as he recognized a tall, broad-shouldered fellow with jet-black hair: the industrialist. His wife-to-be, Blanca Díaz de Antoñana, walked out of the club arm in arm with him, exchanging discreet smiles with other couples. She wore her blond hair in the current fashion: a stiffly lacquered bob, curled at the ends.

Álvaro tugged on Emilia's arm, and they went over to greet the other couple. He instantly noticed a fresh bruise, barely concealed beneath a thick layer of foundation. He was concerned for Blanca and distressed that she had ignored his entreaties to come to the clinic.

"Good afternoon, señorita," he said, nodding his head slightly.

"Doctor Urbina, what a pleasant surprise," she replied in her soft voice. "I trust you're enjoying the festive season with your lovely family."

"Yes, indeed. I look forward to seeing you again at the clinic, should you require my services."

Her husband-to-be looked closely at her, observing the scene without deigning to join in. She smiled, and when they parted without another word, Doctor Urbina thought: *That's it, there's nothing more I can do.*

And yet there had been a hint of something, a lingering look from Blanca. A promise, a "we'll meet again," a silent cry for help. There was a sense of a complicity between them that he had never experienced with another woman, least of all his wife.

The industrialist soon forgot about Urbina's presence. He was unaware that the doctor's family was a few feet behind them in the crowded street and could hear his conversation with Blanca.

"Do you know that fellow?" Javier Ortiz de Zárate asked Blanca.

"He isn't exactly easy to forget. He must be the only redheaded doctor in the whole of Vitoria, perhaps the region."

"Yes, he does rather stick out with that hair. Him and his children. Is he from a good family?"

"I don't know."

"In that case, he isn't," Javier concluded with barely concealed scorn.

Later that night, shut away in his study in the apartment on Calle Honduras, Álvaro took, from a locked drawer, a notebook full of anatomical drawings he had sketched when he was a student. In the back pages, he drew Blanca's face from memory, complete with the bruising and fractures he suspected her arrogant husband-to-be had given her.

The date would remain etched in his memory, because that night he made a decision that, against all odds, calmed him. He climbed into his side of the bed, trying not to touch Emilia's warm body, and he knew that he would finally be able to sleep.

Before drifting into oblivion, he indulged himself, repeating the comforting words over and over like a prayer:

I'm going to kill Javier Ortiz de Zárate.

5

THE CASA DEL CORDÓN

MONDAY, JULY 25

I reached the bar where I was meeting Estíbaliz with time to spare. July was punishing us. A scorching sun beat down on streets that had only recently been swept clean of smashed plastic cups from the previous night's celebrations. The meteorologists were forecasting a heat wave for the next few weeks, even though high temperatures in Vitoria usually didn't last more than a few days.

I went down Cuesta de San Francisco and past the arcades. They were filled with people selling strings of garlic, which left a persistent smell of sulfur in the air and covered the pavement in a sea of dry, white skins. Hundreds of retirees in checked shirts and berets were going home content, a long string of bulbs dangling from each shoulder. That was how it had always been and how I remembered it from when I was little, when our grandfather used to bring us into Vitoria on El Día de Santiago to buy his year's supply of garlic.

I pushed open the glass front door to Toloño's. It had black ceilings, and the list of tapas was written in white chalk on the slate walls. It was very popular, but quiet. It was an oasis of peace, where I often stopped on my way home, and it always calmed me. I would eat and return to my apartment with my stomach satisfied, my culinary needs met.

Estíbaliz was waiting for me on a stool at the curved, light-colored wooden counter.

"I ordered for you," she said. "Irish-style mushrooms, scallops with *gulas,* baked spider crab. Sitting or standing?"

"Sitting, and somewhere out of the way. It's best that nobody hears our conversation."

We chose the most isolated table in the bar, the one in the back corner. Estí devoured a seafood terrine, while I dug into the mushroom mousse.

"What happened with the cyberattack?"

"It was over after a couple of hours, but they still haven't discovered who did it. You can switch the Wi-Fi on your cell phone back on. You need to tell them about the message Tasio Ortiz de Zárate sent you so that they can trace the sender. I didn't tell anyone, but you better do it soon, because the IT people are going through our computers with a fine-tooth comb. Better they hear it from you."

"I know, I know." I sighed, switching on my cell phone. I had twenty-four WhatsApp messages. I tried to ignore the fact that everyone wanted to get in touch with me urgently. "The new deputy superintendent isn't going to like that I went to visit him in prison without mentioning it to her first."

"Give her a chance, it's her first day. I'd be worried about getting things wrong, too."

"Not if your lack of reaction led to the deaths of two more people," I said.

Just then both of our cell phones buzzed. Estí was quicker and answered first. As she listened, her tiny brown eyes stared at me with a strange expression.

"You're a damn wizard," she said to me as she ended the call. Her face was pale.

"What are you talking about?"

"Two more bodies have been discovered near here, in the Casa del Cordón."

The mouthful of *gulas* I had swallowed hit my stomach like

a lead balloon. And it stayed there, bothering me like a stone in my shoe.

"Are you all right?" asked a worried Estíbaliz.

"Yes," I replied mechanically. "I mean no, I'm not all right. Wait a minute, will you?"

I walked poker-faced to the toilet, disguising the hurry I was in. Once inside, I threw up all the food I had eaten.

I didn't want to go. I didn't want to carry out the visual inspection. I didn't want to have to look yet again at two naked young people whose deaths were partially my fault. I washed my face and stared at the failure peering back at me from the mirror.

You're getting soft, I told the Kraken staring at me. *You're not trying hard enough. Who's the clever one now? That wretch or you?*

Thirty seconds later, we arrived at Number 34 Calle Cuchillería. The Casa del Cordón dated from the end of the fifteenth century, when the Catholic monarchs had expelled the Jews. But the prosperous Jewish cloth merchant Juan Sánchez de Bilbao had not only converted to Christianity and stayed in the city; he built a noble mansion that remained gloriously intact over the following centuries and was now one of the best-known sights in Vitoria.

Its curious name came from the Franciscan cord carved around one of the pointed arches. This was one of the facades tourists photographed most, although it brought back much more prosaic memories for me: the hot, greasy bags of french fries served at two in the morning at Aimaru's, the bar opposite.

I used to sit on the steps of the tiny door between the two arches of the Casa del Cordón, the warm bag clutched in my freezing hands. When I was older, I began to take an interest in history (a passion acquired thanks to Tasio), and I discovered that the rich convert Juan Sánchez de Bilbao had ordered the door made significantly smaller so that Christians would have to bow if they wanted to enter and do business with him. A nice, subtle revenge. I have no idea why the most trivial memories come into my mind at the most difficult moments.

That dark day nothing looked the way it usually did. The area had already been cordoned off with red-and-white police tape, and two hearses from the Lauzurica Funeral Home were parked at the top of the street.

At the entrance, Estí and I greeted Ruiz, one of our officers, and went in through the heavy wooden medieval door.

"Was the lock forced?" I asked Ruiz.

"No, it hasn't been touched," he said, shrugging.

The building belonged to the Caja Vital bank's benevolent fund. There were two desks close to the entrance, and the second floor was a strange mixture of big windows, heavy ceiling beams, and columns.

Olano, the judge, came downstairs from the vaulted room, a magnificent chamber with a dark-blue ceiling and small stars carved in between the thick support ribs.

"Are you here to examine the scene?" he asked, grave-faced.

"Yes, sir," my partner said, standing to attention. "We just heard the news."

"All right, I'm done here. The CSU people are taking photos; you can discuss your findings with the pathologist and talk to my secretary about signing the form. What a ghastly way to have your lunch interrupted," he muttered.

Estíbaliz and I glanced at each other and then went up the stairs, holding our breath.

In the center of the room, surrounded by several CSU experts and Doctor Guevara, lay the two naked bodies. As with the previous couple, they were lined up facing northwest. Three *eguzkilores* had been arranged around them, like a small solar system.

"By the beard of Odin," I whispered, amazed, in Estíbaliz's ear. "They killed a Nordic god."

The naked male in front of us looked as if he had just arrived from Valhalla. He was tall with striking blond hair. Blue eyes stared up at the medieval vault's starry sky, and his arms were covered in tribal tattoos.

"This kid spent his father's inheritance on tattoos," my partner said. "What do you think, Unai?"

Kneeling next to Thor's body, I repeated my prayer to myself: *Here your hunt ends and mine begins.*

I took a few seconds, looked carefully at the body, and told her: "Despite all the tough-guy paraphernalia, I think we're dealing with another rich kid. His chest and legs have been shaved, as has his pubic area. I bet he's never gotten his hands dirty in his life. He took good care of himself, and that costs money. But he doesn't match the partner the murderer has given him. I don't think they'd ever meet in life. They look like complete opposites."

The girl was smaller, with auburn hair in a short, almost monk-like cut. My impression was that she was ordinary, the sort of person who went through life unnoticed—the opposite of the fake bad boy caressing her cheek with his huge hand. They could have been twenty-five, but they could just as easily have been twenty-two or twenty-seven.

"What do we have, Doctor Guevara?" I asked, standing next to the pathologist while I continued to scrutinize the couple at my feet.

"To put it succinctly, I'd say it's a double crime identical to the ones from yesterday. I've already e-mailed your colleague the autopsy results on the previous two. The new victims are similar in every detail: It seems their deaths were also caused by asphyxia brought on by multiple bee stings in their throats. They were brought here after death and placed in this position before rigor mortis set in. They've been dead less than three hours. I'll take the bodies with me for the autopsy. I'm curious to see the toxicology results. If they were out celebrating last night, we may find traces of drugs.

"As with the previous victims, their hands and nails are intact, but I've asked for them to be processed. They don't appear to have resisted. They also have a mark on their necks that suggests a needle was used to inject something. I can't find any other signs of violence on their bodies, apart from the fact that their mouths were sealed with adhesive tape, which was then torn off, possibly before they were placed here and once the murderer was sure they were dead. But look, I've made a wonderful find."

Doctor Guevara held out a clear plastic bag containing a motionless bee.

"It's lost its abdomen and internal organs, which means it was one of the bees that killed the girl. I know the director of the Honey Museum in Murguía, so there are a couple of things I'd like to ask him. I'll send you the report as soon as I have it. We're also going to try to trace the *eguzkilores*, or *Carlina acaulis*, but it will be very difficult. We've already tried to trace the ones we found in the Old Cathedral. It's a common plant that grows on mountainsides and in meadows and fields. They could have come from anywhere," she said, casting a final glance at the supine bodies. "Do you need me for anything else?"

"I don't think so," said Estíbaliz. "But keep us informed if there are any interesting developments."

"I will. Good afternoon."

We left the Casa del Cordón as the funeral director's employees went in to remove the bodies. Passersby were slowing up surreptitiously; none of them dared come to a complete halt, but they all cast furtive looks at what was going on at the entrance to La Cuchillería.

Estíbaliz stopped to talk to someone she knew, and we separated with a gesture meaning *See you down there.* I was walking down Cuesta de San Francisco, which was still busy with garlic sellers reluctant to leave their stalls to eat, when a dark-haired, well-dressed man strolled up to say hello. It was Mario Santos, the right-hand man of *El Correo Vitoriano*'s editor and one of the journalists I admit I felt closest to.

We shook hands, and I smiled. I liked Mario. He was discreet, and his articles were always well written. Elegant in style, but above all in attitude. He never blew things out of proportion, and he often played down my slips when he could have made a meal out of them. He was never confrontational at press conferences, and on a couple of occasions he had demonstrated that *off the record* actually meant something to him, to my great relief. Over the years I had come to appreciate him, and although he was a few years older than me, we would sometimes meet in the city center, have a coffee at El Pregón or the 4 Azules, and talk about everything and nothing— Barcelona's most recent game, or the progress being made on the new civic center—without ever really going into great detail about our private lives. He was my go-to reporter.

"How are things, Inspector Ayala?"

"As you see, Mario. Busy."

"And you're worried, I imagine."

"What are you going to publish?"

With Mario, I usually cut straight to the point. He was unlike other journalists, whom I would sound out first. We had a gentleman's agreement.

"We have very little information about what happened yesterday, and nothing about today. Lots of rumors and phone calls. The editor is going crazy putting pressure on me—you know what he's like—but I think this is a very serious matter for the city, so I don't want to publish anything that isn't confirmed. Yesterday was the eve of El Día de Santiago, and today the first celebrations start. The last thing we want is a collective psychosis, especially during the holidays. Can you give me anything now, or should I wait a while?"

"Give me time to meet with my superiors. I promise you'll be the first one I call, okay?"

"I trust you. If the people from *El Diario Alavés* call you, will you tell me before they get something first?" he asked, fixing his small, close-set grayish-brown eyes on me. They studied everything calmly and intelligently. "You can't imagine how badly last night's special edition went down in our newsroom."

I thought it over for a moment, but it was for the best.

"Agreed, you can count on me."

El Diario Alavés tended to be sensationalist, with salacious, biased headlines. *El Correo Vitoriano* was much more sober and rigorous, and the police's affinity with them was simply common sense. The problem was that one of my lifelong friends and a prominent member of my *cuadrilla*, Lutxo, was the news editor for *El Diario Alavés*, and this wasn't the first time we had been at odds over a conflict of interest. Basically, he tried to take advantage of our dinners together to get exclusives for his section, which sometimes led to issues with my superiors over leaks. I was sure I was going to have trouble with him over these new deaths. Not because I was a damned wizard, as Estí claimed, but because ten of the twenty-four WhatsApp messages I had received were from Lutxo. I could sense our friendship was about to get more difficult.

Half an hour later, Estíbaliz and I reached headquarters and went straight up to the deputy superintendent's office. We had to wait while she dealt with calls, but finally she took pity on us and switched off her cell phone.

When she turned her attention to us, we stared into each other's eyes for a second.

Have you seen what we have now? Four corpses? Is that enough for you? I wanted to say to her. But there were plenty of things we still needed to clear up, so it was best to start from the beginning.

"Ma'am," I said, taking a seat, "we've just come from the scene of the new double murder in the Casa del Cordón. First, though, I need to tell you about something that happened this morning. As I was shutting down my computer during the cyberattack, somebody claiming to be Tasio Ortiz de Zárate sent me an e-mail asking me to meet him in prison right away. I went to Zaballa to check that the message really had been written by him and to investigate his possible involvement in the new case. Basically, I wanted to see if his psychological profile fit the one I am building for the person responsible for the crimes committed yesterday and today. I'll write you a full report on the conversation we had there, but I can give you a summary: Even though Tasio didn't openly admit it, I'm sure he was behind the cyberattack. I think his intention was to create a smokescreen to keep our cybercrimes unit busy so that we wouldn't discover what IP address the e-mail was sent from."

I told her briefly about everything we had discussed: the huge number of Twitter followers he boasted about and his offer to collaborate with me in solving the crimes.

"He wants to be a hero in Vitoria again," I said. "He says he wants to help us find the murderer."

"If Tasio was behind the earlier murders," said Estíbaliz, "and if one of his followers is killing couples by copying the same pattern, Tasio could be laying a trap for that individual, hoping that we'll arrest him."

"You mean he could be capable of manipulating his own acolytes?" the deputy superintendent asked.

"That's a possibility," said Estí with a shrug. "To him, people are nothing more than objects—just look at the victims. There was always something impersonal about them. They were no more than numbers in a sequence. He could have manipulated one of his followers into imitating him. It could be someone who would also fit the profile from twenty years ago, so that when he gives us clues as to who the perpetrator is now, they would fit the past crimes as well. Then Tasio would be free, and he would become a hero for helping us. He would get exactly what he wants."

"And why now, when he's finally getting out on parole?" insisted Alba.

"Because he wants more than just his freedom," I said. "He doesn't want to be a pariah, to be public enemy number one. He doesn't want to be the mass killer who gets out of prison just because he's served most of his sentence. He'd like everything to go back to the way it was, as he put it to me, just a few hours before his arrest. He needs to see Vitoria at his feet once again: fame, flattery, social status—that's his goal. He doesn't want to have to hide when he gets out."

"That fits with the fact that he hasn't sold his apartment on Calle Dato," said Estíbaliz. "I checked the property registry this morning. He could have sold it if he had appointed a representative, but the apartment is still in his name, and there's been no change of ownership in the past twenty years."

"That could mean that when he gets out of prison he plans to live there," I said. "Can you imagine what it would be like every time he went out? It's in the center of the city, the busiest pedestrian street in Vitoria. Everybody is going to stare at him, to realize he's back. He wouldn't be able to bear being the villain in his own city."

Alba Díaz de Salvatierra chewed her lip as she listened to me, then stood up and addressed me sharply.

"You are perfectly aware that you should have told me earlier and consulted me as to whether it was wise to visit the prisoner. Wait for me here; I'm going to inform the cybercrimes team. Inspector Ayala, your computer will be monitored until further notice," she said, buttoning up the blue jacket of her tailored suit and leaving the office.

When I saw her go, I let out a lengthy sigh. I stared at the closed door for a few seconds. Despite my frustration, I forced myself to be professional.

"All right, Estí. What were you going to tell me when we were interrupted at Toloño's?"

"I have a list of all the personnel given keys to the Old Cathedral, but the manager told me something that could be interesting. A couple of weeks ago, one of the archaeologists in charge of taking tourists on guided tours asked for a spare key because she couldn't find her set. She claimed she didn't lose them, that she's very careful and never lets them out of her sight. She was convinced they had been stolen during the last tour, at a quarter to eight that evening. By the time the tour finished an hour later, it was almost dark. I can think of a lot of dimly lit places in the cathedral. A crafty person could have stolen her keys during the tour."

"Do we have the names of all the visitors that day?"

"Well, the director gave me a list. But they only record the name of one person for each group, and they don't ask for ID. If anyone went on the tour planning to steal the keys and leave a couple of dead bodies there later, you can be sure they didn't give their real name. That doesn't fit with the meticulous way this perpetrator carries out the crimes."

"We'll have to check the names anyway," I said. "Speaking of which, do we know who yesterday's victims were?"

"Our computer system has been down all morning, Unai. We haven't been able to get anywhere. We have to check hundreds of calls and match the descriptions with the two bodies. But I think we'll know soon enough. For now, to make some progress, I'll try to find a database with the names of all the beekeepers in the region. That should give us a start. Still, there are plenty of people who don't keep bees professionally or sell the honey. In the Gorbea Valley, lots of people keep hives as a hobby. Trying to establish an exhaustive list would be impossible. My father had some hives on our property. Well, he did before the Alzheimer's," she said, lowering her voice, as if doing so would make the diagnosis less painful.

Even though he was still very young, her father had recently moved into a specialized unit at the Txagorritxu assisted living center.

"My older brother must have gotten rid of them," Estí said, twirling her pen between her fingers. "I was always nervous about the bees and never went near them. I'm sorry I wasn't quick enough yesterday when that bee flew out of the victim's mouth. Bees can detect the adrenaline humans produce when we're stressed. They think they're being attacked and then they sting—that's why beekeepers need to be calm or at least be able to control their responses when they approach the hive. I'm such a bundle of nerves, it took quite a few stings for me to learn it was better to stay away."

At that moment, Alba Díaz de Salvatierra came back in. She looked solemn and tired already, and we still had a long day ahead.

"Okay, the cybercrimes team is examining your computer, Inspector Ayala. In the meantime, I'd like you two to tell me your first impressions of these four murders."

"Broadly speaking, there are three possibilities," I said, standing up. I don't know why, but standing helps me express myself. "Or three theories, if you prefer. Theory A: Tasio was the murderer twenty years ago, and this time he is the puppet master. That would imply he's using his influence over someone on the outside. This theory would fit with the Tasio I met this morning: an extremely intelligent individual who is very persuasive and has a high opinion of himself. He has the profile of a messianic leader."

"What would his motive be?" she asked.

"He wants somebody else to be framed, just as he says he was. He's in prison, so he couldn't be the one who committed the most recent crimes."

"Agreed." She sighed. "What's theory B?"

"The next most obvious one: the murderer is his brother."

"Ignacio?" she said in disbelief. "That's impossible, he's one of us, his record is impeccable, and—"

"I know, I know," I butted in. "But let me at least outline the theory, because it's possible. Theory B is that Ignacio is and was the murderer both now and twenty years ago. It's striking that the murders stopped for two decades and have started up again precisely at this moment. Ignacio could have resumed the crimes only a few weeks before his twin is released from prison so that Tasio is accused again. Ignacio's aim is to prevent Tasio from ever being set free. We don't know if Tasio threatened to take his revenge or kill Ignacio when he got out. However little Ignacio seems to fit the killer's profile, we can't ignore what the chronology of events tells us."

"Let's turn to theory C. I don't want to hear any more about this," she said, folding her arms across her chest.

"The final theory is that the killer is a copycat who has no contact with Tasio. An independent, someone new who has joined the twins' game but has nothing to do with them. I don't think it fits. The staging and the paraphernalia surrounding the deaths are elaborate; they've been carried out extremely carefully. That's not something someone can achieve right away. Normally, first crimes are botched. Novice murderers make huge mistakes. In other words, this is not the first time he's killed, and yet, as far as I know, no similar crimes have occurred in the Álava region."

"Okay," said the deputy superintendent. "So let's search for crimes where couples were naked or died from bee stings. Something that's happened that may be clumsier or not so impeccably staged."

"Kraken, you get on that," said Estíbaliz.

"What's this about Kraken?" Alba Díaz de Salvatierra pricked up her ears.

I stared daggers at my partner.

"Are you Kraken?" Alba insisted. It seemed to me that she had gotten very pale.

"It's a nickname I was given when I was a teenager. Why, is it relevant?"

"Yes, apparently it is. After the cyberattack, we monitored the Twitter account you mentioned. I think Tasio left you a message."

She took out her cell phone and showed us the latest tweet from Tasio's account, sent less than half an hour earlier:

> The hero needs a mentor, someone who has followed the same path. It's up to you whether this is a bright mentor or a dark one, #Kraken.

I pinched the bridge of my nose. I didn't find the message amusing. Not at all.

"How arrogant can you get?" I muttered.

"We'll have to go back to the prison and talk to the warden," said Alba. "We need to find out how Tasio communicates with the outside and gives the order for these tweets. We also need to establish if he's breaking the law, or if someone high up in the prison system is protecting him."

"I'll do it," I said. I had thought of a way we could move ahead in our investigation. It might not be orthodox, but it could be much more effective than questioning the warden.

"You can go, but I don't want you to visit Tasio Ortiz de Zárate."

"What?" I said, unable to believe my ears. "He's the only real lead we have right now, and you're forbidding me to talk to him?"

"It's dangerous."

"Dangerous? There's a double-pane security window between us, and guards at the door. What could be less dangerous than meeting with him?"

"I don't mean physical danger. I'm referring to his attempts to manipulate you."

"And you think I'm not prepared for that, that I'm not a professional?" I said. I could feel my temperature rising.

"You heard me. It's not something I'm going to argue about with you. And I want a full report on the conversation you had with the prisoner by the end of the day."

Estíbaliz threw me a look that said, *Leave it, you're not going to win.*

She was right; I had a noose around my neck. Still, I hated the idea that my movements could be restricted in an investigation. The deputy superintendent's absurd caution was going to slow us down, and if the murderer was bent on killing every few hours, then spending all afternoon in the office was like leaving a child unaccompanied in a candy store.

Frustrated, I sat down and waited for her to finish. What did I care?

"Finally," said the deputy superintendent, handing us a folder, "this is the official communiqué from our press department. The only details it gives are the victims' approximate ages and the time their bodies were discovered. We have included self-protection measures, as Inspector Ayala suggested. We're not going to add anything to this press release, no more details. Any progress in the investigation is to remain confidential until further notice."

"Good. I'll send it to my press contact."

"If you have any news, please tell me immediately. You may go now."

———

I left my new boss's office feeling as though I'd just been given a beating, a painful thrashing that would leave me stiff and sore for several days. Estíbaliz was thoughtful as well. I knew her; her brain was already racing at the speed of light.

"Speaking of paperwork, Estí, we need to get the files on the old crimes. Tasio told me something I want to check."

"I already thought of that. I'm on it. Come to my office. I asked Pancorbo to find them for me."

"Why Pancorbo?" I asked. He was a traffic inspector, and I couldn't see how he was connected to this case.

"Because he was Ignacio Ortiz de Zárate's partner. He used to be in the Criminal Investigation Unit. He transferred to Traffic right after the double murder at the medieval wall. I bet that pissed everyone off."

"Pancorbo?" I repeated. I found it hard to relate that gray pencil pusher with someone as brilliant as Ignacio Ortiz de Zárate. It didn't seem to me they could have made a very balanced team.

"Yes, Pancorbo," she said, pushing open her office door.

On her white Formica desk was a folder with a thick sheaf of files in it. Both Estíbaliz and I threw ourselves on them and spent the next half hour poring over the documents until we came to the photographs.

Maybe I wasn't prepared for what I saw.

I wanted to be.

I wanted to think I was. But when I saw the photograph of the newborns, a boy and a girl, naked, each with one hand on the other's cheek, with three small *eguzkilores* surrounding their heads in the tall weeds around the dolmen . . . it was like seeing *them*, the ones who were never born, the ones I never managed to get to know, the ones who still had a thousand names because we'd never had time to choose.

Perhaps more time passed than I recall, because suddenly Estíbaliz's worried face was next to mine. It took both her hands to pry mine from the photo of the dead babies. Apparently I was gripping it so hard that the photograph was stuck, unable to move in any direction, like me on that Avenue of Pines.

"Are you all right, Kraken? Do you want to stop for today?"

"I just . . . I just need some water," I said, jumping to my feet and leaving the room.

A short while later I returned, calmer and more focused. I knew Estíbaliz would never tell anyone about my lapses.

"Okay, let's concentrate on what we can get out of the reports," I said, and she nodded.

When I had finished going through them, I looked up in surprise.

"What's wrong?" she asked.

"There's something strange about the report on one of the last victims, the fifteen-year-old girl. The crime-scene report says there were traces of semen and indications of possible sexual aggression or at least sexual contact shortly before death. That was supposed to be confirmed at the autopsy, but there's no autopsy report here."

Estí looked at me, searched among the sheets of paper she had, and then shook her head. She didn't have it, either.

"Out of the eight murders, why is the only autopsy report that's missing the one for the fifteen-year-old girl?"

A fifteen-year-old girl, Tasio had said.

All of this was new and disturbing to me. I'd never suspected a sexual motive for any of the earlier crimes. That had not made it into the papers.

Who, inside the force, had stolen the autopsy report so that no one would know what had really happened to that young girl?

I glanced at my colleague, who spread her arms in an eloquent gesture.

The time had come to meet, in person, Ignacio Ortiz de Zárate, the honest policeman who had handed over his brother to justice.

Early the next morning, I put on my running shoes and set off through a tranquil, clean Vitoria. It was as if the city wished to stay well away from the crimes soiling its streets. I changed my usual route, because I didn't want to meet . . . But what was the point? I ran down Avenida Gasteiz, parallel to the tram lines, and turned around at Calle Basoa. I was climbing Cercas Bajas when I bumped into her.

I didn't want to stop. Not today, when I felt so hemmed in by her orders.

I quickened my pace and looked the other way when I passed her near Doña Otxanda's Tower, but she greeted me.

"Ishmael."

"Blanca" was all I replied before continuing.

So the parameters of our relationship were established: Inspector Ayala and Deputy Superintendent Díaz de Salvatierra during the working hours.

Blanca and Ishmael in the early morning.

6

NUMBER 2 CALLE DATO

FRIDAY, JULY 29

What do these last deaths have in common? Concentrate on the essentials, and draw up profiles of the victims, #Kraken.

That was the tweet I received over breakfast on Friday. Tasio's account had added almost thirty thousand new followers in the last few hours, and #*Kraken* was one of the day's trending topics. Not only did my dark mentor refuse to relinquish his dose of media fame, but he was arrogant enough to direct me in my investigation.

But that Friday it wasn't Tasio who was the protagonist of the latest drama; it was his brother, Ignacio.

It was a shame he'd left the force shortly after Tasio was sent to prison. Until then, Tasio had been the beloved media star. But a photograph, surreptitiously taken and published on the front page of *El Diario Alavés* twenty years earlier, had turned Ignacio into our hero.

In the photo, Ignacio was raising a hand to his stern-looking face to hide a tear as he entered the courtroom to testify. His jaw was set as he struggled to control himself during what was probably the worst moment of his life. This resigned composure in a man who had been able to see that his twin brother was a serial killer and hand him over to justice moved us all.

What police officer has never wondered, *What if the person I love most of all were a murderer—would I turn him in or protect him?* What if my grandfather had been a sadistic killer during the civil war? While I was training at the Arkaute Academy, I'd read files on Argentines of German descent who were horrified to discover that their beloved grandfathers were Nazi war criminals. How do you fit two such divergent views of reality into your life? Can you still embrace that person, give him a kiss on the forehead, look him in the eye? Do you denounce him? Do you stop seeing or loving someone who has looked after you, who has given you so much love and affection throughout your life?

After his brother's conviction, Ignacio became a presenter on the sort of TV crime shows that were popular at the end of the nineties. He was a demanding journalist, and the shows were completely different from the sensationalism offered on other channels. He developed a good reputation. After that, he vanished from the media. According to rumors, based on what he had been paid by the network, he didn't need to work for the rest of his life. In Vitoria he became highly sought after for civic events. He was always obliging, committed to his new role. Lately, though, I had lost track of him, so when Estíbaliz called me that morning to tell me what she was planning to do, I agreed to join her without a second thought.

Estíbaliz and I drove to Avenida Gasteiz, and by some strange miracle, we were able to park across from the triangular court buildings. We got out and walked to the Zaldiaran, the only Michelin-starred restaurant in Vitoria.

Thanks to Pancorbo, my partner had obtained Ignacio Ortiz de Zárate's telephone number and had made an appointment to see him in his apartment on Calle Dato two hours later. However, as I was morbidly curious both by nature and by occupational hazard, a gastronomic event hosted by Ignacio was too great a temptation to miss. He was partnering with Slow Food Araba, a nonprofit organization focusing on local food. The exhibition was starting at eleven that morning. Estíbaliz and I had shown up dressed more formally than usual so we wouldn't look out of place. She was wearing a cocktail dress as red as her hair, and I was in a slim-fitting, dark blue suit.

We entered the gastronomic temple and strolled down the wood-paneled hallways. The event space was full to overflowing. Hundreds of cell phones raised above people's heads flashed like fireworks at the celebrations in Donostia.

"Can you see anything?" my colleague asked in frustration.

I jabbed people with my elbows and made space for Estíbaliz to stand in front of me.

"Yes, I think our star is having a photo shoot," I said, although I wasn't entirely sure.

Stretching, I finally got a good look at him as he posed for the photographers. Every inch of him looked like my adolescent hero, twenty years later. He had aged well, unlike that human wreck in prison. Tasio looked like his twin brother's beggar grandfather.

There were no lines on Ignacio's face or dark-colored bags beneath his eyes. His well-groomed hair was still the dark blond I remembered, unlike his brother's silvery, unkempt strands. His body was tough and muscular, like an athlete's. He wore an expensive tailored suit with slim-fitting trousers, English suede shoes, and a brand-name wristwatch. His face was perfectly clean-shaven, as though an old-fashioned barber had given him a shave.

It was hard not to admire him. It was also hard for a woman like Estíbaliz not to be impressed. Maybe I felt a misplaced stab of jealousy.

Ignacio was standing and smiling in front of the Slow Food Araba snail logo and slogans. Next to him, artistically displayed on a table, was an array of regional gourmet products. From where

I stood, I could make out tins of Álava black truffles, pots of honey from the Gorbea Valley, small raffia sacks of red beans, and several bottles of the local *txakoli* wine.

Ignacio was talking about all these products with the measured enthusiasm of a veteran jewelry salesman. He nodded and winked, sprinkled his speech with crowd-pleasing anecdotes, invited several lucky spectators from the front row to try the *txakoli*, and gracefully accepted having his photograph taken with the chosen ones, who were grinning like idiots in the glow of his charm.

Once the camera flashes had finished, Ignacio glanced at his watch, thanked everyone with a fleeting smile, and tried to leave the platform.

But he was inundated with a battery of questions from the journalists.

"Ignacio, Europa Press, what do you think about the crimes in the Old Cathedral and the Casa del Cordón? Do you think your brother had anything to do with them?"

We all froze. Maybe the journalist had been too direct. There were a couple seconds of silence, but Ignacio's expression didn't alter. He was still smiling broadly, as if nothing had happened.

"Mireia, you know I'm not going to say anything about that. It's not my job anymore. And now, if you'll forgive me—"

"One last question." A young man with a British accent pushed forward. "For *The Sunday Times*—"

Everybody turned expectantly toward the English reporter. If the European press was starting to take an interest, the pressure surrounding the case might overwhelm Estí and me. But Ignacio didn't seem bothered in the slightest by the appearance of international media.

"I insist," said Ignacio with an elegant toss of his head, "I have nothing to say. I have nothing to do with this unfortunate affair. I thank you all for your interest and your presence at what is such an important event for our region's gastronomy. Good-bye."

Ignacio finally managed to step off the platform, but he was immediately surrounded by a slew of microphones, TV cameras, and members of the public trying to take selfies with him.

"Estí," I said to my partner, "grab him and tell him to go to the men's room. Otherwise he's going to be eaten alive."

I left the event space and asked where the restrooms were. Once inside, I had to wait several minutes before Ignacio entered. He closed the door behind him and leaned against the wall, closing his eyes. He raised his head toward the ceiling and let out a lengthy sigh.

"I'm Inspector Ayala," I said, extending my hand. "We agreed to meet at one o'clock at your apartment, but I think you're going to find it hard to get out of here unscathed. Did you bring a car?"

"No, I came on foot," he replied, grasping my hand firmly. "Ever since El Día de Santiago, people have gone crazy. Everybody's been stopping me in the street to tell me the first thing that comes into their head, but I never thought a culinary event like this could be a trap. I'm afraid it's going to be the same way it was twenty years ago: I won't be able to live my life anymore."

"My colleague and I have a car parked by the courthouse," I said, determined to sound decisive.

"Is it a patrol car? The last thing I need is for people to see me getting into a police vehicle. That would set off even more paranoid conspiracy theories."

"No, it's not a patrol car."

At that point, the police inspector he had once been took control.

"Okay, you're taller and heavier than I am, and you're not in uniform," he said. "Tell your colleague to leave first and bring the car to the restaurant. When you and I leave, shield me with your body and turn your head away from the cameras so they can't identify you. Let's try to keep them from getting the front-page photo they're after."

"Understood."

Five minutes later, when Estíbaliz told us she was in position, we risked crossing the barrier of people waiting at the exit to Zaldiaran. I used my body to protect Ignacio, who was already an expert at escaping the chains that fame brought with it, and as soon as we saw the rear door open, we flung ourselves into the car.

"Do you still want to go to your place?" asked Estíbaliz.

"Yes, we can leave the car in the New Cathedral's parking lot and continue on foot to Calle Dato."

The Ortiz de Zárate twins had inherited their parents' fortune. After their deaths, when the twins were little more than eighteen, they had sold the family company, Ferrerías Alavesas, to the highest bidder. Neither of them wanted to continue in the business. In fact, they didn't need to work, but each had a vocation and followed it: one wanted to be a policeman, the other an archaeologist. Both rose to the top of their professions.

Both bought apartments in the richest part of the city: Calle Dato. Both settled at the top of the street, almost on the corner of Dato and Postas. One across from the other, as if each wanted to reign over his own side of the street. The left-hand side for you, the right-hand for me. Ignacio at Number 2, up toward the Plaza de la Virgen Blanca. Tasio down to Los Fueros. Back then, nobody doubted they would have the world at their feet.

We went up to the third floor in a refurbished elevator, and Ignacio opened the reinforced door to his spacious apartment. The decor was in shades of gray and ochre, very masculine, and it looked as if it had been done by a professional—although I did notice one disturbing detail. I filed it away for later, forcing myself to concentrate on the strategic exploration I was about to undertake.

I didn't like to consider my interviews, whether they were with witnesses or suspects, as interrogations. I had learned from experience that in a small city like Vitoria, people tend to close ranks and follow the code of silence, annoying as that is. As a result, I always prepared a list of topics, starting with the easiest and least awkward and working up to the most difficult. They were like buoys I could cling to until I reached a port that interested me.

I went over the route I had chosen, the points I wanted clarified: the people he had known twenty years before, the media question, the missing autopsy report, and Tasio's imminent release.

"Thank you for having us here, sir."

"Don't be so formal. For heaven's sake, I'm only a couple of years older than you."

"Five," I couldn't help saying.

He looked at me with a swift raise of his eyebrow. I think that was when he realized I knew all the details of the case.

"All right, five then," he said, still studying me. There was a tense silence as we stood in the vast living room. Its restored picture windows looked out onto Calle Dato. "Would you care for a glass of vintage wine? On the Slow Food board, we're working with a wine producer in the Rioja Alavesa who's having a lot of success on the international market. I'd like you both to try it."

"No, thank you, Ignacio. You know we're on duty," I replied.

"I'd love to try it," my colleague said swiftly.

I gave her a hard look. She was as bad as I was at following orders, but we tried to hide that, at least in public.

"You can take a seat. You in this armchair, and you in the other one," he said, pointing to identical, designer black wingback chairs facing each other across an elegant coffee table. "I'll get the wine."

He left us and went to get the bottle.

When he came back, he poured Estíbaliz a glass and sat in the center of the sofa, as if he had placed us on either side of himself to make sure the scene was symmetrical. It seemed an odd thing to do, like a play with a carefully staged set design.

Ignacio sipped his wine and left the glass on the table in front of him. He had also brought another empty glass, which I thought must be for me, but he didn't offer it. Instead, he took a moment to carefully arrange the full and empty glasses in front of him.

Pairs of objects.

In his apartment, everything was decorated in pairs, as if two people lived there rather than a much-sought-after bachelor on his own.

"So you're also on the Slow Food board?" I asked with genuine interest. "It must be fascinating to be involved with regional products."

"Oh, absolutely. We work with local producers without intermediaries: black truffles, potatoes from the Montaña Alavesa."

"Do you work with any honey producers?" asked Estíbaliz as casually as possible.

"Yes. In fact, I look after that product myself," he said offhandedly. "The world of bees is intriguing, don't you think?"

"It certainly is," Estí replied. "At my parents' place we always had a few hives, both for our own consumption and to add to what we earned from the farm. In the Gorbea area, everyone knew a bit about apiculture because it was passed down from generation to generation."

Ignacio smiled to himself, as if we'd told a joke that only he understood. He left his now-empty glass alongside its twin and went over to one of the big windows, where he stood and stared outside, his forehead pressed against the white wooden frame.

"If you don't mind, let's stop beating around the bush. Ask me the questions you've come to ask. I have no intention of obstructing the investigation."

I gave a sigh of relief. This would save me quite a few buoys.

"Thank you for being so direct, Ignacio."

"Even when you're no longer a policeman, what we're taught at the academy stays with you," he said, almost to himself, still staring at the building across the way. "With the four new murders and what happened twenty years ago, I'm sure you must have a lot of unanswered questions."

"I'll get to it then," I said. "First, I'd like to ask you about the media. You can't deny that those first crimes made Tasio's shows tremendously popular. As far as I'm aware, his archaeology program went almost unnoticed initially. But as soon as he began to produce theories about the historical symbolism in each murder, he became a star. Who was in charge when your brother—"

"My twin," Ignacio corrected me, as though I had been disrespectful.

"Sorry, yes, your twin. I was asking who directed his earlier show, the one before his national television deal. That director must have been upset. They believed in him, and then, just when they thought they'd struck gold, he was snapped up by the big boys."

"Are you trying to find a motive?"

"At the moment, I'm simply trying to establish who was around at the time. Can you give me a name?"

"Inés Ochoa," he murmured. "She was the one who pulled the strings at the channel."

"Did you know her?"

"Since you'll find out sooner or later, I might as well give you my version. Inés Ochoa was and still is the program director for our regional channel. And I'm going to anticipate your next question: yes, she was the one who suggested I record those crime shows after I had arrested my twin. At first, I refused. I knew that there would be a flood of criticism in Vitoria; my twin's arrest was too recent. But she insisted that it was the best way to explain what had happened; in the end, she said, the journalists were going to write what they wanted anyway. I thought that if I was in charge, we could do something worthwhile."

"Do you regret it?" asked Estíbaliz.

"Every single day," he murmured wearily.

"So Inés Ochoa benefited from the murders?"

"At first, thanks to my brother, of course she did. Then everything got turned upside down and she was left without her star. Soon afterward she swapped him for me: One twin for the other. Villain for hero. The ratings and the advertising frenzy more than compensated for what she paid me."

"I gather you don't have a pleasant memory of her?" I suggested.

"I don't have a pleasant memory of anything that happened back then," he replied evasively.

"Do you know where we can find her?"

"That question is unnecessary," he replied. "You're on active duty. You can dig up her details in two minutes without any help from me. Ask at the TV station for the Stone Lady. Be careful, though, she's one of those people who always lands on her feet, like a cat. If what you really want to know is if we're still in contact with each other, the answer is no. And don't say hello to her from me."

That's interesting, at the very least.

"I see lots of things have changed in twenty years," I said. "It would be very helpful, and would save us a lot of time, if you could give us a list of the friends you and Tasio had back then. Mutual friends and individual ones. Professional colleagues, relatives. Could you give me a list of, say, fifteen, for example?"

"You want to review the case."

"We're not going to pretend that the key to solving the new crimes necessarily lies within the old ones. But I'd like you to provide me with a manageable number of people for us to interview."

He nodded, lost in thought. There was no longer any sign of the polished public performer: that persona had vanished the moment he crossed the threshold of his refuge.

"That seems reasonable," he finally admitted. "I'll send you the list today. If I were you, I'd be doing the same thing. Anything else?"

"We've seen the files on the earlier murders. The autopsy report on the fifteen-year-old girl is missing," said Estíbaliz.

Ignacio shrugged; he didn't seem particularly interested. "Ask Pancorbo. I can assure you that when I left the force, all the statements and autopsy reports were in their corresponding files. Nothing was missing."

"You don't trust Pancorbo?" my partner asked.

"No, it's not that," he said quickly, with a smile that seemed rehearsed. "I didn't mean to imply Pancorbo took the autopsy report on the girl. What I meant was that I haven't set foot in police headquarters in almost twenty years. I'm sure things must have been moved around. Pancorbo followed the case with me and was essential in helping to solve it. He's the only person I can think of who could give you some idea of when the report might have gone missing. Don't be fooled by his quiet, placid appearance. He's much sharper than he looks, but you'd have to spend hours on a stakeout with him to see it."

"You don't seem to attach much importance to that autopsy report. Don't you think someone could have taken it deliberately? Someone on the inside who might not want anybody to know what happened to that girl?"

"It was a series of eight murders," he muttered, as if repeating a mantra he'd said a hundred times. "And it all happened twenty years ago. You'll have to forgive me, but I've tried to forget the details and the circumstances surrounding the crime. I can't bear this feeling of déjà vu."

"But there was something different about that dead body, wasn't there? You can't have forgotten it. Did your brother know the girl?"

"Not that I know of."

"Did he know any of the children who were killed?"

"Not that I know of."

"Any of the victims' families?"

"Not that you know of," Estíbaliz anticipated.

"They were ritual murders. Don't look any further than that. I also initially investigated possible links between the victims. I spent a precious amount of time on that when I could've been doing something that might have helped us prevent the final murders." He said these last words as though he were biting into a lemon. "They were ritual murders. The *eguzkilores,* the ancient poison, the bodies laid out pointing northwest, the way pagans have done for millennia."

We were finally getting to the heart of the matter.

"And you thought that fit with your broth—your twin?"

"Tasio went through a dark period when he was writing his thesis. He became fascinated by the events at Zugarramurdi. You know, the Inquisition's trials in Logroño in 1610, when eleven local people were accused of witchcraft and burned at the stake. When he was studying in Navarra, he used to hang around a lot with a colleague whose name I can't remember, but he was much younger and very radical—he loved those weird topics. Paganism, occultism, syncretism—all the dark isms you can think of. They had known each other for years. At first their friendship shocked me, until Tasio told me how they had met." He gave us a sidelong glance, as if weighing whether to offer us more information or to keep quiet.

I gave him an encouraging look, and, luckily, he went on.

"From time to time Tasio smoked marijuana and tried other illegal substances as well. I wasn't exactly in favor of it—I always believed in respecting the law—but I didn't condemn him for it, either. I wanted him to trust me so that I would always know what he was getting into. In those days, when he was experimenting, the other guy was his usual supplier. He sold hash in some bars in Kutki. They struck up a friendship, although he was still only a teenager and Tasio was already finishing his studies."

He fell silent, as if it was difficult for him to recall these things.

"Go on, please," I said, afraid he might clam up. "You were telling us that his friend had some extreme pagan ideas."

"That's right. One weekend they went to the cave at Akelarrenlezea, or Sorginen Lezea as some people call it. The cave of *aquelarre*, the witch's cave. The locals can never agree on the name. They wanted to reenact the *aquelarre* ritual, based on descriptions in the texts they were studying, particularly the original witnesses' testimonies from the seventeenth-century trials. They took all sorts of pagan paraphernalia with them: potions, natural dyes to paint symbols on themselves. They also took *eguzkilores*, not merely for protection but also because when the roots are dipped in distilled water, they're supposed to have aphrodisiac properties. They went up there with two girls they were dating at the time—I didn't want to join them. I didn't like that guy at all, he hung out in circles that . . . you know what I mean. By then I was in the police force, so we were natural enemies. I don't know what they got up to that weekend in the cave, but I do know drugs were involved. When Tasio returned, he was nervous, terror-stricken. His pupils were dilated, his limbs stiff; he had trachycardia and palpitations, and his heart was beating like a drum. I stayed with him for a whole week. I wanted to question his friend, but Tasio wouldn't allow it. He wouldn't tell me a thing, although something serious had happened, because they didn't see each other again. I don't know if that answers your question. We never want to see what's coming until it crushes us."

Now came the most difficult question.

"How do you feel about him getting out? Have you been in touch at all over the past twenty years?" I asked, struggling to sound neutral.

He shook his head and looked at me sadly, as if I were a child.

"I turned him in. How do you think he took it?"

I didn't reply. I wanted him to continue talking.

"You don't understand," he said eventually. "I've lived two

lives. One as the twin brother of my other half. The other as an only son. That moment split us all in two."

Good, now the Ignacio I want to see is emerging, instead of the beautiful mask you want to show us.

"If he gets out on parole as scheduled, will you see each other again? Will you renew contact?"

"That's between my twin and me." He turned toward us, unable to hide his discomfort. "I don't want to be brusque, but you must respect my private life. I don't like talking about myself, and this is the toughest thing I've ever had to face. Everyone has gone crazy this week; in the bars, it's all they're talking about. I don't know if I can go through this again. Plus, it's incredibly inconvenient. I have several commitments for las Fiestas de la Blanca: dinners with friends and sponsors of the brands I represent, bullfights, riding in parades. I bought tickets for all these things months ago, but now I think I might just spend the summer at the place I have in Laguardia, until everything calms down."

"And now you're going to politely show us out," I said.

"That's right. Thank you for saving me from getting on my high horse."

"From one police officer to another," I said, standing up and holding out my business card, "could you send me an e-mail with that list?"

I was relying on the fact that our experts had cleaned my computer by now. Tasio could no longer gain access to my messages.

"You'll have it in a couple of hours. I'll cooperate with whatever you want," he said, as though he needed to convince us he was on our side.

Estí and I walked down Calle Dato. The late-morning sun was so hot that our formal clothes were a nuisance, and so were her high heels. She gestured in a way that made me think she was about to throw them at the statue of El Caminante, a ten-foot-tall bronze fellow who had become the city's best-loved souvenir.

"Come in with me," I said when we reached the Goya cake shop. "I need some sugar to help me think."

We went into one of the branches of the oldest confectioner in Vitoria. It was most famous for the *vasquitos* and *nesquitas*, oblong chocolates they had made since 1886. Our ancestors' gluttony had made them the city's favorite ever since.

"Half a kilo of pastries, please, all of them with jelly," I told the assistant, a middle-aged woman with dyed-red hair. As usual, she ignored my request and filled the box with the selection she thought most appropriate.

I left the store resignedly with my box of cakes, and we walked down Calle San Prudencio to pick up our car. We went past Fernández de Betoño's optician office and waited until there were fewer people around so that no one could overhear our conversation.

"Why fifteen, Kraken?" Estíbaliz shot at me. "Why did you ask him for a list of fifteen friends?"

"Nobody has fifteen close friends. Some of those on his list won't be so intimate. I'll start with the last names, the ones he'll have to think hardest about. I won't even bother with the first ones because they'll only have good things to say about him. Let's see if they all close ranks around Ignacio or whether we can find his dark side."

"What do you think of what we saw in there?" she asked. "From a profiler's perspective?"

I sighed and tried to sort out what I had detected. It was no easy task. Ignacio had a complex personality, and of course he had suffered a huge personal trauma.

"I think Ignacio has a kind of split personality. In public, out on the street, he shines. You can't take your eyes off him, pure charisma. His open smile . . . But then in private, at his own home, it's as if he were hollow. He becomes gray, he doesn't smile, and he doesn't even bother to pretend. Did you notice that his voice was much lower? As if he were older than he looks. Then there were several things that seemed almost pathological, like his obsession with two of everything. And did you see that all the objects in his apartment are symmetrical? The furnishings on either side of the hallway, the sofas, the tables, the ornaments. All the paintings are pairs. As if he's half of a whole, waiting for his twin to return and fill the empty space. And he never stopped looking out the window, almost like it was a support mechanism. A psychological reassurance, a means of escape when we were pressuring him. But he didn't look in every direction, just at the building opposite—and do you know what's there?"

"Before it used to be the Banco de Vitoria; now it's the Banco de Santander."

"No, Estí. I mean what's next door to the Banco de Santander."

"The entrance to where his brother—sorry, his twin—lived," she said sarcastically.

"That's right. It's as if he's expecting to see him arrive. He seemed to be keeping a close watch. What were your impressions?" I asked as we crossed the gardens behind the new cathedral.

"That both Ignacio and Tasio are more affected by what happened twenty years ago than they want to admit. The sixty-four-thousand-dollar question is whether they're still so influenced by it that they're eager to start the game again."

"I don't know, Estí. I'd say that today's Tasio is capable of anything, including seeking revenge on his brother and wanting to see him behind bars. The new Tasio is far stranger than the gilded version of the twins you've just seen."

Estíbaliz came to a stop beside the pond behind the New Cathedral, where there was a statue of a crocodile with human hands. She looked around, took off her shoes, and sat on the edge of the small pool.

"Are you all right? I know you're tired, but is there something else?"

"The weekend is coming up; I'm going to stay in Vitoria with Iker. I should go and visit my father in Txagorritxu, but that always makes me anxious."

"Are you doing okay?"

"Yes, everything's under control, Kraken. What about you? I'm worried that seeing so many dead children will affect you."

"It's always hard," I said, loosening my tie and sitting next to her, "but we knew we were going to see horrible things when we joined the Criminal Investigation Unit. We should be able to take it in stride and keep our demons locked up. Estí, do you think you and I are ready for this case, or is it going to crush us?"

"I'll watch out for you, and you watch out for me. Together, we're unstoppable. We just have to focus and make sure our skeletons are kept firmly in the closet."

I said nothing. We were weak.

Estíbaliz claimed she was over her addictions, and I trusted her. But she still had not come to terms with her father's Alzheimer's diagnosis, his rapid deterioration, and his recent move into an assisted living facility. Let's just say we were on orange alert.

"Changing subjects and recapitulating," she said, standing up and heading for the entrance to the parking lot, heels in hand. "What do we have now that we didn't have this morning?"

I sighed and forced myself to concentrate on the double murders again.

"Two new individuals I'd love to visit when we can locate them: Inés Ochoa, or the 'Stone Lady,' and Tasio's mysterious companion in the pagan rituals. Second, a link between Ignacio and the murder weapon: bees. If he deals with a lot of beekeepers and knows that world, it's possible he also knows how to transfer the bees into a container and trigger their aggression with gasoline. But we can't forget that the information about the bees hasn't been in the press yet. Remember, too, that Ignacio lied: he said he didn't remember anything about that fifteen-year-old girl. He was very good at pretending to be unconcerned when I mentioned the missing autopsy report."

"Or he's spent twenty years rehearsing his reply."

"We need to investigate the twins: their family, their past, their circle of friends," I said thoughtfully as I paid the parking-lot ticket. "Nobody did that before, because Ignacio caught Tasio in flagrante and the case was closed."

"That means we have a lot of work ahead of us. Are you going to Villaverde tomorrow?"

"If there's no news and nobody wants me urgently. You know I don't like to leave my grandfather on his own for too long. But if you think I need to be in Vitoria this weekend, tell me."

"I'll be with Iker both days. There are a thousand details to settle for this damn wedding, not to mention the depressing visit to my father. I'll be too busy to worry about things."

"All right, keep your demons at bay."

"And you do the same."

"I always do."

I always do, Estí. That's what keeps me in the land of the living.

7

VILLAVERDE

SATURDAY, JULY 30

Think of the scene as the murderer telling us a story.
What is behind the rituals of these new crimes,
#Kraken?

The next day I set off early for Villaverde, the tiny hamlet with seventeen inhabitants where my grandparents had brought up Germán and me after the death of our parents, so many lifetimes ago.

I liked getting started very early, driving south along the Puerto de Vitoria road, going slowly around the bends in the Bajauri beechwoods, making sure I stayed well clear of the Avenue of Pines, where my life had changed forever.

Villaverde was about twenty-five miles from Vitoria, in the foothills of the Montaña Alavesa, facing the Cantabrian Mountains, or the Sierra de Toloño, as it had come to be called. We locals could never agree with the regional council offices that published the maps of Álava. I grew up admiring the screen of beech, oak, and hazel trees I could see from the heavy wooden front door of the three-hundred-year-old house my grandparents lived in. It was one of those farmhouses with walls a yard thick that kept the icy winter outside, far from our open kitchen fire.

I parked beneath the trellis my grandfather insisted on decorating with tubs of red begonias, even though whenever there was a wind from the south, the poor plants would dry out and he would have to start all over again. He was accustomed to starting and restarting things. Just like his almost centenarian heart, his most important quality was that he kept going.

"Stop moaning and keep going" was his slogan. And that's what he did.

At that time of day Villaverde's steep streets were deserted, but suddenly a horn broke the silence and the Bernedo baker's van climbed the slope to me.

"Morning, Unai. One *hueco* loaf and one *sobao*?"

I was about to take the two steaming loaves when somebody came up behind me.

"I also ordered three *preñados*." I heard my grandfather's raspy voice.

"Here they are. Enjoy," said the deliveryman, closing the back doors of his van and leaving the smell of warm bread floating in the air.

I turned around and smiled. Grandfather knew just what Germán and I loved. Those freshly baked bread rolls filled with hot sausages and their juices were the best pick-me-up in the world after a morning of hard work in the hills.

"What do we have to do today, Grandpa?"

"Come on, your brother got up earlier than you. He's been working in the hazel grove for a while already."

He reached inside the doorway and brought out a pair of scythes.

"Okay, let me get changed and we'll go up there."

I climbed the stairs in a couple of bounds, went into my childhood bedroom, and put on a pair of worn jeans, a white T-shirt, and sturdy boots.

We walked down the village's cobbled streets in silence, scythes slung over our shoulders, while I helped him put his beret on straight. A hefty, vigorous man, he always leaned forward as he strode along in his blue overalls. He was a man of few words: he didn't need fancy language to be right—and he usually was, thanks to his common sense.

"Grandpa, I've brought you some pastries from Goya, but you have to show me the results of your analysis," I said as we went. "What did they say about your cholesterol?"

He shrugged and kept his eyes on the road.

"I haven't looked at them," he lied.

"I see," I said. "That means they were high again. You need to take care of yourself, Grandpa. I'm not going to leave the box of pastries in Villaverde, because I'm sure you'd eat them all."

He twisted his mouth as though he couldn't care less, still staring ahead.

"I'll have to try one or two," he declared, readjusting the beret.

I smiled to myself. "Yes, Grandpa, one or two."

We passed behind the church and crossed the threshing floor where years ago cereals were threshed to separate out the grain. The nearby haylofts had been restored, thanks to the locals' desire to preserve them. At the end of the village we went down a slope to the bridge over the river Ega and entered the land on its banks. The hazel trees were so close to one another that not enough daylight penetrated the canopy, and the branches and weeds were growing so high we could hardly force our way through.

This was where we found Germán, in blue overalls custom-made for him. He was lopping off branches with a scythe as if there were no tomorrow.

My brother and I would have broken our backs working for our grandfather if he'd asked us to. It was the least we could do for him. He was almost a hundred years old, but he was still teaching us with an undemonstrative wisdom I hoped to inherit one day.

"Is Martina coming?" I asked Germán, glancing at the time on my cell phone.

"Yes, she said she'd be here around midday and will have lunch with us."

"Great," I said, smiling. Our small family was very grateful for her feminine touch.

Martina had been Germán's girlfriend for more than four years. She worked in family mediation for Vitoria's Social Services in the Lakua neighborhood, close to my office, and we often had lunch together. She had the gentle, patient voice of those who bestow affection without keeping score, tiny kiwi-colored eyes, and a disastrous haircut that was fortunately growing out. Martina was recovering from an aggressive cancer that had left her bald and weak, but the courage she'd shown throughout her chemotherapy sessions was one of the main reasons I'd come back from the apathy I'd been plunged into after experiencing my own private hell two years earlier.

Watching Martina shave off her long black locks and go to work every day mediating divorces and custody battles, even though she looked like a walking skeleton and was such a mess whenever Germán and I had to pick her up from treatment, helped me get past my cynicism and my lack of will to live. Once more I started to appreciate what I had around me: health, friends, a grandfather, a brother, a sister-in-law, a job that allowed me to remove the scum from our streets. . . .

Sweeping these dark thoughts from my mind, I concentrated on getting rid of all the low branches I came across. Four hours later, we had polished off the rolls, and all the weeds and bundles of wood were piled up at the entrance to the hazel grove. Grandfather took a red apple out of his pocket.

"Show me that eczema, son," he said to Germán.

My brother rolled up his pants leg and showed him a reddish blotch on his calf. Taking out his Swiss army knife, Grandfather cut the apple into four equal pieces and rubbed them on Germán's skin. Then he tied the quarters back together with a piece of string and buried the apple.

"Make sure you rot quickly," he whispered to it.

According to him, in a few days, when the apple had decomposed, Germán's eczema would also be gone. Grandfather used apples for all kinds of things: warts, burns. . . . I had studied science for too long to believe in that kind of thing, and in fact, my grandfather was too pragmatic to put much faith in these superstitions, either, but the truth is that his natural remedies usually worked pretty well.

Once he had finished with his ancestral cure, he lay down at the foot of a tree, got comfortable, and within a few minutes was snoring loudly.

Germán and I also sat down, leaning against the oldest hazel trunk. We were exhausted but jubilant.

"I read about the double murders," he said, plucking a blade of grass and slipping it into his mouth.

"Who hasn't?" I said, staring at the mountains.

"Did they put you in charge?"

"Uh-huh."

"Do you want to talk about it?"

"Not yet."

"Not yet? What's that supposed to mean?"

"It means that maybe someday when the case becomes more complex, when I'm getting pressured because there's no quick fix, when I'm even more stressed about it—then I'll need you. I'll need you to put on your confessor's robe and listen to me because I'll have to tell you things that I can't share with anyone but you and Estíbaliz. But for now, it's all right. I can cope. I'll take a rain check, okay?"

Germán thought this over for a minute, then ran his fingers through his dark hair.

"As you wish." He sighed. "Anyway, there's something I need to tell you, so I'll be quick."

No, Germán, don't start, I thought, rolling my eyes.

"You tend to become obsessed, Unai. I know you joined the Criminal Investigation Unit because you think murders can be predicted, that you can prevent them. But that sounds unhealthy, megalomaniacal even. Somebody has to say it. Since what happened to Paula and the children, you're not yourself. You keep saying crazy things like you should have seen the signs, and I don't even know what other crap. Look, you're my older brother, so get everything off your chest with me if you like. I'm not going to judge you. But don't say things like that in public, not even in your *cuadrilla.* They're our friends, but people talk when you're not there. Don't become obsessed with this case, all right? Make sure to protect yourself: everyone in Vitoria is on edge these days, and even people you know are going to demand things of you. These murders will bring out the worst in people. Beyond a certain point, no one is innocent."

No, no one is innocent.

What could I tell him?

I am my grandfather's grandchild. In the years after the civil war, when Grandfather was the mayor of Villaverde, he went into the blacksmith's house, belt in hand, and taught the blacksmith a lesson, because someone in the village had told him the man was beating his wife.

This happened in the forties, when domestic violence was a private affair. No one called the Guardia Civil if they heard shouting at a neighbor's house, because those upholders of law and order always replied: "It's a private matter between a man and his wife. We can't get involved." That wasn't what my grandfather thought. When I asked him about that incident, he always shrugged and muttered, "He was a coward, beating his wife like that," and then he carried on calmly eating his ewe's-milk cheese and drinking his daily glass of Rioja.

It wasn't that I considered myself a hero. I simply wanted to leave the universe the way it was. Without unnecessary deaths, that's all. I understood the logical mechanism hidden behind the natural order of things, even death—an accident, illness, old age— but I couldn't accept evil creatures making the Grim Reaper knock on innocent people's doors before it was their time.

"Okay, thanks for having the courage to tell me what nobody else dares to say."

"Sometimes you don't make it easy, Unai. I know you've suffered a lot, but the world keeps on turning and people forget your dramas quickly. You can't stay stuck in a rut."

"Not now, Germán. Not now." I put my hand on his arm to stop him.

Germán fell silent. He was intelligent enough to know when it was time to shut up.

My brother wasn't just clever; he was something else. What he lacked in stature, he more than made up for with his quick wit. He knew that if he could take advantage of the first few seconds of astonishment his size created by making a couple of witty remarks—not the same old ones but jokes that really made people laugh—the rest was simple. He might be small, but he was good-looking and one of the most elegant and stylish men I've ever known. Germán could differentiate among four different kinds of necktie knots, and he could take you to task for choosing the wrong pair of socks.

He visited the hairdresser once a week, and his haircut was always a year ahead of mine. Currently he was sporting a hipster look, so the sides were shaved and the black forelock was combed back. He had let his beard grow, but it was better cared for than a hedge at Buckingham Palace.

He was also a connector. Germán knew everyone in Álava,

and everyone knew him, perhaps because there weren't that many people in the city with dwarfism.

It wasn't always this way. I did throw a few punches at kids who harassed him—what's now known as bullying—when he was a teenager and everyone else was a couple of feet taller. I'd do it again. And I'm saying that as someone who never gets into fights, not only because I hate violence but also because whenever you fight, you get hurt as well.

The way our grandfather brought us up was also a great influence: he never made any distinction between us even though Germán was tiny, and he never allowed my brother to feel sorry for himself.

If Germán had to climb aboard the tractor and the first step was a foot off the ground, my grandfather would say, "Stop moaning and get up there." And Germán would find a way to clamber onto the back wheel and slip into the tractor cabin.

When the pedals of the harvester were too far away from Germán's feet, Grandfather helped him make boxwood extensions that he could tie to his boots. They always found ways to adjust his height to the world around him and get on with it.

Germán applied the treatment he got at home to the rest of his life. He had no complexes and a brilliant mind and was kindness itself. He found it hard to get a girlfriend at first, but then everything went smoothly.

He also soon realized that receiving a distinction in his law degree meant he was way above average, not below it, and he enjoyed the feeling. He set up his office in the Plaza América in Vitoria with money he and I had saved from working on Grandfather's harvest each summer. Within a few years he had become the go-to attorney for the city and a fair and much-loved boss to twelve employees. There was no secret to his success: new clients always came to him, because he spent more hours at his office than anybody else.

———————

I suppose we made a strange trio: my grandfather with his beret, my brother with his sharp mind, and me with my . . . who knows what. I've never analyzed myself. I've no idea what my most obvious characteristic is or what the world thinks of me.

Well, now I do. Now I'm the policeman who caught the most famous serial killer in the history of Vitoria. The policeman who ended up with a bullet in the third cerebral convolution of the left hemisphere of his brain.

Tomorrow, they're unplugging me.

Ten days since the shooting and I'm still in a coma. I drew up my will when I joined the police force. I left instructions for my ashes to be scattered from the top of San Tirso, a stone monolith standing on the summit of our mountain range, in view of Vitoria.

I know it's cruel to make my grandfather and Germán climb a hundred and fifty feet of solid rock with my urn. The first part, if you start from the bush about forty feet to the south of the huge boulder, is easy. After that it's more difficult, and coming down is a nightmare. The best way is to jump, but it's high, and you risk rolling down until the boxtrees stop you. It's complicated, I know.

But they'll do it.

They'll find their own ingenious, logical way of doing it.

They'll do it for me.

8

AT MATXETE'S

SUNDAY, JULY 31

Analyze the differences between these murders and the earlier crimes. What direction is the murderer pointing you in this time, #Kraken?

I arrived at Matxete's grill around ten that night. Almost all the *cuadrilla* were already there. We were celebrating Xabi's birthday, the youngest in our group, and we had reserved one of the restaurant's vaulted stone rooms.

As soon as I entered, I realized this wasn't going to be a relaxing dinner: all my friends stopped talking immediately when I came in.

"Hi, Xabi, happy birthday," I said as casually as I could.

He smiled with only the corners of his mouth, then looked away.

I sat at the only spare seat left, at the head of the table, between Nerea, one of my closest friends, and my sister-in-law, Martina, who smiled at me encouragingly.

I ordered a large pork chop to give me strength and waited for the bombs to explode. Everyone was tense, glancing surreptitiously at their cell phones to check the latest news on Twitter as soon as the little blue bird cheeped.

Juan fired the opening salvo. "Aren't you going to tell us anything, Kraken?"

I didn't take it amiss: I saw his rum and Coke was almost gone and, judging from the two other empty glasses on the table, it was his third.

"Don't be so tiresome," said Martina before I could reply. She was always the one to smooth things over. "You know he can't talk about his cases."

"But he should if we're all caught up in this," said Nerea.

Nerea was small and stocky, like a smooth, round pebble. She had a moon face and bangs she had worn the same way since her First Communion. She managed a kiosk on the corner of Postas and the Plaza de la Virgen Blanca, next to La Ferre. She inherited it from her parents. Even though she had a biology degree, she had never worked in the field, because she refused to travel more than a few miles from Vitoria.

"What's wrong, Nerea?" I sighed, looking her in the eye.

What are you going to blame me for?

"There's a serial killer murdering pairs of us living in Vitoria, and the person imprisoned twenty years ago is sending you tweets. Because *you* are the Kraken this lunatic is writing to, aren't you?"

I spread my arms wide: no point denying it.

"What's going on, Unai?" she went on, blowing her bangs out of the way, as she always did when she was exasperated. "Are you going to arrest him, force him to stop? I'm going crazy. I'm scared stiff when I go out at six in the morning to open the kiosk. Can't you make this stop?"

Nerea was screeching at me. She hadn't realized, but she was clutching my wrist and had left indentations in my skin with her nails.

"May I have my arm back, Nerea?"

"Sorry," she said, drawing into herself like a snail. "It's just . . ."

I'm so nervous, Unai. Everybody is talking about the same thing. I can't sell a newspaper without people asking me for the latest information about the crimes, as if I was a TV news program."

"Is it true about the hooves?" Asier the pharmacist wanted to know.

"What hooves?" I asked blankly.

"The hooves of the billy goat. According to social media, it's an occult crime. They're talking about a huge pentagram drawn on the floor of the Casa del Cordón, of dead black cats in the Old Cathedral's entrance. There are all sorts of theories and suppositions, but the most common rumor is that hoofprints were found next to the murdered kids' feet."

Lutxo, Nerea, Xabi—they were all staring at me, hanging on my reply.

"I know this is an extraordinary situation. It seems unreal that someone is killing people on our streets. The city is in a state of panic, just as it was twenty years ago. We all went through that, didn't we? And now I'm the one in charge of the case, but I can't tell you a thing about the Twitter messages. As you well know, I'm not authorized to talk to anyone about that. You're all intelligent enough to understand. Do you want to help solve the case? I'm sure you do, and that's why I need you to behave like good friends, so that whenever we meet the topic doesn't dominate our conversations, so I can relax when I'm not at police headquarters. So when I go to work, I can concentrate and not have to worry about anything else. This isn't going to be easy. I'm simply asking you to rise to the occasion, as you always have."

They all fell silent, suddenly very focused on eating their sea bass. Eventually Asier, always pragmatic and slightly reserved, broke the ice.

"I, for one, agree. I don't want to hear any more talk about the crimes. I've had it up to here with them."

"Thanks, Asier. I wouldn't have expected any less from you."

We spent the remainder of the dinner talking about plans for the festivities in Vitoria. Some of them were in *blusas* and *neksas* groups, and so we tried to fix dates and times and decide which activities to go to.

Shortly afterward, the waiter brought a cake with thirty-five candles. Xabi looked horrified when he saw how many there were, but he puffed out his cheeks, did his duty, and blew them all out. I had begun to sing an out-of-tune "Happy Birthday to You" when Nerea silenced me with a look.

"What's wrong? Is this a birthday or a funeral?"

"I don't believe you, Unai. Xabi just entered the group of people who are at risk: he has a double-barreled name from Álava and now he's thirty-five. And you're congratulating him?" she whispered furiously in my ear.

I fell silent. Everyone was watching to see what I would do next, so I tried to finish my meal and pretend this was just another ordinary Sunday.

The dinner ended as it had begun, with a leaden silence. Lutxo told funny stories about articles they had been unable to publish in his newspaper's society section. He always did this kind of thing when the atmosphere grew tense. He was very adept socially and was more skillful than a matador at avoiding difficult moments.

When the time came for farewells, Martina came up behind me and put her arms around my waist.

"Is everything all right, Unai?" she asked, laying her elfin head on my shoulder.

"Yes, everything's all right, Martina. How's work going? Do you want to get lunch this week?"

"In August not many people want to separate, and everyone leaves Vitoria anyway. It's in September that we get an avalanche of divorces," she said. "That means more work for me and for Germán's law firm. So your brother and I are going to take advantage of the lull and spend time quietly in the city, taking it easy. And, of course, we can have lunch this week. I'll give you a call, okay?"

"Yes, let's do that," I said happily, kissing her on the forehead.

"And, Unai. Don't be disheartened. You can do this and a lot more besides."

She blew me a kiss, fluffed up her unkempt hair, and stepped out into the square.

Before leaving, I went to the restroom. I was standing there, face to the wall, when a young man wearing a white chef's hat came up and tried to hand me a napkin with some writing scrawled on it.

"You're Kraken, aren't you?"

"You're going to have to wait until I finish before I can take that," I said, my zipper still undone.

"I'll wait," he said, glancing around nervously.

As soon as I'd zipped up my pants and washed my hands, he passed me the napkin. I could see his hand was trembling far too much for someone his age.

"Too many joints," he offered as an excuse.

"Before you say anything, I'd like you to tell me who you are and explain who told you I'm called Kraken."

"My name is Roberto López de Subijana. I work here on the weekends. I'm a neighbor of Nerea's, your friend in the *cuadrilla*. Our parents have known each other all their lives. She told us you are the famous Kraken, that Tasio's tweets are addressed to you. My mother and I have drawn up this list of names. We'd like you to read it and take it into account."

"What is this list, Roberto?" I asked, reading a dozen or so first and last names with ages jotted alongside them.

"They're all from our family: my sister is thirty, my uncle fifty-five, my grandmother is seventy-five. All those on the list are of an age to be victims and have double-barreled names from the region."

We don't yet know whether the new victims have double-barreled names, I was tempted to say, simply to calm him down. But that was something I couldn't do: I couldn't give him any information from the investigation. It would be spread all over the city in a few hours.

"But why are you giving it to me?"

"You're leading the investigation. Can't you give them protection?"

"I would have to do the same for several thousand people from Álava who are in a similar situation."

"The thing is, we're all scared stiff. My grandmother has gone back to her village and refuses to come to Vitoria even for a doctor's appointment. Isn't there anything you can do? Why don't you arrest Tasio's accomplice? Can't you trace the Twitter account?"

"Roberto, right? Look, we're doing all we can, but I can't share any information with you."

"Fine. But keep the list anyway. Keep it with you all the time. Then, if one of them dies, it'll be your—"

I cut him off. "That's enough, kid." I didn't want to hear him say what was already rattling around in my brain. "You wanted to give me a message, and I've received it. Crystal clear. Everybody in Vitoria knows someone in the same situation. Just one thing: don't go around the city telling people I'm Kraken. It doesn't help the investigation. Your neighbor Nerea let it slip, but that can't happen again. Don't give me an excuse to cause you trouble because of what you smoke and where you get it, okay?"

The lad reluctantly agreed. By the time I left the restaurant, only Lutxo was waiting for me. He looked at me worriedly, and we walked across the Plaza del Machete in silence. The square got its name from a ritual performed during the swearing-in of the region's procurator-general. From the days of the Catholic monarchs until well into the nineteenth century, it was tradition for the official to face a machete during the ceremony. The implied threat: if he does not fulfill his oath, the machete will descend upon his neck.

We passed in front of a window that displayed a replica of the original machete. Few people were familiar with the relic, and it was so openly displayed that it went unnoticed. Beyond the apse of San Miguel Arcángel Church, behind some railings that had been there since 1840, the replica demanded attention that few people in Vitoria or tourists gave it.

But what was poised over my head was far heavier than a machete and was already shredding my conscience. The boy was right: What was the point of my job if I couldn't protect people who felt threatened, and for good reason?

"Come on, Unai. I'll walk home with you" was all Lutxo said, patting me on the back.

I nodded, and we walked silently across the paved square and down the steps to the Plaza de la Virgen Blanca.

Lutxo was a well-known character in Vitoria. Tough and lean, he had shaved his head as soon as he was old enough to make his own decisions about his appearance. The only hair he allowed to grow was in a vertical line from his lower lip to the tip of his pointed chin. He was accustomed to dyeing this goatee depending on the mood he was in. Recently it had been white. Not silvery, but a shockingly artificial, spotless white.

"Did you go anywhere this weekend?" I asked him, to change subjects.

"I was in Navarra, trying various ascents in the Pyrenees," he said offhandedly.

"Did you explore any new ones?"

"A 7c+."

"Fantastic!" I muttered with a smile. But Lutxo wasn't really listening and didn't smile back. "What's the matter, Lutxo?"

"It was a rather strange weekend, Unai. Iker, your partner's boyfriend, came and brought his brother-in-law."

El Hierbas, I thought, trying hard not to grimace.

Estíbaliz's brother was well known to the police. He had always been an oddball; he managed an esoteric herbalist's store and had had brushes with the law from an early age for trafficking substances that were suspicious to say the least. In fact, I was convinced that Estíbaliz had joined the force to escape her brother's excesses after she had mended her own ways, although I suspected that he still had too much influence over his little sister.

He was a couple of years older than Estí, and I knew him from the days when he wore red dreadlocks and dealt marijuana from his backpack. In his bedroom, when the rest of us had posters of Samantha Fox in a bikini, he had a blown-up photo of Sacamantecas. I always thought it was disturbing that he went to bed every night underneath the brutish face of a local serial killer and rapist.

Sacamantecas was our Álava version of Jack the Ripper, the star exhibit in all the criminal profiling classes I'd attended.

Juan Díaz de Garayo Ruíz de Argandoña, born in 1821 in Eguilaz, a tiny village in the Llanada Alavesa, murdered, raped, and mutilated six women, four of them sex workers, and was garrotted in the former prison of Polvorín Viejo.

For this and many other reasons, I wasn't exactly a fan of Estí's brother, or perhaps I was too protective of my colleague. I was also concerned. Estíbaliz had not spent the weekend with her fiancé like she told me. Why was she lying to me?

"The thing is, coming back from the climb, he persuaded us to take a detour to Zugarramurdi, and we finished up at the famous Witch's Lair, Sorginen Lezea," Lutxo told me as we descended some stone steps. "We spent the night there, and this guy couldn't stop talking about the double murders, filling our minds with pagan rituals. According to him, the perpetrator is calling for a return to more authentic times. That's why he stages these crimes at different places that are important to our regional history. He says it's no coincidence that he started with the dolmen at the Witch's Lair. He told us about the witch who lived there and said that the locals used to toss stones under the dolmen when there was a full moon, as offerings to the goddess Mari. In 1935 archaeologists discovered a large number of pebbles there but said nothing, fearing repression from the Church if they admitted that the old beliefs still persisted.

"He also said it was no coincidence that the crimes started again in the Old Cathedral because of the symbolism it has for this city. Not merely religious, but cultural as well, because it contains the ruins of the original settlement of Gasteiz. He claims it's a warning to everyone living in Vitoria and that the bodies are surrounded by symbols that need to be interpreted." Lutxo said all this in a rush, then paused to catch his breath. "What symbols is he talking about, Unai?"

Lutxo didn't know the poison used in the original crimes was yew or that now the murder weapons were angry bees. He didn't know that the murderer's signature was the three *eguzkilores* placed round the bodies. And that was how it was going to stay for the moment.

"As you know, I can't say anything outside our official press release," I replied as we strolled across the Plaza de la Virgen Blanca.

This was one of Lutxo's usual tactics. He gave me supposedly valuable information and then, in exchange, asked me to give him more details than the other journalists.

"What's going on, Lutxo? Is your boss pressuring you more than normal?"

The editor of *El Diario Alavés* was a mysterious figure, an old-fashioned, reclusive, hardheaded newspaperman. For decades, he had edited the newspaper from the shadows, and I'd heard that the newsroom staff were afraid of him.

"There's a promotion at stake. The deputy editor's post has been vacant since Larrea retired, and I have to go for it. I want that job, and I'm asking you to help me get it, Kraken. I hope you can tell me something, because I'm going to give this case everything I've got, and if you don't help me, I'll have to do it alone."

By now we had reached my front door. I was dying to go up to my apartment and forget the world, the dinner, and my *cuadrilla*, but since Lutxo was now sticking his foot between the doorframe and the heavy, barred wooden door, he clearly didn't think our conversation was over.

"So what are you going to do, Lutxo? Write an article saying El Hierbas's pagan nonsense is true?" I said, shrugging as I turned to go in.

"El Hierbas? You mean Iker's brother-in-law, the Eguzkilore?"

I was about to plunge into the dark hallway, but when I heard that name a shudder ran down my spine.

"The Eguzkilore?" I said, turning back, white as a sheet.

"Yes, that's always been his nickname, ever since he was very young. Twenty years ago, he used to have long dreadlocks, do you remember? Because he's a redhead, he looked like an *eguzkilore*, an orange flower. The name suited him; it was a very graphic description."

"You're right. Very descriptive," I muttered, keeping a poker face. "Lutxo, I'm very tired, and I have a long week ahead of me. Can we leave it there for tonight?"

I said good night and stood in the dark hallway. Although it was the end of July, a cold shiver swept over me.

9

ARMENTIA

VITORIA
APRIL 28, 1970

To everyone's surprise, the day of the San Prudencio festival dawned radiantly, even though Álava's patron saint had a reputation for being a wet blanket. It had long been said that the weather had no respect for the five-hundred-year-old celebration. The saint always gave the procession gathered at the Basilica of San Prudencio, in the Campas de Armentia, a drenching to venerate his relics.

Doctor Urbina had dragged his wife and young sons out of the house early to join the flow of people on Paseo de la Senda who were on their way to see the saint being carried in the procession.

As they passed the Unzueta family mansion behind Hotel Canciller Ayala, Urbina glanced up at the grand windows on the facade, hoping to be able to tell whether the inhabitants were still at home.

He had chanced to read that the palatial mansion was currently the residence of newlyweds Javier Ortiz de Zárate and Blanca Díaz de Antoñana. Apparently the large French Baroque–style square building, which featured oval skylights in the gray slate roof, had been constructed in the early twentieth century by the Zárate family. Urbina wondered about the life Blanca led within those luxurious, decadent walls. Had the beatings stopped now that her husband knew those slanderous stories about la Virgen Blanca were simple village rumors? Had he forgiven her?

A few months earlier, Urbina had also learned that the society wedding had been held in the New Cathedral, that the bishop of Vitoria had performed the ceremony, and that the city's most influential people had attended. It was the event of the year.

He jealously guarded the press clippings, which were the only pictures he had of Blanca. At night, he would spend hours poring over the grainy black-and-white images, trying to discern whether the young woman smiling discreetly behind her veil was happy or terrified.

Blanca hadn't been back to the clinic, and he felt as though he was going crazy. He waited for her next to the Villa Suso at dawn every day, hoping against hope she would turn up for a meeting that existed only in his imagination.

Today he'd spent almost an hour walking arm in arm with Emilia, eyes trained on his two sons, who threatened to disappear amid the throng despite the shock of red hair they shared. Every now and then, between pouts and tantrums, the boys demanded aniseed doughnuts spiked on laurel twigs. Álvaro Urbino kept putting his hand into his jacket pocket in a nervous, unconscious gesture.

It was all right; they were there.

He hadn't forgotten them. He took them with him everywhere, in case he chanced to see her or bump into her in the center of town.

The devotees at the head of the procession chanted Hail Marys at the top of their lungs, while a group of *txistularisi* and drummers brought up the rear, entertaining the stragglers and filling the sunny skies with the festive atmosphere.

They eventually reached Las Campas de San Prudencio, a spacious field where, weather permitting, people spread out checked tablecloths and picnicked in the open air. In fact, the sky was already clouding over, and many were hurriedly unpacking their provisions, one eye on the heavens, lest the rain interrupt their alfresco meal.

The Urbinas laid out their cloth on the side of the field with a view of the basilica and the stalls selling food and refreshments. The doctor looked about furtively for anyone resembling the woman who was constantly in his thoughts.

His wife, Emilia, carried away by the general merriment, prattled on incessantly—a bit too loudly—about the price of *perretxikos* that year at the Mercado de Abastos. Still, she said she was content that for the first time in her life she was able to afford the seasonal mushrooms.

She plunged her stout arms into the hamper and extracted several metal lunch boxes, which contained stewed snails and a *perretxiko* omelette. She had brought *sobao* bread since it kept its shape better than popovers and, for appearance's sake, a bottle of Marqués de Riscal in case they bumped into one of the doctor's colleagues and wanted to offer them a glass of wine.

Álvaro Urbina set out the plastic plates he had bought the day before. He was taking out the knife to slice some bread when he thought he saw Javier Ortiz de Zárate and the bishop of Vitoria enter the basilica together, along with some other elegant gentlemen.

He craned his neck expectantly, forgetting the knife in his hand. Unaware of his sons, dancing about excitedly, demanding he buy them the blessed aniseed doughnuts. Unaware of the aroma of stewed snails in tomato sauce with ham, which hundreds of proud housewives and mothers were serving.

He spotted her standing, alone, in a white knee-length skirt and elegant matching jacket, wearing a simple pair of espadrilles, holding a bag patterned with daisies. She was next to one of the food stands, looking rather lost.

Álvaro placed the knife in the hamper, slipped on his jacket, and said in a mechanical tone, "I'm going to buy doughnuts." Then he disappeared into the field of contented picnickers and made for the little green awnings where vendors were selling punch and hot chocolate with churros. The loudspeakers were emitting an incongruous medley of hymns and "Un rayo de sol" by Los Diablos, the song that was currently driving all the young girls crazy at village celebrations.

He walked straight up to her, determined to forgo preambles and pleasantries. He had so few opportunities to see her—why beat about the bush?

"So you married him," he said by way of greeting. "Just tell me one thing to put my mind at ease: Is it better now?"

Is it better now? she thought, gritting her teeth.

How could she tell him? How could she tell another man what her husband had been doing to her since their wedding night? The beatings hadn't stopped when he discovered that she was indeed a virgin. That wasn't enough.

She had returned from her honeymoon in San Sebastián in a daze. Hadn't anyone at the Hotel María Cristina realized what was going on in their suite? Hadn't any of the cleaning staff reported the broken furniture?

Her elderly aunt had questioned her when visiting Blanca's new home to help find space for her trousseau and all the wedding gifts.

"How did everything go?" she asked, without looking Blanca in the eye.

Blanca didn't reply. She knew this woman wasn't her ally.

"Things will get better. You'll get used to it, eventually," she had said in a burst of candor Blanca hadn't expected from someone so accustomed to keeping up appearances. "Try not to upset him, be a good wife, please him in every way you can. Make sure the house is spotless when he gets home from work and that his slippers are next to his armchair. Try not to let him drink too much. When they drink, it's much worse."

The woman had looked at her niece with an expression that

brooked no further discussion, and Blanca had lowered her eyes in humiliation. She had never imagined that her aunt also had to put up with her uncle's violence. How blind she had been all her life.

Now that she was married, she had female friends: the wives of her husband's friends. Some were dull, others were standoffish, and one or two were cheerful, easygoing, and amusing. But there was nobody she could really talk to or confide in.

And here he was, this attentive doctor. The only person she could speak to openly. If only he had taken her to San Sebastián instead of Javier. She knew that night would have been different. Warm, pleasant, and relaxed. Like him.

"Do you think I have a choice, that I wanted any of this? Tell that to my father and my family."

Doctor Urbina sighed. Nothing had changed.

"Blanca, you mustn't try another stunt like the one at the Villa Suso Palace. Even if you succeed, those steps aren't steep enough to kill you; instead you'd have broken your back and would be stuck in a wheelchair. You won't seek my help, but I'm determined to protect you."

"I don't see how you can, doctor," she said.

Then, all at once, it started to rain. A few rumbles of thunder announced the approaching storm, and the rain fell in sharp droplets that seemed to pierce the ground.

Blanca darted between two stalls while Doctor Urbina stood facing her, oblivious to the downpour.

"Open your bag, look the other way, and act as if we aren't talking."

"Sorry?"

"Open your handbag, Blanca. Trust me."

She obeyed, reluctantly. Álvaro slipped the pills out of his jacket pocket and dropped them into her purse.

"What did you just do, doctor?"

"The white tablets are painkillers. They're for you. Take them after he . . . or before, if possible. It'll hurt less. The ointment will get rid of the bruising, so that you can show your face. I think you're safer outside your house than in it. The maroon capsules are for him. They contain a colorless, odorless powder that dissolves in water. I'd guess your husband is a busy man who works all day and comes home late. Get him to drink it. He'll feel relaxed and drowsy afterward, but not noticeably—don't worry, I wouldn't want to put you in any danger. The drug isn't often prescribed in Europe, but it might save your life."

Blanca looked anxiously at her watch. The cloudburst had emptied the field in a matter of minutes, and small crowds were sheltering beneath the trees along the road and under the awnings. Her husband had been with the bishop and the other officials for a long time.

"Doctor, I appreciate your efforts, but you're putting me in danger. If anyone saw us . . ." She glanced around nervously.

"Keep looking the other way, and listen. Blanca, I'm worried about you. I had no idea your husband was a widower. I read about it in the society pages of *El Diario Alavés* the day you were married, and my nurse told me that his first wife was young like you, and that she was always coming to the clinic."

"What do you mean she was always going to the clinic? Everybody knows she died in a climbing accident."

"I only know what my nurse told me," said Urbina, looking toward the field for a sign of his wife and two sons. "I don't have access to her patient files, but I do know she had a fractured rib and other injuries similar to the ones your husband inflicts on you."

The hairs on Blanca's neck stood on end. How many other people knew? Had her own family concealed it from her? Had they let her marry a violent man? Didn't her father care about his only daughter's life?

"That is speculation, doctor. As far as I know, no one has ever dared question him."

"Don't defend him. One day he'll go too far, and he'll kill you, just like he killed his first wife. It would only take a single blow."

"So what should I do?"

"I said this to you before, but I'll say it again: you can come to me."

He stared straight at her, and at last she had the courage to raise her head and look at the man standing in front of her.

They touched, his damp hand brushing against her slender dry one. For the first time in a long while, they both felt warm.

Doctor Urbina noticed his jacket being tugged, and he swung around, moving away from Blanca.

"Father, Mother is looking for you. The rain ruined the snails," his younger son complained.

He couldn't help noticing the look of hatred the boy gave Blanca.

But his son wasn't the only one. Behind his back, hidden from view, Javier Ortiz de Zárate clenched his fists until his knuckles turned white. It was an instinctive gesture that he wasn't always able to control, and it had happened immediately when he saw his wife talking so familiarly with that red-haired village quack in the pouring rain.

10

LA SENDA

MONDAY, AUGUST 1

You're not going to find the murderer until you discover his motive. And motive, dear #Kraken, is always personal.

It was six o'clock on Monday morning. I had dreamed of more *eguzkilores* than I was able to count, and decided to start the week by running around La Florida Park. My thoughts were always clearer when I was surrounded by trees.

Early in the morning I ran with the sounds of Ludovico Einaudi's piano in my ears. At that hour Vitoria was mine, just as I imagined it. A safe, quiet place that I watched over. Evil wasn't spreading through its monuments, a murderer wasn't preying on its children, its women, its young, and its old. The streets were just deserted pavements waiting for the day. Vitoria's inhabitants could walk without fear, free of anxiety and uncertainty.

My dark mentor continued sending me tweets with alarming precision. At least once a day, his monologue was seen by thousands of eyes desperate for progress. Progress was nothing more than good intentions at this point. Progress didn't come.

Which was why I needed to think. I jogged toward the old bandstand, an octagonal white iron structure where people danced on Sundays beneath the benevolent gaze of the four Gothic kings.

That was where I found her, stretching on the bandstand's metal steps.

"Blanca."

"Ishmael."

I was about to continue through the green labyrinth when she waved me over. I went with some reluctance.

"Tell me something," she said, straightening her black braid. "Why Ishmael?"

I was still jogging in front of her and took a deep breath before I answered.

"Isn't it obvious? Because I'm trying to hunt down the white monster. Why Blanca?"

"Well," she said with a shrug, "it's a version of Alba."

"But it isn't Alba. Why lie?"

"I wanted to stay anonymous. I've just been transferred here, and I don't want to be Deputy Superintendent Salvatierra outside the office."

"But you introduced yourself. You told me your name and asked for mine."

"I was just being polite. Can't we simply be Blanca and Ishmael early in the morning?"

"Do you enjoy having a split personality?" I asked.

"Don't profile me. You make it sound pathological."

"That's what it is. And I'm not sure I like the game. In another couple of hours, we'll meet again, and you're going to keep me tied to headquarters all day. You're getting in the way of my investigation. You'd rather see me filing reports in my office, where I can't make any headway."

"Is that how you feel about me?"

"Yes, Blanca or Alba. That's how I feel. What is it with you? Don't you want to hunt him down?" I said. I felt powerless, and I clung to the iron railings.

"Hunt him down? Arrest him, you mean."

"Sure. But, semantics aside, that's how I feel. Why don't you loosen up a little and let me do my job? I need you to trust me."

Blanca thought this over for a few endless seconds. Then, to my surprise, she agreed.

"All right, I'll get off your back, but I need results. The superintendent calls me practically every hour asking what progress we've made. Can you imagine the amount of pressure that puts on me?"

I lowered my head: I hadn't thought of it from her point of view. Until that moment, I had simply been staring at a wall.

"One last question," she said, "before you disappear into the trees. Why do they call you Kraken? At headquarters, they say it's because you're so good at cornering suspects in interrogations, but when I asked you, you said it was a childhood nickname."

A good observer, I thought.

"That thing about interrogations is a myth. It's true that I do manage to extract more information than my colleagues, but that's because I approach witnesses and suspects from a different perspective. I don't follow the manuals. I don't like the kinesic technique: I think that simply relying on body language provides information that's too vague. Besides, the observer is never impartial, however good the officer, however much they deny their own biases. Honestly, I think it's impossible to enter the interrogation room without having a preconceived idea about the person's guilt. I don't believe in the Reid technique, either: the nine points you're supposed to follow are too rigid. In practice, a conversation is much more organic and imprecise. But try not to believe everything they say about me in the hallways. The truth is going to disappoint you more often than not. Believe me, I'm not exceptional, and having high expectations isn't going to help anyone. You put me in charge of this case because we're facing a series of murders and a profiler can offer a fresh perspective, but I'm not infallible. Far from it. As you can see, even now, there's way too much I don't know about this case."

"Your file suggests otherwise. But you still haven't told me about Kraken."

"Oh, that little mystery. Don't read too much into that, either. I was given the nickname when I was young. The Kraken was a mythological creature in ancient Scandinavia, a kind of giant octopus or squid. It turns out they really existed—recently they've found remains washed up on beaches all over the world. It's just been very difficult to study these creatures because they live so deep underwater. Anyway, the thing is, I grew in pieces, like Legos, with different-size arms, trunk, and legs. At one point, my arms were monstrously long in proportion to the rest of my body. It was only for a while, though; my next growth spurt brought all my limbs into proportion, and my body became the perfect pleasure machine you see before you now." I winked to underline the evident truth of my story. "Or maybe I'm inventing the whole thing and a drunken friend simply thought of the name and baptized me with it just because I happened to be there. It's difficult living in Vitoria without being given some ingenious nickname: Nuts, Spike, Sacamantecas."

"Good. If I'm honest, I find that explanation more reassuring," she said with a smile.

"Were you heading for La Senda?" I asked. I didn't want to cool down too much or spoil the rhythm of my run.

"That was the idea. Let's go."

And so we set off running along the path at the same speed, without talking. I switched off Einaudi: I didn't want to create the kind of memory that would pop up every time I heard the opening notes of this song, at least not yet.

"Why did you start running?" I asked after a while. "Your shoes and running clothes are new, all perfectly matched. So you're a beginner. It's a new hobby."

She peered up at the green tunnel of leaves above our heads.

"I was pregnant for a few months and wanted to regain my muscle tone."

I wasn't expecting that. I gritted my teeth to ward off my own ghosts.

"Well . . . that's pretty good . . ." I managed to say.

"What's so good about it?"

"You must be exhausted with the baby. I'm sure it doesn't let you sleep at night. And you're at work all day and yet you're still worried about being in shape. How old is he or she now, four, five months?" I calculated mentally. "The first teeth must be hellish."

"No, it's not what you're thinking. I was pregnant for seven months. The baby didn't develop properly. It was diagnosed with level-two brittle bone syndrome," she said, not raising her eyes from the wavy red, white, and blue tiles beneath her feet.

"I'm not great with clinical terms."

"My son was not viable. Every day he grew, his bones snapped inside my uterus, and he was suffering. I was given a planned cesarean section, but he lived only a few hours. I can't bear looking at my stomach. I can't bear still having a pregnant body. It didn't bother me when I was pregnant, and it probably wouldn't bother me if he had survived, but now . . . all I want to do is to forget what I had. I don't want to see it every time I'm naked."

I stole a glance at her abdominal muscles under her tight Lycra top. She was blessed with a flat stomach that already looked toned. She was the only one who saw her pregnant belly; it didn't exist in the real world, but it was still in her head.

Body dysmorphic disorder, thought the profiler in me. *Probably only temporary. I hope so, for her sake.*

Do you care about that, Unai? Are you already worried about her? I found myself asking, to my surprise.

Yes, possibly.

Possibly.

I shouldn't, but perhaps.

"That's why you asked for a transfer."

"My husband insisted. I had been at the Laguardia police station all my working life, since I was twenty-four. He works long hours in Vitoria. . . . Well, all hours, really. Why kid ourselves. We were accustomed to seeing each other in the evening, and that was enough. But with the loss, we both had a really hard time. You know that sort of thing either unites or separates a couple. I didn't want it to separate us, but he's withdrawn into himself ever since. It's strange. He hides it, but he was affected by it, too. So now I live here, where I don't know many people. I don't want you to misinterpret this conversation. I won't bother you like this every morning. It's just like I said—I don't know many people."

"That's the problem with Vitoria," I said as we turned around to jog back along La Senda. "The *cuadrillas* of close friends are created in high school, and it's hard to become part of one if you come from somewhere else. It's very insular. You get to know boys and girls when you're fifteen, and some are already going out with each other. The couples change, and when you meet them twenty years later, you find they've mixed in combinations you would never have imagined, and yet no one has so much as looked outside their microcosm to see if there's anyone else for them in the big wide world. That never happens in Vitoria. Marrying outside your group is seen as suspicious. Anyone born more than thirty miles away is what my grandmother used to call '*el forastero*.' It's a word straight out of an old Western movie, but you can hear it in all the villages in Álava. If two pilgrims on their way to Santiago pass through, they're outsiders, even if they're only from Cuenca. If a mattress-maker comes from Salamanca to sell those old-fashioned cotton mattresses out of his van, you'll hear the old folks mutter '*forastero*' with a shrug."

"Well, it looks like now I'm the *forastera*," she said, glancing at her watch. "But what about you? I read your medical discharge report: Are you still in mourning, or are you past it?"

"Have you been investigating me?" I asked, ruffled.

"I'm your superior officer, what do you expect? I was told you were very good, that you work best on your own, and that you get results in complex cases. But they also say that you've been having a bad time recently. So are you completely past it?"

"Of course, look at me." I came to a stop right on top of a yellow shell set into the concrete. It marked the place where the pilgrims' route to Santiago passed through Vitoria. "What do you want me to say?"

"I want you to tell me in your own words, not a psychologist's opinion or a traffic report. Tell me, why did you specialize in criminal profiling after you came back?"

I said nothing. I didn't want to talk, but that wasn't fair. Whether she was simply a casual early-morning running companion or my immediate superior, she had opened up to me without any anesthetic. Could I be equally courageous?

"Thanks to a friend."

"What are you talking about?"

"Why I came back to the Criminal Investigation Unit and specialized in profiling. It was through a friend. I promise I'll tell you about it the next time we bump into each other. It's only fair. But not today. I don't want to talk about it today. I need to prepare."

"Fine, another day, then. It's a deal." She nodded. "By the way, this *forastera* prefers to keep our encounters compartmentalized and not to talk about work when we're running. I think it will help our mental hygiene."

"I agree," I said, although I could see that she was frowning exactly the way she did at headquarters. "But now you're going to add that—"

"In an hour I want to see you and Inspector Gauna in my office. There's important news about the crimes in the Old Cathedral."

"Fine. You know, I don't think our pseudonyms are such a bad idea after all," I said. My mood had improved.

We said good-bye when we reached the Plaza de la Virgen Blanca:

"Ishmael."

"Blanca."

Shortly afterward, after having showered, shaved, and masturbated, I got on my bike and headed for police headquarters in Lakua.

When I reached the office, Estíbaliz and DSU Salvatierra were going through some files on the table, waiting for me.

"We know the identities of all four victims, Ayala. As we feared, the first two were twenty, and the next two twenty-five," said Salvatierra, handing me a report with the details.

"Do we have the autopsy reports?"

"Yes, for the victims in the Old Cathedral. They both died of asphyxia brought on by more than a dozen bee stings. No sign of sexual abuse in either case, no marks, no trace of hairs or fibers. All we have is the composition of the polypropylene adhesive tape used to gag the victims. It's a common acrylic adhesive, so we're not going to be able to trace its origin. Apparently it's the most popular kind of packing tape; almost everyone has a roll of it. It's available at hardware stores and chains like the Leroy Merlin on Boulevard. But there's another interesting detail: both victims were injected in the neck with a liquid flunitrazepam, sold under the name Rohypnol. Does that mean anything to you?"

"The date-rape drug," said Estíbaliz. "Although there haven't been any cases in Spain involving that drug for years."

"Thankfully," I added.

Rohypnol was a sedative twenty times more powerful than Valium. In the seventies, it had become infamous in Miami as a result of its effects when combined with alcohol. It went by many street names: rope, roofies, R2, Mexican Valium.

"That *is* interesting," said Estíbaliz. "Rohypnol was also found in the bloodstream of the fifteen-year-old male victim twenty years ago. It was mixed with alcohol."

"I'd like to add that the autopsy report on the fifteen-year-old girl has somehow been lost. And given the direction the new murders are taking, it could contain vital clues. When we asked Ignacio Ortiz de Zárate about it, he didn't seem to think it was important. He advised us to ask Pancorbo, his partner on the case."

"Do that. Meet with him, and ask all the questions you have about the earlier deaths. He's the most reliable witness we have."

I was still not sure what importance Pancorbo had in all this. But, from our conversation, I'd gotten the impression that Ignacio was deliberately implying there was more to his former colleague than met the eye.

"What about the names of the new victims?" I asked.

"They each have a double-barreled name from the Álava region. A patronymic like Martinez, López, Fernández, or Sánchez, plus a place name from the region."

"In other words, this killer is following the same pattern as the earlier series of crimes," I said.

"Not entirely," said Estíbaliz. "The murder method is different."

"But not much else. And this murderer also leaves the *eguzkilore* signature," I said, watching to see how she would react.

"We don't know that it's a signature yet," she protested.

"It's an element that's pagan, folkloric, whatever you want to call it, and it's been found at the crime scenes because the killer deliberately places the flowers around the victims. The killer didn't use them to commit the murders. That's the definition of a *signature*. And let's not forget that this detail was never leaked to the press. That makes it one of the main pieces of evidence pointing to the fact that we're dealing with the same person, or, at the very least, somebody who is in contact with the previous killer."

"That may be," said Salvatierra, trying to calm things down, "but that doesn't explain why these new murders appear to be the work of the same killer—a killer who is now in prison. It can't have been him, not directly anyway."

"I agree," I said.

"So let's follow this step by step," she continued. "Let's start with the twenty-year-old girl: Enara Fernández de Betoño, an ophthalmology student at the Universidad Complutense in Madrid. Her father has been a fairly important optician on Calle San Prudencio for thirty years. According to the pathologist, they're a well-known family in Vitoria. The girl worked behind the counter at her father's store when she was on holiday break, as was the case in recent weeks. She doesn't appear to have been an outstanding student, but she never had any problems with the police or with drugs, although according to the toxicology report traces of antidepressants were found in her bloodstream, as well as the Rohypnol. You'll have to check with her father to see if he was aware of this. Her mother is on her way to Vitoria. It seems she was traveling in the United States—with her boyfriend, I gather. Talk to her friends, her relatives. I want to know all about her, if she knew the other victim, if they were a couple, or if there is any link between them. I want to know why exactly the killer chose her."

"Where did she live?" I asked.

"In the family home above the store, on Calle San Prudencio."

"How easy," I said.

"What do you mean by that?"

"If the murderer wanted to kill young people with double-barreled names from Vitoria, he didn't need to make things hard for himself by consulting the census or a database. The optician's store already displays the owner's name outside. All the killer had to do was watch for a few days to see whether the optician had a daughter of the right age working with him. They live in the pedestrian zone in the center of the city, which means he didn't even have to follow her in a car to discover her routine, when she went in and out. The day she was murdered was a day when all the young people are out; no one stays home. He could have just intercepted her when she left the store or her apartment."

"Do you think it was someone she knew?" asked Estíbaliz.

"Either that or he is very persuasive, or at least he's someone who seems trustworthy and isn't frightening. If the murderer was a woman, it would be easier to understand why the victim followed her or got into a car. Considering the size of that twenty-five-year-old male Viking killed in the Casa del Cordón, however, I'm beginning to doubt that theory. But what twenty-five-year-old would get into a stranger's car?"

"No one in Vitoria," said my partner.

All three of us agreed on that.

"Still, I think he invites them into some kind of vehicle, and when they're relaxed, injects them with the sedative," I went on. "Once they're unconscious, he drives them out of Vitoria. Maybe he has a house or chalet in a nearby village, somewhere quiet where there are no witnesses. Don't forget he has live bees, or at least access to them, and he knows how to handle them. It's difficult to see that happening in Vitoria itself. He uses gasoline to make the bees angry—he may keep them in a jar or a bottle and may wear a beekeeper suit for protection. He puts the bees in the victims' mouth, tapes their lips together, blocks their nostrils with the other hand, and within minutes they die of asphyxia. After that he strips them and removes their personal effects, puts them back in his vehicle, and deposits them in a place he has already chosen that follows the chronology of Vitoria's history. He lays them down pointing northwest, with their hands in that characteristic position, before rigor mortis sets in. He acts swiftly, carrying everything out with great precision. He may spend a long time rehearsing or planning each step, visiting the Old Cathedral, the Casa del Cordón. He doesn't make mistakes; he wears gloves. He is like a chameleon. He can pass for someone who works for the Santa María Cathedral Foundation or for the Caja Vital Benevolent Fund without arousing suspicion."

"The profiles sound quite similar," said Estíbaliz.

"Or he could pass himself off as a janitor," said Salvatierra. "There are lots of possibilities. Don't just consider the most obvious. I forgot to tell you that the funerals of two of the four victims are tomorrow in Santa Isabel Cemetery, one an hour and a half after the other. And now let's consider the twenty-year-old young man—"

"Santa Isabel Cemetery?" I said, taken aback. "I've never been to a funeral there. I didn't think they buried anyone there anymore. I've only been to the El Salvador Cemetery."

"Both families have had family vaults there for almost a hundred years, and both vaults have room," said Alba. "In cases like that, the city council permits burials."

At that moment, Pancorbo knocked politely on the door and came in.

"Someone by the name of Peio, who says he was Enara Fernández de Betoño's boyfriend, is at the front desk. He says he has something very important to tell us about the crime."

We looked silently at one another.

"Show him in," said DSU Salvatierra. "I hope you two can get something interesting out of him."

"He's in my office," said Pancorbo. "I had to calm him down. He's a nervous wreck."

"Let's see what he has to say."

We found all two hundred and sixty pounds of the boy wrapped around a box of tissues on Pancorbo's desk. He stood out not only because of his size but also because he had freckles scattered over all the visible parts of his skin, as if somebody had sprinkled melanin over his body and round face. He had black hair, flat on the top of his head but cascading down in curls to his shoulders, which were shaking with every sob. He was wearing calf-length camouflage pants and a black T-shirt with a huge picture of Walter White—the protagonist on *Breaking Bad*, who was probably his hero—cooking meth.

"Hello there, Peio," I said. "We've been told you want to talk to us."

"Are you Kraken?" he asked, hiccupping three times in succession.

"Never mind who I am. It's more important for you to tell us why you came here," I said as we sat down. "The first thing we want to say is how sorry we are for your loss. Was Enara your girlfriend?"

"Yes, for the past year," he said, immediately on the defensive. "What's wrong? Can't you see me with her? Was she too pretty or too rich for a kid like me?"

"Nobody was suggesting that. In fact, I think opposites attract," said Estíbaliz, reassuring him. "We don't want to take up too much of your time, Peio. Tell us."

"Enara's parents are at each other's throats over the separation. Three weeks ago, her mother left home with her new boyfriend, or with her old one. . . . I'm not sure how to explain it."

"Well, please try, because I'm lost already," said Estí, smiling to encourage him.

"The thing is, a month ago Enara's mom had one of those high school reunions, where old people get together twenty years after graduating from their fancy schools."

"Right. What school was it?"

"The Company of Mary, I think."

"Are you sure?"

"Yes, that's what it was. The thing is, she met a boyfriend from twenty years ago, and they fell for each other again. He was a handsome guy, much better-looking than Enara's father, who's an insufferable stuck-up pig. He is so weird."

"The optician is weird?" I said. "What do you mean by that?"

"His house is full of animal eyeballs in formalin. It's all very classy, like in a fashion magazine. He loves reminding anyone who will listen that he's spent a fortune on those freak shows. He says that medical antiquities are very much in demand among collectors. Bullshit, he's a nightmare to live with, believe me."

"What happened after the reunion?"

"Enara's mom plucked up the courage and finally left her idiot husband and went to live with her new boyfriend."

"Can you tell us his name?"

"Gonzalo Castresana, I think."

"Okay. And what does this have to do with your girlfriend's death?"

"The thing is, Enara was so fond of her new stepdad that she even began to think he could be her real father. It might be true, because her mother and Gonzalo never denied it. Apparently, the optician had interrupted their love affair, and shortly afterward they were married, and Enara *was* born twenty years ago. Anyway, that was when the problems began. Enara had finished her exams at Complutense and returned home, but her mother had just left to live with Gonzalo. Enara and her father have never gotten along. He's one of those old-fashioned fathers, very bossy. He forced her to study ophthalmology even though she hates it . . . or hated it."

"She didn't want to be an optician?"

"Have you seen her grades?" he said, making a face.

"No, I haven't."

"She struggled, found it hard to pass her exams. There's too much chemistry and physics, and her father was always pressuring her to live up to his reputation as the leading optician in Vitoria."

"Peio, was your girlfriend on anything?" asked Estíbaliz.

"I don't understand your question."

"I'll put it in another way. Traces of antidepressants were found in her body, together with other substances that you could say are not strictly legal. We're not going to give you any trouble. Whatever you tell us stays in this room and won't appear in an official report. But, for her sake, don't lie to me. You may see me as a decrepit old woman, but, believe me, I've burned the candle at both ends and I know what's out there. I'm not going to judge you, but this detail is important if we're going to catch her killer. Did Enara buy any pills?"

"No, no way. She was a saint, a kindhearted person. Ask her *cuadrilla*: She was as good as gold. She trusted people too much. She was too obedient. Well, until a couple of weeks or so ago, when she confronted her father for the first time in her life."

"Did you know about the antidepressants?" I insisted.

"Yes, that was because of her father as well. He sent her to a psychologist. She said Enara was depressed and prescribed those drugs, but her father only did it to get her to concentrate more on her studies. He wanted her to come work with him as quickly as possible."

"How did her father react when his wife left him?"

"I was getting to that. He was schizo: Sometimes he was super-violent with Enara, although always in private, of course. At other times, he was so calm and cold, she was afraid he was plotting something. It was like a battlefield, shouting on their cell phones all day, her father pursuing her mom and Gonzalo. In the end,

Enara's mom and Gonzalo went away until things calmed down a little. But they left Enara at home with that madman."

"From what you're saying, it sounds to me as though he could be bipolar."

"That's it: bipolar. That creep is very bipolar."

"One last question, Peio," I said. "How did he treat you?"

"How do you think? He wanted a rich guy for her, not a fat kid with no education or money."

"Do you have a job?" I asked.

"Of course. I've mown the lawns at the Urturi golf club since I was seventeen, and I'm proud of it."

"That's very good, kid. I've got nothing but respect for some-one your age who earns a living," I said. "But to get back to what brought you here today: What you're trying to say is that you think the father had something to do with your girlfriend's death?"

"Of course he had something to do with it!" he wailed. "It must have been him. He killed the others to throw you off the scent, so people would think the deaths were linked to those dolmen crimes and everything. Go to his house and you'll see the horror show he has there. He's even got nineteenth-century surgical knives and scalpels."

"It's okay, Peio. Here, take these," said Estíbaliz, handing him another packet of tissues when she saw he had finished Pancorbo's.

He blew his nose repeatedly while we waited patiently for him to calm down.

"The evening before El Día de Santiago, Enara told him she was going to live with her mother and her new father as soon as they got back from the United States. Enara was scared stiff, but the optician just acted as if he hadn't heard her or didn't want to know. That really freaked her out. We had agreed to meet on Sunday evening to go out and have a few drinks, but the last I heard from her was that morning, when we spoke on the phone around noon.

After that, I didn't hear anything. She didn't show up or answer her phone again. It was switched off when I called to see why she was late. We were supposed to meet at seven. By nine I was pretty pissed, so I went to her place and buzzed, but nobody answered."

"Where were you supposed to meet?"

"At *The Hole.* I mean that sculpture with the hole on General Loma, next to the Plaza de la Virgen Blanca."

"*The Gaze*, Peio. It's called *The Gaze*," I said with a smile.

It was true that no one in Vitoria ever called it anything other than *The Hole.* It was a gray marble block some twenty feet high with a hole in it. If you looked through the hole, you could see the statue of the Virgen Blanca, and my front door as well.

"Well, that's something else I've learned. I went back several times to the . . . to the sculpture, in case she turned up. I called her girlfriends, but they meet their boyfriends on Sundays, and none of them had seen her. At midnight I was tired of roaming the streets and went home. I spent the night in my bedroom, calling her and sending her WhatsApp messages. Look." He took out a battered cell phone with a cracked screen and showed us an endless stream of one-way messages.

"No one is accusing you, Peio," Estí said gently, like a mother with a small child.

"Just in case. Because of the way I look. I know you cops always suspect the boyfriend. I watch a lot of TV."

"Don't worry, Peio. You don't fit the killer's profile," I said, treating him as though he were a real informer and not what he truly was—a kid overwhelmed by a bad situation.

"Really?" he asked with surprise.

"Really."

"That's good. I was afraid her father would accuse me. Attack is the best form of defense, so I wanted you to hear my version first. That's why I came," he replied, visibly more relaxed.

"You did the right thing. What happened then, on El Día de Santiago?" Estíbaliz wanted to know.

"The next morning, I read about the crimes on Twitter. I even bought the newspaper. Nobody was talking about anything else. I ran to her place. The shop was closed because it was a holiday, so I talked to her father on the intercom. I asked him about Enara, told him I had no idea where she was. But he didn't react. It was as if he couldn't have cared less, even though he was always on her back. I asked him to open the door so I could come up—I didn't want to talk about it out on the street—but he wouldn't. So I had to tell him from there that I hadn't heard anything from his daughter since the day before. I said we had to report it to the police, otherwise we could be suspects."

"You told him that?" said Estíbaliz.

"Yes, that's what they always do in TV series, isn't it?" he muttered, shrugging his shoulders. "The optician said he was the father and he would take care of it, that it was none of my business to go to the police. That I shouldn't meddle in his family's affairs. She was his daughter, but he wasn't concerned that she hadn't been seen all night. I knew something bad had happened to her. Enara didn't even go to the bathroom on her own. Well . . . I think I've told you everything. When are you going to arrest him?"

Estíbaliz and I exchanged glances. Then she stood up and walked to the door. "I think you've provided us with information that will be very valuable for our investigation. I'd like you to leave us your cell phone number, your address, and the best way to contact you if we need anything more. And I'd like to thank you once again for coming in, Peio."

He stood up, pushing back his chair, and stared blindly at Pancorbo's desk, which was littered with damp tissues. He smiled at us, his tiny eyes red from tears.

"It's been a pleasure, especially if you nab that asshole."

I escorted him to the exit, glancing at him as we went. I wanted to see if his grief was real or if he was acting out a scene from *CSI*. I couldn't detect anything that would make me suspect he might be capable of killing four people his own age who were fitter than him, or that he could have set up all the complicated paraphernalia that accompanied the murders, simply to put the blame on a demanding and difficult man.

I went back up to the second floor and opened Estí's door.

"Impressions?"

"I'd say he's telling the truth. He's a little freaky, but . . ."

"A little?" I smiled, raising an eyebrow.

"All right, so he's the goddamned king of the freaks, and I can't see him with a well-brought-up girl like Enara. Maybe he was her first act of rebellion. But it sounds like that family was a powder keg just waiting to explode."

"The most striking thing about his statement is the lack of an emotional reaction from a possessive father who learns that his daughter had been missing all night," I said, leaning forward on her desk. "It doesn't fit; it doesn't fit at all. You would expect him to come running here to report it. In fact, it would have been normal for him to have pressured us to investigate his daughter's boyfriend. Estí, could you find out when Enara's disappearance was reported?"

"Yes, I'll find out. You stay here." With that, she disappeared.

She came back a couple of minutes later, looking puzzled.

"This is really odd, Unai. The report that Enara Fernández de Betoño was missing is the very last one we received. Do you remember how crazy all the parents in Vitoria were? We got a flood of about three hundred calls that first morning. Well, I searched through them, and that one's not there. He only reported it on Friday, July 29. Almost a week after his good-as-gold daughter went missing."

I stared at her, and she stared back. That was our way of giving ourselves the strength for what we thought was likely to follow.

"We'll go in an unmarked car. And take your gun, Estí," I said, looking up the victim's address. "I think we're going to have a very interesting conversation with our optician father."

11

SAN ANTONIO

MONDAY, AUGUST 1

The detective's curse: the answer is in front of you
and you can't see it. Careful, #Kraken, the killer's
showing off. You must have met him.

How was your weekend, Estíbaliz?" I asked on the drive to
Calle San Prudencio.

"Fine," she said absentmindedly.

"Did you and Iker make much progress with the wedding
preparations?"

"Yes, flowers and bouquets. We spent the whole weekend dis-
cussing whether to go with orange gerberas or white arum lilies,
but both are way over our budget." She sighed, sounding bored by
the subject. "That's where we are."

"Hmm, flowers and bouquets."

We parked in the street next to the optician's and got out. His
apartment was on Calle San Prudencio, but the entrance was on
Calle San Antonio.

We went to the front door and rang the bell. No one answered.
We tried several times, then gave up. Either he wasn't at home,
or he didn't want to see anyone that morning, which would have
been understandable.

"Let's see if we have more luck in the store," said Estíbaliz.

We entered the optician's and were attended by an obliging assistant in a white coat with a shiny, tanned bald spot, like a light bulb.

"We'd like to speak to the owner," I said, looking around.

There was no sign of him. There were three other people dealing with customers, but no sixty-year-old man fitting the description of Antonio Fernández de Betoño.

"If you're journalists, we've been told not to say anything to you. You must understand this is a very difficult day for our boss," said the bald attendant, lowering his voice.

"We're not journalists," I said. "In fact, we're from the police. Could you please tell us where he is?"

"The police?" he repeated, swallowing hard. "Yes, of course. Well, in that case, I suppose I can tell you. He's spent the morning going up and down to his apartment, carrying tons of boxes."

"Boxes?" said Estíbaliz.

"Yes, big empty boxes, the ones suppliers like Luxottica or Safilo send with our frames. The store is always full of them; they take up a lot of room."

It happens with some people when they're face-to-face with the police: they become nervous and give information nobody has asked them for. Sometimes it's irrelevant, no more than chatter; but other times it can offer unexpected gifts, snippets we would have struggled to unearth.

"You can ring the bell. He's on the second floor. He might not open the door today, or even answer, but you can reach his landing through a door at the back of the store. Follow me, if you'd like," he said, leading the way, while the other assistants looked on in horror.

Estí and I followed him silently.

We entered a gloomy storeroom, a long narrow cubicle filled with shelf after shelf of glasses cases in all shapes and colors. The assistant took a bunch of keys from his coat pocket and opened a white aluminum door that led to the building's fire escape.

"If you need anything else, anything at all . . ." he said, handing me his business card.

"Thank you, Luis," I said, shaking his hand. He gripped mine too heartily, with that fake assurance they teach in sales courses. "We may be in touch with you if we need further information."

"Creep," said Estíbaliz once he had turned and left.

"With employees like him, who needs enemies?" I said with a wink as we climbed the stairs. "So the optician is at home but doesn't want to open the door for anybody."

"Leave him to me. I'm beginning to want to get to know this gentleman."

"Don't press him too hard, Estí. Agreed?"

"Hmm."

When we reached the second-floor landing, Estíbaliz rang the bell and took out her ID.

"Criminal Investigation Unit. Antonio Fernandez de Botoño, we know you're in there. We want to ask you some routine questions," she said, raising her voice to carry beyond the heavy walnut door.

I put my ear to it and could hear several thuds. Then a man around sixty years old with a bushy, graying mustache opened the door. His serene expression was the last thing we had been expecting.

"Come in. I didn't think you'd be here so soon."

"Forgive us for intruding at a time like this. We know it's awkward. It will only be for a few minutes," I said, extending my hand. "I'm Inspector Ayala, and this is Inspector Gauna. First, we'd like to offer our condolences on your daughter's passing."

"Let's talk in my office, shall we?" Antonio answered calmly, motioning for us to follow him down an endless hallway lined with nineteenth-century anatomical illustrations of eyes.

His office looked like a doctor's consulting room, filled with diplomas and master's certificates in optometry, contact-lens fitting, and vision training. The shelves contained antique surgical implements and a ghastly collection of glass jars filled with different-size eyeballs preserved in formalin.

"This is my collection of vertebrate eyes," he said proudly, ignoring my horrified expression. "On the other side are worms, insects, molluscs. It's the most complete collection of the evolution of the eye in Europe."

"Are you interested in chronology, then?" asked Estíbaliz, peering at a squid's eye.

"Let's just say I like to have things in order," Antonio said, sitting in the main chair in the room and inviting us to take a seat as well.

"Do you have any bees' eyes?"

"I can't bear Anthophila. They always sting me."

"I beg your pardon?" I said.

"Anthophila, or 'flower lovers,'" he explained. "That's the scientific name for those annoying insects. The word *bee* is their common name."

"Thank you for that," said Estíbaliz, although I was sure she already knew what he was talking about. "We've also been told about your surgical collection."

"Yes, scalpels, lancets, metal syringes—I have instruments recovered from Pompeii, the Middle Ages, and the First and Second World Wars, as well as a replica of the engraving of the instruments used by the Egyptians in the temple of Kom Ombo. . . ."

He opened the right-hand drawer of his imposing desk and donned a pair of blue surgeon's gloves. Picking up a small scalpel with a mother-of-pearl handle, he showed it to us as though it were an ounce of gold.

"Some of these instruments still have traces of blood on them.

That increases their value enormously on the antiques market. Can you believe it: Blood from someone who lived in the nineteenth century? That kind of detail fascinates me."

Estíbaliz shot me a furious look. I knew her; she was growing tired of the optician's creepy monologue.

"Let's talk about your daughter," she said.

"Yes," Antonio replied evenly, "I was seeing to that."

"Seeing to it?"

"Yes, getting everything in order. Come with me to her bedroom. That's what the police do, isn't it? Inspect the victim's bedroom?"

We followed him back along the lengthy hallway, and I noticed that the bathroom door was ajar. Antonio kept his latex gloves on, as if he was in the habit of wearing them for long periods. He came to a halt outside a pair of double doors, but as Estíbaliz made to open them, he stopped her with his gloved hand.

"No, not there!" he barked. I think that was the first time I had seen him lose his cool since our arrival. He gestured to a different door. "This was my daughter's bedroom."

How quickly he's assimilated that "was," I noted mentally. Parents usually took days to get that right.

He opened the bedroom door, and we could see a bed frame and a mattress with no sheets or blankets on it. The shelves were empty; the closet doors were wide open, with empty clothes hangers inside. An image of desolation. I don't know why, but the hairs on the back of my neck stood on end. It was as if the Grim Reaper had just slipped behind me to make sure his work was done.

"What about her things?" I asked in the most professional tone I could muster.

"Obviously she won't be needing them anymore," he replied with a shrug. "I think I'm going to redecorate this room, strip out the shelves, and order some glass showcases to put my eyeball collection in."

"I see," said Estíbaliz through gritted teeth. "Did your daughter know someone called Alejandro Pérez de Arrilucea? That's the name of the young man she was found with." My partner had read DSU Salvatierra's report from top to bottom before we left headquarters.

"I haven't the faintest idea. Do you two have children?"

We both shook our heads, although mine was halfhearted.

"Don't ever have any," he snapped.

"You'll admit that your opinion is quite extreme, won't you?" I said, trying to strike a neutral tone.

"It's simply some well-meant advice," he said, taking off his gloves and stowing them in the back pocket of his pleated pants. "If one day you do have children, your center of gravity will shift, your priorities will be turned inside out like a pair of socks, and you'll spend years doing what you think is best. Then that child will grow up. You'll look into each other's eyes and discover you are strangers, that you don't have any idea what is going on in that other person's mind or realize how much harm you can cause each other. It only takes a few words to destroy twenty years of trust."

"Are you referring to your daughter's decision to take her mother's and her new partner's side? Is that why you're so angry with her, because she questioned whether you were her real father?" I said.

"Why do you ask, when I can see you've already been told as much?"

"We'd like to hear your version," I said in a conciliatory tone.

"I don't have a version. All I have is an empty room that I'd love to start redecorating right now, if you would be so kind as to leave me in peace."

"We're just doing our job. Isn't it important to you that we catch whoever did that to your daughter?"

"Frankly, I'm just starting to reorder my priorities. I'll ask you again: Could you please leave? It's going to be a very tough day, and it's only just beginning. As the head of the family, I have to deal with all the practical details involved in the death of a daughter."

"Of course, we're leaving now. Do you mind if I use the bathroom?"

"Don't you have somewhere else—?"

"I'll only be a moment," I said. "It's across the hall, isn't it?"

I raced out of the soulless room before he had the chance to throw me out.

I locked the bathroom door behind me and searched the floor. I thought I had seen something in the shadows under the bathtub as we were coming down the hallway.

I bent down, took out my own latex glove from my inside jacket pocket, and picked up the object: a roll of plastic insulating tape.

"Okay, so what do we do with you?" I said to myself, studying this piece of possible evidence.

I could have taken it and told the optician what I was doing, but I had the impression that, although he didn't seem very keen to talk about his daughter, Antonio had more information to offer us, and I didn't want to arouse his suspicions. I could also take it without telling him, but if he'd been using it when we rang the bell and, as I suspected, hastily threw it into the bathroom, that would be the first thing he looked for when Estíbaliz and I left, and I wanted him to go back to whatever he'd been doing.

In the end I decided to tear off a couple of inches of tape and put it in a big evidence bag. Then I flushed the toilet, turned the faucet on and off, and left the bathroom in a hurry.

The optician and Estí were waiting for me in the apartment's foyer, looking serious. The front door was open.

"Thank you for everything, Antonio. If there's anything more you wish to tell us, you know where you can find us," I said, extending my hand once more.

"I know, I know. And now, if you'll excuse me. . . ." He stroked his bushy gray mustache with what seemed like barely controlled impatience.

We traveled down in the elevator without a word. Estíbaliz's gaze met mine in the mirrored paneling.

"It's him," she whispered.

"We don't know that yet."

"His reaction isn't normal," she insisted, folding her arms across her chest.

"Yes, it is. He's in denial. However strange it may seem, it's the first stage of mourning. You've seen it hundreds of times in training, and there's a huge stack of reports on cases just like this one."

"None that have been this brutal. It's not normal, Kraken. He gets rid of any trace of his daughter only a few hours after he finds out she's dead. Who does that?"

"How about a father who is accustomed to controlling everything but who, in the past few weeks, has seen his wife leave him for an old boyfriend from the Company of Mary, his daughter question his paternity, and then that same daughter turn up naked and dead in the Old Cathedral?"

"I don't get it," she said, untying her braid, then tying it again. "Doesn't he seem suspicious to you? He's hyperorganized, obsessive, and meticulous. He's fascinated by the morbid aspects of death, and he knows how to use surgical implements. He fits the psychopathic profile you've been drawing up from the beginning. And he has a motive, Unai. He could have killed his daughter out of pure animosity toward her, or because he feels like he no longer controls his family, or to hurt his ex-wife. We've seen it before. That's how a murderer behaves, how a murderer thinks. All that ritual crime paraphernalia is to distract us, to camouflage his daughter's death, to try to make her seem like one more victim in the double murders of the Old Cathedral and the Casa del Cordón."

But my mind was already focused on other, more pressing matters. All those arguments, but there was no way to prove anything without solid evidence.

"Let's stay in the car and watch until he comes out. He's spent all morning filling boxes, but he's hidden them so well that we didn't even see them in his apartment. I bet he takes them out of his garage in his car. Call headquarters and see what vehicles he has registered in his name."

"Do you think he's going to take them out now?" asked Estí as we emerged from the building onto Calle San Antonio.

"This afternoon he has the funeral and his relatives are arriving. I think if he's going to get rid of anything, he's going to do it now."

While we were keeping an eye on the garage from our car, Estíbaliz received the license numbers of the optician's two vehicles: a silver Audi A4 and a white Mercedes van.

After two hours of waiting in silence, Estíbaliz broke the trance.

"Unai, I'm going. It's one o'clock and I haven't eaten all morning. I'm going to PerretxiCo for a couple of *pinchos*. Do you want me to bring you a roll or something to keep you going? We have a lot to get through today. If he hasn't appeared by now, I doubt if—"

"Shhh," I said, pointing. "Start the engine."

At last, a white Mercedes van with tinted rear windows and a license plate that matched the information we had emerged from the garage. Estíbaliz waited for him to get a few yards ahead, then pulled out to follow at a safe distance.

The Mercedes headed for the southern exit to Vitoria, and we tailed it for less than a mile. Estíbaliz was concentrating on her driving, and my mind was racing.

"Estí, do we still have each other's backs?" I asked point-blank.

"Why are you asking me that now?"

"I don't care if you lie to me about what you did last weekend—I don't tell you everything, either—but are you telling me all you know about this case?"

"I don't follow, Kraken. Spit it out, will you? Neither you nor I like beating about the bush."

"Good, that means I can save my breath. Estí, why didn't you tell me your brother is called the Eguzkilore?"

I was watching her face as I said this, but she was a good poker player.

"Let's set aside the fact that I'm furious because you don't trust my family. Why don't you tell me why you suspect my brother? Couldn't this just be a coincidence?"

"I wanted to ask you directly and hear you deny it."

"Deny what, Unai?" she growled.

"That your brother's mind is full of pagan ideas, that he runs a herbalist's shop and very likely knows how to prepare an infusion of yew poison, that he's been obsessed with other serial killers like Sacamantecas since early childhood, that he's spent his entire life surrounded by beehives, and knows how to handle them perfectly well . . ."

"How can I deny all that? It's true, and it's also true that he has a record for possession. Is that where you're going with this?"

"And for dealing, Estíbaliz. He has a record for dealing."

"All right, that, too. But he's been rehabilitated. Does that make him more of a suspect than your average inhabitant of Vitoria?"

"Yes, statistically it does, but that's not what makes him a suspect in this case. You can't ignore this many clues. Not to mention the Rohypnol. Wouldn't it be easy for him to get his hands on some and to know its effects?"

"Unai, I admit that Eneko is one of a kind, but do you really think you're talking to the sister of a serial killer?"

"Look, I'm not going to say anything to Salvatierra for the time being. But I want to talk to him. You're not going with me, and you're not going to tell your brother anything, because if you did you would be obstructing an investigation and would be taken off the case."

"Only if you blab. How did this conversation start? Oh, right, you were asking me if we still had each other's backs?"

"And I'm doing that, Estí, believe me. I know you're going through a difficult period with your father's Alzheimer's, and I'm sure that El Hier—that Eneko must also be affected, no matter what I think of him. But I have to check him out, just as you would if you suspected my brother were involved. I just want to cross him off the list and forget him, okay?"

"Can't you see that this guy is a thousand times more suspicious?" she said, pointing her chin at the white van a hundred yards in front of us. It began to slow down, and Estíbaliz did the same.

"That's why we're here, Estí. I hope to God it is him and this butchery will stop. But all I see is a father in denial. He may be a jerk to his family, but I can't see him killing three more young people just to conceal the fact that he murdered his daughter, and I can't see him stage-managing such a perfect copy of Tasio's crimes in only a few weeks."

"I think those questions are going to be cleared up right now," said Estíbaliz.

The van turned off the Peñacerrada Highway and went around the Gardelegi dump, where all the waste from Vitoria ended up. Several carrion birds circled the mountains of garbage while municipal trucks scratched at the city's filthy innards.

"What's he doing?" my partner whispered as she turned off behind him.

"I think he's trying to get into the oldest part of the dump, the part they no longer use."

The van finally came to a halt a few hundred yards ahead. Our car was half-hidden around a bend.

Antonio Fernández de Betoño got out, opened the van's rear doors, and began to unload big, brown cardboard boxes.

I took the small Konus binoculars out of the glove compartment and watched Antonio's movements at the edge of the dump.

"What can you see?" asked a frustrated Estíbaliz. "I can't make out anything from here."

"At the moment he's opening the box he's carrying and throwing what was in it onto the garbage heap: clothing, high heels—"

"He's disposing of evidence, Kraken. We have to stop him right now," she shouted, opening the car door to leap out.

"No, wait!"

All the cardboard boxes were marked with the brand names of optical firms. They must have been the ones the attendant had said he saw the optician carrying upstairs that morning. But now our suspect had returned to the van and was beginning to unload smaller boxes. These were black, and it didn't seem as though they could contain many personal effects. I wanted to know what was in them.

"Unai, if you don't arrest him, I will," said Estíbaliz. "I'll give you two minutes."

"It makes more sense to see what he's trying to get rid of. We can't arrest someone just for dumping things."

"Inspector Ayala!" she hissed. "One minute and forty seconds."

I concentrated on the smaller boxes the optician was hastily riffling through.

"They're not boxes!" I said. "They're office files. Now he's going back toward the garbage."

"Okay, let's go!"

"Wait! My God! He's throwing away—"

"What?"

"They look like old newspaper clippings."

Estíbaliz turned the ignition and sped to where the optician had parked. When he saw our vehicle coming toward him, he looked up in a panic. He tried to run back to his van, but Estíbaliz braked and jumped out in front of him.

"Stop there! Police!"

She drew out her HK 9mm service pistol and pointed it at his head. I knew Estí well enough to be sure that, for the moment at least, she had no intention of shooting him, but the optician was smart to raise his hands above his head. In our quarterly firing range practice, no one could beat her when she was focused. Her eyesight was legendary; she never missed a target.

Antonio Fernández de Betoño stood still, sweating. He was so terrified that even his mustache trembled.

"Don't shoot! This is only an environmental offense. I don't think it deserves a bullet."

"Quiet," said Estíbaliz, her gun still trained on him.

I ran toward the garbage heap, pulled on a glove, and picked up the yellowing press clippings the optician had dropped when he attempted to run away.

They related to the double murder at the dolmen, the village of La Hoya, the Valle Salado . . . everything about the original murders. There were also more recent articles about Tasio Ortiz de Zárate's imminent release.

I walked up to the optician and waved the cuttings at him. He nodded and lowered his head, acknowledging defeat.

"Antonio Fernández de Betoño, we're going to have to examine all this material, and we're asking you to accompany us to police headquarters. I am arresting you on suspicion of the murder of your daughter and of Alejandro Pérez de Arrilucea."

12

THE GREEN RING

Monday, August 1

You're already crossing the first threshold into the
world of magic. What are the murderer's rules?
What's inside his brain, #Kraken?

Our suspect was handcuffed and waiting in the interview room at the Lakua headquarters. Estíbaliz was frowning at him through the glass window. Antonio Fernández de Betoño seemed stunned to have been arrested, and yet he still had that strange serenity that so riled my partner.

He was examining the handcuffs with curiosity, as if they were one of his nineteenth-century surgical implements and he was trying to discover the release mechanism that would allow him to leave.

"Let me interview him on my own."

"No, he's mine. You're not convinced he's the one. You'll be too soft on him."

"Look, this is me you're talking to, Estíbaliz. Me. If this guy is guilty, I swear I'll get a confession out of him. You won't give him any option. Admit it: you're too set on it being him."

She threw up her arms and fixed her brown eyes on me. There were days when those eyes dug deep, and this was one of them.

"This has nothing to do with you wanting to pursue my brother, if that's what you're thinking."

I shook my head, my forehead pressed against the glass, staring at the optician.

"What you or I think isn't going to alter reality. Let me go in there on my own. With you, he's bound to clam up completely. You've been too hostile toward him from the outset. He has an apathetic profile; it's not going to be easy."

It's not going to be easy.

Estíbaliz nodded without another word, and I went into the room.

"We are here so that you can clear up a few details. I'll get straight to the point," I said, sitting down across from him. "I can't even begin to understand the stupidity of what you just tried to do. If you wanted to get rid of a few bits of paper, you could have burned them."

"That was my intention," he said, staring into my eyes. I found that odd—people guilty of murder never look you in the eye unless it's to challenge you, and that wasn't the case here. "My first stop was at Gardelegi to throw away the clothes and all the bad memories I had of my daughter. To me, they were nothing more than garbage. Then I wanted to drive to Treviño, where there's a picnic area with barbecues. I guessed no one would be there on a Monday morning, but it's August, so I couldn't be sure there wouldn't be groups camping, and honestly . . . I was sick of it all and didn't want my relatives or employees to discover I'd been gone a long time. That's why I tried to get rid of all those clippings. I knew that if you searched my house and found them, it would be very hard to explain what they were doing in the hands of the victim's father."

"Give it a try."

He turned his handcuffed hands around and stared at his fingernails, as if expecting to find something unusual under them.

Then he sighed. He was preparing his reply: either it was a lie, or it was related to something that was such a distant memory, it was an effort to recall.

"I became obsessed with the case twenty years ago," he said finally. "One of the babies killed in the double murder at the Witch's Lair dolmen was the son of a *cuadrilla* friend of mine. When he disappeared from the neonatal unit at the Vitoria Clinic, it was traumatic for everyone. Shortly afterward, my daughter was born. We had the same health insurance and the same doctor, and she was born at the same clinic. I was terrified she might be abducted and murdered like the other two. All of us parents who had young children felt the same way. I read every word that was published, as we all did, for God's sake. I don't know why I kept it. I suppose I'm a bit of a Diogenes and find it hard to throw away the things I collect."

"I'll need you to give me your friend's name to corroborate your story."

"Whenever you like. He doesn't like to talk about it—you know how we men get. He's separated now. They never managed to get past it."

"Let's say I believe you." I forced myself to continue. "What I need now is for you to give me a good alibi for where you were on July 24. Your daughter's boyfriend says that the last time he talked to her was around noon."

"I was with the *cuadrilla* of veteran Blusas, in our locale. We made lunch, ate, had a few drinks, played cards, and then went out at eight in the evening."

"Can you give me a list of everyone who was there? It's essential to determine whether we keep you here or allow you to go home."

"Give me a pen and let's get this over with as quickly as possible. Tomorrow is my daughter's funeral. I don't want anyone to hear that you brought me here. You know what this city is like."

I was watching him, trying to get inside his brain from the few clues his body language offered. As far as I could tell, he wasn't faking anything. I don't think he was even worried about whether we would charge him—he was in another world, with other concerns. That the police might think he was the murderer seemed unimportant; he was astonishingly uninterested in whether we would find him guilty.

At that moment Estíbaliz entered, giving me an urgent look I knew well. I excused myself and left the room.

"The superintendent is hopping mad. He wants to see us," she whispered in my ear, as though the suspect could still hear us.

"Now, when I'm in the middle of an interrogation?"

"Yes, now!"

We went up to the third floor, to the office that had the best views. Both Superintendent Medina and Deputy Superintendent Salvatierra were waiting for us, stern-faced. I still couldn't fathom why they looked so serious.

"Do you mind explaining why on Earth you are questioning Antonio Fernández de Betoño?" growled the superintendent.

"We're doing our job, sir. The boyfriend of the twenty-year-old female victim came to headquarters this morning and told us he suspected that her father was guilty of the crimes. Inspector Gauna and I went to his home to check his version of events. He was behaving oddly, so we followed him to the Gardelegi dump, where we saw him getting rid of his daughter's personal belongings as well as a lot of press clippings concerning the double murders that took place twenty years ago."

"And that was enough to arrest him? For heaven's sake!" snorted Medina, undoing a button on his jacket and loosening his tie.

"We just have to check his alibi: he states that on the day in question he was with his *cuadrilla* from midday to evening. As soon as he writes their names down for me—"

"Of course he was in our locale, Inspector Ayala! He's one of my closest friends. We were together from the moment he came into the kitchen and we put on our aprons to prepare the sea bass. Do me the favor of releasing him at once, and discreetly! That man doesn't deserve to be treated like this; it's only been a few hours since he was informed of the death of Enara, of his daughter. I want you to be proactive, but don't make any more gross mistakes like this one. Concentrate on those suspects who really fit the profile. And stop bothering the families of the victims! We cannot make this kind of mistake. We're in the spotlight, and any slipup is going to be front-page news around the world. Our press department is already struggling with *Le Monde*, *The Washington Post*, and even *The Sunday Telegraph* from Australia. I want to see progress, inspectors, not blunders like today. You may go."

The three of us filed out. Estíbaliz shot me a despairing glance.

"I'll tell the optician he's free to go."

"Inspector Ayala, accompany me to my office, will you?" said DSU Salvatierra.

I followed her in silence. Everybody seemed to be glancing at us out of the corners of their eyes: uniforms, other inspectors. I felt like a small goldfish in a bowl—a strange, fascinating object.

"Shut the door."

"With great pleasure, ma'am," I said, blocking the view of several colleagues peering surreptitiously into the office as they passed by.

"I'm sure I don't need to tell you this must never happen again. You are not to bring anyone in without a convincing reason," she said, repeating the superintendent's warning as she sat down. "A *more* convincing reason," she added.

That day she was wearing her long, dark hair loose. It made her look years younger, and I found her far more attractive than I wanted to. It took me a couple of seconds to react.

"I totally agree," I said, forcing myself to concentrate once more.

"Are you agreeing with me as if I were an idiot?" she asked, possibly surprised at how meek I was being.

"Not at all. It's just that I've never believed these crimes are circumstantial. That's why I never thought the optician fit the murderer's profile. I'm telling you, the key to all this lies with the twins. We have to avoid distractions and start investigating them."

"That's precisely what I wanted to talk to you about. I spoke to the prison warden, and she insisted that the prisoner has no privileges or access to the Internet. When I argued that he was obviously in contact with somebody on the outside who is composing the tweets on his behalf, she told me that we would need a judicial order if we wanted to restrict the visits he receives. To do so without that order is illegal and a violation of the rights he still has in prison."

"What impression did you have of her?"

"She was very correct, but I think that she's protecting him for some reason. Be that as it may, we can't do anything there. So we're trying a different approach. A few days ago, we asked the cyber-crimes unit to close the @scripttipsfromjail account. The people at Twitter agreed and explained the legal process we need to follow in such cases, but they warned us it could take several weeks."

"It's a waste of time," I said. "Even if it were closed, it would be of no use."

"Why do you say that, inspector?"

My God, how awful it felt to hear her call me "inspector."

"Because Tasio, or rather his accomplice, is using the hashtag #Kraken, which has spread across social media. Anyone who wants to comment on the double crimes is using it. It's unstoppable. We can't ask Twitter to delete all the tweets using that hashtag. If the original account were closed, Tasio would continue to communicate with his followers by opening another account and using that hashtag. It would only take a few tweets to convince them it was really him. We could close a second and a third account, but that would take weeks. He'll always be a step ahead. As my grandfather would say, you can't build walls against the sea, or doors in the countryside. Believe me, I hate the fact that the name Kraken is on every cell phone in Vitoria and throughout Spain more than anyone, but as far as social media goes, we simply can't win. What about the IP address he used?"

"Bad news there as well. The technical experts are still working on it, but they say it's untraceable."

Untraceable, okay. If there's no other way, I'll have to use it.

"If I understand correctly, you're saying that Tasio must have a good hacker working for him."

"Yes, you've understood absolutely correctly," she said, staring at me with those dark eyes. Did she want to say something more? Was Alba in charge, or was Blanca struggling to make her presence felt in that stuffy office?

I forced myself to look down at her wedding ring. It didn't look right on her hand. Not that ring, at least.

"You have to allow me to speak to Tasio Ortiz de Zárate again. There are key elements in this case that he seems very keen to share. We shouldn't neglect that line of investigation."

"You know I'm worried he might manipulate you."

"That won't happen, and even if it does, I'll give you a full report of everything we talk about on each of my visits. Inspector Ruiz de Gauna knows me well, so I'd like you both to monitor me. If any aspect of my behavior makes you think that the convict is leading me on or that I'm starting to show symptoms of Stockholm syndrome, simply order me to stop communicating with him. I promise I'll do as you say."

I had never spoken like this to a superior officer, but for some reason, I was sure her shoulders were broad enough to take her weight and mine.

Alba's face took on a serious expression, and she cracked her knuckles as she thought it over.

"All right, get in touch with the penitentiary and ask for a visit for today. Let's see if you can bring back something that will help our investigation."

"I think I can," I said, glancing at my watch. "And now, if you'll excuse me, I've arranged to meet one of the people who knew the twins twenty years ago. Ignacio gave me these names, so I'm not expecting any surprises, but I want to gain a more precise picture of what they were like back then. As for what they're like now"—I sighed—"I think I have some idea."

"What are they like now, Ayala? Share it with me."

"Two strong-willed men who are at odds with the bright future they faced two decades ago. Two men who are intelligent and clever and who have, in their own way, survived a tsunami. Do you remember that line from *Damage*, the Jeremy Irons movie?"

" 'Damaged people are dangerous, because they know they can survive,' " we said in unison.

"Wow, I didn't think that . . ." I muttered, scratching the back of my neck.

"That I would know it? What, you've never had a DSU who was a film buff?"

"No, I've never had the pleasure, I admit it." I stood up, forcing myself to break the spell. "I have to go."

It was hot in there, far too hot.

"Of course. Good afternoon, inspector."

Half an hour later I was surprised to find a heavily pregnant woman waiting for me. She was pushing a baby carriage with an infant in it. I had contacted Aitana because she was one of the last names on Ignacio's list, and besides, I was interested in a female perspective on the twins' world.

I had done some research on her. She was the daughter of the former head of dermatology at the Hospital de Santiago, and now she was competing for the post.

Over the phone, Aitana had insisted we meet somewhere in Vitoria's Anillo Verde, a ring of parks used for walking, biking, and jogging that surround the city.

We had chosen Zabalgana in the west, a quiet wooded island with ponds and lots of footpaths.

Aitana was about forty years old. She appeared to be on the heavy side, with dyed blonde hair, flattened against her skull, and skin darkened from a tanning bed. She was smoking continuously, a cigarette stuck between two tense fingers that pointed up to the cloudless sky in a *V* for victory.

I introduced myself briefly, and we set off through a grove of oaks and junipers. She was nervously trying to calm the baby in the carriage.

"His name is Markel; my parents are bringing him up. The thing is, I spend long hours in the hospital and hardly get to see him. Besides, I don't like children," she offered as an excuse, blowing a cloud of smoke over the child.

"So I see," I said.

I must admit that meeting this witness—a pregnant doctor who smoked and seemed so uncaring—left me puzzled. Even from a distance her class and upbringing were obvious, but something about her didn't fit. It was as if she was very damaged inside.

"Ignacio told his *cuadrilla* that a detective would call us. If you don't mind, ask me the questions you've prepared, and I'll answer. I think the baby is hungry. If he goes on crying like that, I'll have to take him to my mother's so that she can feed him."

"I understand," I said. "Were you part of Ignacio's circle or Tasio's?"

"More Ignacio's. When we were eighteen, I was his girlfriend for a few months. The three of us were friends in the same *cuadrilla*, but I always had more to do with Ignacio."

"What were they like?"

"Ignacio was a gentleman. Tasio did as he pleased. He was full of himself, especially a few years later, when he became famous because of those TV shows. Tasio was promiscuous; all the girls in Vitoria hung around him when we went into the bars on Calle Cuesta. He could leave with anyone he wanted. In fact, that's exactly what he did. And then . . . then there were the rumors about the twin thing."

"Rumors?" I said. Luckily, Aitana seemed more than happy to tell me about them, as if she had been holding back the story for years.

We strolled through the park, staying in the shade and enjoying the cool vegetation and the small lake, where dragonflies chased each other in their mating ritual.

"Yes, erotic rumors. Apparently they liked twin girls, and apparently all of them within a radius of seventy miles had been in Tasio's bed. Threesomes, with Tasio and Ignacio. Ever since they were little, they always tried to fool people because they looked so much alike. Ignacio told me they used to swap places at school. The teachers at Sacred Heart grew tired of their pranks and put them in different classes. The twins hated it. To them, it was an insult, because they thought they were inseparable. Ignacio told me that he was ten when this happened, and he couldn't imagine spending even a few hours apart from his brother. He didn't think it was physically possible, and he was ill, in a state of shock, for weeks after it happened. He was vomiting and had a fever. He said the doctor didn't know what diagnosis to give his parents.

"And, yet, Tasio thought of how to use this to their advantage. They would each study half a subject. Then, on exam days, they would switch places, and each of them would take the exam twice. They had any number of tricks: they would both ask to go to the bathroom at an agreed-upon time and then swap their uniforms and name tags before going into the other's class. They'd take the exam and swap back again. They liked to play that game all the time. In the *cuadrilla*, we grew accustomed to it. People were tired of constantly being tricked, but the twins were who they were. No one could stop them; they were untouchable. Their father was one of the wealthiest men in Vitoria. Our parents always told us to try to get along with them, to stay friends, to invite them to our birthday parties. My parents were very proud when I started going out with Ignacio. That was the best thing one could aspire to socially in this city."

"What do you think of them now?"

"About Tasio, what everyone thinks: that he was an egocentric creep who it turned out was completely crazy and liked to kill children. As for Ignacio, it must have been incredibly hard for him to turn in his brother. He suffered a lot. We tried to support him as best we could in the *cuadrilla,* but as usual here, the topic was taboo. In Vitoria we talk about everything except what's important. Our mothers bring us up with the slogan, *For peace, a Hail Mary*, which means you look the other way and keep quiet like a coward. That's what we do, and we're very good at it. . . . Anyway, to get back to Ignacio, then there was that television thing. It took us all by surprise; he was quite shy really, but he forced himself to be extroverted to keep up with his brother. Then, suddenly, Ignacio was the new hero, and everyone stopped him in the street to congratulate him. He took on Tasio's personality, although he was more restrained. As I already told you, he was always a gentleman. It's not as if we stayed close friends after our relationship finished, but we've been in the same *cuadrilla* for more than twenty years, so we see each other every week at dinners and so on."

"Fine," I said when we reached the end of the walk and were back in the city. "I just wanted to get an idea of what the twins' friends and *cuadrillas* were like. Thank you for being willing to talk to me. I'll leave you my card; feel free to give me a call if you remember anything else . . . and good luck with the birth."

After drinking a few pick-me-ups in Rincón de Luis Mari with my sister-in-law and enjoying some respite from the case with her tales of separation, I got into my car and drove to Zaballa.

Tasio was waiting for me on the far side of the security glass in Room Three. A guard sat next to him.

"About time, too," said Tasio in his drawling voice. "Did you do your homework?"

"Have we made peace since the last time we saw each other?"

"We're condemned to understand each other, Kraken. You've come back; that means you need something from me. And, it goes without saying, I need you to solve this case. That's why I try to point you in the right direction every day," he said in a placatory tone that I was hearing for the first time.

"You mean the tweets you send me that are read by all of Spain and a good deal of the world?"

"That's right."

"What exactly do you mean by discretion? Did they teach you that in your criminology course?"

"You're upset," he said, smiling faintly.

"I'll get over it. And, as you say, it would be good for you if I were heading in the right direction."

"What do you want from me?" he asked, staring down at his nicotine-stained fingers.

"You have acolytes, admirers who've been following you for twenty years."

"Is that what you've heard?" Another faint smile, and he blew smoke down toward the floor. He was pleased to have his celebrity status recognized.

"Tell me about them all."

"We don't have enough time," he said, enjoying his starring role.

I was tired of this.

"Tasio, you offered to collaborate, and I'm giving you the chance to have your moment of glory on social media. I'll explain why I want you to tell me about your admirers: The crimes you were accused of and those taking place now have similar elements. That means that it's the same killer, or someone who was connected to the investigation twenty years ago, or that you have shared the details of the court case with someone and that person is imitating the first murderer to incriminate you once more. Wake up, Tasio, because this is happening again. It's real. If we can't find any other suspects, public opinion and my superiors will be keeping you in their sights. You have a lot to lose. This isn't an arm-wrestling match between us. I'm on the outside, and you're in here. You're smart enough to realize you should stop trying to bluff me."

We stared defiantly at each other for a few seconds. Long enough for him to give way.

"All right," he said eventually, crushing half a cigarette in one of the ashtrays. "What exactly do you want?"

"Give me all the letters you've kept from anyone who has been in contact with you since you've been in here. That would be a good start. It would show me that I could trust you and would ensure that I keep visiting you. It doesn't matter how many tweets you write every day. I can ignore them, because you don't have any real power. I can let you continue to be a voice crying in the wilderness. You do understand that, don't you?"

"You know I do. You'll get those letters. They're garbage—they mean nothing to me. I'll give you all of them."

"Do you think I'll find anything to rescue me from all that garbage?"

"Most of them are crazy, people obsessed with the crime. I wouldn't give them the time of day if you paid me. But you're doing your job, and I would do the same."

"Fine."

"Kraken . . ." he said after a while, his hand sweeping the air, "this is going to get worse."

"What do you mean?"

"The longer it takes for you to catch him, the harder it will be to anticipate his next move. We're in the late Middle Ages already; as I see it, there are several other locations he could use in the medieval quarter. But things will get much harder when he reaches the nineteenth century: the closer you get to the present day, the more buildings still exist, the more opportunities for him to stage his murders. There will come a time when you won't be able to predict anything."

"Does that worry you, Tasio?"

"I want to get out of here, damnit!" he thundered. "I want to get out, but he's going to find a way to frame me again! Are you blind? The fiesta days begin this week in Vitoria. Don't you see? This time he's trampling on all our rituals, all our customs. The celebrations are going to be a bloodbath."

No, Tasio, I can only hope you're wrong about that.

"Tell me something," I said, interrupting his rant, "and calm down. You're scarier when you're calm."

He glared at me. A ferocious look, as if he were going to disembowel me. It was like something out of a nightmare.

"Whatever," he finally said.

I plucked up my courage. I had swum from buoy to buoy, but now I was close to the taboo subject. Double or nothing.

Go for it, Kraken.

"What if it was your brother? What if he was the one who set a trap for you? Don't tell me the thought hasn't crossed your mind in the past twenty years. You studied criminology, you became obsessed with the case, you've spent two decades in a cell going over conspiracies, motives, suspects, profiles. So why aren't you trying to convince me of what's right in front of you? Wouldn't it be normal to try to do to him what he did to you? 'It was him. He was jealous of me. He was a policeman. He planted the evidence. He knew the reports. He tampered with them'? Ignacio could have done it, he had everything in easy reach; all he needed to do was point the finger at you. Tell me you didn't threaten him. Tell me you didn't swear to be avenged when you got out of prison. Tell me Ignacio has no reason to be afraid when you're released and you see each other outside, away from the cameras."

I took a deep breath, studying his reaction. Tasio was a pillar of salt.

I kept pressuring him. Was this going to be a moment of catharsis, or was it too soon for Tasio to crumble?

"Tell me you've never wondered whether he was the one doing it and whether he's trying to incriminate you now so that you won't be released. He'll find a way to make it look like you're the puppet master. You're running that risk with your cyberattacks and your Twitter account. You're showing people that you're a ubiquitous devil who can get people on the outside to do things for you. Tell me something, Tasio: If twenty years ago somebody set a trap for you, how long do you think it will be before he manipulates public opinion and makes you look guilty again? And have you honestly never imagined for a moment that such a person could be your own brother—who, by the way, is getting on just fine in Vitoria without you?"

He sat in silence, refusing to look at me. He smoked a cigarette with exasperating slowness. I was at the point of leaving when he finally spoke.

"Do you have brothers, Kraken?"

"Don't pretend. You know my nickname. You must know whether I have brothers."

Leave Germán out of this, Tasio. You haven't seen me in kamikaze mode yet.

"But you're not identical twins."

"No, we're not."

"Then you can't understand what my twin and I have. It has nothing to do with the brotherly feelings between you and Germán."

"You said his name." I choked back my anger. I hated any veiled threat against those closest to me: Grandfather, Germán, and Estíbaliz were untouchable.

Sacred.

Nonnegotiable.

Off-limits.

This had nothing to do with them.

"I knew you were going to notice that. It's my way of showing you I'm still one step ahead. Let me continue."

"Shed some light on it for me."

"What I'm trying to make clear to you—and it's very important you understand this—is that in here we're not going to talk about my twin, or of what he and I have pending when I get out of prison. It's too private. What happened between us is something we'll sort out separately. We're the only inhabitants of a planet neither you nor anybody else has any right to visit. I want that to be clear, because after this we're not going to talk about it ever again. If you want to investigate him, get on with it. Do your duty, that's what I'm expecting. But I'm not going to give you the slightest reason to do so."

Or maybe you're so twisted that everything you've done until now has been calculated precisely so I reach the point where I think it's up to me to investigate him and find him guilty. Because a vendetta on your part would be too obvious.

"All right, Tasio. That's clear. Now I want you to go back to your cell and look through all the letters you've received. Save me some work and give me your own list of suspects. Prioritize the most likely ones, but don't leave anyone out. And have your Twitter contact send me a list of your most active followers, and the most vehement commenters—everything that you instinctively think a seriously damaged person might be behind."

In fact, Tasio's account was like an enormous strip of flypaper, despite how awkward it was to be gradually losing all anonymity thanks to that blessed hashtag. That was why I hadn't urged the deputy superintendent to close it. If the murderer was vain, he would be prowling around everything related to the crimes and the investigation.

"You have influence in here. I'm going to ask for all your admirers' letters, so go through them quickly. We're close to the grand finale; you can sense it, too."

"I'm glad we speak the same language," he said, smiling at last.

"I'll see you soon, Tasio," I said, standing up. "This time you're the one with homework."

With that I should have left the prison, but there was something I still wanted to do. I wanted information, but I wouldn't get it through official channels. So I strolled over to the guard at reception and said casually:

"I was about to leave, but first I wanted to say hello to Jose

Mari. Do you know if he'll be in the cafeteria at this time of day?"

"Go and have a look."

In Álava, the name Jose Mari belonged to probably 10 percent of the male population over forty-five. I couldn't go wrong.

I walked over to the block he had indicated and entered the room where the prison staff met to have coffee or a snack. There weren't many people at five in the afternoon. From the counter, I gazed at the small groups seated at the tables and chose a skinny guard sitting on his own, finishing a can of Aquarius, absorbed in the soundless TV screen on the wall.

Prison staff weren't a good source of information. They rarely told the police anything. The worst thing in a prison, whichever side of the bars you were on, was to be a snitch. I knew I had to take a more creative approach.

I waited for him to come up to the counter to pay and then intercepted him.

"Do you know if there's a coffee machine around? The waiter in here is ignoring me."

He looked up, busy on his cell phone.

"Are you new here? I haven't seen you before."

In a couple of seconds, I took in several details: no wedding ring and a photo on his cell phone of a pretty young woman who, based on her age, could be his daughter or niece but wasn't. Her pose suggested she was something else entirely.

"I don't work here, at least not yet." I smiled. "I came to see if I might have any luck swapping jobs. I work in the Basauri penitentiary, but I'd like to transfer here. I've found myself a girlfriend in Vitoria . . . we haven't been going out long . . . but, well, you know how it is."

"I've been there. Well, I hope you get lucky and we end up colleagues. There's a machine at the exit. Come on, I'll go with you."

We left the cafeteria. Fortunately, there were no other prison staff around.

"What's it like, working here?" I asked, as I inserted a coin into the machine.

"We're getting used to the changes. It's a supermax prison now, and it has its eccentricities," he said noncommittally.

"All prisons do, believe me. I've been at Avila and Logroño. Listen, what's it like having someone famous behind bars?"

"You mean Tasio?" he said, looking around.

"Yes. Doesn't the press bother you?"

"For the moment, the press is manageable. But inside here, he's like a god. He's overprotected, a legend. Some say he's a good guy, even though he sometimes acts tough to show how much power he has. The inmates respect him; some are afraid of him. You only have to see him to understand: he looks like a lunatic with that wild stare, like someone who could cut you up into little pieces and sprinkle you on his salad. He's like Charles Manson; there are women who write to him asking to see him face-to-face. He likes that, although he usually sees them only once. As far as women go, he's one of the most active prisoners we have."

"What it is to be famous."

"You said it." He shrugged.

"And what about this crap that he has a Twitter account?" I went on, rotating the fiendishly hot plastic cup in my hand. "I don't believe it. I bet it's a fake."

He looked around him to make sure nobody was listening.

"I have a theory about that. It must have been that good-looking kid, that boy genius."

"What boy genius?"

"You know, the one in the newspapers for that Internet fraud with credit cards. The hacker, don't you remember?"

"Now that you mention it, I think I do. What ended up happening with him?" I tried to remember the case, but cybercrimes weren't my thing. I eventually recalled a short report about it from a few months earlier.

"The kid began his brilliant criminal career at the tender age of sixteen. He fleeced anyone who left their credit-card details on a fake website selling soccer shirts signed by First Division footballers. After a flood of complaints, they managed to catch him, but he was very slippery. They must have had their work cut out for them, because by the time they got him, he was an adult, and so he was brought here. He looked about twelve or thirteen, one of those kids who hasn't grown up yet, with no hair on his balls or his face. He looked like a cherub or a model, dark-haired and blue-eyed. I reckon he could've been a YouTube sensation, with that angelic face. But he was tempted by the dark side."

"And you're telling me this because . . ."

"Yes, I was getting to that. The warden made Tasio his buddy, which was a smart move. Inmates love fresh meat, and the queens here would have made a meal of him—you know what I mean. Tasio took charge and kept him under his wing, so that nobody touched the kid during the six months he was in here. That Twitter business began just after the boy was released. That's why I think they're in it together; they must still be in contact."

"What did you say his name was?"

"I don't remember, but it's a common name. What I do remember is that his hacker handle was MatuSalem. Yes, that's it: MatuSalem. I remember now: his name was Maturana, like the village near the wetlands, and he changed it to MatuSalem, after that place where the witches were in the States. He was a little weird; there was something sinister about him. He looked like a Goth or something."

———

As soon as I reached the outside parking lot, I called an old friend.

Occasionally I had no other option but to turn to certain collaborators who were outside official channels.

My collaborator was sixty-six years old. Her white hair was dyed purple. She was so good at hacking that she had been able to produce fake documents for a wedding—to her deceased partner of forty years—that had never existed. The local council had refused her a widow's pension, and she was having trouble staying in the apartment they had shared their entire life.

I had discovered her forgery last year during my search for an assailant who stayed in a room she rented out. I told her about it, and thanks to her courage, I was able to capture the man and keep the city's women a little safer.

Her nom de plume was Golden Girl, or Urreszko Neska. She was a legend in black-hacker forums, although many people didn't believe she existed. Until she retired, she had worked for a security company subcontracted by Cisco Systems. The worst mistake anyone could make was to underestimate her computer knowledge on the basis of her age or her dotty old-woman's appearance.

"I need you to search for someone who is hacking my e-mail and for a Twitter account."

"That's what I like about you: straight to the point, as if every moment counts," said Golden Girl in her venerable old lady's voice.

"Maybe they do. Have you heard of MatuSalem?"

"You like making life difficult for me, don't you? That boy is hard-core. It's not going to be easy. What can you give me?"

I supplied her with the details she asked for. Golden Girl had the sort of instinct that comes with age, which meant she could immediately tell when something was urgent.

"And a favor. I'm using my laptop to investigate, and I'm sure that MatuSalem has found a way into it or has mirrored it. I don't want him to be able to see what I'm doing. Can you make me a firewall that I can use starting tonight?"

"Doubting me is an insult. Is it that serious?"

"Pretty much. Is this senior citizen going to astonish me yet again?"

"You know you have this golden girl at your feet, Kraken. I'll call you as soon as I can triangulate that spring chicken."

13

THE VITORIA CLINIC

VITORIA
JUNE 1970

Doctor Urbina was consulting a medical text in his office when his nurse, Felisa, knocked on the door. Puzzled, he looked at the clock. He was done with his last appointment and was preparing to go home.

"Doctor, a patient wants to see you," said the nurse in her rich voice. "Shall I send her in, or have her make an appointment for another day?"

"Who is it, Felisa?"

Felisa's right eye drooped slightly because of a botched sinus operation that had ruined part of the eye socket. She had a few gray streaks in her black hair, which was always kept in place with tight curls, and like many women her age who were going through the change of life, she was on the heavier side.

"It's Señora Ortiz de Zárate, Doña Blanca."

The pages of the heavy volume slipped between Urbina's fingers, and the red-leather cover shut without his realizing it.

Quietly clearing his throat, he reopened the book.

"Tell her to come through. I was planning to stay late this evening."

The nurse looked at him with the discreet intuition she'd acquired from working in hospitals for nearly twenty-five years.

"You don't mind if I go home, do you?"

"You can go, Felisa. I'll lock up," he replied quickly.

The nurse left, and at last Blanca entered his clinic.

She looked completely different. Maybe it was because summer had arrived, and she was wearing a light dress with a bright psychedelic design, or maybe it was because, for once, her expression no longer hid suppressed pain. For the first time since she had become his patient, he saw what looked like a semblance of happiness in her face.

"Doña Blanca. I'm so glad to see you! Are you feeling better? You know what I'm referring to." She had taught him things no one else had: to be sincere, to look her straight in the eye, and to enjoy the few meetings Fate would allow.

"I came to thank you for everything you've done for me. These past few months have been a lot more . . . bearable."

She lowered her voice instinctively, although no one could have heard them in his office with the door shut.

"Did you use what I gave you?"

"Yes, and I think you were right when you said it might save my life. I no longer need the tablets or the ointment, but I'm running out of the maroon capsules. They keep him sedated in the evenings. He goes straight to bed when he gets home. He blames his workload and doesn't seem suspicious."

The doctor unlocked a small drawer in his desk.

"I was planning a chance encounter, Doña Blanca. You've saved me a lot of walks," he said, laughing.

"You don't need to be so formal, Álvaro, at least when we're alone. I believe you know me better than anyone else right now."

He relished her words, perhaps more than he should have. And, better still, Blanca knew and remembered his Christian name.

Álvaro ran his fingers across his ginger eyebrows, trying to clear his head and not look at her. She seemed to delight in the gesture, because she grinned at him like a young girl.

"Here, this should last you a couple of months." He took the bottle from the drawer and handed it to her.

Blanca took it from him, deliberately letting her hand brush against his. They remained like that, on either side of the desk, not knowing what to do next. Neither wanted to end this caress. They each had longed for it over many lonely nights.

"I don't want you to think that I only came here for this bottle, Álvaro. I came because I wanted to see you," Blanca declared boldly.

She was tired of paying for something she hadn't done, tired of playing the role everyone expected of her, tired of not caring that Javier might one day beat her to death.

She was tired of obeying men who were hard, cruel, and strong. Tired of being sad, of being afraid. What had happened to the care-free little girl she'd once been? She was tired of being a last name and a punching bag, a vessel for semen. This was her first act of rebellion, and she wanted it to be with Álvaro Urbina.

For once in your life, she told herself, *forget about what other people might think. Haven't you earned this with blood and tears?*

Álvaro looked into her eyes questioningly, but all he saw was a woman whose mind was already made up. He stood without saying anything, slowly went over to the door, and locked it. Then he turned around and hung up his white coat.

Blanca sat on the examination table, undoing the buttons down the front of her dress one by one. Then she was naked. In her wedge heels, she was the same height as Álvaro. He took her hand and gently began to kiss the knuckle of her forefinger.

He continued to kiss along her extensor tendon and moved up her arm, following the cephalic vein. He curled his tongue deliciously into the crook of her elbow and, much later, reached her deltoids. He strayed along the line of her collarbone, and by the time he arrived at her trapezius, his erection was almost excruciating.

For the first time, Blanca understood what being ready for a man meant, because when Álvaro gently penetrated her, all she wanted was to remain in that sterile office and never go back to her married life.

14

SAN VICENTEJO

Monday, August 1

He points the way, and you follow. Always behind, always behind, #Kraken.

Night had fallen, but my day was not over yet. I changed vehicles and drove to Villaverde in my Outlander, along back roads I had traveled a thousand times since childhood. I headed south along the Puerto de Vitoria road and entered the Treviño region, with its almost deserted villages and small Romanesque churches that had withstood centuries, surrounded by harvested fields of wheat. When I reached San Vicentejo, the dark mass of the mountains I knew so well appeared. I accelerated, hoping Grandfather had not yet gone to bed. I passed through the beech trees that formed an arch where the road curved near Bajauri. By day, their tall trunks and leaves covered the slopes, giving it a fairy-tale appearance; but at night it looked more like a witch's den.

When I reached Villaverde, the golden glow from half a dozen streetlights accompanied me up the hill until I parked the car beneath the trellis.

I whistled as I climbed the stairs, my laptop case slung from my shoulder, and Grandfather whistled back. I found him in the kitchen, shelling a sack of almonds. He liked to make *garrapiñadas* with them, adding water, Las Cadenas aniseed, and sugar. Then he gave them to Germán and me to take back to Vitoria. *For the difficult days*, he always told us, shrugging and turning away to get started on another chore.

"How are things, Grandpa?"

"You're here at this time of night and on a Monday, young'un? What did you forget?"

I sat opposite him on a cane chair that had been mended countless times.

"Grandpa, can I use the loft for some research? I've got a lot of photographs I don't want to keep in my apartment."

Grandfather never said yes or no directly.

"Let's go up there and see," he said, stooping as he stood up and walked over to stairs so worn from twelve generations of shoes that they were bowed in the middle, each like a tiny wooden valley.

Grandfather kept the upper floor of the old house spotless. The varnished, dark wooden beams were exposed, and the original stone walls were unplastered. He still had a few small fox and wild boar skins from back when postwar hunger made him a poacher. No one could understand how they had remained intact half a lifetime later, and if asked, he did not explain.

The loft also contained my boxes, mementos I did not want to throw away, things I had no desire to see again because they made my heart clench but that I knew I had to keep.

"Grandpa, can you open up the Ping-Pong table while I find what I'm looking for?"

"Of course, son."

This mythical table had been part of the philosophy that Grandfather had instilled into Germán and me. As a teenager, my brother barely reached the height of the table's green surface, whereas my disproportionately long arms did not have enough space to wield the racket properly. I felt hemmed in when I had to play sports in restricted spaces, but this game forced us to compensate for our weaknesses and concentrate on tactics to win the point and then the game. Even then we could sense that the world wasn't always going to be as accommodating as our family, and so we spent our summers trying to thrash each other until we collapsed in exhaustion and Grandfather brought us the old wineskin and allowed us to have a swallow.

I moved all the boxes until I found what I was looking for at the very bottom: the box with *Tasio* written on it in my teenage handwriting.

"My God, it's been a long time!" I exclaimed, staring almost reverently at the cardboard box.

By then Grandfather had set up the table in the center of the room. I opened the box and began to take out newspapers and VHS tapes.

"Do you think you can make the videotape recorder and the old TV set work up here?"

Grandfather shrugged. He loved old-fashioned electronic challenges.

"Let's see," he said with a smirk.

He went over to the corner and, from under some cobwebbed plastic sheets, pulled out a videotape recorder and a TV set that had long since been replaced by more up-to-date models.

While he was doing this, I took the front-page photographs I had cut out two decades earlier and arranged them on the vast table.

What would Estíbaliz think if she discovered the evidence of my obsession with Tasio? Would she have arrested me as she had the optician? Would I be added to her list of suspects?

I had photographs of Tasio's arrest, Ignacio's appearance in court, and all the places the dead children were found: the dolmen, the store in the village at La Hoya, the salt pans in the Valle Salado, and near the medieval wall's gate, in Cantón Carnicerías.

I had to stop myself from gagging as the forensic photographs of the children's bodies flashed through my mind. During all those years, I had thought only of the twins and the historical route the murders had traced. But now I was the detective, not a spectator fascinated by the double crimes. The forensic team's cold lights showed only too clearly the harsh reality of bodies not meant to be stretched out on the ground, naked and poisoned.

"You're working on the case of those two sly foxes—those twins—aren't you, son?" my grandfather asked from behind my back.

I nodded without turning around.

He came over to the table and picked up one photograph of Tasio and another of Ignacio, who were literally identical in those years.

"Which is the docile one?" he asked.

"Neither of them were very docile. They both chased the girls. I think they were arrogant rich kids."

"But one of them dominated the other. When two lambs are born in the same delivery, one leads the other wherever it likes. The other is docile. Always. Which of them is the dominant one?"

"They're not sheep, Grandpa. Sheep are dumb creatures, but this guy is the smartest person I've ever run into," I said, pointing to Tasio's photograph. "I don't think he's the docile one. No way."

"Then it's the other one. I'm sure of it. And you know what I always tell you: every good question starts with 'What if.'"

This was a lesson Grandfather had instilled in me since childhood. It was his way of passing the López de Ayala family's common sense on to me.

"All right, I'll play: What if . . ." But I couldn't continue. I wasn't ready yet.

"Don't be such a coward. Say out loud what keeps you from sleeping at night. Last Saturday you were thrashing about in bed worse than a wounded wild boar."

I sighed.

"What if, in fact, it was Ignacio who was the dominant one? What if he set a trap for Tasio, incriminating him with evidence he had planted?"

"You need more what-ifs."

"What if Ignacio did it because he was jealous? What if the docile one became more famous than the dominant one? Wouldn't Ignacio have liked the success and fame Tasio enjoyed?"

Satisfied, Grandfather patted me on the back.

"I think you've got enough to start with. I'm going to bed, but the TV is set up if you want to use it. Good night, son."

"Good night, Grandpa," I muttered, too focused on what I was doing to listen to his weary footsteps descend the stairs.

I opened my laptop and went onto the Internet. Golden Girl had sent a brief text message: *All clear.* So I began to research the twins' family: Their father's business, their mother's family. Addresses, dates of birth and death, clinics, schools, universities they attended, clubs they were members of . . .

There was a profusion of society-page articles about their illustrious parents: their engagement, their wedding. Photographs of their mother, Doña Blanca Díaz de Antoñana, a blond, elegant-looking woman, as ethereal as a Basque sprite or a Nordic elf. The twins had inherited her features and her patrician attitude. Their father, the industrialist, was big, broad-shouldered. In all the photographs from the seventies he looked self-important, tense, as if he was focused entirely on his business and nothing else mattered.

As well as being wealthy and influential, some of Javier Ortiz de Zárate's forebears could have been characters out of a dark legend. Don Enrique Unzueta, the father of the twins' great-grandfather, had left a small town in Álava at the beginning of the nineteenth century to become a powerful landowner in Cuba. He had even been appointed mayor of Havana. Three times married—twice to his own nieces—he was awarded the title of marquis when he returned to Spain, but in Cuba he was notorious for being one of the richest and most powerful slave traders. Over a period of twenty years, he shipped thousands of African slaves to the Caribbean islands and, in response to pressure from British ships that were chasing the slave ships, opened up new routes and brought in Chinese laborers. An entrepreneur in the slave trade. Horrific.

I found a documentary about the former Álava estate in Cuba, which was where he ran his human-trafficking business. Nowadays almost three thousand people lived there; 70 percent were African or mixed race. A quarter of them were named Unzueta—apparently, he had also been extremely attentive toward the female slaves. Every August 21, they still celebrated the Fiesta of the Absentee Landlord from Álava. He couldn't have left many fond memories.

Once I was satisfied with the information I had sifted through, I shut down my computer and began to watch the videos I had recorded of Tasio's historical and archaeological TV programs.

"All right," I said to myself, "let's get on with it."

I inserted the first tape and felt a sense of déjà vu when I saw Tasio in his office, talking about the ghost village of Ochate.

We had grown up with the legend of a village that was deserted as a result of three epidemics: cholera, typhus, and smallpox. Later it became famous for UFO sightings, neo-pagan tourism, and the paranormal sound recordings brought back by reporters from esoteric magazines. Tasio played the scientific archaeologist, using facts to refute the falsehoods that had turned the village into the most famous ghost town in Spain. However, he also mentioned a curious discovery made by a topographer who was measuring the area. The ruins of the church of San Pedro de Chochat de Ochate and the chapels of two nearby villages, San Vicentejo and Burgondo, formed a perfect isosceles triangle: exactly 1,750 yards between the chapels, and 875 yards between them and the ruins of Ochate.

After that, Tasio concentrated on the chapel at San Vicentejo, a small Romanesque wonder that had been attracting experts for decades. He described the stonemason's markings and the strange Eye of Providence, an architectural oddity that consisted of a small round opening above the apse framed by a triangle.

It was then, as I was watching the images from the exterior of the small chapel, that I thought I spotted a tiny detail that seemed familiar. I rushed to the videotape recorder to pause it; it had not been used for so many years that Grandfather had been unable to find the remote control. There was definitely something there, though it wasn't very clear: even Tasio hadn't mentioned it in his interview with the old stonemason who had overseen the latest restoration at the end of the eighties.

I switched off the lights and ran downstairs. Grandfather was snoring in his bedroom, so I jumped into my car and drove off toward San Vicentejo, which was located off the highway on the way back to Vitoria.

When I reached the tiny hamlet with half a dozen houses, I turned down the slope that led to the meadow where the chapel sat. I got out of my car and could have sworn I was the only person in the village, surrounded by the sounds of the night and a sky so free of light pollution that I could see galaxies that had exploded billions of years ago.

I took my small flashlight out of the glove compartment and walked around the chapel. At the back, above the apse, I found what I thought I had seen in Tasio's program: a stone carving of a man and a woman lying down, each with a hand laid in a loving gesture on the other's cheek.

15

AVENUE OF PINES

TUESDAY, AUGUST 2

The key to the new crimes will lie in what is different this time. What do the dead whisper to you, #Kraken?

I hardly slept that night. The bed seemed small, and my apartment was tiny. I needed some air, so I went out onto the balcony, but still I couldn't seem to get enough into my lungs. I was excited by my discovery, because sometimes, just sometimes, you know you're on the right track. You find a pattern, and all of a sudden you're certain.

It was still dark when I jogged down the stairs, but adrenaline was pounding in my veins. It felt as if I were inside a huge loudspeaker at a percussion-heavy concert.

I let off steam by charging up several inclines. That got me in a rhythm, and I ended up kamikaze-like near Ciudad Jardín. At that time of day, the streets were so empty I could have run down the middle of the road without an incident.

I found her near the university buildings. She'd been waiting for me. I had worked up a sweat; she was just warming up.

"Let's go down past the villas on Calle Álava," I suggested, getting my breath back. "I owe you a story today."

"Your friend's story," she said, slowing down to run along-side me.

"That's right."

I had prepared myself to bare my soul when I met her that day. It was only fair.

Only fair.

She nodded, and we slowed to a walk as we passed the most sought-after houses in the city. Built in the twenties to resemble the elegant mansions of Biarritz, they were now worth between two and three million euros, although there were few sellers and still fewer purchasers. Tall hedges meant we could only glimpse red- or green-tiled roofs, white walls, and wooden beams as solid as the fortunes of the families living there.

"His name was Sergio," I began. "He was in the same San Via-tor *cuadrilla* as me. We had been friends since the first year of ele-mentary school, from the age of six. He was a good kid: shy, quiet, on the plump side, and not very good at soccer. When the school became coed, the arrival of girls really upset the male ecosystem. Nobody understood how he was one of the first guys to get a girl-friend. Sara was Sergio's opposite: black curls, always talking . . . very bossy, very determined."

"Go on," said Alba.

"Against all expectations, they became one of the most stable couples in our *cuadrilla,* and they married when they were quite young. She was from Bajauri, close to my own village. Whenever they had a free day, they used to go to Sara's grandparents' house. She always said she wanted to visit all the villages in Álava, and she insisted they take the car to see a different one every weekend. Sergio would have preferred to remain quietly at home, though. He liked to stay and have a drink in Vitoria on Saturdays, eat a few *pinchos* at midday on Sunday, and spend the afternoon dozing in front of the TV, bingeing American television."

I slowed down even more to take a few breaths. I was exhausted, but it felt good. It took my mind off the painful story I was telling.

"Three years ago, Sara had a bad asthma attack. It was a Saturday night, and they were alone in the house at Bajauri. They had left her inhalers back in Vitoria, and in those days, there was scarcely any cell phone coverage in the area. Sergio went desperately from door to door until he found someone with a landline and called emergency services. The ambulance took forty minutes to arrive. It must have been more terrifying than I can even imagine. Sara was cyanotic by the time they arrived, and there was nothing they could do to save her."

"I'm so sorry," murmured Alba.

"We all were. In the *cuadrilla* we were very worried about how Sergio would react. Sara was the one who held the reins in their relationship; he allowed himself to be led. We had no idea whether he would ever get over his loss. But Sergio didn't react at all. We didn't see him shed a tear, not at the vigil or the funeral or even when she was buried in Bajauri Cemetery. It was as if he wasn't even aware that Sara had died."

"Was he in denial?"

"You could say that. The following Thursday, while we were having supper at Tximiso's, he told us he wanted to visit all three hundred and forty-seven villages in Álava Province. He would start in the northwest and come down diagonally, from Ugalde in Araia County, to end up in Oyón. Every weekend from then on. We all thought it was a great idea. We wanted to take care of him and support him, so the first weekend the whole *cuadrilla* went with him. We had time to visit five villages: Ugalde, Llodio, Zubia . . . That was the start of a routine that lasted months."

I glanced at Alba. She was staring fixedly at me as she listened to my story.

"I once went into his house. It was exactly the way it had been when Sara died. There were photographs of her everywhere; you could feel her eyes on the back of your neck as you walked down the hallway or around the kitchen. Sergio had gotten rid of the TV in the living room and instead had hung up a map of Álava. It was covered with black thumbtacks stuck in the villages he had already visited. Eventually the first anniversary of her death arrived. He pretended not to notice. He didn't even organize a Mass in her honor. By then only a few of us were still accompanying him to visit the villages on Sundays. We all wanted to do something different, but my wife, Paula, insisted we shouldn't leave him alone."

"Your wife."

"Yes, my wife," I repeated. It had been a long time since I had used such an everyday word. "As I was saying, as the months went by, Sergio's map was filling up with black thumbtacks. He went to probably five villages every Sunday. After awhile the only ones left were in the Rioja Alavesa region, on the far southeast of the map: Oyón, Moreda, Yécora, Laguardia, and Viñaspre.

"I'll never forget it. It was a very special week for Paula and me. We had been trying for a baby for a couple of years, and we'd finally had to go to a fertility clinic. That was hell for Paula, a real roller coaster, and I felt completely helpless. All I could do was accompany her while she was tortured. Then one day we heard good news. A few weeks later, it became doubly good: we were expecting twins. Out of three embryos, two had survived. We were terrified, afraid of losing them, and so we told no one in the *cuadrilla*. Still, those were the best months of my life. We had a secret we didn't want to share—we had the future at our feet. Nobody knew, except my grandfather and my brother, Germán."

She waved for me to continue. I gazed up at the sky, where the deep indigo typical of Vitoria's dawns was already losing its intensity.

"Paula was very active," I went on. "She used to go climbing with Estíbaliz. She was very fit, and so, during the first months, her pregnancy was barely noticeable. By the twelfth week, the twins had taken shape. They were so perfect. . . . We wanted to know what gender they were, because Grandfather was redoing my cradle and my brother's. Paula and I were in a whirlwind of activity. We wanted to have our children's bedroom prepared well in advance, to make it real. We went for the fourteen-week checkup. By this time her belly had begun to grow a little, and her abdominal muscles were giving way. The ultrasound revealed more than we could have hoped for: a boy and a girl. We were so emotional, almost hysterical, and we knew we had to tell people. That weekend we were going to announce it to everyone, and I bought Paula her first maternity dress. It was real. Finally. it was real."

Alba nodded silently. I knew my memories were reminiscent of her own.

"That Sunday, Sergio was even more silent than usual. Now I think there were signals that I had ignored. Paula tried to get him to talk, while I kept thinking: *What are you going to do next Sunday, when there are no more villages left to visit?* But I didn't dare mention this to him. Sergio was walking more slowly than usual; he touched the sides of the buildings, stared at the portico of Oyón's church as though the stones were whispering to him in a way that neither Paula nor I could hear. My wife suggested we go to Calle Laurel in Logroño to eat some *pinchos* and return to Vitoria afterward. Sergio begged us to go with him to Bajauri. We were traveling in Sara's car, an old SEAT 127 that Sergio refused to send to the scrapyard. We accompanied him to the cemetery, where he stood in front of Sara's crypt. He did something then—something that seems clear to me now, but back then . . . I thought it just meant my friend was suffering. He fell to his knees with his arms outstretched—it was like that painting by Goya, *The Third of May.* It was a gesture of surrender, but I failed to realize it. Paula ran to lift him up and tried to comfort him, but Sergio didn't see her. He didn't even weep. We thought it would be best to return to Vitoria."

"And did you get there?"

"No . . not all of us. We got into the car, and Sergio insisted on driving. We couldn't talk him out of it. I ended up in the front passenger seat, with Paula sitting behind. All three of us were uncomfortable. We didn't know what to say. The journey didn't last long. As soon as he entered the Avenue of Pines, Sergio accelerated, and then he swerved at ninety miles an hour. We crashed into one of the thickest pine trees, one to the right of the road, just after the firebreak. I don't know if you know it, but it's always stood out to me. Sergio died instantly; at the last second, he had unbuckled his seat belt, and he was crushed by the steering wheel. The SEAT didn't have rear seat belts. I don't know how we could have been so thoughtless; it's something I've never forgiven myself for. Paula was thrown through the windshield. Her head slammed into the tree trunk. Half of her body was draped across my left shoulder. I was wearing a seat belt. I was conscious, but I couldn't move. I stayed trapped in that bloodbath until the ambulance arrived and brought us back to Vitoria. Both of them were dead. And so were my children. I had nothing worse than whiplash and scratches from the broken windows."

"I'm . . . I'm so sorry."

"I know. Let me finish. I've gotten this far, and now I must tell you everything. I don't know whether I lost consciousness; afterward I was told I had been alone for almost forty minutes. But I swear I saw Grandfather out hunting with his shotgun in the pines. When he saw the accident, he came running over. He calmed me down, told me not to look at Paula but to keep my eyes fixed on him, and to take deep breaths, that the ambulance was about to arrive. My head was cold, so Grandfather took off his beret—something he never does—and put it on me. Later, in the hospital, when I asked my brother, Germán, about Grandfather, he told me he was on his way to Vitoria. That weekend he had gone to the spa at Fitero in Navarra, many miles away. He goes once a year for his rheumatism. When Grandfather arrived at the hospital, neither of us mentioned how he had helped me in the car. But I think that—this is going to sound crazy. I don't believe in miracles, I'm not a religious person, and I don't believe in being in two places at once, but I do think that part of my grandfather was there with me, like a splinter of consciousness. I don't know how to explain it. He didn't leave my bedside until I was released from the hospital. He didn't say much; he was simply there. He left everything unfinished in Villaverde. But occasionally we would look at each other, and I swear we both knew what happened on the Avenue of Pines. I've never told anybody this, and I don't know why I'm telling you now."

"Well, someone has to say this. I suppose you've considered that the whiplash could have caused hypoxia, and the lack of oxygen to your brain could have produced that hallucination."

"That's what I tell myself every night. The only thing is . . ."

"What?"

"Grandfather arrived at the hospital without his beret. I had never seen him with his gray hair uncovered. Even Germán was surprised and commented on it."

"And . . . ?"

"When I was released from the hospital and they gave me back my clothes, my grandfather's beret was among them. How do you explain how an Elósegui beret—the brand he always wears—was in that old SEAT 127?"

"There could be a thousand explanations. You're a detective. You have more than enough imagination and common sense to come up with something," she said, although I could tell she didn't believe what she was saying.

"I wasn't alone, Alba. He was with me. He didn't leave me on my own. He never has, and he never will."

"But someday he'll no longer be here. He must be very old. You know he'll go before you."

"No, you don't understand. My family is very long-lived. My great-aunt is a hundred and two and has no intention of dying. Grandfather's uncle Gabriel died at a hundred and four back in the sixties, when life expectancy in Spain was little more than sixty. You may not believe me, but it's engraved on his headstone in the Villaverde cemetery. He lived forty percent longer than most people in his generation. Grandfather is going to be one of the first supercentenarians; I'll be ninety and he'll be a hundred and fifty and still roasting chestnuts."

Alba shot me a tender glance, even though she didn't believe me. How could she, when she didn't know Grandfather?

"After the funerals, I was put on leave and went back to Villaverde with my grandfather. I thought a lot about Sergio and his refusal to mourn, the pathological way he postponed it for so long, how eventually it didn't matter to him if he took his friends with him. He simply couldn't face life without the goal Sara had set for him. It wasn't just suicide; he killed another three people at the same time—he became a mass murderer. I was determined to learn from that experience. I consciously struggled through the five stages of grief: denial, anger, bargaining, depression, and acceptance. I went through all of them. And they hurt. Each of them hurt, but I never thought that my life ended there on the Avenue of Pines because my friend and my entire family had died in that accident.

"I was left with the feeling that Sergio's suicide could have been avoided, and with it the deaths of Paula and my twins. It was at that point I decided to take up criminal investigation and specialize in profiling. The other thing that changed was that I could no longer bear the sight of dead bodies. You're my superior, and I shouldn't be telling you this, but when I see them, I get sick. It's a physical reaction."

"You'll get used to it. Most people feel the same way at some point in their career."

"I don't want to get used to it. That's the point: I see it as my penance, the price I have to pay for having done my job badly, for not realizing in time."

I was talking too much, and I knew it. And in a conversation, the person who talks less is the one with the upper hand. That was one of my mantras in interrogations, and now I was consciously falling into my own trap.

I couldn't stop. I didn't want to end the conversation there, feeling bare and vulnerable. I had to finish.

"I started to train in criminal profiling, to study nonverbal communication and motives. Sometimes they are so predictable and transparent that it's as if we're going through life with speech bubbles above our heads, like in comics, but nobody can be bothered to read what we're screaming. Do you know what resilience is?"

"The ability some people have to get through bad experiences and find the good in them."

"Since then, I've worked very hard to be a better detective. I've forced myself to help that experience make me a better person. But I'm no saint, and the dark side to all this is that I no longer trust my friends. I don't think I'll trust anyone around me ever again. Not because I believe they want to harm me intentionally. Paula and I were the only ones who continued to support Sergio after almost two years, the only ones who still accompanied him most Sundays. And yet Sergio didn't spare any thought for us when he hit that tree. His suicidal urges, his need to end his life, was stronger than any feeling of humanity or gratitude toward even his closest friends. We didn't see it coming. At first, I told myself it was unpredictable. Later on, I looked at the statistics of the modus operandi of suicides. Most prefer to literally throw themselves into the void. But Sergio lived on his building's second floor and worked in a store at street level. In Vitoria, there was nowhere he could reach a height that would kill him—at least not without leaving his comfort zone. There are also those suicidal individuals who cut themselves. Sergio was scared of needles, and he hated the sight of blood. So that wasn't an option. That leaves us with hanging. Sergio was no good at knots; he had particularly poor manual dexterity. His hemispheres were crossed, and he was never really able to distinguish right from left. He couldn't follow specific instructions and shied away from any physical work."

"Where is all this leading?"

"I'm getting there. I want to become so good at reading profiles that if Sergio were in front of me now, I would put him on suicide watch because of the imminent risk that he would harm himself. And, of course, I wouldn't let him drive a car. That's why I love my job more than ever. Murderers, delinquents, abusers—they're all predictable, and that's good for me. I feel secure when I'm faced with them, because I always expect the worst possible reaction, and they usually don't disappoint me."

"So we're opposites. You believe in prevention. I'm much more of a fatalist."

I looked at her, puzzled. "What do you mean?"

"I firmly believe that once a murderer has decided to kill, there's nothing we can do," she explained, absentmindedly toying with the whistle around her neck. "He will always find the way and the moment to do it. We all go through life unprepared. It could be a knife to the stomach on the street or in a doorway. A poisoned drink, a simple exchange of bleach for white wine. A hit man firing off two shots while you're stopped at a traffic light. A cell phone charger wrapped around your neck. Generally, for an ordinary citizen, there's no way to avoid being murdered, if somebody has decided to kill you. I like to study the cases we have, the crime scenes I visit, and think about the practical way the victim could have escaped a murderer. But I don't fool myself: however well prepared I think I am, the killer's motive will always be stronger."

"That's precisely why I believe in trying to prevent crimes," I insisted stubbornly. "That's why I'm obsessed with catching him before he can continue."

"We can't possibly protect everyone in Vitoria who is thirty years old and has a double-barreled name from Álava. There are 4,634 people who fit that description. Despite all our warnings to take precautions, two will die, because the killer will find our weakness. So far, the murderer has anticipated everything we've done. He'll find a way to kill them."

"That's not how a deputy superintendent should think," I protested. "What scope does that give me?"

"You're chasing him. It's obvious he's been planning this for a long time. I don't think you can prevent the next murders, but I do believe you can solve the previous ones. And that, paradoxically, will put a stop to the next ones."

"I don't know whether that's a compliment or a reprimand. At any rate, we're not keeping to our agreement."

"I know that, Kraken." She looked down at her watch. "And I'm going before I break any more promises. I'll see you in a couple of hours."

With that she disappeared down the street in her white leggings, striding along in her slightly flat-footed way.

Watching her go, I felt more alone than usual. If it had been another woman, I would have invited her to regain her strength with a big breakfast, the kind that leaves you feeling good.

Sometimes it happens. You fall for someone. You fall when you don't want to; you fall for someone you shouldn't. It has nothing to do with willpower or intentions, or with how suitable the person is. It must be pheromones, something slippery and intangible but real. And that was happening now. It meant that, as an emancipated, self-sufficient man, I was obsessed with the sound of her sneakers as she ran, a rhythm I could recognize when she approached along the dark, deserted streets of our parallel, silent Vitoria. It meant I was waking up every day with a hard-on like a teenager and jacking off in the shower after every run. And I knew I was on the verge of returning to evenings spent seeking out one-night stands. I was two Fridays away from doing it and I knew it.

To ask for a transfer at that moment was unthinkable. This was the most important case of my career, and I was painfully aware that the murders were going to continue, so how could I allow the monster to get away with it?

How little I imagined then that the individual in question had not the slightest interest in letting me get away, either.

16

THE ANGEL OF SANTA ISABEL

TUESDAY, AUGUST 2

You're in the second act: evidence, allies, enemies.
The hero's most personal stage. Trust your first
instinct, #Kraken.

It was a scorching day from first light. There was no trace of a breeze. It was as if the city were inside a glass bottle that had been left out in the sun. The heat wave that had been forecast didn't even compare to what we were experiencing.

We had set up an undercover operation that would begin early that morning, with vans recording outside Santa Isabel Cemetery, in the Zaramaga neighborhood.

Estíbaliz was waiting for me by the iron gate at the entrance, wearing street clothes and dark glasses. Soon afterward the optician Antonio Fernández de Betoño arrived, accompanied by various members of the city council. He barely glanced in our direction before moving on, unperturbed, as if he were conducting a guided tour of the burial ground.

Behind him relatives escorted, presumably, his ex-wife. She was leaning on several friends and seemed inconsolable, although she was wearing such large sunglasses that it was hard to see her expression. Enara's friends were also weeping. Peio was on his own, stuffed into a suit that was much too tight, his hair in a ponytail. He dropped damp tissues into every trash can he passed. He looked disconsolate, out of place.

My partner and I followed the mourners silently, keeping a close watch on everything.

Santa Isabel Cemetery dated back to the beginning of the nineteenth century, and to walk among the ancient tombs was like visiting a time when statues of praying children and weeping virgins whispered stories that were guaranteed to keep you awake at night.

"Last night I watched some old videos of the first programs Tasio Ortiz de Zárate made. He was talking about churches, archaeology."

"Did you find anything?" Estíbaliz asked in a low voice. We stood at a prudent distance from the family's vault.

"Possibly, Estí, possibly. I'll explain when we get back to the office, when it's calmer. But for now, what do you remember about Ochate?"

"The ghost village? We went to visit it when we were young, like everyone else did after the UFO sighting. I remember getting goose bumps as I approached it. Whether it was the epidemics or something else that caused people to leave, there was no doubt it had a . . . malign atmosphere, I suppose you'd call it. I also remember that when the double murders of the dolmen and La Hoya began, people in Treviño County said they had seen the same strange lights around the famous abandoned tower at Ochate again."

"Did your whole family go?"

Estíbaliz lowered her sunglasses and gave me one of her hard stares. "What you're really asking me is if my brother has any connection to Ochate, Kraken. Don't play games with me. I'm not one of your witnesses—I'm your partner. If you have anything linking my brother to the crimes, tell me now."

"I don't have anything. The thing is, though, in that region, in an area spanning only a few miles, there are several phenomena that could be related to the crimes. Your brother's name always comes up when pagan or esoteric subjects are mentioned. That bothers me as much as it does you. I simply want to be able to cross him off the list once and for all."

"Or incriminate him."

"No, I don't want that at all, but I'll have to pay him a visit at some point. I'd prefer to tell you, but as I already said, I don't want you to warn him. That way I can eliminate him as a suspect, and we can pursue other lines of inquiry, okay?"

Estíbaliz's only response was a grunt, so I set off down one of the walkways to try to find the vault where the newspapers said Tasio and Ignacio's mother had been buried in 1989.

I passed one of the cemetery's most famous epitaphs: FOR THE RECORD: I DIDN'T WANT TO.

"Which of us does, my friend, which of us does?" I said quietly to the tomb's inhabitant.

I eventually found what I was looking for. The door was in bad condition, but the Unzueta family's granite pantheon was still impressive.

I was disturbed to find that the vault made the hairs on the back of my neck stand up. I shrugged my shoulders, but the feeling remained. I wasn't sure where it came from, until I raised my head and saw the angel.

On top of the domed roof, a stone angel followed me with its eyes. Dressed in a tunic, wings folded, it was carrying a trumpet in its left hand while its right arm was raised to the cloudless sky.

I moved a couple of yards to the left, but the angel was still staring at me. It was only an optical illusion, but it wasn't the angel's gaze that disturbed me as much as the uncomfortable feeling inside my chest like heartburn or the start of a heart attack.

"You have to be brave to stand in front of it. Aren't you afraid the angel will point to you?" said a voice behind me.

Wheeling around, I came face-to-face with a man in his sixties wearing coveralls and carrying a watering can in one hand. His other arm was missing, and his face was leathery from many hours spent out in the sun.

"Should I be afraid of a statue?" I asked, relieved, because the arrival of the gardener had put a stop to the cold current running through my body.

"I can see you're not familiar with this cemetery's legends. Don't you know this is the famous angel of the Unzueta vault? It lowers its arm and points to those doomed to die."

It sounded vaguely familiar, but I'd never paid much attention to it.

"Tell me the story. It sounds interesting."

"In fact, it's quite frightening. Come with me and don't stand in front of the angel. It makes people feel bad," he said, leading me away. "See the apartment buildings across from the cemetery? People can look out onto the pathways, the tombs, and the vaults from their balconies or bedrooms. Thank goodness we no longer have burials every day. Nowadays, they all go to El Salvador Cemetery. Can you imagine what kind of effect it would have on a person, to witness mourners weeping for their loved ones every blessed day?"

After a few yards, we came to a halt. Even though this gentleman had only one arm, I guessed he must do his job well. As we walked, he occasionally stopped to pull a few tall weeds, and he didn't seem bothered by the midmorning sun burning our backs.

"You say that, even though it's precisely what you do."

"I had a hard time until they opened the other cemetery. I didn't choose this job, but I couldn't find anything else when I came to the city from my village. All I knew was farmwork, but I was the youngest of four brothers, so there was no land for me to inherit. Besides, after a threshing machine took my arm, the people in the village thought I would be useless in the fields. I couldn't drive tractors or harvesters, so where could I go? I'm used to it now. I almost consider myself a gardener, but I can never forget this is a cemetery, an *ilherri*. If you understand Basque, you'll know that means 'city of the dead.' They're the ones who inhabit this place. I simply try to keep it looking good. I keep my tools in the hut at the back, as far away from the tombs as possible. I prefer to keep my distance."

"What were you saying about the angel?" I asked, trying to steer the conversation back in that direction.

"It's not very pleasant, but I'll tell you. It's said that one day a little girl who lived in the building opposite looked out her bedroom window and saw the angel lower its arm and point to a man passing along the street near the cemetery entrance. At that very moment, a truck veered up onto the sidewalk and hit the man, and he died on the spot. The girl became hysterical and told her mother, but she didn't believe her. Some time later, the girl again saw the angel lowering its arm, this time pointing to a man reading a newspaper on that bench over there. She wanted to go down and warn him, but she didn't get the chance, because the huge cross that hung above the Atauri family vault suddenly came loose and fell on top of the poor man, killing him. After that, the girl began to suffer panic attacks; her mother was very worried about her. Then there was one of those storms we occasionally get here, with thunder and lightning. The girl was in her bedroom and came out to look at the cemetery. That day the angel turned, and the poor girl saw it was pointing straight at her. She began to scream and called her mother to tell her what she had seen. Her mother did all she could to calm her and help her go to sleep, but the following morning . . . she found the girl dead in her bed. Rumor has it she died of fright or anxiety, but nobody knows for sure."

"It's a fascinating legend." I glanced at the angel out of the corner of my eye. "What about you? Do you believe in that kind of stuff existing beyond the grave?"

"I'm no fan of the dead, but the living are worse. Take those twins, the ones responsible for the fact that today the cemetery is filled with families weeping over their children. Did you know they're descended from the slave trader whose remains are here?"

"Yes, I'd heard something about it."

"They're just like their great-grandfather's father. As children, they were little devils. And if you had witnessed what I saw in this very cemetery when their mother was buried, you'd be hard-pressed to deny that bad blood runs in their veins and that it's passed on from parents to children."

I was dumbfounded. At last I'd found a direct witness from two decades earlier.

"What exactly did you wit—" I started to ask him, but Estíbaliz came running up, cell phone in hand.

"You have to see this, Kraken!" she said, coming to a stop in front of me, breathing heavily.

"Could you excuse us a minute?" I turned back to the grounds-keeper, but he had already disappeared, slipping away among the tombs as if he had never existed.

I drilled Estíbaliz with my eyes.

"I think we've just lost an important witness. What is it now?" I asked, more annoyed than I cared to admit.

She stared at me as she got her breath back. I wouldn't have said she looked happy, but I couldn't help noticing a glint of tri-umph or relief in her eyes that had not been there earlier.

"A witness? Oh, the gardener? Forget him, you have to see this," she repeated. "This changes everything. We have to speak to the twins, to both of them. They've been hiding the truth for twenty years."

"What's this about, Estí?" I asked, trying to appear interested. But the old man's words were still echoing in my brain.

"See for yourself," she said, holding up her cell phone. "And let's go get a copy now."

"Is this another special edition of *El Diario Alavés*? What did they publish this time?"

I looked at the screen and could scarcely believe my eyes.

I read the headline, but I didn't understand it. I couldn't grasp what it meant, what those few harsh words were trying to convey.

THE MEDIEVAL WALL MURDERS:
A CASE OF JEALOUSY BETWEEN TWO BROTHERS
OVER AN UNDERAGE GIRL?

"You need to see the photographs, Kraken. This time there's no doubt; it's not speculation. The newspaper has photographic evidence. The murdered fifteen-year-old girl from twenty years ago had a relationship with both Tasio and Ignacio. And they lied to us: they both denied they knew her. Ignacio even denied to our faces that he remembered anything about the file on the girl. How could he not remember?"

"Wait, wait—" I held up my hand to stop her. "Too much information for me all at once, Estíbaliz. Give me a minute."

"All right. Just look at the photos. Look at those little twenty-five-year-old angels taking advantage of a fifteen-year-old minor."

I opened the link to the newspaper's digital edition. There couldn't be any doubt; it wasn't faked. Ignacio Ortiz de Zárate, in police uniform, was canoodling with Lidia García de Vicuña behind a tree on Paseo de la Senda, like a furtive couple. And, in another image, Tasio was entering his front doorway at Number 1 Calle Dato. The street looked deserted, and he had his arm around Lidia's waist, cuddling and joking with her.

17

MONTE DE LA TORTILLA

VITORIA
JULY 1970

This was the first time Blanca had driven. Álvaro's rickety Citroën DS was less daunting than her husband's enormous Isotta Fraschini. Besides, she knew Javier would never allow a woman to take his car. When necessary, his manservant Ulysses took on the role of chauffeur. Ulysses walked with a limp and had a dropped shoulder, supposedly because he'd been injured in a fight and had to have a kidney removed. He reminded Blanca of a crow—a slightly sinister man who responded to her with croaking sounds. His other job was to keep an eye on her when she met up with her new friends, as if she were a little girl and might get lost if left on her own in the city.

With Álvaro, it was different. Since their affair had begun in the clinic, they had been obliged to meet outside Vitoria. They favored short excursions in the doctor's car to Monte de la Tortilla, a small promontory less than half a mile south of the city, where, on clear days, there was a view over the Alavese Plains.

Like the other young couples with no apartment of their own, they drove to that lonely spot, draped towels over the car windows, and made love on the imitation-leather seats. Afterward, their naked bodies slick with sweat, they would turn on the listeners' program on Radio Vitoria, where someone would invariably request

"Let It Be" by the Beatles, who were already threatening to break up, or "El Condor Pasa" by a duo with an unpronounceable name.

"We can't go on like this," Blanca said, gazing up at the roof of the car from where she lay in the back seat.

"Why not? This is the best thing that has ever happened to me. Don't you feel the same way?" Álvaro replied, slipping into his underwear in the driver's seat.

"Yes, of course I do. You know I do. That's why we can't keep seeing each other in a car on a hilltop. The police could drive by at any time and arrest us for public indecency. It's too dangerous."

"What do you suggest?"

"I told you that my aunt died last week and that we weren't very close. Still, I'm her only niece, and she left me an apartment. The place is furnished, but it's too fussy for my taste. I told Javier I want to redecorate, that I'd like to renovate the living room so that I can invite my friends over in the afternoons, as a change from going to the club. He likes the idea. It reassures him to know that I'm shut inside four walls, out of public view, while he's at work."

"So you have an apartment?" Álvaro straightened up.

"Yes, the only problem is its location. It's at Number Two Calle General Álava, the art nouveau building on the corner of Calle San Antonio. It's right in the center of town, Álvaro. Anyone could see us coming and going. I have the excuse of overseeing the improvements, and you could always pretend to be visiting a patient in the area. But we can't be seen together—we'll have to arrive and leave half an hour apart. And you must always carry your medical bag. If I phone your office and let it ring four times, it means that day I can see you and I'll be waiting for you at the apartment."

"Four times," Álvaro repeated.

He liked the idea.

Blanca nodded. "We're taking a huge risk. I have no idea what Javier would do if he found out, although I can imagine. Do you want to . . . do you think we should keep seeing each other, take that risk?"

Álvaro climbed into the back seat in his socks and underwear. It was a fiendishly hot July day, and his hair was soaked with sweat. The car was like a furnace.

"Blanca, you know I can't think straight when I'm with you. I used to be a gray man with a gray life—don't change your mind on me now. I will, if you will. There will be plenty of time for us to regret the consequences," he said, stripping again and pressing himself between Blanca's thighs.

He turned his body around, and she licked his erection while he nuzzled the downy blond hair below her belly.

18

THE STATUE ON CALLE DATO

TUESDAY, AUGUST 2

We need to talk. Don't let yourself be prejudiced by anything you hear about me, #Kraken.

Somebody had told Tasio—someone inside the prison must have given him the news—because when I met him in Room Three, he was in crisis mode, pacing up and down, ignoring the chair. His teeth were clenched so violently I thought his skull might explode at any moment. It took him a while to notice I was there, waiting impatiently for him to sit down.

"Now there's no way I can go back to Vitoria, even if I prove I'm not the murderer. To everyone I'm a damned pedophile, and they'll never forgive that," he said, phone in hand, staring down at his fingernails.

"You should have thought of that before you went down that route. You were a twenty-five-year-old television star; she was fifteen. What did you think would happen?"

"You don't understand. She was different, very advanced for her age. We were going to wait the two years and seven months until she reached adulthood and then make it public. I would have been forgiven. When Lidia turned eighteen, the difference in our ages would have been forgiven."

"Of course," I replied, "just like they forgave your great-great-grandfather for marrying two of his nieces. Is that how it is? Is it your birthright to do as you please, because of the family you were born into?"

"So now we're in a class struggle, without my realizing it?" he said, looking up. "Are you going to get sanctimonious because you're the grandson of farmers?"

I didn't bother to respond. That day, Tasio had lost all his power and was firing blindly.

"Be careful, Tasio. You know as well as I do that you've just renewed your claim to the title of public enemy number one. Maybe you haven't been told what's happening on Twitter right now, but your followers are deserting you in droves. Before, it was subversive to follow you; now it's simply disgusting. There's a new trending topic: #TwinMurderers. That's how you're being described. And that's far gentler than what's making the rounds on social media: girl rapists, perverts, child killers."

Tasio's eyes narrowed. He didn't like that at all.

"I can leave you here and never listen to your theories again," I said. "Or you can tell me what I need to know. It's up to you now, more than ever. Think it over. I've got a lot of people to see today."

Tasio was clever enough to know when he was beaten.

"All right. You came here for something," he said at last. "What do you want?"

"Tell me what happened between you and Ignacio and Lidia García de Vicuña. I'm sure that in the coming days I'm going to have to listen to many different versions, so why don't you start by telling me the truth?"

"The truth . . ." He lit a cigarette, then immediately crushed it out in one of the ashtrays. "The truth is that Lidia went out with Ignacio first. For him, she was nothing more than a little bit of fun, even though he usually respected the rules. Even I was surprised that he was going out with someone so young. But he introduced her to me and . . . According to her ID, Lidia was fifteen, but mentally she was older than either of us. What she and I had was different, I don't know how to explain it. I lost my head. I decided to risk everything for her. To keep it a secret so I wouldn't cause her any harm—"

"No harm? She was murdered, Tasio."

"Yes, that's right. Unfortunately, that's right. She vanished at midday one day, in the midst of the media storm I was involved in: my shows were becoming more and more popular, and Vitoria was in a state of panic because of the murders of the two children. People worshipped me for trying to unravel the possible historical links to the murder scenes. I remember the last show I recorded. Lidia had been found dead near the medieval wall, with a fifteen-year-old boy who was like a child compared to her. I was in a state of shock, but I had to hide it. I couldn't tell anyone, not even my twin, but inside all I wanted to do was disembowel myself and eat my own innards. The director pressured me into making that stupid show as quickly as possible. I had to analyze why the murderer had chosen that site. The history of medieval Vitoria, the restoration of the battlements—I can't remember what I managed to record. I know filming was interrupted when several police officers came and arrested me in front of the whole team. I couldn't understand it. I asked where Ignacio was. They told me he had issued the arrest warrant."

"So then you thought it must be revenge. That he'd found out you had stolen his girlfriend," I said, tossing him the noose and waiting for him to put his head through it.

Come on, give me something I can use.

"You're wrong. Ignacio would never have had the courage to kill her. You've studied so many murderers' profiles—you must be sick of them. Ignacio doesn't have the right profile, he's . . ."

He's your beta. Is that what you're trying not to say? That as the alpha male, you can't imagine how a beta like your brother could do the dirty work himself?

"You're still defending him, after twenty years?"

"Believe me, right now, I'm alone on this sinking ship and I'm only looking out for myself. I'm not defending him, but if I let you believe he was the culprit, you'll be wasting time and you won't catch the real murderer. Tell me, Mister Genius: Who leaked those photos to the newspaper? Who gains by having them published? Ignacio? Me? This is the coup de grâce for both of us! We're done for! Whoever is behind this is celebrating with Dom Pérignon as we speak."

"You have enemies. Any relative of the children you killed, or anyone who doesn't want to see you become a media star again. You've been found guilty of eight murders and you're going to be allowed out on parole soon. Do you really think people are going to applaud you because you've reinvented yourself in prison? I can think of hundreds of reasons people might try to make life impossible for you, Tasio."

He gave me a look of frustration.

"I'm trying to stop you from only seeing what most people see. Can't you understand that you're the only possibility I have of getting out of here with some guarantees?"

So there's no way you're going to say anything bad about your brother. Let's try a different tack, or this visit is going to be completely useless.

"Speaking of thinking outside the box, I want to talk to the archaeologist now. Do you remember the show you devoted to the triangle formed by the chapels of Ochate, San Vicentejo, and Burgondo?"

"Of course. We didn't have much of an audience, because we were just starting out and didn't know what tone to give the program, but the content was interesting. It was the approach that I wanted, in fact."

"What do you mean?"

"Well, beyond UFO sightings and supposed biblical plagues, I'm still convinced that part of Treviño County was an important area for the different peoples who lived there—a mystical, telluric place. Despite the fact that I'm too much of a scientist to believe in that sort of thing, I still think that, for its inhabitants and those who built churches there, the area had something special, that it was a hub for meetings or encounters."

"You interviewed an old man, a master stonemason who'd been involved in the restoration of San Vicentejo. But in the video, you never mention his name, and in all the shots where you're talking to him, he always has his back to the camera. Was that an editing choice?"

"He asked to remain anonymous. That happened often with our older guests. He was very discreet. Why are you asking?"

Because one of the stone sculptures is an exact representation of the crimes, you damned egotist, and I want to know if you got the idea there or if the real murderer is even further ahead of us than we thought.

"You're in no position to ask questions. You need to decide if you want to help me with the investigation, Tasio," I said, weary of so much resistance. "Do you remember him or not?"

He gave a lengthy sigh.

"Yes, I remember him. Let's see . . . he was called Tiburcio, Tiburcio Sáenz de Urturi, from Ozaeta. I remember him because he didn't seem to fit."

"What do you mean?"

"He wasn't just a workman—he was an expert in medieval buildings. He knew a lot about medieval symbolism, and he was an open book when it came to the meaning of all the images in the chapel. A kind of idiot savant, if you'll forgive the expression."

"Do you know where I can find him?"

"You're asking me twenty years later? If he's not dead, he could still be living in his village, or in some old folks' home. There can't be many left with that name. I bet you can get an address for him before you've even left the parking lot."

"There's only one way to find out," I said, standing up. "Tell me something: What are you going to do with your Twitter account now that everybody is going to vilify whatever you write?"

"You know I have no Twitter account. But if I did, I'd continue sending you messages and contacting you to try to guide you in your investigation. Yes, that's what I would do, Kraken."

I nodded and left the room.

As soon as I got into my car, I called Estíbaliz. We had sent two officers to Ignacio's apartment on Calle Dato to ask him to present himself at our Lakua headquarters to answer questions about the latest developments.

"What did Ignacio say?" I asked.

"Ignacio hasn't said anything. He's not at home, or at least, there's no sign of life. He's not answering his cell phone, either, or any of the other contact numbers we have for him. I'm going to his villa in Laguardia with two men. If we don't find him there, we'll have to ask Judge Olano to issue an arrest warrant."

"All in due time, Estí. I don't think we have enough to convince the judge yet."

"You don't think lying about his relationship with one of the victims is enough?" she shouted through the cell phone.

"I think he owes us an explanation, but all we have are some photos that show them touching. That's not proof of murder."

"What is it with you and the twins, Unai? Aren't you suspicious of them now?"

"You'll understand when I explain this afternoon in the office. Now look for Ignacio, and if you find him, put as much pressure on him as you can. I've got a lot of visits in front of me."

Almost an hour later I reached the center of Vitoria. I entered a huge building on Calle General Álava and went straight to the top floor, where *El Diario Alavés*'s newsroom had been located practically since the dawn of time.

When the boy in reception saw me, he seemed to panic. I suppose he recognized me, having seen me with Lutxo at some time or other, or maybe the Kraken hashtag was more effective than I imagined.

"I'm looking for Lutxo."

"He's at his desk," he said, flustered. "I'll tell him you're here, if you like."

"No, there's no need. I'm sure he'll be delighted to see me," I said, heading down the hallway. Every head lifted as I went by.

I found Lutxo at the far desk, talking at two hundred words a minute with smoke coming out of his cell phone. He was enjoying his moment of fame—he seemed more than happy, exultant even.

It took him some time to realize I was there: perhaps it was the expectant silence that grew around us that finally made him look up and see me.

"Listen, I'll call you later. Something urgent has come up here," he told the person on the other end of the line. He ended the call. "You were quick off the mark, Kraken."

"You're the one who was quick off the mark, Lutxo."

"Let's go into the conference room; it's empty," he said, getting up from his desk.

The rest of his colleagues turned back to their screens, pretending to concentrate on finishing their articles before the edition closed at seven.

Lutxo shut the door behind us. Through the picture windows I could see San Miguel Arcángel Church overlooking the roofs of the medieval quarter.

"Go on, spit it out, friend," he said. "But don't shout, because here the walls have ears."

"Friend? You've played a dirty trick on me, *friend.* You published what you published without consulting me about how it might affect my investigation. What's left of our collaboration now, *friend*?"

"Collaboration, Unai? What do you mean by that? You haven't given me a thing, not a thing."

"Because we don't have anything, for God's sake!" I shouted, forgetting where I was and who I was with.

"Well, now I've given you something, and you can start doing your job. All of Vitoria and half the planet is waiting for you to get on with it. I've done my part."

I turned my back on him, trying to regain my composure as I looked at the outline of tiled roofs.

"I didn't come here to cause a scene. I'm here as a police inspector in an ongoing investigation. The newspaper where you work has published an article signed by you with photographs of a man who was found guilty of murder, along with one of his victims. How did those photos come into your possession?"

"You know how we protect sources."

"Don't rile me, Lutxo. That damned source could hold the key to stopping the murders. Don't you care that he could go on killing? Who was it? The Eguzkilore?"

"The Eguzkilore?" he repeated, puzzled. "No way. I mean, not that I know of."

" 'Not that I know of'? Are you telling me you don't know who sent them to you?"

He stroked his white goatee in frustration.

"It's hard to lie to you, Unai."

"Then it's simple, Lutxo: don't. Who gave you those photos?"

At that moment we were interrupted by the sound of knocking

at the door. A well-dressed man peered in. Lutxo stiffened as soon as he saw him.

"Is everything all right, Lutxo?"

"Everything's fine, boss. My visitor was just leaving," he said, his eyes imploring me to say nothing.

So I was finally in the presence of the mythical, hermetic editor of *El Diario Alavés*, a powerful man whom few people had seen in recent decades. He looked too normal and unremarkable to fit with the dark legend that had grown around him.

I left the meeting room without looking at Lutxo. I took the stairs, as I always did when I needed to think things over quickly. For the rest of the world at least, the latest news was the most important thing, but I was determined to get beyond the headlines.

I just needed time to slow down. I needed time to get something solid together.

My cell phone buzzed. I looked down at the number and decided to answer.

"Good afternoon, Inspector Ayala. Do you have a moment?"

"Not much of one. What are you going to publish in *El Correo Vitoriano*?"

Mario Santos appeared to think this over and then answered in his usual calm way.

"Are you in the city center? Maybe we could meet. I'm also in a hurry today; my editor is crawling up the walls."

"We could meet in Usokari's in five minutes, if you like," I said. "I haven't eaten yet."

A short time later, as I was polishing off my five *pinchos*, Mario appeared. He sat down opposite me at the most discreet table in the bar, facing Calle del Arca.

"I imagine you've read the special edition of *El Diario Alavés*," he said by way of greeting.

"Did you know anything about it, Mario?"

He was someone I could ask straight out. He wouldn't hide anything.

"I'd be lying if I said I didn't. Those rumors have been circulating around the newsroom for twenty years now. People knew the twins liked young girls. When Tasio was accused, Ignacio played his cards very well with the television crews, and everyone stayed quiet. But in some circles, there was always a suspicion that the fifteen-year-old victim could have been one of their girlfriends. Back then, people turned a blind eye to certain things. Right up until the day he was arrested, Tasio was untouchable, and after that, so was Ignacio. In *El Correo Vitoriano* we weren't interested in interviewing people who wanted to talk. We didn't want to repeat gossip. With the bodies of eight young people on autopsy tables, why stir up things further? The important thing was that the crimes stopped."

He waited for me to finish my slice of tortilla, calmly stirring his milky coffee.

"But now we have to say something about it, don't we? We're adopting a far less aggressive tone, but our readers want more news from the paper. But, inspector, I don't want to do so behind your back."

"I can't stop you publishing anything; the photographs are there. All I can tell you is that we're pursuing other lines of inquiry as well."

"I thought it would be sufficient for you to focus on the twins," he said, finishing his drink.

I looked at him, puzzled. Mario didn't usually commit himself like that.

"Tell me, Mario, is your boss pressuring you that much?"

"I'm trying to keep him in check, but he wanted to give the crime-of-passion story a big splash today. It's only logical. I called you out of personal consideration: I don't want to do anything that will disturb official channels. I see our relationship as a long-term one—the world isn't going to come to an end tomorrow, not even with this case. I don't want to destroy our connection by publishing anything that makes an enemy of the police."

"Let me tell you, it's a relief to find a journalist who thinks the way you do. Look, I'll keep you up to date, and if I have anything that can be published, I'll call you, as I always do."

"I'm counting on it, inspector," he said, glancing down at his watch.

He went over to the counter, paid for his coffee and my *pinchos*, and left. I decided to get an ice cream at Breda's on the same street. Finishing my lunch with something sweet was the only thing that could rescue my day.

I was just leaving Usokari's when I got a call I hadn't been expecting. It was Aitana, Ignacio's pregnant ex-girlfriend.

"Inspector Ayala, there's something I want to say, something I haven't told you," she whispered in her croaking smoker's voice.

"Is it important?" I asked.

"It's very important to me. And for you, too, I think. Have you read the newspaper?"

Who hasn't?

"Is this about the twins?"

"Of course."

"I know maybe this is asking too much, but today I don't think I'm going to have time to meet. Could you tell me on the phone, or at least give me some clue as to what it's about?"

It took her a few seconds to reply.

"All right." I heard her blowing out smoke. "Tasio and Ignacio swapped me."

"I'm sorry, could you explain?"

"I haven't told anybody this in twenty-seven years, but they swapped me. That was one of their games: they always boasted they could swap girlfriends and no one would even notice. But when I started going out with Ignacio, I didn't think he was capable of

EVA GARCÍA SÁENZ

it, at least not with me. We were only eighteen, but we were more serious than Tasio, with all his one-night stands. Around that time their mother died. Her death hit Ignacio very hard, and I was at his side. I simply never thought Ignacio would do something like that to me. That was why I broke it off with him."

"What happened exactly?" I asked as I walked down Calle Dato.

"One day Ignacio called me to go over to his place—you know, the Unzueta family mansion, where the twins were brought up. He did that a lot when he knew nobody was going to be there for a few hours. We used to have sex like crazy in his room. That day, Ignacio opened the front door and asked me to go up to his bedroom, then disappeared. When I got there, it was quite dark, and he was already in bed. I joined him without saying anything, but I thought there was something strange about him—some unexpected reactions, gestures he didn't usually make—but I went along with it. It was only afterward, when he began to talk, that I realized it wasn't Ignacio."

"How did you know? I don't want you to think me inappropriate, but I have to ask."

"It's not a problem, it's not as intimate a question as it might seem. As soon as he opened his mouth, I knew it was Tasio. His voice was different; he spoke more quickly and in a more relaxed way than Ignacio. It was terrifying to find myself lying naked in bed with someone and realize it wasn't who I thought."

"So what did you do?"

"I started shouting that he wasn't Ignacio. He laughed and admitted he was Tasio. He said he'd wanted me, and his brother had accepted. That they had debts to each other and this was how they paid them. I ran out. I picked up my clothes and got out of there. I was furious for days. Ignacio didn't even defend himself when I broke up with him. All he said was that I knew who I was going out with, as if everybody tacitly accepted swapping like that, except for me."

I took a deep breath. Suddenly, an ice cream didn't sound nearly as appealing. Nothing appealed to me. I walked on for a few steps, then sat on the bench in front of a bronze bullfighter. At least he seemed like someone I could trust.

"Did you go to the police?"

"The police?" She laughed. "And say what? That we'd had a great time? That it was a rape I'd agreed to?"

"Aitana, you were duped into having sex with someone you didn't want to have sex with."

"I know. That's what I tell myself every morning when I get out of bed. It's what my psychologist recommended, and I do it. I'm ready to testify against them. I've kept quiet since I was eighteen, trying to hide how disgusted they made me feel every time I went out with our *cuadrilla* and they were there, because they were untouchable. But I don't want to stay silent anymore."

"Why did you keep seeing them? Why have you been defending Ignacio all this time?"

"What do you want me to do? Not be part of my *cuadrilla* anymore? You live here. You know what it's like."

"What are you going to do now?"

"Frankly, if there was a crime, the statute of limitations would have kicked in by now. But just telling you is a big step for me. I feel relieved. Before, I'd always been ashamed of what happened. Now, for once, I've done what I should do. That's enough for me."

"I don't know if this is any consolation, Aitana, but what you've just told me is a big, big help. I want to thank you for being so honest," I said, and bid her farewell.

The bronze bullfighter looked at me. I could have sworn he was left with a bad taste in his mouth as well.

When I reached my office, there was no sign of Estíbaliz, so I went to look for Pancorbo.

"I'd like to talk to you about what you remember of the medieval wall murder."

"No problem. Fire away," Pancorbo said, as though he had been waiting for our conversation for some time.

"Was the semen found in the vagina of the fifteen-year-old girl Ignacio's or Tasio's?"

"Tasio's."

"Was that what led Ignacio to arrest his brother?"

"Chronologically that was the trigger, of course."

"What do you mean?"

"I knew Ignacio was fooling around with a very young girl, although I didn't realize she was a minor and she didn't look it. She was very well developed, and I never imagined Ignacio would be so stupid or so sick. Anyway, he was tremendously discreet and took lots of trouble not to be found out, but you know how things are between colleagues. When you spend so many hours together, you can spot their mood swings, their lies, when they're not really there."

"Yes, I know. We've all been through it," I said awkwardly.

"The autopsy report hit him hard. He was beside himself, although we didn't talk about it. He would never have admitted anything, because he would have been jailed for corrupting a minor. Then we discovered the yew poison, and everything started moving quickly."

"What was discovered?"

"Ignacio had keys to Tasio's apartment on Calle Dato. We went there while his brother was busy recording his show at the TV studio. I found a plastic bag with yew leaves in his office, carefully hidden behind a clay *eguzkilore* hanging on the wall. That was enough for Ignacio to order his arrest. Then the forensic team found Tasio's prints on the bag, and the yew leaves matched the poison found in the eight bodies. The fifteen-year-old boy and girl were apparently drugged beforehand, I suppose so they wouldn't resist when they were forced to swallow the poison."

"What about the girl's parents? Why didn't they go to the press? Why has it never become public that Tasio had sexual relations with her before she died? With everyone so enraged at Tasio, it would have been normal for her parents to have added fuel to the fire."

"I'm sure her parents knew that she had been with one of the twins, or perhaps even that she had been with both. They kept quiet because they were afraid of the social stigma. Their daughter was dead, but she was a martyr, a victim. And Tasio was sent to prison without the scandal ever seeing the light of day. I can understand why they didn't want to stir things up."

"Yes, so can I," I had to admit. "Tell me something: Do you think that Ignacio got rid of the girl's autopsy report so that the sexual motive wouldn't come out?"

"I want to be fair to him. I don't owe him anything, and he doesn't owe me a thing, either, but I want to be fair to my former colleague. It would be easy to feel indignant, just like the people sounding off in all the bars. But if I want to be an honest policeman, I'd have to say I don't have the faintest idea."

"You've been a great help, Pancorbo. I'm really grateful."

"Anytime," he said, and I left him alone in his office in front of a screen I knew he wasn't really looking at.

I quickly called for a meeting, and shortly afterward DSU Salvatierra and my partner were waiting for me in the second-floor conference room. Estíbaliz got the ball rolling.

"We haven't been able to trace Ignacio, and the house at Laguardia was locked. We still haven't managed to persuade Judge Olano to issue an arrest warrant. We'll give him a few more hours, but we need to concentrate on finding incriminating evidence."

Then it was my turn. I filled them in on my conversations with Tasio, Aitana, and Pancorbo.

"We all need to take a step back and look at everything that's been going on since the night before El Día de Santiago as if we are neutral observers who don't care who committed the murderers."

"What is your thinking, inspector?" said Alba.

I looked at her for a couple of seconds longer than necessary. She looked tired, and so was I.

"Ma'am, we seem to be linking premeditated serial crimes—with anonymous victims that meet only two conditions: age and name—with a crime we're now expected to believe was one of passion. But the fifteen-year-old girl also met the other two conditions, which means the crime-of-passion interpretation seems false. I simply don't believe it."

"Explain yourself, Unai," said Estíbaliz, frowning.

"There's somebody else behind this, and it's not the twins. If the last crime was one of passion, what were the prior victims? Why were they all certain ages, and why the typical Álava surnames? That girl was going to be a victim from the start."

"I agree, but that doesn't exonerate the twins," my partner said.

"Let's suppose it was Tasio. It doesn't make sense for him to plan to kill his girlfriend and his twin's former companion from the outset, and then try to conceal it ahead of time by murdering seven more kids and camouflaging the scenes with pagan paraphernalia. Not to mention that he left traces of his own semen. Doesn't that seem too stupid?"

"But it does fit with Ignacio being the murderer," Estíbaliz said. "Let's imagine that Ignacio wanted to kill his ex-girlfriend for sleeping with his brother. He must have planned everything from the start: killing those other seven children and staging them as historical crimes, allowing his ex-girlfriend to see Tasio, and then killing her so that the autopsy would reveal traces of Tasio's semen. Then he could have planted the evidence in a bag with his brother's prints on it in Tasio's office, where he knew Pancorbo would find it. It all fits."

"That's possible, but what about what happened today? As I see it, if one of the twins is the killer, this is the worst mistake he's made in twenty years. Whoever sent those photographs to the newspaper followed the twins before that girl was killed and kept the evidence for two decades. Then, today, he makes it public. The pictures didn't come from Tasio or Ignacio. Those photographs don't merely damage them—they destroy them. There's no way they can come back from this. No one is going to forgive them for being pedophiles. It couldn't have been them. There must be a third person who is determined to incriminate and destroy them both. First he framed Tasio, and now he wants us to think Ignacio is the killer. We have to look ahead to what he's going to do next, not backward."

"So what do you suggest, inspector?" said Alba.

"We have to find Ignacio and verify the alibi he gives us about his whereabouts on El Día de Santiago and the night before. At the same time, we must continue investigating the twins' background from birth to age twenty-five. We have to find the real motive. Someone very intelligent and very patient wants to destroy them. This is the most complex bit of profiling I've ever come across; a cooling-off period of twenty years implies that the murderer is a psychopath who is able to control his emotions over an extremely long period. I don't think he's making a mistake, and I don't think he'll stop. I think that what we've seen up to now is just the start of his plan."

19

TXAGORRITXU

WEDNESDAY, AUGUST 3

Don't join in his game or allow yourself to reconsider things now. Concentrate on your first leads. Follow them closely, #Kraken.

I went out for another run at six the next morning. Las Fiestas de la Virgen Blanca were starting the next day, and the streets would not be as empty as I liked. I preferred them to be almost deserted.

Almost.

But that day there was no sign of her running along the streets of the city center with her black mane of hair, so I concentrated on my routine, and an hour later I was back at the Plaza de la Virgen Blanca, planning to head home. Then I remembered something I still needed to do, so I walked to the kiosk on the corner of Calle Postas, where my friend Nerea was opening up the shop, displaying newspapers in the stands.

"Good morning, Nerea," I said from behind her.

She jumped and whirled around in a panic.

"Kraken! I mean, Unai, you scared the life out of me," she said, her hand flying to her chest.

"Yes, that's exactly what I wanted to talk to you about. About Kraken, and scaring people, and the fact that you can't keep your mouth shut and are turning me into a celebrity without my consent."

"What are you talking about, Unai? I haven't talked to a lot of people about you. . . . Well, only a few, like everyone else," she said, blowing her bangs out of her eyes.

I closed the gap between us, trapping her between my body and the counter. The kiosk was small, and I was being deliberately intimidating. We were friends and I was fond of her, but I couldn't allow her to keep behaving so thoughtlessly.

"Nerea, you have to stop. I understand that people come to the kiosk and ask you questions. The whole of Vitoria may be talking about it, but that's no reason to show a photo of me to passersby and tell them I'm Kraken. Don't you realize the danger you're putting me in?"

"Danger?" She shrugged. "A few minutes of fame doesn't hurt anyone. A lot of people would be happy about it, so don't be like that."

I pressed even closer, although my T-shirt was wet with sweat.

"You don't get it, do you, Nerea? This isn't gossip in some magazine. Haven't you considered that the murderer may have talked to you, and that by showing him my photo you may have led him to me? You may have put me in harm's way. You may have told someone who told someone who told someone who told someone. Tell me: If anything happens to me, will you be able to sleep at night?"

She swallowed hard. "I'm sorry, Unai. I never thought of it like that. Are you serious?"

"Unfortunately, yes. My job isn't a game, and these crimes are real. Even though what you're doing isn't criminal, you're a step away from no longer being someone I consider a friend. If I hear that you're showing my photo around again, you will have crossed the line and you can forget our friendship. I'll never have anything to do with you again."

"Shit, I'm so sorry," she said, cheeks flaming. "I had no idea."

"I know, Nerea, I know. But you have to stop."

She bowed her head in shame. "You have my word, Unai. From now on, I won't open my mouth."

That'll be difficult, I thought. But at least I knew she was going to try. Nerea was good at heart, although I had my doubts about her willpower.

I said good-bye and ran back to my apartment.

My destination that morning was the Txagorritxu assisted living center. A quick search on my computer had revealed the whereabouts of Tiburcio Sáenz de Urturi, an eighty-six-year-old widower born in Ozaeta with no other family in the world.

I didn't want to tell Estíbaliz where I was going because I didn't want to spoil her day. Her father was in the Alzheimer's unit at Txagorritxu, and I knew how difficult my colleague found her visits there. Estíbaliz was from a dysfunctional family. She never talked about it, but I knew her father had been abusive and his Alzheimer's diagnosis elicited a mixture of concern and relief.

The facility was very close to my office, but I decided to drive and park inside the grounds, which were surrounded by pines and other trees that provided shade for several of the residents, who were conversing or dozing on wooden benches.

I went in and approached reception, where I learned that Don Tiburcio's room was on the second floor. The elevator was as slow as the senior citizens inhabiting this microuniverse.

When the elevator door finally slid back, I was confronted by three hallways. I didn't know which one to choose, so I pushed open one of the glass-paneled doors to try to find a nurse.

I caught sight of a young man in a light blue uniform who was pushing an empty wheelchair, and I was about to approach him when I heard my name being whispered close behind me.

"Kraken," said a deep voice.

I whirled around, taken aback. In front of me was a man who didn't seem to be that old. He was wearing slippers and a Deportivo Alavés soccer shirt. It took me a moment, but I finally recognized him by his red hair, which was turning white at the temples. His brown eyes, identical to his daughter's, looked at me with what I thought was a mischievous glint. It seemed to me that inside the sick patient was someone intelligent, or sporadically so, desperately trying to get out.

"You're Señor Ruíz de Gauna, aren't you?" I said, not really knowing how to manage the situation. I couldn't remember Estí's father's first name.

"Kraken," he said again. He must have remembered me from when Estí and I were young. Our *cuadrillas* would sometimes get together forces to climb Monte Gorbea or San Tirso.

"Excuse me, young man! You're not allowed in here if you're not a relative of one of our patients," a thin female nurse who was taller than me said sharply. She went up to Estíbaliz's father and led him to an empty wheelchair.

"I'm looking for Room 238, but it's probably not around here, is it? Could you tell me where it is?" I asked, casting one last look at my colleague's father. It seemed to me that, now that the nurse was present, he was pretending to appear vacant.

"Exit this wing and head for the blue hall across the way from you," the nurse said.

I did as I was told and, shortly afterward, found the right room.

I knocked on the door and waited for a while, but no one answered. I knocked again, more loudly this time, and finally heard a reply.

"Who is it, then?"

The voice was weary, empty. I opened the door and saw an old man doubled over in his metal wheelchair. He had coarse white hair and pronounced cheekbones in a skull-like face that must have once been pleasant but was now consumed by age. He still had the weather-beaten look of those who have always worked outside, but he was dressed in an incongruous suit and tie, as if he was expecting a visit or was the guest of honor at some municipal event.

"Don Tiburcio?"

"Who's asking?" he said expectantly.

"I'm Inspector Unai López de Ayala. I'm investigating a case, and I believe that your knowledge of the chapel of La Concepción de San Vicentejo could help me."

"Has something happened to the chapel?" he asked, obviously concerned.

"No, don't worry. The building is still in perfect shape. Do you remember a man named Tasio Ortiz de Zárate?"

"The TV archaeologist? How could I forget him? He was a whirlwind. He pestered me until he convinced me to go on that famous show of his. He was a good sort, though. No one ever imagined he would end up the way he did. He belonged to one of those families that . . . you know, one of those families that have always been here, whom nobody thinks anything bad could ever happen to. I . . . Well, I always believed in more equality, for a start. But don't just stand there, come and sit with me," he said, pointing to a small wooden chair next to a window that looked out on a flat roof covered in white stones.

"I've been told you were in charge of the chapel's last restoration, and that you're a stonemason, an expert craftsman the likes of which no longer exists, as well as an expert on the chapel's iconography."

"Yes. You see, my family comes from a long line of builders," he said mechanically, as if he had given the same explanation thousands of times.

"If you could talk to me about it, I'd be very grateful."

"A talk?" He smiled to himself, like a cheeky little boy. "Young man, could you open that closet?"

I obeyed without understanding and discovered a box decorated with pilgrim's shells behind three suits.

"Bring me the box, will you?"

Don Tiburcio opened it and took out a heavy iron key. It was just like the one the few of us left in Villaverde used every month when we climbed the bell tower and rang the Angelus.

"It's a replica, given to me by a member of the family during the restoration. They were so pleased with what I'd done that they let me go in whenever I liked, although I haven't been there lately, since I no longer drive. Young'un, you wouldn't happen to have a car with a big trunk, would you?" he asked mischievously.

Half an hour later, we reached San Vicentejo.

Don Tiburcio was smiling in his seat as my Outlander went down the highway bordered by oaks and beech trees. The track narrowed, becoming greener still and bringing a breath of freshness to the summer morning.

I left the SUV on the side of the road, unloaded the wheelchair, and pushed Don Tiburcio down to the grass meadow surrounding the small Romanesque chapel.

"Well done, young'un. This chapel is *unicum*, unique. What exactly do you want to know about this strange marvel?"

I pushed his chair to the rear of the chapel and stopped in front of the curved bulk of the apse. I pointed out the reclining couple affectionately touching each other's cheeks several feet above our heads.

"Can you tell me what that carving means?"

His brow furrowed in what looked like surprise, and I caught him glancing at me in a way I couldn't interpret, as if he was trying to figure me out.

"Those two specifically?"

"Yes. Do they symbolize something?" I insisted.

The old man stared up at them, as though he had known them all his life and they were simply meeting once more, or maybe he was saying good-bye to them—I wasn't able to tell.

"Of course they symbolize something. They are the soul of what this building is trying to tell the world. Everything around them is based on their story. They are an iconographic representation of the hermetic couple, or alchemical marriage. The only other example is at San Bartolomé in Rio Lobos, in Soria Province."

"Isn't this a Knights Templar church?"

"Yes, it belongs to their order. And what we have in front of us is a typical military-order building. All the experts agree on that. But its stones contain many other secrets. You have to read it like a book. In the year 1162, the date it was probably built, ordinary people didn't have access to books, so they read images. We have lost the ability because we don't have the key to it, but I can help you see what I see. It's not that complicated. In fact, this is a basic, foundational story. It tells us of the prototypical couple, Adam and Eve, as well as of original sin and its consequences. It's simply a re-creation of Genesis. Let's go inside: the story begins on the presbytery wall."

He took the huge key out of his jacket pocket and held it out to me. I pushed his chair around to the wooden entrance. The lock creaked, but the key eventually turned, and the door opened.

The interior was twenty yards long at most; there was barely room for four rows of wooden pews. Daylight filtered in through three narrow windows, and the ochre-colored stone lent the chapel a warm glow.

Don Tiburcio murmured a few words I couldn't catch, a kind of prayer he kept to himself. Then he began to propel the wheelchair around the perimeter of the chapel, as if reaching this place had given him renewed strength.

"You just have to follow the corbels on the inside of the apse.

First, can you see? The outline of a young, beardless man. That's Adam in his youth. The next corbel is a spiral-shaped flower. Here there's a female face with a wimple—that's Eve. The first couple are going through the different stages of life. The next one shows two unrecognizable, mutilated figures. I never discovered what they meant and didn't add anything to them in the restoration. Then there is another flower, a small rose blossoming and turning to the sun. After that, another flower in a spiral shape like a swastika, and then two beings emerging from a flower."

For a few seconds, I held my breath. All the flowers looked like *eguzkilores*. Flowers of the sun.

"What's the symbolism behind all the flowers?"

"It's the Garden of Eden surrounding the couple before their expulsion from Paradise. It's universal but, at the same time, very specific. You, my lad—have you never felt expelled from your own paradise? It happens to all of us at some point."

I was determined to show no emotion, so I cast aside my memories of the Avenue of Pines. I had no idea if I was with a master of the order or simply an expert, and so I decided to play the role of a young man without a past.

"And, finally, there's the corbel with the figure of a bee, the emblem of chastity. Beeswax was used to make the Easter candles for Holy Saturday, when Christ's triumph over death was celebrated."

I tried to remain composed so my voice wouldn't betray the cold shiver that had run down my spine at these words.

"So the animals and the plants inside here are . . ."

"Yes, they convey a moral message, as does the nudity of the couple. We're talking about the origins of humanity, something sacred. This, my lad, is the narrative of the first couple and the consequences of original sin. That's why the chapel is filled with male and female visages. They represent different ages—some are young and fresh-faced, some are bearded. Then the couple commit sin and are punished. Then they fall literally into disgrace, as they are shown on the outside wall of the apse: prostrate and with the schematic figure of the tree of good and evil. A tree that can be an apple tree, or a yew. In the Middle Ages several different species were portrayed, so I couldn't tell you which one is shown here. But they are not on their own: the couple have each other, which is why they are laying their hands on each other's cheek."

I remembered the photographs from the crime scenes—the naked couple comforting each other, framed by an isosceles triangle and surrounded by their Garden of Eden in the form of *eguzkilores,* and finally the plant or animal symbols used in the murders: the yew, the symbol of immortality, and the bee, the symbol of chastity.

I was reading the killer's novel as he wrote it—each double murder was a chapter I'd failed to interpret.

But what was the murderer's goal? To continue the tally, killing people aged thirty, sixty, even older? To wipe out the oldest people in Álava? According to the census, there were twelve men and fifty-eight women over a hundred years old. Surely only a few would have the double-barreled name or be the exact age the killer required. At least we would be able to protect them, especially the men. But reaching that point would mean sacrificing forty people, and that was far more than my conscience would allow.

I helped the old man leave the chapel and locked the heavy door behind us. I drove back to Txagorritxu, glancing at Don Tiburcio out of the corner of my eye every now and then. He had opened the side window and was caressing the breeze with his hand, as though conducting an orchestra. Maybe he was saying good-bye to that route, or maybe he realized this could be his last journey in a car. Until that moment I had never really asked myself what it meant to still be alive at an age like his, to be "in the firing line," as my grandfather used to say.

We reached the nursing home's parking lot, and I unloaded his wheelchair while he waited with the patience that comes with age. I lifted him into it; he was little more than skin and bone.

"Don Tiburcio, do you think there are other people who know as much about the chapel as you do?"

"Who are still alive? Because I learned all that"—he sighed in frustration, as if trying to calculate the years in his mind—"many years ago."

"Yes, preferably still alive."

"The only person I can think of is the apprentice I had during the renovation work. He was a plump red-haired boy, a little clumsy," he said without thinking, but I had the impression that he immediately regretted having told me even this much.

"A redheaded kid? Do you remember his name?"

"No, of course not, that was a long time ago. Besides, he wasn't the kind of kid who attracted much attention. He was silent and calm, but I always thought he was very bright. When I started explaining the symbolism, he took it all in, and that encouraged me to continue. What I remember most is that he was a very solitary sort, and I had the feeling that his father used to beat him badly: his body was covered in bruises. You used to see that a lot more often in villages; fathers were much harsher. Sometimes they were little more than animals. I think that, although the work he did for me was backbreaking, carrying sacks and doing all that heavy lifting, it was a relief for him to spend time away from his home—"

I interrupted him. "Do you think his name might be written down somewhere?" He was being deliberately vague, and I knew this wasn't going to get us anywhere.

"No chance. The council contracted me because they had an agreement with the family that owns the chapel. He was underage, so I paid him in an envelope without any contract or pay slips. He was always dressed like a beggar—I got the impression that he handed over the money at home and they gave him nothing. Now you must excuse me. The journey's exhausted me and I don't think I can answer any more of your questions," he said, gesturing for a nurse to take him inside.

He said good-bye with a firm, old-fashioned handshake, but I couldn't help noticing that he moved his little finger away from the others and stroked the back of my hand.

It might have been an oversight on his part, possibly a habit after a long life of rituals, or maybe he was trying to tell me something I had known for a couple of hours already.

I nodded and left.

I knew that he would protect the boy, that it would not be humanly possible for him to give me any reliable lead to track down his apprentice.

So now we have an undocumented red-haired ghost, I thought with satisfaction as I headed for my office. *And that's a lot more than we had yesterday.*

20

THE CAMPILLO MURAL

WEDNESDAY, AUGUST 3

Are you delving into the deepest cave yet, #Kraken?

I was climbing the curved staircase to the entrance of the Lakua headquarters when I got a call from a blocked number.

I stared at the screen for a few seconds, wondering whether to take it. In my line of work, you never know if that kind of call is going to be a blessing of new information or the start of a long series of fresh headaches.

"Drop everything you're doing and go straight to Campillo."

"Is that you, Golden Girl?" I asked, recognizing her voice.

"The Etxanobe Garden: I've located him, Kraken! And when I say *located*, I mean you'll find him there right now. Who would have thought that a police officer would ask me to pull off the most difficult hack I've ever had to do? This kid is too much for my brain. I've never seen anything like him."

"You'll have to explain, Golden. I don't understand what you're saying."

"MatuSalem is literally untraceable. I've never come across anything like it before. But life has taught this old witch to look at the big picture. He uses several fake identities. But he has a nickname similar to another nickname that looks like another nickname. He's a young guy, and he's no hermit. I mean he has a life. He goes out. He does things that other kids his age do."

"Such as what?"

"Such as belonging to the Brigada de la Brocha de la Ciudad Pintada."

"Aren't they the volunteers who paint murals in the Old Quarter?"

"Bingo, Kraken. Today they're putting a layer of antigraffiti paint on the mural in the Etxanobe Garden at Campillo. The one that depicts the game of cards."

"*The Triumph of Vitoria,*" I said. It was one of my favorites.

"That's it."

"I owe you one, Golden."

"You do. I'm already thinking of creative ways of collecting it, ones your bosses wouldn't like a bit. Why is everything fun illegal?"

I smiled and ended the call.

It took me less than fifteen minutes to rush to Campillo, only a few yards from the medieval wall and the Old Cathedral.

I reached the garden at the top of the city, and from there I could see that they had put metal scaffolding up the seven floors of the facade that looks over Calle Santa María. Half a dozen volunteers were busy with their paintbrushes at different levels of the scaffolding. I stood there, trying to work out which could be the elusive MatuSalem.

Then I spotted him.

A teenager dressed in black was painting the hair of one of the three figures in the mural.

I walked slowly over to the bottom of the scaffolding and found a woman who appeared to be in charge. I went up to her and showed her my badge.

"Inspector Ayala. Don't say anything. I'm going to climb the scaffolding to talk to one of the volunteers, but I don't want to scare him, so I need you to act like everything's normal," I said, speaking slowly and softly so that she would understand.

The woman—who had an Afro and rainbow-colored pants—looked bewildered, but she nodded her head without a word.

I started climbing the side of the scaffolding. Several of the volunteers gave me puzzled looks. I reached the top and stepped out onto the platform. The youth was concentrating on applying a coat of varnish to the wall, but he looked up with a start when he saw me. He ran the few feet to the opposite end of the platform, trying to escape, but I caught up with him and seized his arm.

"We're just going to talk, MatuSalem. I only want to talk."

His mouth drew into a taut line. He didn't like having an adult give him orders, or maybe he just didn't like police. He was small and thin and couldn't have weighed more than fifty kilos, but he did look like a Pre-Raphaelite angel. He had almond-shaped blue eyes and a smooth face that was so perfect, anyone would turn to admire such pure beauty.

"So you're the famous Kraken?"

"Since you've been making yourself at home in my hard drive, I'm guessing your question is rhetorical."

Although I had him pressed against a wall three stories above the ground, he kept glancing to the side, as though calculating whether to jump.

"You're a pig. You couldn't possibly trace me."

"You're not the only one with supernatural computer powers, MatuSalem. Take it as an indication that you've been underestimating me."

"All right. My friends here are looking at us, and I don't want you to give away one of my most useful identities. Can you pretend we're old friends catching up?" he muttered between clenched teeth, looking around.

"That seems reasonable. You know I came to talk to you about Tasio. If you'd like, we can skip the part where you pretend you don't know what I'm talking about, then deny everything, and then, when I tell you I can prove it, you admit it proudly. We've put you away once; you know what that's like, and so do I."

"Shit, you waste no time," he said, scratching his neck.

"That's because I don't have much of it," I said. "People are being killed just a few yards from here, and your former cellmate is an integral part of this tragicomedy."

MatuSalem was one of those people who never looked straight at you. His eyes were always roving; he was a mental recluse, someone who put barriers between his hyperactive brain and the outside world.

"It's not Tasio. It wasn't him back then, and he isn't in contact with any apprentice outside the prison, like some of you think," he finally murmured. "I don't like anybody murdering children or couples. But it's not Tasio. He was well and truly framed twenty years ago. He's had enough on his plate trying to survive in the slammer."

"Why are you defending him? You're the typical economic delinquent. You like intellectual challenges, you defy authority by thumbing your nose at the law, and you earn just enough money to live on. But you don't have the profile of someone who would empathize with other delinquents, much less a sociopath convicted of murder. Come on, Maturana, tell me the truth."

"The truth? I defend him because he defended me when the people who should have didn't want to know what was going on," he said angrily. "Inside, the pedophiles wanted to have a party in my honor the day I arrived—they'd won the lottery with a young virgin like me. The first night I went in for dinner, all their dicks stood on end. I knew I wasn't going to get out of there intact. The only question was whether I would survive everything waiting for me. Tasio stopped them in their tracks. He scared the crap out of them and left them praying to the Virgin of Fatima. I literally owe that guy my life, and neither you nor the fuckin' state security forces were there to defend me, so don't give me any grief. To me he's the fuckin' Godfather, and I'll pay him homage until my bones drop off."

Okay, Kraken, change tack, you're up against a brick wall.

"I didn't come here to make life difficult for you, even though I could. You were put away for credit card fraud. Now you're out, and the first thing you've done is collaborate with a prisoner found guilty of eight murders. No one could say prison taught you to give up your criminal ways. I presume that even now you're up to something illegal that I could arrest you for, and you know it. But I came here to make a deal with you. I want a list of Tasio's most suspicious Twitter followers."

"Is that all?" he exclaimed. "A list of the top followers?"

"You've been in contact with all of them. I'm sure that, with your remarkable brain, an alarm goes off when you see certain individuals. It would take my cybercrimes team forever to analyze them all, but you've been pretending to be Tasio for months, so you know them. You know which followers are just morbidly curious about the crimes and which ones are really sick. I don't just want their accounts; I want their IP addresses. I want you to identify the most suspicious users, and do it quickly. Check them against our records—I'm sure you made a copy when you hacked into the police computers. And tell me immediately if any of them have a criminal record. Do we have a deal?"

"So I'm going to be a police informant? I'm not even twenty; I don't want to go down that path this soon. Everyone I know who works with the police ends up in trouble. Somebody on either side gets angry, and the informants always get it in the neck," he said, folding his arms across his chest.

"You won't be an informant. I'm not going to tell my superiors or anyone else about you. You're more useful to me if your name doesn't appear in any report. That's the way I work. I have other collaborators outside official channels, and they're almost as good as you. But you're unique."

I was off the mark: egotism was not his weakness. MatuSalem was still not convinced.

"Plus, this will be your chance to return Tasio's favor. You're convinced he's innocent. If you help me pursue other lines of inquiry that can prove it, you'll be helping to get him released as soon as possible. Come on, I need to know if I can count on you."

"Do you know what's on this mural?" he asked, pointing to the figure of the young woman he was varnishing.

"Three people playing a game of cards. Why are you changing the subject?"

"It's all about trickery, Kraken. It's about beating a cheater, about being faithful. Look, I'll show you. You have to see it," he said, going to climb down the scaffolding.

I followed close behind. We went down a couple of levels until we were at the center of the mural.

"It's inspired by a sixteenth-century painting called *The Cheat*. The great lady, who symbolizes Vitoria, is playing cards with a man who is not only cheating but is showing his trickery to the public. Look."

It was true. Above the figure of the lady ran an inscription in Gothic characters: *Victoria*, the first name that King Sancho IV gave our city. The figure of the man was hiding two cards behind his back, one with a dog on it and the other with three dogs. Beside him was an inscription reading *Fraudulentus*.

"The servant, the figure I was working on, symbolizes the people of Vitoria, who warn their mistress of the trickery. Can you read her inscription?" He pointed upward, and I had to step away from the wall to see it properly.

"*Fidelitas*," I said out loud.

I turned back toward the boy, but he was no longer on the scaffolding. He had vanished.

Swearing, I jumped from the second level and landed on the ground. I ran out of the metal gate and onto Calle Santa María, but he had already reached the Montehermoso Palace, hundreds of yards ahead of me.

"Damn it!" I shouted in frustration, giving up on the idea of chasing him.

The best hacker in the city had tricked me. I had let him escape without knowing which side of the game he was playing on.

21

NUMBER 2 CALLE GENERAL ÁLAVA

Vitoria
July 1970

Javier Ortiz de Zárate loosened his tie as he entered his bedroom and perched on the king-size bed. He had been in a foul mood for days. He was sure that Apaolaza was going to sign a contract with the German company, damn him, despite his repeated denials earlier that day. If the deal went through, Javier could lose 15 percent of his business.

And yet he sensed something else was going on. There had been too many secret meetings between the other partners, too many sales reps postponing product presentations using the same flimsy pretexts. Javier had thought about sending Ulysses and a couple of his friends to interrogate the employees at Ferrerías Alavesas. People accused him of not trusting anyone, but that mindset had gotten him to where he was today.

"Blanca!" he yelled from the bedroom, losing his patience. "Are we ever going to eat tonight?"

He heard his wife's brisk footsteps on the stairs. Then she put her head around the door, but she didn't venture inside.

"Benita set the table. We can eat whenever you're ready," Blanca said matter-of-factly.

Javier continued to stare into space after his wife had hurried back downstairs.

What was wrong with the stupid woman? Why couldn't she give him any children? She was too thin; he had known it all along. Her narrow hips would never produce an heir. The same thing had happened with his first wife, María Luisa. He seemed to be a magnet for women who were as sterile as mules. A discussion with his lawyer, Joaquín Garrido-Stoker, had revealed few options. To annul a marriage based on deception, Javier would have to prove that Blanca knew she was infertile before they were married. That proof would have to be medical reports. Javier had already sent Ulysses to search through the documents in Blanca's room. He had even rummaged through her old bedroom at her parents' house. But the search had yielded nothing. It was pointless. Why would she keep evidence of her infertility? She must have destroyed any documents.

He could think of only one solution: a heart-to-heart talk with her gynecologist, Doctor Urbina, even though Javier despised the man and everything he stood for. Why had Blanca chosen a country doctor, when they could afford the very best? According to Ulysses, Blanca visited Urbino regularly; perhaps she was undergoing fertility treatments. Damn right. It was her duty, after all. What else did she have to do all day?

Javier was forty-two and had no heir. He was the laughingstock of Vitoria. People were even questioning his virility. But he couldn't think about that now . . . maybe after dinner. He had been feeling tired and achy lately, and he had a knot in his stomach that no amount of seltzer would ease.

Gazing at his upturned palms, Javier noticed with surprise that his hands were trembling, and that his squared-off nails had turned blue. Then, the muscles in his stomach spasmed, and dark, blood-filled vomit spewed onto the bedspread and the carpet beneath his feet.

That was all he saw before a sharp pain in his throat closed his airway and he fell back, unconscious.

———

As Doctor Urbina was finishing his meeting with the pharmaceutical salesman, the telephone rang four times. Álvaro hid a smile. He had no more appointments, so he could spend a few hours with Blanca at the apartment.

However, when the ringing started again and didn't stop, he frowned and picked up the receiver.

"Doctor Urbina's practice, how may I help you?"

"Javier is at the hospital." He heard Blanca's voice at the other end of the line.

He's coming for me. The terrifying thought sprang out of nowhere. *He's coming for me.*

"Would you excuse me, Jorge?" he asked the salesman. "I have an emergency call. I'll send you the order tomorrow."

He waited until Jorge left the room. "How . . . how did he find out?" Álvaro whispered into the mouthpiece. "Did someone see us together? Was it his driver?"

"No, you don't understand. Javier is seriously ill. He's been admitted to the hospital. They think he's been poisoned. I can't speak for long. The police came here to question me. I'm calling from a payphone, so I don't have much time. I told them I needed to inform his family. Whatever you do, don't come to the hospital.

"Just tell me one thing, Álvaro: the capsules I've been giving him these past months—are they sedatives, or have I been slowly poisoning him?"

Álvaro Urbina's mouth went dry. He wanted to say something, but his lips wouldn't move.

"For God's sake, Álvaro! Have we been poisoning him? Are we guilty of attempted murder?"

"No, the drug I gave you is undetectable. They can run all the tests they want, but they won't find anything. It won't even show up in an autopsy. Rest assured, they can't touch us, Blanca."

He heard a nervous sob on the other end of the line, a dog barking in the distance, and, after she had recovered her composure, Blanca's cold voice.

"Good-bye, Álvaro. We must never see or speak to each other again. The police suspect that I, or one of his business partners, had something to do with this. I never want to see you again, even if you have made me a widow."

"No, Blanca, wait. Let's meet at the apartment. . . . Blanca!"

But there was no one on the other end of the line.

The local press covered the event discreetly with a few lines at the bottom of one of its inside pages:

> Industrialist Javier Ortiz de Zárate was taken to the Vitoria Clinic yesterday. Although the reason for his admission remains unknown, unofficial sources suggest a possible poisoning or ingestion of toxic substances caused him to suffer multiple-organ failure. He is currently responding well to treatment at the above-mentioned medical facility.

Álvaro reread the seven lines of the month-old newspaper clipping to make sure he hadn't overlooked any details. He had heard nothing else from Blanca, but nurses at the hospital had told him that her husband had been discharged after ten days.

Still, Álvaro continued to scour the newspapers' obituary columns and to listen to Radio Vitoria's news bulletins, all while telling himself that if the wealthiest man in Vitoria had died, everyone would know about it.

The only thing that made his life bearable were the small doses of morphine he injected each night. Although the drug helped him sleep, his difficulty concentrating was bringing him to the edge of medical negligence.

One afternoon, on his way back from a premature birth that had turned out to be a false alarm, Álvaro found himself outside the doorway to Number 2 Calle General Álava. He had no recollection of heading in that direction. This was the first memory lapse that he was aware of, and it made him uneasy.

When he noticed that the couples strolling by were staring at him, Álvaro finally roused himself from his daze. He felt in his inside jacket pocket for the keys to Blanca's apartment.

Climbing the stairs to the second floor as if in a trance, he opened the door with bated breath. Perhaps Blanca still went to the apartment when she needed to be alone. Perhaps she waited for him every afternoon when she knew he would have finished seeing his patients. Perhaps she had left him a message that had been sitting unread for weeks. Why hadn't he thought of that before?

Perhaps . . .

But the silence of those silk-lined walls drilled into his temples, and soon his only thought was of instant relief.

And so Álvaro sat on the floor, propping himself against the sickly vanilla wallpaper, with his back to the busiest street in the hateful city. He removed his necktie and wound it tightly around his freckled upper arm.

He opened his scuffed leather medical bag, which was too shabby for such an elegant place, and took out a nearly full vial of morphine. He had created a fake prescription card. So the pharmacist on Calle Postas gave him all the opiates he wanted.

Slowly he injected himself, relishing the cold sensation as the morphine entered his vein, bringing the welcome amnesia. The ceiling blurred, as though there had been a silent earthquake.

And finally, after waiting for so long, the darkness arrived.

22

THE MONTE GORBEA NATURE RESERVE

WEDNESDAY, AUGUST 3

Are the stakes higher now, #Kraken?

I was walking through the medieval quarter of the city toward headquarters, still furious that I'd let MatuSalem escape, when I got a call from Estíbaliz.

"Unai, you need to get here. I'm at Ignacio's farmhouse between Murguía and Altube. There's been a fire."

"But wasn't the house you went to yesterday in Laguardia?"

"This is another one. Since we still couldn't find him, I looked in the council's land registry files and cross-checked with property deeds. I discovered he has a farmhouse and land on the slopes of Monte Gorbea in the name of one of his event-promotion companies. I wanted to see if he was here so I could talk to him. But when I arrived, the rear part of his land was burning. The fire service from Murguía is already taking care of it."

"I'm on my way," I said.

Shortly afterward I was driving through Abechuco toward Echavarri-Viña, along a road shaded by oak and holm oak canopies.

When I reached the huge restored farmhouse on the slopes of the Gorbea Nature Reserve in northern Álava, the firefighters were busy putting out the few remaining flames behind the building.

The stone farmhouse was set inside a large beechwood, and there were no neighbors nearby. It was built in the traditional style, with a pitched tile roof and a wooden balcony. The wooden entrance ended in a pointed arch, with an *eguzkilore* protecting the household, as was typical for Basque farmhouses.

"What happened, Estíbaliz?" I asked as I clambered from my car.

I took off my jacket. The heat from the recently burned ground made it impossible to get any closer.

Two firefighters signaled for us to stay back. All that was left was the smell of smoke and black scorched earth.

"The fire was started deliberately. It was restricted to a small area. My guess is Ignacio did it."

I looked around carefully. The area surrounding the house was well cared for; it was obvious the owner spent a fortune maintaining this property.

"Why would Ignacio want to torch his own farmhouse?"

"I don't think he wanted to destroy the house. I think he knew the fire department would get here quickly. What he wanted to burn was in the land at the back."

"I don't think there was much there, Estí."

She shook her head, staring intently at the burned patch of ground.

"Wait until they let us get closer, and I'll show you."

We stood there patiently while the firefighters doused the area, and then we approached the officer in charge.

"May we go in now? Inspector Ayala and I would like to have access to that area," said Estíbaliz, pointing to the smoldering ground.

"I advise you not to walk on the burned section; it's still very hot," said the firefighter, shaking his head. His face was bathed in sweat, and as he was talking, he wiped his forehead on his sleeve.

Estí was insistent. "Do you have any extra pairs of boots?"

"Maybe. I'll look in the truck to see if I can find anything, but I'm not sure they'll be your size."

A few minutes later, he came back with masks we hadn't asked for and two pairs of enormous boots. We put them on anyway, adjusted the face masks, and walked to the center of the burned patch.

"What exactly are you looking for, Estí?"

"I'm looking at what's left of those pieces of wood. Can you see them?"

"Yes. What do you think they were?"

"I want forensics to process the scene. From what's left on the ground, I'd say four small, rectangular wooden constructions were completely destroyed by the fire."

"I don't follow you yet, but I'm trying," I said, scratching my neck.

My back was soaked in sweat. We were walking on an inferno.

"I think they were beehives, Unai. Simple pinewood flow beehives. I think Ignacio had four active hives that he burned to destroy all traces of them."

I looked around, still at a loss.

"What about the bees?"

"It's a very cruel way of getting rid of them, but I imagine he put them to sleep with a smoker first. The fire chief also thinks the fire was deliberate and that it spread outward from the center of this field. It's unusual for someone to burn ground like this. The grass, even these tall shoots, wilted close to the area where the fire started. Everything points to this location, even the stones in that small wall marking the boundary—they're blacker on the side the fire came from. And there are signs that accelerants were used: Do you see those stains in concentric circles? The whole area needs to be searched for traces of gasoline, oil, diesel, or kerosene. Here in the hills, everyone has something like that."

"Kerosene? Why would anyone keep kerosene in the house?"

"Believe it or not, the old folks still think it's a good remedy for arthritis. When I was little, the *amatxos* used it to get rid of head lice. If an accelerant like that were used, the high temperatures would mean there will be nothing left of the bees, unless we get lucky and find a dead specimen farther away. If there are lots of them, we could conclude that four hives were burned. Do you remember the day of the Slow Food presentation? Ignacio told us only he dealt with other honey producers. Why did he lie to us?"

"If you're right and Ignacio deliberately burned these beehives, then either he's the murderer or he knows that this time the murder method is bees. That's interesting, because that fact hasn't been released to the press. We need to get a search warrant for the farmhouse as quickly as possible. If he had hives, he must have other beekeeping tools. You know more about this than I do, but wouldn't he need specialized equipment to handle them?"

"Of course. Spatulas, scrapers, gaiters . . . I don't think he burned them, because that would have left some trace, and he knows it. I agree with you: we need to talk to Judge Olano and get that warrant. But frankly, I don't think Ignacio would have left his equipment anywhere near here. He was a police officer. He knows you can't get rid of all organic clues."

"What would you do?"

"Follow me. There's nothing more we can do here."

We went back to the police car, where she took a map of Álava out of the glove compartment.

"You and I are going to check out the garbage containers on the reserve's hiking trails. But I also want patrols sent out the A-624 toward Amurrio, and others toward Villareal, Miñano. I want to cover all four directions. The fire was in a very small area, and it was burning when I arrived, so it had to have been started less than an hour ago. Ignacio could still be transporting something linked to the crimes or other items he doesn't want us to find. Unai, this could be the place he brings his victims. It's isolated, there are bees, and there's enough room to park a vehicle. I'll put out a call with his license number, and we can run a search to see if he has any other properties in his companies' names."

"All right. You drive. You know this area better than I do."

We drove down forest paths, stopping every time we saw a garbage container.

We discovered the object in one of the camping sites. Hidden in a black industrial garbage bag were a smoker, a beekeeper's hood, a couple of well-worn jackets, a pair of rubber-soled boots, and gaiters with zippers.

23

THE LANTERN PROCESSION

Thursday, August 4

By this stage, the villain's power is channeled through associates, henchmen, minions. . . . Be careful, #Kraken.

For the inhabitants of Vitoria, this is the greatest day of the year. The Celedón, a man wearing a floppy beret who represents the Álavan people, descends from the tower of San Miguel Arcángel Church on his umbrella and crosses the sky thanks to a system of pulleys. Then, at six in the evening, the lighting of the *chupinazo* rocket signals the start of las Fiestas de la Virgen Blanca. I took advantage of the day off by getting up early and going for a run.

I came across Blanca, or Alba—who knows which—running along Siervas de Jesús. Was this a chance meeting? For days I had been wondering if she planned her runs around a possible meetup. I hoped she did, although I wasn't sure.

"Do you have a route planned today, or can you improvise?" I asked by way of greeting.

Meeting MatuSalem at the Campillo mural the day before had given me a good idea.

"I have room to improvise. What are you offering?" Alba asked.

"I'll show you my favorite murals. What do you think?" I said, my eyes fixed on her for longer than necessary.

"Sounds good. Let's go," she said, staring into my brown eyes. There wasn't much to see in them, but I took it as a good sign.

We jogged to Fuente de los Patos. Alba liked to compete, and every so often, she challenged me to a sprint, by the end of which we were both out of breath. I hardly need to say how this affected me.

We clattered across the medieval cobbles of the oldest part of the city until we reached the Plaza de la Burullería. The huge mural there depicted medieval fabrics with intricate ancient stitching.

"It's called *A Stitch in Time.*"

"A nice name," she said, catching her breath with her hands on her knees. Her long braid was sticking to her back from perspiration. "But . . . they're only old cloths."

"Don't underestimate it. This is one of the thirty best murals in the world," I said, my pride slightly wounded. I hadn't managed to impress her.

Come on, Kraken, you can do better, I challenged myself.

"All right, I'll show you my favorite."

We jogged as far as the medieval wall, and I led her into the interior gardens. The mural there was special. Not just for what it depicted—*The Shortest Night*, La Noche de San Juan at midsummer—but also for the bright blue background it provided for the joyful procession of Vitoria's medieval inhabitants.

"It's the summer solstice, the pagan feast. Can you see the bonfires, the processions? Every detail is important. Look at the entrance gate in the wall. It doesn't look that way now; it shows it as it must have been in the Middle Ages. It's pure magic, Alba," I said without thinking. As I folded my arms across my chest to admire the mural, I felt her arm brush mine.

I had not realized we were closer than a deputy superintendent and an inspector should be. In every respect.

Where was this leading?

"I didn't tell you, Unai, but it's my favorite mural, too. Because it's La Noche del Alba, I suppose."

Unai. She had just called me Unai. Not Ishmael, or Kraken, or Ayala.

"So why not come and watch the Lantern procession from my roof tonight?" I said enthusiastically. "I live on the square, next to the Virgen Blanca restaurant. Will you come? It's magical, almost dreamlike. The Plaza de la Virgen Blanca is silent apart from the prayers of the faithful. There's a spectacular light show thanks to the colored-glass lanterns, the blue light from underneath the monument to the Battle of Vitoria, and the warm glow from the ancient streetlights in the square. It's enough to make even the staunchest atheist think twice."

"You do a good job selling it," she said with a smile. "I'm almost tempted to accept your invitation."

"Seriously, it's a unique occasion. Think it over. The procession starts at ten o'clock. You'll have to call me at half past nine if you want to get into my building. At that point, the square will be emptier after the rocket is launched, but later it's impossible to get through."

"All right. Let me . . ."

I know, your husband. You have to think about where your husband will be then and whether you can lie to him to be with me.

At exactly half past nine, I heard the entry phone buzz and, with a mixture of disbelief and excitement, waited for her to climb the three floors to my apartment.

"You came." That memorable phrase was all that occurred to me.

"I think you have something special to show me," she said.

I had never seen her dressed in anything other than her running gear or her uniform. Leggings and a T-shirt, or a tailored suit. I had the impression that on this occasion Alba (or Blanca, who knows?) was dressed in her own style: skinny jeans and a tight top, her black hair worn loose, not much makeup.

"That's right. Let's go up to the landing on the fourth floor; the tenant is never there."

She walked behind me up the stairs like an obedient accomplice. When we reached the landing, I took a stepladder out of the shared storage room and placed it underneath the trapdoor leading to the roof.

"Follow me?" I asked, knowing she would.

I climbed outside and sat on the sloping orange tiles. She climbed up, poked out her head and then the top of her body. She looked at me incredulously.

"Are you sure this isn't dangerous?"

"I've been up here a thousand times and have never had a problem. You just have to be a bit careful."

"I'm not sure if this is safe," she muttered to herself.

I had no idea whether she was referring to that moment or to our odd relationship.

She pushed herself up and sat beside me on the roof.

"Have you noticed what a special atmosphere there is in the square already?" I asked, pointing downward. "The procession will start any minute now. They've put up an altar on the corner of the steps to San Miguel. When all the lanterns are grouped around it, there'll be a short service. They usually prevent access to the balcony where the marble niche with the statue of the Virgen Blanca is, the place where we . . ."

Where we first met, I was going to say, but then I thought better of it.

"Where we usually stop and stretch," I backtracked.

"I remember," she said, and I knew she was thinking about the same moment I was. Sometimes our memory sticks thumbtacks in apparently trivial moments, and they remain fixed forever, although forever seems like a long time.

"What's that they've placed at the feet of the Virgen Blanca?" she asked.

I looked in the direction she was pointing, although, given the distance and how dim the light was on the balcony, all I could make out was a vague white blotch.

"I don't know. It looks like a sheet or a piece of cloth. Maybe it's to show where people should put their flowers."

"Perhaps," she agreed.

At our feet, the square was gradually filling with people lining the path leading to the church.

"It's strange," she said, hugging her knees. "We're right in the center of a city in the midst of a celebration, and yet we're invisible."

"Don't worry, it really is impossible for anybody to see us unless they're in the building across the street, but even then the light is so dim they'd only be able to make out two shadows. No one would recognize us."

"I know, and I understand. On the one hand, I feel very exposed. But I hear what you're saying: nobody will find out."

Once again, I was sure she was talking about us in general. Her doubts, everything she stood to lose, the little she had to gain.

"Do you remember 'Lau teilatu'? 'The Four Rooftops,' that Itoiz song they used to play at all the village fiestas in the north twenty years ago?" I asked.

"Of course, who hasn't fallen in love to that song?" she said with a smile.

"Who hasn't had great sex listening to it, the great sex we used to have when we were kids, when we didn't think about the before, during, or after."

"Irresponsible, authentic sex. A whole generation, I reckon." She laughed nostalgically.

"This is like being in one of the verses of 'Lau teilatu.' Every time I come up here, that song comes to mind: *On four roofs, the moon in the sky and you, looking up at it.* . . . I brought it for you."

Taking my cell phone out of my back jeans pocket, I handed her an earbud, then inserted mine. Now we were connected by a song that only the two of us could hear. We were far away from the silent worshippers several yards below our feet. That was the closest I had felt emotionally to anyone since the Avenue of Pines.

"*—And we'll be happy again in the fiestas of any village,*" she translated from the Euzkera as she listened to the Basque ballad.

"If only we had met at one of those village fiestas," I dared to say. "I used to go every year to the one in Laguardia—how come I never saw you? Tell me, is it too late now? You're married, I'm a widower, and both of us have children we never got to bring up. Is it too late, Blanca?"

"I don't know. I never thought I'd be asking myself that question at my age, but . . ."

She didn't finish her sentence. I waited, but she wasn't ready. She had just been transferred to Vitoria a few weeks earlier. It had only been a few days since we started running together in the early morning, and even less time had passed since the first new crimes brought us together professionally.

Sometimes calendar time has nothing to do with the mental or emotional time we experience.

"Why don't you come back here on the night of the Perseid meteor showers? It's unbelievable. You lie here at three in the morning in mid-August and wait for the shower of stars. Last year I counted forty-three."

"I don't believe you," she said doubtfully. "I don't believe you can see them from here. There's too much light pollution."

"Yes, you can. In August, Vitoria is empty. There isn't as much light from the apartments, and it makes a big difference. On August twelfth the sky is clear, and at about four in the morning you can see the shooting stars of the Lagrimas de San Lorenzo. You have to believe me, Alba."

She thought this over for a moment, or at least she was kind enough to pretend she was considering.

"Unai . . . you know I won't be able to," she said eventually, hugging her knees.

I know, at that time in the morning you'll be sleeping with your husband. I was only dreaming about not feeling so alone.

"And I know when one shouldn't insist with a lady."

"I thank you for that, then," she said.

"Listen, here comes the procession." I removed the earbud from her ear.

As I did so, I brushed against her, and she didn't pull away.

The worshippers began to appear on Calle del Prado. They were dressed in white with red handkerchiefs around their necks, and they walked in pairs, carrying big glass lanterns. The first ones had blue and gold star-shaped sides. Then came green, red, and yellow ones. Finally, a few red and blue stragglers. From our vantage point, the procession looked like some kind of Santa Compaña, but more beautiful, colorful, and solemn than its Galician counterpart.

"You know something? When I'm up here, I like to imagine I'm a sentinel. I like to think I can protect them all," I said with sudden frankness.

She tilted her head worriedly.

"As your boss, I'm glad you're so obsessive. I know you haven't been thinking about anything else since the murders started."

"Since they started again," I corrected her.

"All right, since they started again. That's your hypothesis, and I trust you. On the other hand, I'd rather you weren't so mentally and emotionally involved. You can't protect an entire city on your own. Remember: if the murderer has decided to continue killing, we'll only be able to catch him because of his mistakes, but that won't help us prevent future crimes. These murders are too well planned to imagine that the killer leaves anything to chance."

"That's the worst comedown I've ever had with a girl. Do you think we could listen to 'Lau teilatu' again and get back into a mystic mood?" I said wistfully.

She laughed, with that frank laugh I remembered from the morning I met her, when she was trying to be someone else, or to recover herself, who knows.

Then she did something I wasn't expecting. She snuggled between my legs and leaned back against my chest. I folded my arms around her and laid my head on her left shoulder. It felt so good to be that close.

Then we were caressing each other without saying a word. What would have been the point? I didn't want to hear her excuses. She had so many good reasons not to continue that I would have had to admit she was right. But I didn't want to do that, either. Not here, not this night, on this roof looking out over Vitoria. The touch of her tight jeans beneath my hand, my zipper almost bursting, her soft breathing in my ear . . . my lips on her neck that was as wet with perspiration as it was when she was running.

We would have ended up on fire on those roof tiles had it not been for what happened next.

First, we heard a man shout hoarsely. Then there were screams of panic, and chaos ensued.

Bewildered, Blanca and I peered over the edge of the roof. We couldn't understand what was going on. It was like being expelled from paradise by an alarm clock.

We saw the priests running from the stairs leading to the niche where the Virgen Blanca stood, abandoning the temporary altar, cassocks flapping.

From so far away, we could see that someone must have discov-

ered the white sheet, because it was no longer visible. Several people
had formed a tight circle around something and were gesticulating
hysterically near where the sheet had been.

We looked at each other, wondering what to do, and then
Alba's phone rang.

"Deputy Superintendent Salvatierra. What is it?"

My boss had taken control. The magic had fled from our rooftop, and everything that had happened only seconds before seemed
terribly out of place.

Alba listened to the urgent voice on the other end of the line.
When she ended the call, she was a different person.

"Inspector Ayala, two naked bodies have been found at the
foot of the Virgen Blanca niche, on the balcony outside San Miguel
Arcángel Church," she told me flatly. "I informed them that I am
in the area, and so I'm going down to the crime scene. Call your
colleague. The duty magistrate, pathologist, and forensic team are
already on their way, and a couple of patrol cars are about to arrive
to clear the terrace and cordon it off. We need to try to stop people
from taking photos on their phones—we don't want the details
leaking to the press. That would hamper our investigation. I'm
going down."

She moved away, opened the trapdoor, and started to descend
without waiting for me.

"I'll come, too."

"We can't arrive at the same time. The entire city is in the
square; someone we know would see us coming out of the same
doorway, and nobody in the police should suspect we are together."

"All right. You've already said you're in the area, so you go
down first and approach the scene from the steps. I'll come out a
few minutes later and take the tunnel that runs under the Arquillos,
next to the Toloño. I'll approach from the right, and I'll say I was
watching the procession."

"Let's do that, then," she agreed, and disappeared down the stairs.

I called Estíbaliz and gave her the news. She was having dinner with her fiancé at La Riojana in La Cuchi. A couple of minutes later, I tentatively opened the front door and went out into the square. The procession had come to a halt. The people carrying lanterns were awaiting orders, not knowing what to do.

Everyone was talking in small groups. I could see the consternation on their faces and hear how feverishly they were speaking. I was dismayed that a single person could be so powerful, could turn such a solemn, unique moment in Vitoria into a time of terror.

Pushing my way through the crowd, I managed with difficulty to reach the small arch that most people never noticed. I leaped up the steps, and in a few minutes, I was on the scene.

Alba was already there. She had had the presence of mind to stand to the left, and I found her giving orders to a couple of uniforms who had already arrived.

We started clearing the area. According to regulations, we should have established a cordon forty yards from the crime scene, but it would have been impossible to avoid photographs. Cell phone cameras were flashing all around me, and so I simply moved the curious onlookers who were hypnotized by the two naked bodies.

When we finally managed to cordon off the area and I was able to concentrate on the two new victims, I knelt on the gray cobblestones and repeated my silent prayer:

Here your hunt ends and mine begins.

This was the third time in the span of only a few days that I had said it. How many more times would that monster oblige me to repeat it?

But for the first time, when I looked at the canvas the murderer had laid out for us, I was able to interpret clearly the picture I saw before me.

The couple were lying at the feet of the Virgen Blanca. They were naked, almost certainly thirty years old, each with one hand laid on the other's cheek to comfort them and the purity of bees in their throats punishing them for original sin. Three *eguzkilores* formed an isosceles triangle to represent the Eye of Providence.

The all-seeing eye.

24

THE DAWN ROSARY

VITORIA
AUGUST 1970

Álvaro Urbina woke at six. Emilia had insisted they go to the dawn rosary, and he hadn't had the strength to refuse. Not even his near-overdose in Blanca's apartment had managed to shock him out of the torpor he had been plunged into for the past few weeks. Maybe he had wanted her to find him passed out on the floor. Now it was all the same to him. Summer or winter, fiestas or funerals.

It was all the same.

He let himself be swept along by the flow of people walking behind the Blusas carrying the Virgen Blanca to San Miguel Arcángel Church. A pair of standard bearers on either side guided the procession with huge white flags. Several priests in black cassocks and altar boys wearing starched chasubles chanted songs and prayers with a zeal he found tiresome at this early hour.

Álvaro was on his way home, arm in arm with his wife, staring absentmindedly at the ground, when his eyes enountered a familiar pair of high heels. Swallowing hard, he looked up and saw Javier Ortiz de Zárate and Blanca Díaz de Antoñana.

To his astonishment, Javier beamed at him. He seemed completely recovered from the incident that had led to his time in the hospital. Blanca also gave him a friendly smile, and yet she shot him a warning look that he found hard to decipher.

His clinician's eye instantly detected a change in her. He had seen it hundreds of times in his other patients: Her breasts were fuller, and the veins on her chest were bluer and thicker beneath her pale skin. He glanced at her swollen ankles and at the hated wedding ring tight around her finger.

"Doctor Urbina! How nice to see you!" Blanca's husband said cheerfully, slapping him on both arms. "I imagine my wife has been to your clinic since we had the good news. I'm most grateful to you for your attention. We were starting to lose hope."

Álvaro responded swiftly to the situation, putting on his doctor's face and smiling with deliberate restraint.

"Yes, indeed, my congratulations. A pregnancy always blesses a newlywed couple's home with joy."

"Actually, I have an appointment with Doctor Urbina next week," Blanca said, her eyes trained on her husband. "Until then, if you'll excuse us. We're on our way to have an ice cream at La Italiana, assuming they are open this early. All I think about these days is eating the special tortillas at Naroki's followed by a milkshake from Casa Quisco."

"Until then, take good care yourself, señora. Make sure you drink plenty of water during the hot weather. You're retaining a lot of fluid, and you don't want to risk fainting. And for heaven's sake, wear some sensible shoes," Álvaro added, completely assuming his role.

Javier gave a satisfied smirk, and the couples parted company.

A few days after this encounter, Blanca walked into his office early in the morning and closed the door behind her. Álvaro dropped his pen and tried to say something, but she spoke first:

"You're a doctor. You know there's no way of telling if the child is yours or Javier's."

"Blanca . . . you should . . ." He tried to stop her, but she was already ensconced in the chair opposite him.

She stared at the medical books piled at one end of the large desk, and the words came out in a rush.

"The police have dropped the investigation. They say they can't prove if my husband's poisoning was an accident or not, but Javier won't let it rest. That's why I came here: to warn you that we have to be extremely careful. And that I have no choice but for you to oversee my pregnancy. Javier would be suspicious if I changed doctors now. Two of his business partners were attacked recently. Neither reported it, but their wives are friends of mine and they told me all about it. Both incidents appeared to be muggings: a group of masked men followed them, demanded money, but then beat them and slashed them with a knife. I know Javier suspects one of them might have tried to poison him, because I heard him tell his driver Ulysses. But I'm terrified, for myself and for you, Álvaro. If he ever found out what we did, there's no telling what he might do. He wants this child more than anything in the world, and he hasn't laid a finger on me since I became pregnant, and yet—"

Just then, Doctor Urbina's nurse, Felisa, stepped out from behind the white screen and restrained Blanca with a gesture.

"Stop there, Doña Blanca. Don't say another word. You can rest assured my lips are sealed, but let me leave the room now. If I hear any more, this will become my problem, too."

Felisa gave Doctor Urbina a stern look, and he frowned as he pinched the bridge of his nose. Then he heaved a sigh and waved her away. "You may go, Felisa. We'll talk later, if you don't mind."

The nurse left without another word, pulling the door closed behind her.

As soon as they were alone, Blanca buried her face in her hands. "God, all I do is complicate things! I don't think I can go on," she said.

"I think we can trust Felisa. Unfortunately, we have no choice but to rely on her discretion. However, I'm not sure it's such a good idea for me to oversee your pregnancy and the delivery of your child. Supposing your husband finds out about what . . . about what happened between us?"

He used the past tense, pursing his lips as he tried to conceal the pain it caused him.

"I told you: The only thing that matters to him now is having this baby. I think he's afraid to make any changes. He wants you to be in charge. We'll have to grin and bear it for a few months. Limit yourself to being my doctor and carrying out the necessary checkups, and after the birth, we'll never see each other again. I'll raise this boy, or this girl, regardless of who the father is. You'll go back to your family, and we'll forget this ever happened. It's the safest solution for everyone."

Álvaro took a while to process the news. Then, fed up with the whole thing, he simply gave in.

All right, Blanca. This is the end of the road.

"Very well, I will oversee your pregnancy, in accordance with you and your husband's wishes," he said eventually, trying to keep his voice even. "I'll start by requesting a blood test to make sure everything is in order, and then we'll calculate your due date. Please go behind the screen and take off your clothing from the waist down. You may cover yourself with the sheet."

No sooner had Blanca left than Felisa entered Doctor Urbina's office and, for the first time since he started working at the clinic, she sat down in the patient's chair.

"I wish I hadn't found out about this, especially in this way, doctor. But I lived through the civil war and have witnessed more violence between neighbors than you could imagine. You were a baby then, and hunger was probably the only thing you experienced. My job as a nurse is to see, hear, and keep silent, and yet there are times when keeping quiet only makes things worse. I've already mentioned that I treated Don Javier's first wife with Doctor Medina. I've told you about her injuries and that Doctor Medina kept quiet, as was his custom. However, I haven't told you everything.

"She came to see the doctor because she couldn't get pregnant. I was there when he examined her. Due to a congenital malformation, her uterus was the size of a pea. The poor woman wasn't to blame, but Doctor Medina insisted it was her duty to tell her husband the truth. We gave her an appointment for a week later, but she didn't show up. She didn't cancel, either, which was strange behavior for such a courteous, dependable young woman. Some time later, I read her obituary in an old newspaper I'd found in the waiting room, and I asked around. She had jumped off the Gujuli Falls that same weekend. Do you know how unlikely that is? The woman couldn't say boo to a goose; the slightest noise or raised voice scared her. You know the type I'm talking about: the kind of person who asks permission to breathe, who's terrified of being a nuisance. Like a whipped dog that won't even pick up a discarded bone without looking to its master for approval. So I can't imagine her going anywhere near the edge of a three-hundred-foot drop."

"What are you insinuating, Felisa?"

"That a leopard doesn't change its spots. Everybody knew her husband was free with his fists, but they turned a blind eye because he comes from a wealthy family. Everyone knew that no one gets away with making a fool out of Don Javier Ortiz de Zárate. I've said too much already. If it's all the same to you, I'd like to go home now."

Blanca's long, slender body gradually filled out, her belly tightening under the weight of the pregnancy. Come the fall, the relationship between Doctor Urbina and his patient had changed from an initial self-conscious aloofness back to the friendly intimacy of before. The crippling fear they had experienced was a vague memory they chose to ignore. They were looking ahead. Simply looking ahead, awaiting the probable due date.

One morning, Doctor Urbina received a call. Four rings. Then silence.

I'm waiting for you was Blanca's unspoken plea.

I'm waiting for you.

That afternoon, Álvaro went to meet her. As a precaution, he looked up and down Calle General Álava, and when he was sure he couldn't see anyone he knew, he took out the keys he still kept and entered the building.

Blanca was waiting for him, naked in bed, just as he remembered her. It was not an afternoon for words; there was no situation they needed to discuss. There were only two bodies seeking refuge from their fears, comforting each other.

It happened the following evening, when Álvaro was on his way back from seeing his last patient. The wind had picked up, and as he made his way down Avenida Generalísimo toward his house, he thought he heard whispering behind him. His family had recently bought a three-bedroom apartment on Calle Honduras, in one of the residential areas off the main avenue, near El Pilar. The area, full of gray concrete towers surrounded by trees and green spaces, stood behind the foundations of what would become Colegio San Viator.

When he reached the end of the avenue, Álvaro glanced anxiously over his shoulder. There were very few people around, and yet he thought he heard footsteps. So he crossed onto a stretch of sidewalk where a few bars were still welcoming customers who wanted a final aperitif before they went home to dinner.

He negotiated the last crosswalk in the lighted area, and continued along the gravel path bordered by trees and hedges that led to his apartment building.

Once again, he heard noises behind him, and this time he felt scared.

"Who's there?" he shouted in alarm, wheeling around.

But the single nearby streetlight illuminated nothing more than shadows from the trees, and so he quickened his step until he was almost sprinting along the walkway to the entrance to his building.

Three men wearing scarves over their faces stepped out from behind the columns. They were thickset; all he could see were their eyes. One slowly pulled out a knife with a long, thin blade. He had none of the quick, nervous gestures Urbina would have expected from a mugger or addict.

The other two men surrounded him. The doctor shouted for help, but nobody came. He thought he recognized a familiar figure propped against the concrete wall about twenty yards away, watching what was about to happen.

25

THE BALCONY OF SAN MIGUEL

THURSDAY, AUGUST 4

Can the villain also be a trickster, a shape-shifter
who can change history? Open your eyes, #Kraken.

It was an intense night. Someone had uploaded an image of the murdered couple on Twitter, and everyone on social media was a detective now, trying to identify the victims. Social media had baptized the latest killings "The Crime of the Virgen Blanca," and created a new hashtag, #CVB, which was competing with #TwinMurderers and #Kraken to be the highest globally trending topic. The major international newspapers also tweeted about the latest murders, from *Corriere della Sera* in Italy to *Clarín* in Argentina. A third double murder in less than two weeks once again put us at the epicenter of international news.

Various theories were trending, many pointing to Ignacio as the killer. By now, even though I had not given any information to Mario Santos, and certainly nothing to Lutxo, it was public knowledge that Ignacio's whereabouts were unknown.

His lifelong friends turned out not to be such good friends when it came to being discreet; they had spread the news to the four winds that he had not been to any of the pre-fiesta dinners organized by his *cuadrilla*. Everyone knew his cell phone was out of service, and the assistants in the stores next to Number 2 Calle Dato told anyone who cared to listen that Ignacio had not been in or out of his apartment for days.

Many of the tweets were calling on me for an explanation: Where is Ignacio, #Kraken? Why haven't you arrested that pedophile?

However, none of his family or friends had reported him missing, and since we didn't have an analysis of the beekeeping accessories we had found, we had no justification for issuing a warrant for his arrest.

Other trending theories pointed to Tasio as the guilty one. They supported the original theory that he was the puppet master for an acolyte on the outside. For days, there had been a spontaneous attempt to collect signatures for a petition to prevent Tasio from being released on August 8. No one seemed to care that his temporary parole would last less than a week; everyone had decided he was bound to abscond, and we were criticized for not initiating legal proceedings to prevent it. According to social media, we were inept, and I was the worst of the lot. I couldn't deny there was some truth in that.

After bringing the superintendent up to date, DSU Salvatierra called us in for an urgent meeting. It was plain from her weary face that her boss was turning the screws on her.

There were dark lines under her eyes, her jaw was tense, and her expression showed grim determination. The weight of the world was on those warm shoulders that, only a few hours earlier, had pressed against my chest. Day still hadn't dawned when my partner and I entered headquarters, the strain showing on our faces as well.

"The two victims have just been identified," DSU Salvatierra

told us, handing out two reports as soon as Estíbaliz and I were
seated.

"So quickly?" asked Estí.

"There hasn't been time for their parents or relatives to report
them missing," I said.

"They've been identified on social media. And, yes, they were
both thirty years old. Their friends raised the alert when they saw
the images that had gone viral on the Internet. They contacted the
families and verified that no one knew where they were. By now
several photographs of their faces have appeared online. The *cuadrillas* they belonged to were already worried because neither one had
turned up in the bars where they had promised to meet and they
weren't answering their cell phones.

"All this happened less than an hour after the news about the
two new bodies exploded on social media. Mateo Ruiz de Zuazo's
mother and Irene Martínez de San Román's parents got in touch
with us. I saw no need to prolong their suffering, and so, rather than
making them wait until tomorrow, I had them taken to formally
identify the corpses. Unfortunately, they all made positive identifi-
cations. Now we're waiting for the autopsies to confirm the results
we're almost certain we already know: death by asphyxia caused by
bee stings to the throat, the presence of Rohypnol in their blood,
and little else that will be news to us."

"Who are the victims this time?" Estíbaliz asked.

"Until a few hours ago, Mateo Ruiz de Zuazo was a lecturer
in marketing at the Basque Culinary Center. He commuted from
Vitoria to Donostia. He lived here alone in an apartment, but he
had lunch or dinner with his mother in the El Pilar neighborhood
every day. He has no police record, not so much as a traffic fine;
his mother says he has never had any drug problem. In short, a
normal healthy man. Very sociable and easygoing, he liked sports
and mountaineering, and once again, he was very trusting. The last

time anybody saw or heard from him was yesterday morning, when he agreed to join his *cuadrilla* after the celebrations started. Apparently, he didn't like to join in the fiesta because he couldn't bear the cigar smoke. According to his mother, his father was a heavy smoker and died of lung cancer. That was the only thing Mateo was really passionate about."

"So it's the usual profile. Is the woman the same?" asked my partner.

"I'm afraid so. Her case is especially tragic, because Irene Martínez de San Román just turned thirty yesterday. She's dead because of a single day. Her mother keeps insisting that thirty years ago the doctors moved her delivery date forward because the baby was in a breech position and had stopped growing, that her due date was in fact August 15, and if the doctors had respected that, her daughter would be alive now."

"It's curious what parents cling to when they've lost a child," Estíbaliz said.

Alba and I glanced at each other, as if jolted by an electric shock. Then we looked at Estíbaliz, but she was still studying the report Alba had passed to us, oblivious to our pain. How could she understand? It was like talking to a soldier who had never been to battle.

"Irene had said she would join up with her *cuadrilla* to watch the Celedón descending. When she didn't appear by five thirty, her friends became suspicious and started calling, trying to locate her. They got in touch with her parents, who didn't know where she was, either. By the time the news appeared on the Internet, her parents were about to come down to police headquarters. Like everybody else, they were pretty much obsessed with the double crimes and were very worried their daughter might be . . . Well, you know, on the list of possible victims. I refuse to adopt the terminology that's appearing in the press, the media, and the Net: the list of the condemned, the chosen ones."

"I'm starting to wonder what the profile is for a person who abducts people aged twenty, twenty-five, and thirty," said Estíbaliz.

"What I wonder is how they can be such easy targets," I said. "We're waiting for the latest autopsies to confirm it, but there doesn't seem to have been a fight or a struggle with any of the victims. This guy must be a wizard, a chameleon, someone who can win people over without arousing any doubts or suspicions."

"He's a psychopath. Stop acting as though you admire what he's doing," Estíbaliz protested.

"I'm simply stating facts, Inspector Gauna. I'm trying to put myself in the position of six young people who died because they thought they could trust someone."

Estí looked apologetic, but we were both exhausted. There was no point starting an argument now.

"For once Twitter has helped us," I said, changing the subject and looking at Alba.

She shook her head. "It hasn't helped in the slightest. The leaked images showed we'd been careful not to reveal, like the *eguzkilores*. Now the entire world has seen them. That's given rise to a whole flood of neo-pagan theories. Experts in Basque mythology have been giving their opinions when no one has asked for them; the TV stations have found a rich vein that will keep them busy for weeks. This might create a very dangerous precedent. The superintendent is looking at steps we could take to stop these images from circulating, including potentially getting Judge Olano to ask a judge to rule that they are part of an ongoing investigation.

"Before he kills again," said Estíbaliz. "The Vitoria fiesta days have started: five days of pure chaos, with thousands of people in the streets. We're not going to declare a state of war, so this could be a bloodbath. People are scared. What does the murderer hope to achieve by choosing to kill right now? Does he want las Fiestas de la Virgen Blanca to be canceled?"

"Obviously he's attacking all our rituals, our customs, all the historic sites in the city. He hates everything to do with Vitoria."

"I agree with you," said Alba. "The scene of the crime takes us another step forward in this city's history. The Virgen Blanca's niche was built in the eighteenth century. Beyond that, the victims appear to have been chosen simply for their age and surnames. There doesn't seem to be a personal motive for any of the murders."

"That's only if we discount Lidia's murder and the circumstances surrounding it," said Estíbaliz, folding her arms across her chest. "Or are we going to leave out the prime suspects yet again?"

"We still have nothing, absolutely nothing, that points to their guilt."

"Other than Ignacio's burning his beehives, and basic common sense," my partner insisted.

"Well, you'll have to bring me more, and quickly, inspectors," said Alba, standing up as if to dismiss us. "This situation must not continue. It can't. We have the eyes of half the world on us, expecting us to stop these crimes. The superintendent isn't just struggling with Spanish television. The international press is covering the double murders, and their correspondents are already here to report on the week of las Fiestas de la Blanca. And you can't imagine how insistent the people from the BBC, Europa Press, and Reuters can be when they decide to devote time to a story.

"You two go and get some sleep, if only for a few hours. Tomorrow is going to be very busy. I want you functioning at your best, completely clearheaded. I need you to follow up each line of inquiry we have. Look at them again; maybe you've missed something. From now on, I'm going to judge you on results, not on effort. And finally, we're going to begin an operation to keep people away from all the historic buildings from the nineteenth century. It's not going to be easy. That's almost the entire Ensanche, which is precisely where most people congregate during the fiestas."

"I have something to share with you," I said, despite my weariness. "It's a line of inquiry I'm just starting to explore, but things are moving so fast I haven't been able to tell you about it so far. Now is as good or as bad a moment as any other."

"So what is it, Ayala?" said Salvatierra, sitting down again.

I told them about the carvings in San Vicentejo and my visit to the chapel with Don Tiburcio. When I mentioned concepts like the Eye of Providence, the hermetic couple, and animals as moral symbols, Alba raised an eyebrow. Estíbaliz didn't seem pleased when I spoke about the red-haired apprentice.

"You don't have anything" was all she said. "In fact, the only connection we have to that stonemason is thanks precisely to Tasio. Doesn't that incriminate him further?"

"If it incriminated him, Tasio wouldn't have told me his name. He would have claimed he couldn't remember it after all these years, and I couldn't have done anything to identify him."

"So what do you conclude from all this?"

"Don Tiburcio Sáenz de Urturi is a Freemason, probably a Grand Master or a Grand Secretary. Don't look at me like that, it's no secret that there's at least one lodge in Vitoria. It's called Manuel Iradier. They began meeting decades ago in a farmhouse at Respaldiza, in the north, close to Amurrio."

"Are you trying to tell us that the person committing these crimes is also a Freemason?"

"No, if he were, Don Tiburcio wouldn't have given me that information so openly. I think the murderer could be the apprentice he had during the restoration. I think he was impressed by Don Tiburcio's ideas, and he has copied them in his own historical stagings, possibly to incriminate Tasio because of his work as an archaeologist. But the crime scenes are his reinterpretations. What we can see is a diagram of his mind, his cognitive map, a snapshot of what his world must look like, his problems, his traumas, whatever they are. Don't forget that murderers have a cost-benefit logic: For him, everything he does has a meaning, from the signature to the modus operandi. Every effort he makes brings him a reward if it gets the result he wants."

"So do you think this is a Masonic crime or not?" my colleague insisted.

"I don't, but I think it's directly inspired by the medieval iconography in the San Vicentejo chapel. Without meaning to, the person who deciphered the imagery of the medieval stonemasons planted the seed of the crimes we're now struggling with."

"Unai, with all due respect, I think you need to get some rest. I want to be able to count on your excellent profiling. Do yourself a favor and sleep in a little. Some nights are so long, it's like a lifetime has passed since they began. Today is one of those," said Alba, standing up again and drawing our meeting to a close. It felt as if she was somewhere between my boss and my almost lover.

We nodded and waved good-bye. We left headquarters like three zombies, unwilling and unable to speak. The first light of day was breaking on the eastern streets of the city.

I flopped like a jellyfish to the Plaza de la Virgen Blanca. The *cuadrillas* were on their way home, but there was none of the joy I knew so well, none of the celebratory atmosphere, no drunks trying to pick up lampposts they'd mistaken for people.

People were staying in groups. Girls were going home in twos, threes, and fours. Everybody was staring at their cell phones as they went along.

The atmosphere was totally different from las Fiestas de la Blanca I had known throughout the thirty-plus years of my life.

I cursed the power a single brain had to change the lives of so many people, most of whom had nothing to do with whatever motivated him. I was horrified at the ease with which the sick determination of one person could turn an entire city upside down.

But more than anything else, I cursed the person who had interrupted what Alba and I had been on the brink of starting on those four roofs of ours.

MIRACONCHA AVENUE

FRIDAY, AUGUST 5

He's acting rashly. Look for mistakes, because if
he hasn't made any at this point, I swear I give up,
#Kraken.

I woke up and went to Mentirón's, at the foot of the square, for
coffee and a croissant. This damn case was interfering with my
rituals.

The waitress, a young girl with thickly painted eyebrows and
hair pulled back into a dark bun, brought me a sheet of paper along
with the coffee I had ordered

"You're Kraken, aren't you?"

"Would there be any point in denying it?" I said wearily.

"No. Someone I trust told me who you were," she said, sweeping back a lock of hair that was bothering her.

"I suppose this is a list of your relatives and friends who are
thirty-five," I said, sleepily eyeing the paper with the bar's logo
on it.

"I just want you to look at the names. They're real people who
are important to me, not just names on the news that will be forgotten as soon as there are new victims."

"They're all real people. None of them are just names on a list,"
I said, as if I were talking to a child.

"Well, then, put those twins away once and for all. Both of them, and make sure they don't have any contact with each other. I don't know what you're waiting for."

I pinched the bridge of my nose. Perhaps my alarm clock had not gone off, and this was just another nightmare—but in that case the coffee wouldn't smell as good as the one I had in front of me.

"You do realize you're making it hard for me to want to come back here for breakfast?"

"That might be better anyway. Everyone is staring at you. You're scaring away the customers."

That's enough, I thought.

I gulped my scalding coffee, giving myself a painful burn that would last all morning, and forced down the stupid croissant in four bites. I left a few euros on the metal plate and stood up, ready to escape.

I was reaching for the door handle when the waitress grabbed my arm. Disconcerted, I turned around.

"What on Earth do you think you're doing?"

"My boyfriend is on that list. We're expecting a baby. Please, keep him in mind. You can't leave an unborn child without a father. Can't you understand how anxious I am?"

Her words burned like acid in my veins.

"Would you like some advice?" I said, losing patience. "Tell him to get out of Vitoria. Right now. He shouldn't be here until—"

Until a thirty-five-year-old couple turns up dead, I was going to say, but could I admit my failure? How could I confess to a stranger that I didn't think the murders were over, either?

Her face turned pale as she thought over what I'd just said.

"Yes, you're right," she admitted. "To hell with his job and his boss. This is a matter of life and death. Thank you, Kraken."

With that she rushed out of Mentirón's like a tornado, cell phone in hand.

Half an hour later, I had just sat down in my office when I received a call from a number that I didn't recognize.

"Inspector Ayala. My name is Antonio Garrido-Stoker, calling from the Garrido-Stoker Law Firm in San Sebastián. My client is Don Ignacio Ortiz de Zárate."

"I'm listening," I said, trying to conceal my astonishment.

"Since August 3, my client has been staying in my private residence in Duque de Baena, behind Miraconcha Avenue. He has instructed me to get in touch with you personally. I would like to schedule a videoconference, this morning if possible. Due to recent developments, my client wishes to clarify his situation as swiftly as possible."

"Is Ignacio with you?"

"That is correct. In fact, he is standing beside me at this very moment."

"Since this meeting will cover legal matters, I would like my immediate superior, Deputy Superintendent Alba Díaz de Salvatierra, and my partner, Inspector Estíbaliz Ruiz de Gauna, to be present as well."

I heard some whispering at the other end of the line.

"My client says he was counting on that. Shall we speak in half an hour?"

"Yes, in half an hour," I said, and the attorney ended the call.

I hurried to Alba's and Estí's offices to let them know about the call and to give us a few minutes to prepare.

At the appointed time, the three of us were waiting in front of my computer screen. It had been scanned by our IT experts, and I had secretly called Golden Girl to make sure MatuSalem couldn't record our conversation and pass the information on to Tasio.

When we finally established contact, we could see Ignacio in a suit and tie, as impeccably dressed as if this was a business meeting.

The man next to him, the famous Garrido-Stoker Junior, looked more like a Wall Street shark than a young pup from a long line of lawyers who were legendary in every court in northern Spain. His dark curly hair was combed back with lots of gel, exposing a broad forehead. His jacket would have delighted my brother, Germán.

The Garrido-Stoker family are experienced, high-powered lawyers who represent the large fortunes of the Basque country. The senior partners' fees are well beyond what an average or even comfortable salary could afford. They play in a different league.

Behind the lawyer we could see a garden with symmetrical hedgerows with a view of La Concha Bay and Santa Clara Island.

"I am Deputy Superintendent Salvatierra," Alba introduced herself. "Our team from the Information Technology Central Crime Unit is recording this interview, as it forms part of an ongoing criminal investigation. Do I have your express consent for us to record our conversation?"

Ignacio and his lawyer exchanged a rapid glance.

"I don't think that will be a problem," said Garrido-Stoker. "If you have no objection, we will also record it. That's routine."

"You have my permission," said Alba. "Could you explain your client's current situation and the reason you reached out to us?"

"Naturally. I understand you must be very busy this morning. We all wish to see progress in the investigation. We have a long-term relationship with our client; in fact, his father was my father's client. Don Ignacio Ortiz de Zárate came to us on August third when he decided to leave his residence in Vitoria following the publication of slanderous material. We have initiated legal proceedings against the newspaper. In addition, anticipating that a series of crimes could resume, we thought it best to accommodate him in our private residence. That is where we are now. Given the nature of our work and the importance of the affairs we deal with, we have strict security measures in place. CCTV cameras cover the property twenty-four hours a day, including the exterior, the garden, and other recreational areas.

"What I am endeavoring to make clear is this: Don Ignacio has voluntarily agreed to be monitored at all times. He has not communicated with anyone via cell phone or landline since he has been with us. Nor, as you will be able to verify, has he had any access to the Internet. This morning our delivery service sent you recordings of all his movements, starting from the day he arrived. Your experts will be able to corroborate that there is not a single moment when my client has not been monitored. In this way, we intend to demonstrate conclusively that he could not have committed last night's murders."

Stunned silence followed. None of us knew how to react.

"This guy is slyer than a fox," Estíbaliz whispered to me, breaking the spell.

"Inspector Gauna, I simply wanted to get the ball rolling," said Ignacio, approaching the camera with a gesture identical to the one his brother had made when I visited him in prison. "I think we are all caught up in a lengthy game. Although you may not believe it, you are as much of a pawn as I am. But I'm twenty years and hours of reflection ahead of you, and I refuse to play a passive role. I've already paid a high price for events that had nothing to do with me. I have no intention of becoming the scapegoat for these crimes."

Alba glared at Estíbaliz. My partner pursed her lips and said nothing.

"We would like to ask your client several questions. We understand that you've been preparing his defense, and it would help our investigation if he could clear up a few things," I said, in a placatory tone. What sense did it make to get out our knives with that shark swimming around?

"You may proceed," said the lawyer.

"On August third, a fire broke out on one of your client's company's properties close to the Murguía municipal boundary. This was one day after the publication of the photographs you referred to earlier. The same day, as you have just told us, that your client arrived at your residence in San Sebastián. Was your client aware of this event?"

"Yes, he was burning some stubble. My client maintains that the fire was under control and that when he left there were no more flames. A strong southerly wind was blowing that day and the atmosphere was very dry. In fact, news bulletins reported a spike in fires all over the Basque country. My client cannot be blamed if a spark from the fire caused more damage. Be that as it may, if you charge him with an environmental misdemeanor, our law firm will undertake his defense for that as well."

"Our technicians are still analyzing the debris," I replied, "but we would like Ignacio to clarify whether there were four beehives in the burned area."

"This line of questioning is not relevant. If you agree, my client will not clarify that point."

Is it because Pancorbo tipped you off about bees as the murder method and you don't want us to find out how much you and your client know about our investigation? I was tempted to ask.

But I didn't. It was only a suspicion, and I didn't want to show my cards to such an expert poker player.

"Last week we didn't ask Ignacio this question, but now it seems relevant," said Estíbaliz. "Where was your client on July twenty-fourth and twenty-fifth?"

"He was at his house in Laguardia and then at his apartment in Vitoria," the lawyer shot back. They had been expecting the question.

"Do you have any witnesses who can back that up?" Estí asked insistently.

"I'm afraid not. Those were quiet days when my client did not meet anybody. But not having an alibi for those days doesn't make him guilty."

"Would you agree, however, that it places him in a difficult position?" said Estíbaliz.

"I have agreed to defend him because I am absolutely convinced of his innocence, inspector. The lack of an alibi does not present a major obstacle."

"Very well, then let's proceed to the most delicate aspect of this case. Did your client know Lidia García de Vicuña?"

"My client will not answer that question. The deceased's parents have yet to make a complaint. Even the publication of images proves nothing."

"We could not disagree more strongly," Estíbaliz responded, shaking her head. "At the very least, the photos show that your client and the young woman knew and trusted each other—something your client explicitly denied to Inspector Ayala and me. That constitutes an obstruction of justice."

"Are you considering taking legal action on that particular point?" the lawyer inquired.

"We reserve the right to do so. If that were the case, you would be informed in due course," said Alba.

"Ignacio," I said, speaking directly to him and ignoring the lawyer, "Tasio has admitted his relationship with Lidia and confirmed that she was your girlfriend first, but that she was only one of many. He told me that by contrast his relationship with her was serious, that it was a long-term one, that your brother—"

"My twin," Ignacio interrupted, unable to restrain himself.

"That your twin was prepared to wait the two years and seven months for her to come of age. He had high hopes for the relationship and was risking a great deal. Were you aware of this?"

I observed him closely. He was growing nervous: the pleasant breeze apparently blowing in Donostia was beginning to trouble him, because he kept pushing a lock of blond hair behind his ear.

I decided to press the point, to see where it took us.

"He believes you decided to arrest him on the day you received the autopsy report—which is currently missing—stating that the semen found in the girl's body was Tasio's. He also believes that you faked the evidence proving his guilt—that is, the yew leaves that matched the poison used for the crimes. If you went to his home as a relative who had an extra set of keys, that's fine. However, by taking another police inspector and conducting a thorough search without a warrant, you violated several laws. I don't understand why the judge didn't rule that your actions were unlawful. What do you have to say? Was that the reason, Ignacio? Did you arrest Tasio because you discovered he and your girlfriend were betraying you?"

Ignacio's face transformed into a mask of pain. He stood up suddenly, knocking over the chair. His knuckles were white. He started shouting, but the lawyer quickly switched off the sound.

A few seconds later, the call was interrupted and, to our astonishment, we found ourselves looking at a blank screen. We stared at one another in silence, but thirty seconds later the lawyer reappeared.

"I'm sorry," he said with a smile that appeared genuine. "I'm afraid there was a technical glitch. I think we can continue now from where we left off."

"Oh, I see, a technical problem. Well, Tasio Ortiz de Zárate had just confessed to his relationship with a minor and stated that your client had also had an affair with her," said Estíbaliz.

"My client will not respond to these baseless accusations. If any legal action were taken in this regard, our law firm would undertake our client's defense."

"I believe we have covered almost all the points we wished to raise," I said. "Although, tell me something, Ignacio, and let's hope we're not interrupted by another technical malfunction. Tasio is getting out of prison in three days. Are you hiding in a bunker in San Sebastián because you're afraid he'll come after you?"

This time, Ignacio was prepared. He stared at me through the webcam, and his face betrayed no sign of emotion.

"My client is not going to answer that question."

"I insist. Ignacio, are you scared that your twin will seek revenge?"

"I think we had better draw this meeting to a close. As I have said, you will receive the recordings on a CD later this morning, addressed to Inspector Unai López de Ayala. Every day you will receive a similar package with twenty-four hours of recordings that will show my client within the boundaries of my properties at all times. On principle, he is not going to leave here until this situation is resolved. I beg you to carry out your duties qiuckly. No one enjoys being under house arrest, however pleasant the views of Donostia. My client used to have a life; it's my job to see that he recovers it."

"Agreed," said Alba. "Thank you very much for your cooperation. If we need to consult you about any new developments, we will be in touch with your firm."

"Please do so," said the lawyer. "Have a good day."

The communication was cut, this time for good.

"Conclusions," said Alba, turning toward us.

"We can rule him out as the murderer," I said.

"But not as the person behind the killings," said Estíbaliz, shaking her head. "He could have hired someone to commit the murders in exactly the same way in order to point the finger elsewhere."

"That's too twisted," I said, voicing my thoughts.

"Everything in this case is too twisted," she retorted.

"For now, he's under control sixty miles away. That, at least, seems like good news. But you're right, all this legal posturing doesn't eliminate him as a suspect, not for the crimes twenty years ago and not for the first two in the most recent series," I said.

"And let's not forget he has no alibi for July twenty-fourth or twenty-fifth."

"Just because he wasn't with anyone doesn't make him a suspect," I insisted.

"Oh, come on! Not even you believe what you are saying. He's such a sociable person. Until the day before yesterday, everybody wanted him for official events. Now you're telling me that on El Día de la Blusa and the night before he hadn't planned to meet anyone, not even his *cuadrilla*?"

"Maybe, after the way his *cuadrilla* has betrayed him, he didn't want to give us any names because he's afraid they might incriminate him?" I said.

"As interesting as this is, I'm going to end this meeting," said Alba. "We all have a long list of urgent tasks to get through this morning. If there is any progress in the investigation, kindly inform me at once."

We agreed, and Estíbaliz and I stood up.

I was alone in my office, so I opened my e-mail to see if I had received any messages.

Among the dozens waiting to be opened, one stood out: yet again, the sender was *Fromjail*.

I opened the e-mail to find a Tasio anxious to meet me:

> Kraken, I think I've just spotted a coincidence that might interest you. I'd like this to be my final contribution to the case.
>
> Come and visit me right away. There's no time to lose.

27

THE CALLE
HONDURAS TOWERS

VITORIA
OCTOBER 1970

The man with the knife snuck up behind him before he had a
chance to turn and run.

"Not a sound," he whispered.

Álvaro dropped his bulky doctor's bag, which fell to the ground
with a thud. He raised his hands slowly in surrender and felt the
tip of the knife dig into the left side of his throat, close to the aorta.

"You can take everything. I won't put up a fight."

The man and his two accomplices were dressed in black. There
was nothing conspicuous about them, no distinguishing characteristics, except that the stocky fellow was brachycephalic, with a flat
back to his skull.

"First, the wristwatch, easy does it," said the tallest of the three,
drawing closer.

Álvaro did as the man told him, trying to control his nerves
and prevent his hands from shaking.

"Now your billfold," the man with the knife said. "Hurry up,
we don't have all night."

Álvaro handed it over, remembering with incredible relief that
only a few days before he had removed the newspaper clipping
about Blanca he had been carrying in his wallet for months. It

had been an intelligent move, and he clung to it now in his blind panic.

Just when Álvaro thought the mugging was over, the beatings started. While the two smaller men held his arms, the third man aimed his blows at Álvaro's upper body, leaving his face untouched. He withstood two punches to his chest, but the third one caught his ribs and he doubled over.

Afterward, the kicks came thick and fast. He protected his head with his hands, curled in a fetal position on the ground. The blows to his back were less painful, but those to his genitals winded him, leaving him giddy and nauseated.

The man with the knife crouched, waving the blade in Álvaro's face. He was sure that was the end. He wouldn't live long enough to pay back the thirty-year loan on the apartment above their heads.

Then the man plunged the blade into Alvaro's left thigh, piercing his flannel trousers, his freckled skin, several blood vessels, and three inches of muscle fiber.

"Keep your hands off what doesn't belong to you, quack," Álvaro heard the figure watching from the shadows say before vanishing behind the columns.

It was very dark, and he couldn't trust his senses, but Doctor Urbina could have sworn he recognized the limp that characterized Javier Ortiz de Zárate's driver.

Once the men left, Álvaro turned his attention to stanching the wound in his thigh. He dragged himself into the bushes beside the path and opened his bag, which his attackers had left. He took out a bandage and wrapped it as tightly as he could around his leg. Then he lay in the undergrowth for several hours, until he was sure Emilia had gone to bed. His wife was easily frightened, and if he told her he had been attacked near the entrance to their home, she would never walk alone there again.

———

Álvaro started to live in fear. He invented excuses so he would never be alone, and he tried not to let his wife and sons go out without him. He avoided the city center and refused his more prosperous colleagues' invitations for a drink on Calle Dato or for tapas at the Txapela, no matter how enticing the aroma of fried squid was after attending Sunday Mass at San Mateo.

And he steered clear of Calle General Álava.

On the day of her five-month checkup, Blanca showed up at the clinic with her husband.

Álvaro lowered his head. He felt like the whipped dog Felisa had described. He didn't have the strength to confront Javier Ortiz de Zárate.

He'd had enough.

So this was how Zárate kept a man, a firm, a city under his control.

"How are you, doctor? Is everything going well?" Javier shook his hand, a little too forcefully, Álvaro thought.

"Everything's fine, Don Javier," he replied, without so much as a glance at Blanca. She remained silent, cowed by her husband's presence. "What brings you here?"

Javier sat down without waiting to be asked. Blanca remained standing, her belly protruding.

"I wanted to see for myself that everything is in order. I'm referring to my wife's pregnancy."

"Yes, of course. The latest blood tests are normal, although a couple of the results surprised me. With your permission, I'd like to examine your wife," Álvaro said, terrified. He stood up, disguising the limp caused by the stab wound.

"Go ahead, doctor. Carry on."

Javier looked straight at him, and Álvaro sensed a provocation in his words. A kind of perverse challenge. The game nauseated him, but he managed to suppress it.

"Now, let's see about this heartbeat, Doña Blanca. If you would sit down on the examination table and unbutton the lower part of your blouse, please."

Blanca obeyed without saying a word.

"Lie on your left side. I'm going to find your baby's heartbeat," he said, probing the zone between Blanca's navel and pelvis.

He palpated her belly, looking for an area that was harder and flatter, which might indicate the baby's back, but the one he found seemed rather small.

Nevertheless, he concentrated his search there, ignoring Javier's questioning looks, and listened for a rapid heartbeat.

It was then he discovered two separate heartbeats, both faster than their mother's.

"Doña Blanca, you are expecting twins," he managed to declare.

"Twins?" Javier exclaimed. "Twins! Like my uncles Ignacio and Anastasio. It runs in families, doesn't it? I've heard that if the father has an uncle or aunt who is a twin, he is more likely to produce them as well."

Statistics showed that the likelihood of having twins came from the mother's side, but Doctor Urbina said nothing; he just nodded wholeheartedly. The absence of doubt in Javier's mind about the twins' paternity was Álavaro's life insurance.

"Quite right, Don Javier. You have perpetuated a special family legacy. I think you already have names for your sons"—Urbina congratulated him but stopped short of clapping his muscular back—"assuming they are boys, of course."

Javier looked at him, offended.

"And what else would they be, doctor? Don't bother me with gloomy predictions. They'll be boys, just like their father."

"Of course they will be," murmured Álvaro, not wishing to contradict him.

When the industrialist and his wife finally left, Álvaro had a panic attack. A concerned Felisa administered a sedative and helped him lie down on the examination table until his heart rate slowed.

A few days later he received a call. The caller let the phone ring four times, then hung up.

How could she know what he had been through?

He did not go to the Calle General Álava apartment. He spent the next few weeks in a state of lethargy, counting the days until Blanca's due date.

Álvaro was a bundle of nerves waiting for Javier and Blanca's next appointment. Even the small dose of morphine he took shortly before he they were due to arrive didn't help.

At exactly twelve o'clock, Blanca entered, wearing an orange, black, and brown dress with flared sleeves that disguised her curves beneath its generous folds.

"My husband couldn't come. He had to go to Sestao, the blast furnaces, at the last minute. We're on our own."

"Good, let's proceed with the examination," he replied, refusing to look at her.

"You didn't come to the apartment when I called. You've left me, haven't you?"

I've left you? he thought, feeling helpless. "I think he knows. It's possible that he knows," said Álvaro. He rose from his chair, suddenly tired of it all, locked the door, and lowered his pants in front of Blanca.

"What . . . what are you doing?" she asked, embarrassed.

"Two months and five days ago, twenty-four hours after our last meeting at your aunt's apartment, three men mugged me in my doorway. They beat me up and left me with this scar. A fourth man was watching, directing them from the shadows. I think it was your driver. I didn't report the incident. Ever since your husband was admitted to the hospital, I haven't wanted the police anywhere near me."

Blanca clapped her hands over her mouth, unable to take her

eyes off the red gash on Álvaro's thigh. The blood drained from her face.

"Maybe he'll do the same to you once you've had the twins. For God's sake, Blanca! Your husband probably knows all about us, and after the birth, he'll finish what he started."

Blanca leaned her elbows on the desk and closed her eyes, shaking her head as she tried to collect her thoughts.

"I want nothing more to do with this," Álvaro went on, pulling up his pants and fastening his belt. "I'll keep my word and deliver your sons or daughters. But after that, I don't want to know. I . . . I'm thinking of escaping to America."

"What about your wife and sons?" she asked.

"I'm a registered doctor. I have life insurance. Besides, physicians' widows and orphans are well looked after. She'll receive a generous payout, and she and the boys can go back to her family in the village. They'll live simply, but they will want for nothing. They'll be better off without me."

"What about your sons?" insisted Blanca. "Are you prepared to abandon them?" She wasn't thinking about the two flame-haired boys she had seen with him on two occasions, but about the twins she was about to have.

"My sons? They're becoming a couple of spoiled brats here in the city. They're constantly asking me to buy them things. I'm not a very affectionate father, Blanca. I'm a shy person, and I find it difficult to show my feelings. But I'm little more than a billfold to them. In the village there are no shops, kiosks, or toy stores. For a long time, I've been thinking they'd be better off there. As for Emilia, look at her. She is incapable of adapting. My colleagues' wives laugh at her behind her back; they don't ask her over for coffee. It's only natural, she left school before she learned how to do basic math. She talks too much . . . she'll never be happy in Vitoria.

"I'm not asking you to come with me, because I know you'll

refuse. Some people know how to take the beatings; they learn to put up with them as time goes on. That is their strength. But they don't know how to run away—the very thought of an unfamiliar world paralyzes them. I think you are one of those people."

Blanca kept a troubled silence.

"You see, you can't say I'm wrong. I'm tired of being a whipped dog. I can't do this anymore."

The remainder of the appointment went as planned. Doctor Urbina read the results of her most recent blood tests, listened to two tiny heartbeats, and advised Doña Blanca to get plenty of rest.

28

ZUGARRAMURDI

FRIDAY, AUGUST 5

I'm waiting, #Kraken.

Tasio was waiting for me in the usual room. This time he had a number of old envelopes and handwritten letters spread over the counter between us. There was something new in his expression as well, a gleam in his eye that an optimist would have called hope.

"This time the killer struck in the eighteenth century, on the balcony of San Miguel. Have you thought of guarding potential sites for the next murders?"

We're on it, but what good will it do?

"What did you find, Tasio?" I said, ignoring his question. "I hope it's important. I have a hell of a day ahead of me."

"That's precisely why I called you here so quickly. I heard about your meeting with my . . . collaborator. You gave him a job to do, one that you gave to me as well. So we've compared results and we've found something I think is important to share with you, but it's going to be hard for you personally to accept this conclusion. I want you to be open-minded and to think like a detective, okay?"

"Are you really asking me to be open-minded?" I almost laughed. "Here I am, listening to you, when everybody else thinks you're a murderer and a pedophile."

He gave me a hard look. Usually that would have intimidated me so much that I wouldn't have been able to speak, but today Tasio was less forbidding than usual.

"Several decades ago I had a colleague for my esoteric explorations. We used to be great friends, but things ended badly, even though he continued writing to me during my early days in prison, expressing his support and his pride at the sacrifices I made to keep the flame of paganism alight in this region. I ignored him—I never answered any of his letters. There's a whole range of people who admire serial killers. Some just want to feel close to danger; others admire you for having had the courage to act out their fantasies. A lot of women come on to you for sex—nothing more, nothing less. Others want to heal damaged individuals; that's their emotional trigger. They have a long history of relationships with alcoholics, drug addicts, and chronic or terminally ill people. And finally, though fortunately not very common are the most dangerous of all: those who would like to be the murderer. These admirers think getting in touch with a serial killer is the first step toward gaining access to the criminal underworld. He was one of them. After we had . . . certain differences, I began to think he really was dangerous and mad."

"So far you haven't given me a thing."

"Be patient, Kraken. We're getting there. MatuSalem has discovered a link between his nickname and his Twitter account. I had no idea he was following me on social media, but in fact he's one of my most active followers and the first to publish the image of the victims of the Virgen Blanca crimes. That means he must have been close to the scene."

"But why would he draw attention to himself like that?"

"These crimes are very visual. The murderer makes the scenes public because he wants us to admire his handiwork."

"That's strange, people say the same thing about you."

He ignored my comment, and went on: "This individual has a criminal record for drug trafficking; that's why we started looking into him."

"Okay, now this is starting to interest me."

"We were surprised when MatuSalem discovered his real name and verified that he is your partner's brother," said Tasio, peering at me to see how I would react.

"Excuse me?"

In some ways this was the best possible news, because at last I had concrete proof of his link to the case. But it was also the worst, because of the effect it would have on Estíbaliz.

"His name is Eneko Ruiz de Gauna, although he's known by several nicknames. I knew him as the Eguzkilore and El Hierbas. In fact, he must still use that one, because @elhierbas is his Twitter handle. There's no sense hiding anything from you at this stage: twenty years ago Eneko was my pusher. Although he was only a kid, we shared an interest in the region's pagan past and we saw quite a lot of each other. Nowadays he's the manager of a store below Doña Otxanda's Tower—"

"I know that," I interrupted. "But what evidence do you have to support what you're claiming?"

"It'll be in your inbox before you leave."

"Fine, Tasio. If you think he's capable of something like this, tell me about him. But I also need to know why your friendship ended so abruptly?"

"We had a bad experience at Zugarramurdi." He looked away. "It's not a pleasant memory."

"Yet another reason for you to tell me."

"Eneko was a fundamentalist when it came to anything esoteric. He was also a faithful proponent of using drugs to alter perception, very much like the creative experiments Aldous Huxley conducted with peyote or mescaline in the fifties. I don't know if you've read *The Doors of Perception,* but it was on his bedside table. I was interested in the anthropological aspect of Zugarramurdi, but Eneko took it to extremes. I should have seen it coming.

"There were four of us—two couples. He led us in a ceremony, an ancestral rite based on the confessions of the people accused of witchcraft in the Logroño trials. I never thought they were genuine: The confessions were largely obtained by force, if not by torture. Most of the accused were terrified and simply said what they thought was necessary to collaborate with the Holy Office during the Inquisition. They expressed the fantasies and imaginary worlds of people of the seventeenth century. But El Hierbas took everything literally. He instructed each couple to strip and hold hands. He placed *eguzkilores* on the ground and gave us a potion to drink. That was when the nightmare started."

"What nightmare?"

"Whatever he gave us was a paralytic drug that brought on hallucinations. I imagine the dismal atmosphere inside the cave contributed to it, but it was the most terrifying experience I've ever had. I couldn't move, although I was still conscious. I could see shadowy figures at the edges of my vision, presences I knew weren't really there, but I felt vulnerable because I couldn't move, and the figures seemed threatening. . . . In all honesty, they were petrifying. I was also scared that the paralysis would spread to my lungs and I would suffocate. The experience lasted several hours. Eneko was the first to be able to stir again: we lay there naked, watching him weave his way among us chanting, while we were unable to move a muscle. I swear that at that moment I wanted to—"

"Kill him?"

Tasio took a deep breath but didn't fall into the trap. "We were dying. As soon as we could get up, the two girls and I got dressed and left in my car. After that, I didn't want to have anything to do with him. That's why, when he wrote me these letters, I ignored him."

He held up the letters on the other side of the security glass.

I pointed to them. "I'm going to need the correspondence as well."

"They're all yours. I don't want them. They'll show you just how rotten someone's mind can be."

I glanced at my watch. It was late. I started to get up and say good-bye. "Thanks for this. You get out in two days. Will you stay nearby?"

"Are you asking if I plan to abscond?" he said with a smile.

"I just want to know what to do if I need you for anything else . . . unofficially."

"I'm not going to mess everything up now. I've served most of a sentence for murders I didn't commit, but I'm forty-five years old and I can still enjoy something that resembles a life when I'm finally released for good," he said, as if I had offended him.

"I bet it's not the release you were expecting."

"No, it's not. Nothing is what I was expecting. Everyone in Vitoria hates me because of Lidia. For twenty years, I've been dreaming about walking the streets of the city. I don't think I'll be able to do that now. But you know how to reach me if you need to, Kraken. Nothing you haven't done until now."

With that he stood up, motioned to the guard supervising the visitors' room, and disappeared.

I left the prison and called my partner. We agreed to meet in front of the New Cathedral. I didn't want any witnesses to hear what we had to say to each other.

We met, both looking serious, by the Plaza de Lovaina. All around us, the *cuadrillas* were cavorting through the streets to the sound of blaring brass bands.

"It seems strange that people are still having fun despite what happened here last night," I said. "Perhaps it would be better for everyone if the fiestas were canceled."

"But maybe that's the real purpose of the fiestas. Despite disasters, deaths, and wars, life goes on. Maybe that's what our ancestors wanted to teach us. Whatever happens, we need to celebrate La Noche de San Juan, Christmas, Easter Week, a birthday, an anniversary," Estíbaliz reflected. "Come on, Kraken, let's go in."

There was a hidden garden on Calle Magdalena that few people visited. Inside stood a giant sequoia that was over a hundred and sixty feet tall. It took five people holding hands to encircle its trunk. Estíbaliz had introduced me to this quiet corner years earlier, when the word *partner* began to mean something more than "work colleague," and I stopped seeing her simply as a friend from my deceased wife's *cuadrilla*.

We sat on our bench, staring straight ahead. The noise of the fiesta was muffled; it sounded almost like a memory. I didn't know how to begin the conversation.

"Estí, I've just come from talking to Tasio. You're not going to like what he told me, but I wanted to speak to you before I report it officially."

"My God, that's the worst preparation for bad news I've ever heard. Go on, spit it out."

You asked for it.

"Do you remember the episode at Zugarramurdi that Ignacio told us about in his apartment?"

"Yeah."

"Today Tasio told me the same story, from his point of view. He talked about a drug that kept them paralyzed for hours. And the mysterious kid who gave it to them was your brother."

"What?"

"Did you know your brother and Tasio were friends?"

"He's my brother. He has his own life. I've never kept an eye on his friends, especially when I was young."

"He was already a good-for-nothing back then, Estíbaliz. He used drugs and sold them. We all knew it."

"Is that all you have to tell me, Kraken?"

"No. Here is a man whose nickname is Eguzkilore, like the signature at the crime scenes. He lives by and for the esoteric, the pagan. He used to write admiring letters to Tasio when he was sent to prison and now is one of Tasio's most active Twitter followers. And this person was at the crime scene yesterday only minutes after the bodies were found. In fact, he was the first person to upload the images of the victims."

Estíbaliz gritted her teeth.

"You knew, and you said nothing to me," I went on. "You knew it was his Twitter account."

"That doesn't implicate him. Other people uploaded the images, but you don't think they're guilty."

"Estíbaliz, the evidence is mounting. Lutxo told me that last weekend your brother was determined to go back to the cave at Zugarramurdi, that he was talking about the double crimes, and that everyone thought it was weird for him to be so excited about them."

"Eneko is like that, Kraken. He's extreme: it's all or nothing. He expresses himself violently, and there's no filter between what he thinks and what he says. Yes, he's a difficult person, but—"

"Hear me out, Estí. I'm finding this as hard as you are. I have more things on my list: He knows how to deal with bees, because you two were brought up with them. As you said, he dealt with them, because you were too nervous and they stung you."

"That doesn't make him a serial killer."

"He's also used to handling drugs and knows the effects of many different ones. That would give him easy access to Rohypnol. And now he has a store in the center of the city, below Doña Otxanda's Tower. His van is well known in Vitoria. He could have easily transferred the bodies from there to the Old Cathedral, the Casa del Cordón, and the balcony of San Miguel Arcángel Church without arousing suspicion. And last but not least, he has red hair. Or he did. Just like the stonemason's apprentice. Don Tiburcio told me he suspected his father used to beat him. I'm sorry to have to say all this, Estíbaliz, but there are too many coincidences to ignore. Do you know if your brother worked at San Vicentejo one summer?"

"I can't say he did, but I can't rule it out, either. My brother began to earn a few extra pesetas early on. Sometimes he would go down to the Laguardia region for the grape harvest; other times he repaired roofs in villages. But I can't follow your reasoning, Unai. I really can't. Do you seriously believe he committed those crimes twenty years ago, when he was no more than fifteen?"

"At fifteen your brother was already as tall as a man, and the victims were babies, children aged five and ten, and two not very strongly built fifteen-year-olds. He could have easily done it. Who would have suspected that a fifteen-year-old kid could throw a whole nation into a panic?"

She shook her head again. "You don't have anything, not a single piece of real evidence, not even a fingerprint. Nothing places him at the crime scenes. You've told me about coincidences that you're determined to twist until they fit your version of events."

I sighed and leaned back against the bench.

"Think like the profiling expert you are, and come up with a motive," she insisted. "You're always saying that the motive for a crime is personal, intimate. What motive could my brother have had for killing all those children years ago or the adults our age now?"

"I think the red-haired youngster who listened to the stonemason's stories embraced the occult paraphernalia. He created a scenario inspired by the imagery of the chapel at San Vicentejo. He's portraying his own journey of initiation as the different ages of man. Each crime scene is a physical projection of his mental state."

"And how does implicating the twins fit into your theory?"

"Your brother wanted to get revenge on Tasio. Maybe because he was bitter that Tasio wouldn't join him in his occult games. They went to Zugarramurdi with two girls. If one of them was your brother's partner, I'm sure that at least one of them was a minor. Your brother must have known about Tasio's problems, and that's why he killed Lidia García de Vicuña. What better way to implicate Tasio and defy the twins?"

"None of this holds water, Kraken. Your reasoning is weak. To do what he's doing, to have planned everything to destroy the twins' lives, my brother must hate them. Otherwise, it's too much trouble for such a feeble motive."

Estíbaliz's words made me doubt my theory.

"You're not convinced, either, are you?" she said, taking my chin in her hand. "I'm looking you in the eye and I can tell that there's a sliver of doubt, that you're not one hundred percent convinced. Unai, I know you're going to dismiss what I'm about to say. You don't like it when somebody tells you something straight out, but here goes: Tasio Ortiz de Zárate has brainwashed you. You should never have been given this case—you've always had an unhealthy obsession with Tasio, which makes you easy prey. You joined the force because of him, because at twenty you thought you had solved the case. Paula told me: it was something about you she didn't particularly like. Tasio makes you feel like the chosen one, and now he's leading you around by the nose. He's had twenty years to think everything over. Do you really believe that anything that happened this week was a coincidence?"

"Don't bring Paula into this," I said. "She has nothing to do with it."

"And neither does Eneko."

"But he does, Estíbaliz. It seems your brother does have something to do with it."

"Don't you realize what's going on? Twenty years later, and it's the same thing: I'm about to hand over my brother. I'm not Ignacio, and I won't follow his lead. I will not give up like he did when he was faced with circumstantial evidence. I'm going to follow other lines of inquiry, which is what a sister should do."

I stood up and looked at the sky, trying to rest my eyes. All I could see were the sequoia's leafy branches.

"Let me think about it over weekend, Estíbaliz. I need to let all this settle. I've been putting this off, but I'm going to talk to your brother. Just talk, but I'll have to inform the DSU. If my brother were a suspect, you'd do the same thing. You'd have to do it. We can't let our personal affairs blind us."

Estíbaliz stood up as well. She looked at the ground and kicked a small pebble.

"Can't let our personal affairs blind us. Kraken, it's strange to hear you say that."

With that, she slipped away like a snake.

Did she know something was going on between Alba and me?

29

THE UNZUETA MANSION

VITORIA
FEBRUARY 1971

The people of Vitoria would remember that February first for many years to come, because it was the biggest snowfall of the century.

There weren't enough snowplows to clear the city's main roads. Emergency services workers got up an hour early to dig out SEAT 600s and Renault Toros from beneath three feet of snow. Then, armed with bottles of alcohol, they scraped the ice off their windshields with pieces of hard plastic and a great deal of patience.

Doctor Urbina was in his office, poring over a handbook on mammary diseases, feeling almost glad to be able to enjoy a quiet morning. All his patients had canceled their appointments. Felisa was rearranging the instruments on his shelves for the third time, somewhat ill at ease being idle.

The telephone interrupted his reading, and he picked it up absentmindedly.

"Doctor Urbina's practice, how may I help you?"

"Doctor Urbina!" Javier Ortiz de Zárate's voice boomed. "I need you at my house this instant! My wife has gone into labor."

Thirty-two weeks, Álvaro thought, making a mental calculation. He didn't need to verify the date; he had thought of nothing else for months.

"Today of all days? Heavens! This is a little premature, even for twins. You must bring her to the hospital as soon as possible. I'll book an operating room right away," he insisted, trying to steady his nerves.

"You don't understand," replied Javier. "I'm telling you to come here at once. No vehicles can get beyond Paseo de la Senda, the roads are under three feet of snow, and the plows haven't reached us yet."

"Don't worry, I'll call for an ambulance myself. The drivers are trained to deal with these situations."

"I've already called, and the ambulances are all busy. Evidently there are a lot of casualties, people slipping or being trapped in their homes. You need to come here to attend to my sons!" Javier yelled.

All right, thought Álvaro. *All right.*

"How is the mother doing?" he inquired, his tone shifting.

"Well, she's in labor, screaming her head off."

"Have her waters broken yet?"

"Please be more specific, doctor. I know nothing of such things. I thought she would take care of everything."

"Has there been any clear liquid?" he insisted.

"No, there's been blood; the bed is soaked. But that's normal during labor, isn't it?"

Álvaro leaped from his chair. "I'll try and get to your house with my nurse. Stay by your wife's side. We're leaving the clinic now."

He slipped into his coat, took all the basic equipment for an emergency delivery that would fit into his medical bag, and called for Felisa. She was already pulling on her snow boots with a look of concern.

It took them almost an hour to cover the half mile separating the clinic from the Unzueta family mansion. They entered Paseo de la

Senda, where in some places they had to wade through fresh snow. Despite her age, the hardy Felisa seemed at home in the situation and strode ahead. She had probably grown up in a village in the mountains, and Álvaro realized how little he knew about her life.

When they reached the entrance to the mansion at last, Javier was waiting by the iron gates.

The main door to the house was in a side street off Paseo de la Senda. A thick hedge, now laden with snow, hid the garden from the prying eyes of passersby.

Ulysses was busy shoveling the snow on the driveway into mounds. Suppressing a shudder, the doctor raised his coat collar and walked by without looking at him.

Álvaro ran upstairs, alerted by Blanca's screams. When he reached the bedroom, he found her lying in bed, semiconscious in a pool of blood, the first baby's head already crowning.

Blanca looked at him in relief, her hair plastered to her sweaty brow. She didn't have the strength to talk, only to steel herself for the next contraction.

Felisa followed a few steps behind Doctor Urbina, carrying his bag. Observing the scene, she turned to Blanca's husband and said in a firm voice:

"Don Javier, fathers cannot be present during labor. Don't worry, I'll bring your sons to you as soon as they're born. This is a multiple birth and will take several hours. Go down to the kitchen and ask them to give you a cup of tea, or a brandy."

"I'm not going anywhere! I want to make sure my sons are all right. Do you think I'm squeamish about a little blood?"

"I'm sure you aren't. However, we make no exceptions. Fathers aren't allowed in an operating room, and my job during a home birth is to keep you away. It's for the good of your sons, Don Javier. You wouldn't want us all to get flustered and for the babies not to get enough oxygen, would you?"

"No, but make sure you see to it that my sons are born healthy.

I won't forgive any medical negligence when it comes to my sons."

"Then we're agreed you should wait outside," Felisa said, closing the door on him without waiting for a reply.

She went over to the bed, where Álvaro had started telling Blanca to push.

Álvaro was also in a panic. Under normal circumstances, he would never have agreed to attend such a high-risk delivery outside a hospital. There was every chance that one of the babies would have a problem, or that the mother would bleed to death. And yet, having seen the silent warning, the unspoken threat, on Javier's face, he knew what would happen to him if one of the babies wasn't born completely healthy.

The scar on his leg was unusually painful, probably because of the humidity from the snow. It was excruciating. He had never been as lame as that morning.

He didn't dare speak freely to Blanca, for fear her husband might be listening outside the door, so he employed a language of silent glances and, when necessary, squeezed her hand.

She seemed to understand and clung to him with all her might.

The first baby was a boy, blond like his mother, slender and with an oval face. Álvaro suctioned the fluids from his mouth and handed him to Blanca.

She lay back on the bed, smiling, the weight of the tiny infant on her chest. She longed to fall asleep, to close her eyes and rest for a while, with the warmth of Álvaro's last gift to her: their first baby son.

"You have to keep pushing, Doña Blanca," Álvaro said, interrupting her reverie as he forced himself simply to be her doctor. "There's one more to come." Blanca rallied.

Felisa wrapped Ignacio Ortiz de Zárate in a blanket, and they continued with the delivery. Twenty minutes later, Tasio was born, identical to his brother.

Álvaro clamped the umbilical cord before cutting it.

They placed the twins on either side of Blanca, and Felisa and Álvaro looked at each other with relief. The babies had strong lungs, good muscle tone, and a heart rate that exceeded a hundred beats per minute: their Apgar score was eight, which wasn't bad for premature twins.

Hearing the babies cry, Javier started to pound on the door.

"Is everything okay? Why won't you let me see my sons?" he shouted, becoming frantic.

"Don Javier, we're making your wife comfortable, and we'll open the door in a moment!" shouted Felisa, without moving from Blanca's side.

"Felisa, you take care of the babies, I have to make sure she expels the placenta," Álvaro said anxiously.

Something wasn't right; he could sense it.

He had delivered several sets of twins, but Blanca was still having contractions.

"It's not possible," he whispered, when he realized what was happening. "Felisa, come here. I think there's a third baby."

"A third? How can that be?" she said in a low voice. She wanted to avoid another outburst from the master of the house and feared what would happen if he learned the news.

"I think his brothers must have hidden the heartbeat from me, because they were in a more exposed position. He's in a different amniotic sac and seems to be presenting headfirst, so with any luck she won't need a cesarean." He was concerned for Blanca. She had lost a lot of blood, and he didn't want to risk performing surgery outside an operating room.

He drew closer to Blanca and spoke to her slowly, to be sure she heard him.

"Blanca, you're having triplets. The baby's head is almost crowning. A few more pushes and it'll all be over, I promise."

He allowed himself to plant a last kiss on her brow, while Felisa pretended not to see.

A few minutes later, the third baby was born. It was another boy. No one had been expecting him, so no one had even thought of a name for him.

Álvaro helped his little head emerge, and when he saw it, his mind went blank. He forgot that he was a doctor, he forgot that he was in a slave trader's mansion, and he forgot that an irate husband was pounding on the door, eager to regain control.

In a state of shock, he held up the baby, still joined to its mother by the umbilical cord, and showed him to Blanca.

The boy looked nothing like his brothers.

Blanca and Álvaro stared at the infant in horror, not knowing what to do. The baby had a mop of red hair identical to Doctor Urbina's. Javier Ortiz de Zárate was on the other side of the door, threatening to break it down.

30

CASA DE LAS JAQUECAS

MONDAY, AUGUST 8

This is one of the worst stages on the hero's journey: the dark night of the soul, the most difficult decision. #DoItRight, #Kraken.

I was not in the best mood. After spending the weekend going over how to deal with Estíbaliz's brother, I had decided to follow my professional ethics, even if it hurt. Even if I lost her.

I stayed in Villaverde, because I didn't want to go back to Vitoria. I was fleeing its noisy atmosphere, fleeing the embarrassed way my *cuadrilla* treated me, fleeing my sleeplessness over the main fiesta weekend.

At least the heat wave had abated—on Sunday the temperature dropped by almost fifteen degrees, which was a relief to everyone.

Germán and Martina came for Sunday lunch with Grandfather and me, using the excuse that they were bringing me the special Virgen Blanca cake, a delicacy made of strawberries and cream mousse, with toasted meringue. It was something I never missed. I was silently grateful for this apparently unruffled support. Martina was telling us she had finished her chemotherapy treatments, and now she just had to go back for a checkup in six months.

"Why don't you get away for a few days in August to cele-brate?" I encouraged them. "Go somewhere where it's really cool, where the heat doesn't melt the asphalt."

I wanted to get them as far away as possible from the daily horror Vitoria was experiencing, from the fiestas, from the veiled threat the murderer posed for us all.

"You know, we might just do that, Unai," said Germán thoughtfully. "Come with us."

You know I can't.

"That's not a bad idea," I lied. "We can talk about it after the fiestas."

I knew I shouldn't have gone out for a run early that Monday morning. The streets wouldn't belong to me; they'd be ruled by drunks and those engaged in last-minute sexual encounters. But I couldn't bear the fact that Alba and I had reached a stalemate, and I hated the coldness her position forced her to assume when we met in her office.

I put on a thin hooded top and leaped out into the square while it was still dark and cool. I ran along the pedestrian streets and around the medieval quarter. I decided to stay away from the bands and headed for La Florida Park. On my right, the park's thick tree trunks protected couples from indiscreet eyes as they lay in the grass, frantically offering true love even though they had just met half an hour before.

After thirty minutes I felt ridiculous and slightly pathetic for thinking these things at my age and so, frustrated, did an about-face when I reached Casa de las Jaquecas, at the start of Paseo de Fray Francisco de Vitoria. Each of the Atlases holding up its balcony had a hand on his head as if in pain. I also had a headache from thinking so much and getting nowhere.

Then I saw her. The city was still dark, but the deep indigo sky heralded day. Alba was running with her earbuds in, ignoring several men who whistled and made unintelligible comments as she ran past. Then she saw me.

Then she saw me.

"What are you listening to?" I asked, falling in step with her.

"'Wonderwall,' the Ed Sheeran version," she replied, passing me one of the earbuds.

And you're my wonderwall, I thought to myself.

"Why are you listening to that?"

"It takes my mind off things. This week is crucial, Kraken."

I came to a stop, sick of everything. The white cable tugged at her, forcing her to stop beside me, beneath one of the huge horse chestnuts lining the walk. I have no idea how old it is.

"I don't want to be Kraken now! I don't want you to talk about the case. I don't want you to ask me about trauma, or my wife, and I don't want to know anything about your husband. I want more than a few minutes in the early morning to talk about who we are," I almost shouted. I was astonished at my fury—it had just spilled out.

"Do you know what *wonderwall* means, you idiot?" she said, standing there, arms akimbo.

"It's a kind of therapy practiced in certain British psychiatric hospitals," I said. "A wall where the patients put photographs of relatives, friends, or places they want to live."

"That's not what I was referring to. A wonderwall is a person you're completely obsessed with because they inspire you like crazy," she said, poking me in the chest.

Then she pulled my hood up and did the same with hers.

"Is that an invitation to kiss you?" I asked.

Sorry, but you're my boss and I need to know if you're sure.

"Half of Vitoria knows you, so we can't do this in the middle of the street," she said, her face hidden in the dark shadows of her hood.

"All right."

All right.

"Okay, so let's see who can reach my doorway first," I suggested. "If we go quickly, I bet the people out now are too drunk to pay attention to two obsessive runners."

Alba didn't reply but set off down the street toward the center of the city. She was good at sprints, and it took me a while to catch up with her and match her strides. We ran the thousand yards in a little more than four minutes.

We reached my still-dark doorway at almost the same time. I took out my keys and concentrated on opening the door on my first attempt, so I didn't seem completely useless. Alba was about to head down the hallway toward the stairs, but I knew that wasn't a good idea.

"No, here," I called out, my crotch throbbing.

"Here?" she asked doubtfully, still breathing heavily from the race.

"Don't worry about the noise: My neighbors are a hundred years old. They're deaf as posts."

I think we had sex too furiously, without affection, like soldiers who are angry because they've been sent to the front and know they're about to die. Maybe that was how we felt, resentful of the lives we were leading.

She pushed her hand into my running pants and gripped my erection. I did the same with her, slipping my fingers into her moist body and taking hold of her.

"Let's see how elastic your leggings are," I said.

We touched one another, our hands trapped in our clothes, staring into each other's eyes the entire time. It was as though we were creditors reclaiming an ancient debt.

I thought I was going to explode. I had had sex with other women, of course, but those times had been soulless. With Alba it was different. It was like another one of our conversations: frank, without anesthetic, and with no pretense at politeness. *This is what I am, and this is how I do it. I don't even expect you to like it,* she seemed to be telling me.

But I did like it. God, I liked it so much. Her way of taking me, with no regard for gentleness or coy looks, drove me wild.

Alba didn't ask permission. She simply took what she needed from me to reach her climax, and then she was strong enough to allow me to take what I wanted.

I positioned her as if I were going to frisk her, raised her arms above her head, seized her hands in mine, and pushed them against the door, almost as if she were being crucified. I used my knees to spread her legs, so that she was staring at the few remaining minutes of darkness coming in from the Plaza de la Virgen Blanca, where hundreds of locals were streaming past right in front of us on the other side of the doorway, completely oblivious to the incredible fuck that was about to take place behind that heavy wooden door.

"This is for calling me an idiot," I whispered in her ear, pulling down her leggings. What did she expect after she had insulted me like that?

I bit her earlobe, which was already burning hot. I ran my hand up the triangle formed by her thighs, then turned it over and let the back of it stroke the skin still in the shadows. I moved my hand up to her groin, gently stroking until it was as wet as I wanted, then let two fingers push inside her. I could sense her body trembling, and I couldn't wait any longer to penetrate her. Alba threw her head back but could move little else as I clasped her hands again above her head. I took her by the chin and turned her toward me. Her mouth sought mine, and she moaned as much as I did.

"God, you move so well, Unai," I think she groaned.

We weren't superheroes and didn't last very long. I think we wanted each other too badly, because we climaxed almost together, and then there was only my labored breathing in her ear and my Kraken's embrace crushing the body of this woman who had thrown me into such confusion in the past two weeks, and with whom I had just had fabulous sex in an old doorway.

"That's the best view I've ever had," she said with a slight smile. She snuggled between my arms, as if asking me to embrace her even tighter.

"Mine was better. I could see your back as well as the square," I said with a laugh, laying my head on her shoulder.

"Day is dawning," she said, as if it wasn't obvious.

"Alba, like your name."

"Aren't you going to let me come up to your apartment?"

The spell was broken.

"If you really insisted, I'd let you, but I'd rather not," I said. I was uneasy and released my grip on her. Why lie?

"All right," she said. She sounded distant again, as if my reply was of no importance. She put her leggings and sports bra back on, then her T-shirt and sweatshirt, almost as if I wasn't there.

She didn't turn around, just raised her hood and slipped out into a Vitoria where it was already day. She lowered her head and sped off, every inch a running fanatic who refused to change her routine even for las Fiestas de la Virgen Blanca.

The sound of the door slamming echoed for a good while. I stood in the doorway gazing into space, my shorts around my knees.

You really are an idiot, Unai.

I went up to the third floor, opened the door, and looked around the apartment. How could I have let her see the state my life was in?

And what state are you in, Unai? I asked myself for the first time in a long while.

It was only then I realized just how damaged I was.

How I had not managed to turn the page.

Framed photos of Paula were everywhere. All along the hall-way, on the TV stand, the right-hand table by my bed. I sat on the mattress and picked up another framed image. A 4-D scan of our children. Sepia outlines that suggested a nose like mine, lips like Paula's, tiny hands I had imagined clutching mine.

I felt dreadful. I felt dirty and sweaty, and I smelled like a quick fuck and shared saliva. I got into the shower, and then I realized that Germán was right: I hadn't gotten over it. I had been fooling myself. I stepped out of the shower, still dripping wet and covered in soap. I didn't even think about grabbing a towel; I just went straight back into the living room. Dismayed, I saw my apartment through someone else's eyes: it was a shrine, a shrine to Paula and our children.

I collapsed in horror onto the sofa, soaking it in. For the first time I looked around my apartment—where until now I had thought I had recovered from their deaths—with the clinical gaze of a professional profiler.

I had built my own wonderwall, a wall I could escape into and convince myself that Paula and our babies were still there.

I don't throw things in anger, especially because they've been paid for thanks to a dangerous job. But right then, I was on the verge of and destroying everything in front of me. I looked at the family I had once had and knew they didn't deserve that.

So I choked back my anger and tears. I took a box from under the bed and put all the photographs from my past life into it. I had to keep going. I had to cross the line, to let it pass, to let them go.

I found a thick marker, taped up the box, and wrote *Paula and the kids* on it. I shaved, dressed, had breakfast, and went down to the parking lot carrying the box. I put it into the Outlander's trunk. I would wait for it to gather dust in my grandfather's attic in Villaverde.

————

When I reached the Lakua headquarters, I was in a foul mood, lost in my own thoughts. I had no desire to speak to anyone, so I went straight to my office and buried myself in the backlog of reports.

Estíbaliz poked her long red bangs around the door and came in tentatively. She immediately saw there was more weight on my shoulders than simply our difference of opinion over her brother.

She came over to me, openly studying me, but she stayed quiet. I think she knew me well enough not to throw fuel on the fire.

"Have you seen the news about Tasio?" I asked.

"What do you mean, about Tasio?"

"He's being released from Zaballa in five minutes. All the Spanish TV channels are there, as well as several from Europe and America. I think there are even two from South Africa."

"You're joking."

"No."

"Look, I don't know who's done what to you today, but let's watch his release live. Maybe that will help you snap out of it," she said, pushing me aside with her hip and leaning over my computer to open the link. "Let's see SuperTasio again after twenty years. You didn't think you'd be the only one who had a chance to see him, did you? There's lots of interest in what he looks like after all this time."

"If you only knew . . ." I said listlessly.

We sat watching a Spanish news channel. They were transmitting live, and we could see the entrance to the supermax prison. It was packed with TV crews from around the world and people holding posters calling for Tasio's head. There was barely room for the inmate to emerge.

As always, Tasio exceeded all expectations.

Behind the white CNN and BBC News vans, a black stretch

limo with tinted windows suddenly appeared. At the same moment, a hooded figure came out. He was tall and wore an expensive suit, but his face was invisible in a hooded Barbour jacket.

Despite booing from the crowd and microphones getting in the way of his walk to freedom, Tasio remained impressive even with his face hidden. He elbowed his way through to the limousine, one of the back doors opening just as he came alongside.

"I have to admit he has style," said Estíbaliz.

"You don't know the half of it," I replied, glancing at her. "And now, Estí, I'd like to finish this report. We can talk later."

She caught on immediately and left as rapidly as she had come.

I didn't want to deal with her, not today. Even though my heart sank at the idea, I had decided to question her brother, Eneko.

Noon arrived, and I didn't feel like going into the city center to eat, so I had a few snacks in a bar on Avenida Gasteiz and finally made up my mind to call her.

I was calling my boss, not Alba. I decided I'd rather talk on the telephone than see her face-to-face.

So I stood staring at the leafy green walls of the Palacio Europa, took my cell phone out of my pocket, and dialed her number.

"Are you alone?" I asked.

"No, but we can talk, Inspector Ayala," she replied in a steady voice. "Tell me what you have to say, if it's important."

"We have a suspect," I said, trying to concentrate on work. "Tasio Ortiz de Zárate brought this person to my attention, before he got out of prison."

"And you trust what Tasio Ortiz de Zárate tells you?"

"Ma'am, I think that we could have something solid."

"Describe this person to me then."

"Male, aged thirty-five," I said. "He used to go with Tasio on pagan jaunts, and now he owns a store selling esoteric objects below Doña Otxanda's Tower. His profile is a perfect match to the one I've drawn up."

"Are you going to arrest him now? Do you need me to get the judge to issue a warrant? Because to do that I need something more concrete to give him."

"Let me talk to him first. There are a few things I need to clear up, but I will inform you as soon as I'm done. I think . . . I think we're close to solving the case. At least that's what I'd like to believe."

"Me, too, Inspector Ayala," she said. In her words there was no trace of the warmth I knew so well.

Alba hung up, and I walked up Calle Badaya toward Cercas Bajas.

Not even I had the slightest notion of what I had just unleashed with that call.

31

DOÑA OTXANDA'S TOWER

MONDAY, AUGUST 8

Nowadays, Doña Otxanda's Tower houses the Natural Sciences Museum. Restored in the sixties, the square medieval tower is a faithful copy of those that had dotted the Álava region, like the Tower of Mendoza and the Varona family tower.

Next to its heavy wooden entrance, gold lettering advertised Eneko Ruiz de Gauna's herbalist and bookshop.

Through its dark windows, I could see a collection of crystal balls, amulets, and sachets of infusions, as well as secondhand books on everything from the Knights Templar to Basque mythology and ufology.

The tinkling of bamboo canes announced my arrival as I crossed the threshold. An *eguzkilore* hung from the doorframe, but unlike those I had seen in northern farmhouses, this one was hanging inside. It was as if the outside world had to protect itself against what was stored here.

The shop was crammed full of *santería* candles, boxes of herbs with handwritten labels, necklaces to ward off the evil eye, and hundreds of antiquarian books piled from floor to wooden ceiling. The air was filled with the heady scent of incense, with an underlying hint of marijuana.

I climbed several steep stairs to the back room. I couldn't recall ever having been in this kind of place before.

"The famous Kraken," someone said behind me. It was an unpleasant voice, like a crow cawing.

"The famous Eguzkilore," I replied, turning to face him.

"No one calls me that anymore; there's no resemblance now," he said, shrugging and taking a drag on his joint.

It was true. The red dreadlocks that Eneko had once sported were long gone. Rapid hair loss had swept them away, and now Eneko had a shaved head with an *eguzkilore* tattoo on the nape of his neck.

Eneko was as tall as I was, with sharp cheekbones, but a stocky body. He was wearing a pair of purple pants and had the bloodshot eyes typical of those who smoke strange substances. Still, his brown eyes could not have been more alert.

"Come through, I don't want my customers to see me with a pig."

I looked around to see if I could spot any of the customers he was talking about, but I couldn't see anyone else in the store.

"Did you come for the mandrake root?"

"For what?" I asked, nonplussed.

"For the order."

"What are you talking about?"

He stared at me for a few seconds, brow furrowed.

"Nothing, pig. Forget it."

He pulled back a glittering gold curtain, and we went into a strange cubbyhole that was even more cluttered than the store. There was an unmade double bed, a wooden table with invoices strewn all over its rune-carved surface, and thousands of photographs of paranormal events stuck on the walls. The candles in several seven-branched menorahs provided the only light. Obviously, there was room for every belief in Eneko's head.

"This is my office. We can talk freely here. So why did you come, Kraken? To thank me for my help in identifying the latest victims?" He sat on the table, taking one last drag on his joint.

"Not exactly," I said, wandering around the dimly lit office trying to see if there was anything interesting in the images papering the walls. "One line of inquiry in the current case concerns the triangle of San Vicentejo and the chapels at Burgondo and Ochate. You study these things: you can't be unaware of Ochate."

"Nobody from around here is. It's part of the cultural heritage of several generations."

"And how did it influence you?"

"I'm convinced that region is a center of power. I was part of several groups who recorded paranormal sounds there. Some were quite good quality. But then people lost interest and the groups split up," he said. I thought he was being deliberately vague.

"Tell me, did you ever work on the restoration of the chapel at San Vicentejo?"

"What are you talking about, man?" he protested. "Why don't you get to the point? I'm still not clear on why you're here."

All right, so there's no way of linking you to San Vicentejo.

"Let's just say I found a link between you, Tasio Ortiz de Zárate, and Zugarramurdi," I said, changing the subject.

He turned his head away, as if trying to avoid an unpleasant memory. "I was only a kid. I don't know what that crackpot has been telling you, but a lot less happened than he likes to claim."

"Well, it seems he hasn't found it easy to forget."

"He never understood my desire to return to ancient customs. Once we were wizards; now I run a herbalist's store. I'm frustrated by the way people like me, those of us who are more in tune with what the eye can't see, have lost power. I don't know why I'm sharing these things with you. If you don't have any more questions, I'm going to politely ask you to leave. I've only allowed you to come in here because of the respect I have for my sister."

"Respect? If you'd respected her, you wouldn't have gotten her involved in your drug dealing."

"What's wrong? Are you fucking her?" he said, standing up to confront me.

"What are you talking about, you cretin? I'm trying to take care of her, while you drag her down."

"Be careful. You weren't there when our father used to beat the hell out of us. I was the one who protected her then."

"Protected her? Is that what you were doing when you forced her into your corrupt world?"

"The drugs anesthetized her, made her stronger. Don't be so narrow-minded. You know nothing about it—all you can see is that they're illegal."

"Stop your gibberish. You've turned her into a master of self-destruction."

Just then I sensed someone behind me. I turned my head and saw it was Estíbaliz.

She glared at me, lips pressed in a tight white line.

"Is that what you think of me, Kraken? How wrong you both are! How wrong."

As I turned toward her, she vanished down the stairs. I ran after her, but she was too quick. By the time I reached the street, she was nowhere to be seen in any direction. I ran up Calle de las Carnicerías, looked into Calle Herrería, and a few minutes later Zapatería, but the only people I saw were having a good time or getting ready to join the procession of the Blusas.

"Wait, Estíbaliz!" I shouted, although I didn't have the slightest idea where she had gone.

I dialed her cell phone. Once, twice, a third time.

She didn't pick up. I knew she was more disappointed than angry with me.

So I turned back toward Doña Otxanda's Tower, ready to finish my conversation with Eneko.

When I arrived at the herbalist's, I saw the glass door was ajar, just as I had left it when I ran after Estí.

"Eneko!" I shouted. "Do you have any idea where your sister could have gone?"

But Eneko Ruiz de Gauna was nowhere to be seen.

He had disappeared, leaving his store wide-open, and a policeman completely at a loss.

32

IZARRA

VITORIA
FEBRUARY 1971

Álvaro Urbina turned and looked behind him at the bedroom door. Javier's shouts had roused him from his stupor.

"I know you've done something to hurt my sons, doctor! Let me in!"

"But how is this possible?" Blanca managed to say, despite being in a state of shock.

"Triplets usually come out like that: two are identical and one is different," whispered Felisa. "Is there another way to leave the house? Besides the front door?"

"Yes, if you go through my dressing room to the study, there are stairs that lead down to the back of the house," replied Blanca.

"Listen, there are married couples who would raise this child as their own," whispered Felisa. "I know one in Izarra. I don't mean a legal adoption. Doctor Urbina, you know that at the clinic sometimes we break the rules if an unexpected situation arises. There are always unmarried mothers from good families who have hidden their pregnancies and come to the clinic to give birth. In such cases, we give the babies to desperate couples who haven't been blessed with children. This couple has been waiting for some time. Doctor Medina always used to do it, and I see, hear, and keep quiet. If Don Javier discovers this redheaded baby, he'll kill you, Doctor

Urbina. He'll kill everyone in this room: his wife, the three babies, and me. I'll take the boy home. Tomorrow I'll go to Izarra to give him to the couple, and we need never speak of this again. Nobody was expecting triplets, and the twins are the spitting image of their mother, so she can raise them as her own."

Álvaro looked at Blanca, her tired arms struggling to hold all three babies.

Then he picked up the red-haired child and examined him closely. He was almost identical to his two sons as newborns; Álvaro was certain the child would grow up to look like him.

"Blanca, you're their mother, and you'll be the one bringing them up," he said, leaning over and brushing her hair from her face. "You have to decide."

"They're your children, too, all three of them," she replied feebly.

"He's going to kill us, Blanca. Your husband won't let the babies live if he sees all three of them."

She closed her eyes. She wished she didn't have to think, she wished she could end everything, and yet she couldn't. Two children's lives depended on her passing them off as Javier's sons.

"All right, Felisa, take him," she said at last. Then, overwhelmed with exhaustion, she fell back weeping on the sodden pillow.

Felisa wrapped the little redhead in one of the blankets Blanca had laid out for his brothers, emptied Doctor Urbina's leather bag, and placed the child inside.

She slipped into the dressing room, leaving Álvaro alone with what could have been his family: an exhausted first-time mother and identical twins.

Just at that moment, Javier burst into the room, forcing the lock and flinging open the door with such force that the handle crashed against the wall.

He looked around for his sons, but Doctor Urbina blocked his way.

"Everything turned out well. You have two sons who are in perfect health, given the circumstances. The initial tests also look promising. You may go over to their mother to see them. She is exhausted after the hard work of labor and needs to rest. And please close that door; it's essential the babies stay warm."

Javier looked askance at him and approached the bed, where he found the babies also asleep, wrapped in a blue blanket that wasn't quite big enough for both of them. He didn't dare touch them but rummaged inside the blanket to make sure all their limbs were present and correct.

"Good. Everything looks fine. You were so quiet in here I was beginning to fear the worst."

"We were simply doing our job, in the interest of your sons, Don Javier."

"Speaking of which, where's your nurse? I didn't see her leave," he said, glancing about the room.

"She rushed back to the clinic to fetch some equipment," he replied. "Your wife still requires care."

"Why didn't she leave through the front door like everyone else?"

"Without wishing to offend you, Don Javier, you were in a such a nervous state we couldn't risk letting you enter the room. It was a delicate moment for your sons. She preferred to go out the back way. I'm sure you understand, she's an elderly woman and has a great deal of respect for you."

"Yes, yes, I see," said Javier dismissively. "What remains to be done? Can the nurse manage by herself?"

"Yes, she will look after the mother and make sure the babies thrive, but right now these three need to rest. We'll let them sleep for a few hours, and as soon as the roads are passable, we'll take them to the hospital to be monitored. Since they're premature, they will need to stay in the neonatal unit until they've gained some weight and their lungs have grown a little stronger."

"But they're all right, aren't they?" Javier insisted. "They look rather small to me."

"This is a normal size for twins, considering they are slightly premature."

"Good," Javier said at last. "In the end you did your job and brought my two sons into the world. Who would have thought it?"

"It seems so, Don Javier."

And now what, Javier? Now what?

"I don't think there's any reason for us to meet again, in which case you can leave my house straightaway. Ulysses will drive you back to the clinic."

The doctor flinched, tried to muster a smile, but couldn't.

"Don't concern yourself. Besides, I doubt he'll be able to drive in this snow, even in a car like yours."

"The plows were here half an hour ago, and the streets are clear now. I'm not giving you a choice, so don't make me insist. I'll accompany you myself."

Álvaro shot a glance at Blanca and the two babies at her bosom. All three were asleep, oblivious to everything.

That was the last time he saw them.

A week later, a tiny announcement reporting the disappearance of Doctor Álvaro Urbina appeared in *El Diario Alavés,* placed there by his grief-stricken wife, Emilia Aranguren.

No one in Vitoria ever saw or heard from him again.

Six weeks later, the directors of the clinic determined that Doctor Urbina was unlikely to show up and a new doctor arrived from Bilbao.

The outgoing young gynecologist belonged to three generations of doctors from a prestigious Basque family. A charming,
capable fellow. By the time Doctor Goiri's plaque had replaced
Doctor Urbina's, scarcely anyone in Vitoria remembered the red-
headed doctor.

33

EL CAMINANTE

TUESDAY, AUGUST 9

*I*t *was just a sexual adventure, a bad decision, a summer fling—a mistake as far as my job is concerned. Nothing more. I'll go to her office today and tell her never again. I'll tell her to go back to her lukewarm, silent husband, the invisible man, Señor X.*

That was what I told myself when I woke up early.

I couldn't get her out of my mind. I was fooling myself, pretending I didn't care, that it didn't tear me apart that she slept with another man, took showers with him, went shopping, did the laundry with him, wore a ring that meant she had promised herself to him.

Pretending I didn't wish I was invisible, inaudible, intangible, so that I could creep into her bed, make love to her until she was warm and exhausted and fell asleep in my arms, even if afterward I had to return to my empty apartment.

Because, yes, this time I was the other man.

The stupid lover who could touch but didn't have the right to anything else. Not to late-Sunday-morning breakfasts in bed, not to introduce her at *cuadrilla* dinners, or to hold hands in the last showings at one of the movie houses on Calle San Prudencio.

I knew it was a stupid thing to do at this time in the morning, but I sent her a message.

Are you out for a run?

Yes.

Where are you?

It doesn't matter. Where shall we meet?

**In the gardens at the back of the
Unzueta mansion, the side gate is open.**

When I saw her thumbs-up emoticon, I ran to have a shower
and raced down the stairs.

When I arrived, Alba was already there, a shadow waiting for
me, arms folded across her chest, next to the hedges bordering the
gardens. She didn't seem to be in a good mood.

"What do you want? Another opportunity for a quick fuck?"
she hissed.

"What are you talking about? It wasn't a quick fuck."

"No? So what do you call taking me from behind and then not
even letting me go upstairs for a shower? I didn't want to sleep with
you, Unai. I wasn't begging you to commit yourself."

"You didn't want to sleep with me?" I roared. "Thanks a million, I feel flattered. Tell me, would you let me into your home?"

She turned pale, not knowing what to say.

"Come on, Alba. Let's go and have a fuck in your doorway—
although of course I haven't the slightest idea where that might
be—and then you let me up into your apartment. Okay? That way
I can get into bed with you and your husband. Wasn't he waiting
for you for his morning fuck?"

"Do you really think I had sex with him yesterday, with your
semen still inside me? You have no idea, Kraken. No idea about
me or my marriage."

"For heaven's sake, don't call me Kraken. I'm sick of all these
nicknames."

"You are? Then stop behaving like a brainless cephalopod."

"Don't even think of judging me. You're the one who's married. Don't play games with me, Alba. Either you're with me or you're not. I don't want to be the lover. It's—it's humiliating that this is what you've turned me into."

"Well, then, stop looking at me the way you do in my office!"

"What's wrong with the way I look at you?"

"I can't get it out of my mind, Unai," she whispered, still angry. But she came closer to me. "I can't get it out of my mind."

Her voice was quavering in a way that disarmed me completely.

"Neither can I, Alba." I sighed. "I can't get the way you look at me out of my mind, either. We shouldn't allow ourselves to get caught up in this; we're not children. There are other people involved. I don't want anyone to get hurt."

I don't want anyone to get hurt. . . .

How ironic, especially bearing in mind what came next for all of us.

I don't want anyone to get hurt.

"I came to apologize," I said eventually. "And to tell you I'd love it if you came up to my apartment."

"We're going to be late for work," she said, glancing down at her wristwatch.

"I know, we're in a real bind, but . . . just come and sleep, will you? I've never taken anybody up to that apartment. I moved there after I lost my wife more than two years ago. I want you to come into my bed and for us to sleep together, even if it's just for half an hour. That's what I want, Alba. You know you're not just a quick fuck for me, don't you?"

"Do you realize everything I'm risking?"

"I know, a lot more than me."

She fell silent.

"Let's go, then, before daylight," she said finally.

So we ran back to my door, but this time I let her go up to the third floor without even kissing her or holding her hand. I didn't even take her clothes off. I turned around in my bedroom and let her undress while I did the same. When I knew she was between the sheets, I followed her, but all I did was hold her. We fell asleep pressed tightly against each other, until my cell phone's alarm told us those golden minutes were over.

Alba got dressed again while both of us pretended I was still sleeping. In her running gear, she knelt down on the parquet floor on my side of the bed, turned my head toward her, and hugged me without a word.

Then she pulled her hair into a ponytail and left. I lay there staring at the hollow her back had made in the sheets.

It had been such a long time since I'd seen that.

I remember I went to work that dark day feeling relieved: las Fiestas de la Virgen Blanca would be over soon. If the murderer was timing his atrocities to coincide with important dates in Vitoria's calendar, he would have to wait until the first week of September, when the FesTVal took place, perhaps, or until the Medieval Market at the end of that month.

Just one more day. I just needed to keep a close watch on the streets of the city for one more day, and then concentrate on finding Eneko Ruiz de Gauna.

Estíbaliz and I were not exactly getting along. Neither of us was good at pretending, and seeing her reproachful face reminded me that we were ruining our friendship.

Eneko didn't answer his cell phone, but Estí refused even to contemplate reporting him missing. First, because he had deliberately disappeared and was possibly hidden in some farmhouse or cave. Second, because my partner didn't want to give the game away and make him visible.

My brother called me at work first thing in the morning.

I noticed a worried edge to his voice that he didn't bother to hide.

"How did it go last night, Germán? Did you go out?"

"Yes, our whole *cuadrilla* went out. It's a very strange atmosphere. As you can imagine, people are only talking about one thing. I'm sure you don't need to be reminded."

"Yes, let's talk about something else." I looked away from my computer screen.

"I took the day off. I agreed to meet Martina for lunch in Deportivo Alavés to try some of their traditional tortillas with chorizo. Martina hasn't arrived yet. She was up late last night. I think she wanted to stay out all night. I was calling to see if you wanted to join us."

"I'm touched by the way you look after me, brother," I said with a smile, rousing myself. "But today's pretty complicated for me. Maybe tomorrow, when we lower the alert level."

"Oh, come on, Unai. The fiestas will be over tomorrow. Why don't you live a little?"

"This from the man who's always first in his office at the crack of dawn."

"All right, all right. At least I tried. Take care, and we'll see each other on Saturday in Villaverde."

"Yes, Saturday in Villaverde. Enjoy the tortillas."

"Don't worry, we will," he said, and ended the call.

It was five in the afternoon by the time Estíbaliz and I reached Calle Dato. The Blusas' last parade was the most popular: it was usually the day things got messy.

The processions began exactly on the hour. The first *cuadrilla,* the Bereziak, started the parade from the start of Calle Postas on a special float: a gaudily decorated old truck from which they threw flour at the spectators on both sides of the street.

Within a few minutes, Calle Dato was filled with people covered in flour, and the sidewalks were white as well. Even the trunks of the magnolia trees and the sturdy wooden benches were hidden under a layer of white powder.

My partner and I tried not to be affected by the joyful atmosphere surrounding us. We had deployed plainclothes officers and uniformed police to the most emblematic buildings throughout the city, to try to help people feel a little more secure on their own streets.

There was also more of a TV and press presence than usual. It seemed as if the whole world was interested in las Fiestas de la Virgen Blanca. Reporters were everywhere, interviewing anybody who had a theory, however harebrained, about who the murderer might be. The streets in the city center were crammed with media vans, all parked illegally, which meant a lot more work for the Traffic Unit.

After the Bereziak came the Biznietos de Celedón, the Jatorrak, and the Desiguales. The parade lasted for barely forty-five minutes, but it left Calle Dato under a fine white blanket and the spectators in high spirits.

Estíbaliz and I said nothing to each other—the wall between us left us feeling awkward. We walked down Calle Dato as the crowd dispersed along Calle General Álava and San Prudencio.

It was when we reached the Plaza del Arca that I saw something that made the hairs on the back of my neck stand up.

At the foot of El Caminante was a white sheet that people were avoiding, passing on both sides so as not to step on it.

"Do you see that?" I asked Estíbaliz, my throat dry.

"I hope this is just a macabre joke the Blusas are playing, because it looks like there are a couple of bodies under the sheet."

"Let's get the area cordoned off before we uncover anything. It's going to be hard to prevent people from seeing what we're doing."

"We have to try, though," said Estíbaliz, calling for a patrol car.

In a few minutes we had roped off all the entrances to the Plaza del Arca, from Calle Dato to both sides of Calle San Prudencio and the small alley leading to the bookstore and J.G.'s bar.

I couldn't help staring anxiously at the two human shapes under the sheet.

"I hope they're dummies, Estíbaliz. I'm starting to think this is no joke—they haven't moved this whole time."

She glanced again at the sheet and then looked back at me. I could see she shared my apprehension.

"We'd better get on with it, then," I muttered. "If they are dead bodies, we'll have to call the judge, the pathologist, and the forensic team."

Estíbaliz handed me a pair of latex gloves. We lifted one end of the sheet, the farthest from El Caminante's enormous feet.

The first things we saw were an *eguzkilore* and a bald male head covered in flour. The white dust blurred the features, as if it were an anonymous puppet waiting to be painted.

My colleague stared at the head in disbelief. "It can't be."

"What is it, Estí?"

"It can't be," she repeated, then took the man's head in her gloved hands and exposed the nape of his neck.

The back of his head had been on the ground and had no flour on it. We saw the *eguzkilore* tattoo.

"It's my brother!" she shrieked, throwing herself on him. "It's my brother!"

Her scream drifted high above our heads. We soon heard people shouting hysterically all around the cordoned-off area.

I clutched her to me. "We don't know that, Estíbaliz. We don't know that. Come on, you have to move away. It's a dead body. We have to wait for the judge and the pathologist."

"It's him, Unai! It's him. No one else has a tattoo like that—

it's my brother," she yelled. Beside herself, she began to cover his forehead with kisses, smearing her face with flour and tears.

"Estíbaliz, you have to stand back. You can't contaminate a dead body like that. Come on, I'm here for you," I said, grasping her chin. "Come on, Estí. Look at me. Take deep breaths."

I forced her to look me in the eye and to breathe as I did. I was dimly aware that beyond the cordon, onlookers were raising their cell phones above their heads and taking photos that would travel across the world in a few seconds.

It was like living in a damn reality show. Like having a TV camera on your shoulder and never being able to switch it off.

Judge Olano didn't take long to reach us. He certified the deaths of a man and a woman, both of whom were covered in flour. I allowed the pathologist to register all the details, which in principle seemed to be the same as the earlier crimes, except for the flour drenching them.

I led Estíbaliz to one of our vehicles. She stared at the ground, unable to respond to any of my questions.

I called her fiancé and explained the situation. He came to fetch her.

I was about to leave that dreadful scene and escape the bronze giant's accusatory gaze when my brother called.

I shouldn't have taken the call at that moment. I shouldn't have become emotional, but I needed his support.

"I've just seen Twitter, Unai. Is it really Estíbaliz's brother?" he said in a rush.

"We don't know for sure, Germán. I'm going with the pathologist to the Basque Forensic Institute in the Palacio de Justicia. I hope we can identify the body there."

"How is Estíbaliz?"

"I think she's going to hate me for the rest of her life. I was convinced her brother was the murderer."

It took a couple of seconds for Germán to react.

"What's that?"

I knew I had said more than my job permitted, but what the hell, it was Germán. My brother.

"We both know I shouldn't be telling you this, but that was what I thought. The line of inquiry I was following led me to him. But now nothing fits, Germán. I've got nothing. I'm back to square one, and Estíbaliz is never going to forgive me."

It took my brother some time to assimilate everything I was saying.

"All right, Unai. Don't freeze now, take it step by step, the way Grandpa taught us. One thing at a time and end the damn day the best you can. That's why you've got such broad shoulders, right?"

"That's right," I said, slightly calmer.

"I know I shouldn't bother you with my concerns now, but I called because I'm worried about Martina. She didn't show up for lunch and isn't answering her phone."

"If she stayed out all night, maybe she fell asleep," I said, although I wasn't convinced. Alarm bells had started to go off in my head. The shock of finding Eneko's body had meant I hadn't paid any attention to the female victim.

"You know that's not like her. She may like to party, but she still always keeps her word. And I don't think she could still be asleep at six in the evening. I went to her apartment, but there's no one there."

"Could she have stayed with someone from her *cuadrilla*? Didn't she have to work today?" I said, swallowing hard. I tried to hide my concern from Germán, to keep my voice level. It couldn't be, could it? It was too remote a chance. Too remote . . .

"No, we both took the day off. Maybe you're right, and she's sleeping at Nerea's. I don't want to keep you. Call me if you need to, will you, Unai?"

"Yes, I will. I have to go to the Palacio de Justicia now; they're about to remove the bodies. We'll talk later." I realized I was repeating myself. Let's just say my stupefaction had reached a dangerous level.

Half an hour later I was with the pathologist in the autopsy room.

Eneko's body, still covered in flour, was stretched out on the stainless-steel table.

"What about the woman's body?" I asked her, looking around anxiously.

"It hasn't been brought in yet," said Doctor Guevara, intent on choosing her implements. "I'll get started on the male."

She began to wash Eneko with a small showerhead. Little by little, the flour was washed off his face and neck. I approached to get a better look.

"I've heard it's Inspector Ruiz de Gauna's brother," said the pathologist. "Can you confirm that?"

"Yes, it's him. There's little doubt about the identification. The deceased had a unique tattoo on the back of his neck. Could you lift up his head?"

She took hold of Eneko's head and twisted it to one side. She directed a stream of water at it, and the *eguzkilore* tattoo was clearly visible.

"Was he thirty-five years old?" she asked.

"Yes, I'm afraid he was on the list of—"

"Possible victims," she finished the sentence for me.

"Tell me, doctor, does he present the same characteristics as the previous bodies?" I said, trying to concentrate, even though all I could think about was that the door was opening and they were finally bringing in the body of the dead woman.

"Yes, at first sight, it does. Look, inspector, there's a small puncture on the side of the neck that could have been made by a needle. Of course, we need to carry out a thorough investigation, but I'm afraid that it's the same pattern."

"You may well find traces of other drugs in his blood," I warned her. "He had a record for dealing drugs and was known to be fascinated by all sorts of illegal substances."

"Understood. In any case, I don't think that will change the cause of death. As with the other victims, the glands in his throat are swollen. I'm not expecting any great surprises."

"Well, his father is incapacitated with Alzheimer's, his mother is dead, and his other brother left home many years ago. The only family he has left is Inspector Gauna. I'll call her so that she can make the formal identification."

At that moment two members of the Institute came in and carefully lifted the second body onto the steel table.

"Let's see what we have here," muttered the pathologist, starting to clean the flour from the body's face and close-cropped hair with the showerhead.

She washed her forehead, her open eyelids, her nose and mouth.

I swayed, lost my balance, and had to steady myself against the table where Eneko Ruiz de Gauna lay.

The murderer's latest victim was my sister-in-law, Martina.

34

THE PRADO PARK

TUESDAY, AUGUST 9

The pathologist shot me a worried look as I slumped against the steel table. I wasn't even aware I was touching Eneko's lifeless body, recently washed and still damp.

I jumped up in a daze, the rear of my jeans wet.

"Are you feeling all right, Inspector Ayala?"

"This woman is . . . she's . . . Martina López de Arroyabe. She's my sister-in-law, my brother's fiancée."

The pathologist's face froze. "Are you one hundred percent certain?"

"She is recovering from cancer. You'll find her fingernails are discolored from the chemotherapy, her feet are swollen because she's been retaining fluids, and her eyebrows are just starting to grow back," I reeled off the list while staring at a white floor tile and trying not to be sick.

"Can you tell me where the toilets are, please?" I managed to say.

It felt as if a large rock had settled in my stomach. It was tearing me apart. I couldn't stand up straight.

"Up the stairs on the left. Would you like me to go with you?"

I ran up the stairs, head spinning, unable to respond.

I rushed into the restroom and ran to a toilet. But as much I wanted to, I couldn't throw up. I wanted to be sick, and then to sleep, to obliterate the fact that I had ruined my brother's life.

I don't remember much after that. I collapsed onto the shiny tiles, blood rushing to my burning cheeks, and it was so hot. Perhaps this was my hell, and I was the Devil?

Because that's what the Devil did, wasn't it?

He hurt everyone who crossed his path.

I was the kiss of death. Everyone in my life died. My parents, my wife, my children, my sister-in-law—even my best friend's brother was dead because of me.

I didn't hear her arrive. Someone pried my arms from my knees and grasped my chin so firmly that I finally had to raise it and see her.

"Unai," whispered Alba, crouching next to me, "you have to come with me. You've been in the women's bathroom for two hours. Doctor Guevara called us because your cries could be heard all over the Palacio de Justicia. You've had a panic attack. There's an ambulance waiting to take you to the hospital."

"I don't want to go to the hospital, Alba. I don't need to." Some part of my brain answered automatically.

"Yes, you do. You need to be checked out and at least given a sedative. Don't make things more difficult than they already are." Her voice was gentle, like a mother talking to a child.

"I don't want a sedative. I have to . . ." I was returning to the real world. "I have to make a phone call. I have to tell my brother before he finds out from someone else."

"Unai, you're not in any state to make that call. The paramedics are outside waiting for you. Let's take it step by step. I'll be right next to you, if you want." There was a silent plea in her words—to let myself go, to allow her to be in charge—that made me feel something I wanted to resist.

"All right, Alba." I got to my feet more unsteadily than I

was willing to admit. "Let's get out of here. I think I need to be looked at."

We got into one of the glass elevators that dominated the center of the Palacio de Justicia. It looked like a space capsule, and it slowly took us down two floors. All the while employees walking along the hallways glanced at us surreptitiously.

"Do you feel better, Inspector Ayala?" asked Alba when the elevator reached the ground floor. Her voice was no longer gentle and intimate. We were surrounded by people, and Alba was DSU Salvatierra once again.

I turned toward her and looked her in the eye. This wasn't the first time I was lying to her and, the way things were going, it wouldn't be the last.

"I think . . . I think I'm going to need that sedative. Thank you, deputy superintendent, for having come in person. I really appreciate your concern."

"I'm afraid I can't go to the hospital with you, inspector. The superintendent has called me in for an emergency meeting. He's been waiting for me at headquarters for some time now."

What she was really saying was "I can't expose myself by going in the ambulance with you."

"Don't worry, I think I can get myself there. Thanks for your help upstairs," I said. Then I walked over to the Osakidetza paramedics waiting for me in the fierce sunlight, suffocating in their hi-vis jackets.

I glanced behind me. Alba was staring at me from the glass entrance to the Palacio de Justicia, but her cell phone rang and she turned to one side for privacy.

"Are you waiting for Inspector Ayala?" I asked one of the young paramedics seated on the rear of the ambulance.

"Yes, has he come down already?"

"It seems he's feeling better. I'm his colleague, Inspector Ajuria. If he's not down in ten minutes, you can go back without him."

"All right, we'll wait." The paramedic shrugged.

I was still dazed and found it hard to walk normally, but I managed to get out of Alba's sight and cross the avenue toward the Prado Park.

I passed families heading for the stalls pushing strollers, and kids carrying cotton candy and launching colored spinners into the air.

All that happiness and light was too much for me. My world was much darker, and I was about to drag someone else into it. Someone who meant a lot to me. Someone who meant everything to me.

I looked for a quiet bench in the shade and dialed my brother's number.

"Unai, how are you? And how is Estíbaliz?" he asked.

"Germán, where are you exactly? I'd like us to meet. I need to . . . I need to talk to you," I managed to get out.

But my brother knew me too well. He knew all the shades of my voice.

"Unai, what's going on? What happened?" he asked in alarm.

"Stay calm, Germán. Stay calm." I tried to slow him down. "I just want us to meet right now, to talk face-to-face. I don't want to have this conversation on the phone. Where are you?"

It took my brother only a couple of seconds to read between the lines.

"Tell me it isn't so, Unai!" he said, his voice cracking. "Tell me it wasn't Martina."

I got up from the bench, feeling powerless, still trying to reassure him.

"Germán, calm down and tell me where you are. I'll be there right away. I don't want you to be alone."

"No! No!" he yelled, starting to panic. "Tell me it's not her, Unai! Tell me, for God's sake!"

I sighed, defeated.

"I didn't want you to find out like this, Germán. I'm sorry, so sorry. But you have to tell me where you are."

I let him weep on the far end of the line, trying hard to contain myself. I closed my eyes, put my hand over my mouth. I controlled myself for his sake, for my brother. I had to be strong for him.

I had to do it. He had done the same thing for me when I lost my wife.

In the first few hours after the murder of my beloved sister-in-law, I was able to keep my mind occupied by taking care of all the formalities. To save time on phone calls, I got in touch with Nerea, knowing that within a short time not only our whole *cuadrilla* but most of Vitoria would know.

I called Grandfather and asked him to take care of Germán for the next few days. He arrived from Villaverde within the hour and managed to find Germán, although I don't know how he did it. Yet again I admired his ability to get things done and wished I had it.

I wished I had it.

Then I called Alba, pretending I was still at the hospital. I asked for permission to go home and rest. I knew she would agree. I was exhausted, and I didn't want to argue.

I just wanted to let myself go, to drag myself home at eleven, right when the Celedón was getting ready to climb the night sky above the Plaza de la Virgen Blanca. The worst Fiestas de la Virgen Blanca in all Vitoria's history were drawing to a close.

35

THE MONTE GORBEA CROSS

WEDNESDAY, AUGUST 10

They did not hold a Mass for him. Eneko had never wanted anything to do with the Church, and we were all aware that he would have been spinning in his grave if we had buried him in a Christian cemetery.

Estíbaliz followed the advice they had given her in the Alzheimer's unit at Txagorritxu and didn't tell her father that his elder son had died. Since there was no other family member to consult, she decided to have him cremated and to carry his ashes up to the cross on the summit of Monte Gorbea, one of the goddess Mari's haunts.

Even at midday, the faunas accompanying the urn were scary: alternative customers of the herbalist store, potheads, Goths, and ladies with rainbow-colored hair dressed in white tunics chanting in an incomprehensible language.

My colleague led the procession, escorted by Iker, her fiancé. They were wearing climbing gear: black Lycra leggings and tops, magnesium bags strapped to their waists.

They were going to climb the cross, even though it wasn't allowed. At that moment I was the only representative of the law in the area. It was as if Estíbaliz were silently challenging me: *Are you going to arrest me? Are you going to stop me?*

She had not answered any of my calls since I had lifted the white blanket by El Caminante's feet.

I found out about the funeral because Lutxo talked to her fiancé. That was also how I learned that she didn't want to see me. Not only had I lost my best friend, I was unlikely to recover my work colleague, either.

Still I went. I'm not one to hide. If someone wants to smash my face in, let them, especially when they have every right to do so.

So I followed the hellish group at a safe distance, and we began the ascent.

As we climbed, the trees gradually gave way to the bare mountain with the cross on its summit. About seventy-five feet tall, it was like a small Eiffel Tower. The cross had stood there for a century and was a common destination for climbers in northern Spain.

However, as we approached it, something strange occurred. I rubbed my eyes to make sure it wasn't an optical illusion.

"It's Eneko! It's his aura!" screeched an old lady who was drawing on a roll-up cigarette containing heaven knew what: "It's red! Can everyone see it? Can everyone see the cross moving?"

Although what she was shouting was incredible, it was also true: the cross was red and it was swaying, like the snow effect on a TV screen when the signal is lost.

Swallowing hard, I joined the procession and approached the cross's four iron feet.

As I drew closer, I discovered the explanation: A plague of ladybugs covered the ironwork. Several thousand red shells twitching crazily because of the heat, making the monument appear to be alive.

The insects didn't discourage Estíbaliz. She put the urn with her brother's ashes into her backpack and began to climb. The rest of us held our breath. I stood next to Iker and silently pleaded with him to accompany her.

He must have agreed, because in a few seconds he caught up with her by the last struts on the cross, seventy-five feet above our heads.

Estíbaliz didn't wait for prayers or chants. She unscrewed the top of the urn and poured out the ashes. They drifted down onto the ladybugs, causing many to fly off.

I imagined Eneko would have found a mystical meaning in this, perhaps it would have been irrefutable proof of the transmigration of souls. Yet the only empirical truth was that the Eguzkilore was no longer there to tell the story, thanks to a murderer who had me completely bewildered.

We descended the mountainside in silence, Estí and her fiancé in the lead, followed by the entourage, while I brought up the rear, several yards behind and lost in my troubled thoughts.

I didn't realise Estíbaliz had dropped back until she was alongside me. By now we were in the beechwood. The tall branches provided a little shade when the ground and my head were burning.

Iker looked back at her with concern, but Estíbaliz tilted her chin at him to indicate he should keep going. She and I slowed until the others were farther ahead, and then we stopped in a clearing dappled with green.

"Say what you have to say, Estí. Come on, spit it out."

She stared at me, furious. Her face was haggard from lack of sleep, and her hair seemed even redder than usual.

"If I tell you what I'm thinking, you'll probably never speak to me again, Kraken," she said, snarling.

"Say it, Estíbaliz. We may just agree on something for once."

"It was your fault!" she shouted, her hands pummeling my chest. "My brother is dead because of you! You got him into this, and the murderer has been laughing at you!"

I tried to restrain her, but Estíbaliz fought like an alley cat. She was much quicker than I was, like a squirrel on caffeine. I grabbed her from behind and held her to try to stop her from hitting me.

"Laughing at me, you say?" I whispered in her ear. "No, Estí. He's not just laughing at me. He's killed my brother's fiancée; he's killed your brother. This is way more than some macabre joke. He's made it personal."

"Kraken, if you don't let me go, I swear I'll hurt you."

"I know."

"Then watch out," she said, raising her knee. She raked her heel all the way down my thigh and shin, scraping off the skin as she did so.

When her heel stamped on my instep and made me howl with pain, I let her go. "Shit, Estí! You'll leave a mark," I said, peering down at my injured leg.

She turned away, ready to walk on. "You've already left a mark on me, Kraken."

Stretching out my arm. I grabbed her wrist.

Just then I realized our shouting had attracted the Eguzkilore's friends and we were surrounded by people taking photos on their cell phones.

"I'll pulverize anyone who takes a photo, do you hear me?" I bawled, my patience exhausted. "No cell phones! I've had it with all these phones!"

In a rage, I rushed up to one of the Goths, planning to snatch his cell phone. He stepped back and raised his hands.

"Don't get mad, man. You don't need to worry about me. I'm not going to upload anything," he said with a beatific smile.

"That's it, the show's over. Could you all go down to the parking lot and give us some privacy, please?"

The small crowd dispersed and renewed their descent.

"It's fine, Iker. I'll be down in a minute," Estíbaliz told her fiancé.

As soon as we were alone, I approached her so that nobody could hear us. "We have to figure out what to do about this case,

Estí. You have several days' leave due to you because of your brother's death—are you going to take them?"

"No chance."

"Do you want to keep going, or have you had enough?"

"I want to catch him now more than ever. Don't you?" she asked, her voice so choked with rage I could barely recognize it.

"You can't imagine how much."

"Well, then let's get him. Let's get Tasio once and for all."

"Do you really think it was him?"

"For God's sake, Kraken! He gave you my brother's name, got out of prison, and a day later killed him and your sister-in-law. Don't you see the connection, or would you like me to draw a diagram?"

It could be. I may have to accept the evidence and start thinking Tasio is the devil everyone says he is.

I do not want to say anything about Martina's funeral. There are some things that . . . I prefer to keep to myself. They hurt too much to make public.

I remember that after the work colleagues, Martina's parents, the press, curious onlookers, the authorities, and the members of her *cuadrilla* had left, Germán stood next to the square lid of her niche. I had ordered a marble plaque with the inscription *We'll never forget you,* together with her name, a photograph, and the dates of her birth and death, but it would be several weeks before it was ready.

Grandfather and I stood without moving next to Germán, enduring the scorching sun that brought out great pearls of sweat on Grandpa's forehead under his beret and had long since soaked the back of the black shirt I always wore for funerals.

"Now we are all widowers," said Grandfather as we continued to stand there a couple of hours later.

"Maybe we're cursed," I said.

"Don't be ridiculous. It's just that life's a bitch," said Germán.

"All that's left is to be worthy of them," Grandfather added.

That's difficult, Grandpa. I'm just a rotten guy who doesn't deserve a family.

"Come on, sons. We ought to get back and have a drink. You two look like ghosts. Germán, we will eat something at Unai's. I've brought some *txixikis* from Paco the butcher."

The mention of his favorite food brought some comfort to my brother. It was good for him not to be alone in his apartment, where everything would remind him of Martina. With us he could weep as much as he needed. In his ninety-four years, Grandfather had endured hundreds of burials and mournings. It was soothing to follow his sensible decisions about what to do and to forget that we were adults for a few hours.

If I am as faithful to the truth as I wish to be, I have to admit Martina's death also brought moments that restored my faith in humanity. A wave of solidarity and consternation surrounded me: no one in my address book failed to call me.

No one.

They were concerned about me and my brother. Their consolation gave me goose bumps, because I understood that pain unites people, possibly even more than happiness does. We quickly forget that, ungrateful wretches that we are.

There was one particularly emotional call from Mario Santos, the journalist on *El Correo Vitoriano*. Up until then, we'd had a purely symbiotic relationship in which I gave him information for his newspaper and, in return, his measured articles did not misinterpret our investigations. There was a necessary distance between us. But not that day.

"Inspector Ayala? Is this a good moment to talk?" he asked when I answered.

"As good or as bad as any other, Mario. Do you want something?"

"I'm not calling today as a journalist, Unai," he replied, using my Christian name for the first time in years. "Tomorrow's edition has gone to press. My article has been written and dispatched. I wanted to tell you how sorry I am about what happened to your sister-in-law."

"Well," I said in surprise, "thank you for that, Mario, I mean it."

"I can't imagine what you must be going through right now. Nobody is prepared to die so young. I don't know how families keep going," he murmured, his voice choking with emotion for once.

"It's ironic, but I think that, in some way, we felt prepared for Martina to leave us. She had a devastating cancer that she fought like a tiger, but there were moments when . . . I don't know if you're familiar with that illness . . . we thought she had only weeks to live. She always recovered. Even though she didn't look as if she had the strength to do so, Martina recovered. That's what makes it so cruel that she was killed at the very moment when the doctors said she was cured."

"All this seems too awful to be true, Unai. I only hope—and I trust you in this, my friend—that you catch the murderer once and for all and bring these tragedies to an end."

That's what I hope, friend, that's what I hope, too.

36

SALBURUA

Thursday, August 11

The deputy superintendent called us into her office first thing. She gravely offered her condolences and then asked us to accompany her down to the parking lot, where she led us to an unmarked car.

"Where are we going?" asked Estíbaliz, crawling into the back.

"We're going to get some air at Salburua. The office atmosphere can be suffocating, don't you think?"

This wasn't a good sign. Maybe what she had to say was so serious that she didn't want the rest of our colleagues to see our reactions as we left her office.

I climbed silently into the front seat. I tried to anticipate what was coming, but until DSU Salvatierra told us what this was about, I had no idea how to defend myself.

We soon reached the Salburua wetlands. I must admit that Alba's idea was a good one—being surrounded by so much green cleared my mind. There was nobody there after the fiestas, so we were able to walk in silence for a while. Alba led us down an out-of-the-way path.

"I'm afraid we are here because of the latest turn of events," she began. "I won't hide from you how alarmed the rest of the police force are after the last murders, or the pressure we're getting from

above. I don't want to seem insensitive, inspectors, but I need to get
to what's worrying me, because I have to update the superintendent
as soon as we get back to headquarters."

"Go on, we're listening," said Estíbaliz, who was walking
beside her.

"First of all, Inspector Gauna, thank you for returning to work
without taking the leave due to you. But do you two think you
should continue on this case? I have serious doubts about your
suitability. Naturally both of you are emotionally affected by the
deaths of your family members. The public and Judge Olano are
going to watch every step you take very closely."

"What do you think, ma'am?" I asked, staring at her. "You are
our immediate superior, so I'd like to know your opinion."

"No kid gloves, Unai?" she said. I was surprised she used my
first name in front of Estíbaliz.

"Please."

"I don't think you have anything. From the start, Unai, you
in particular have disregarded the prime suspects—the twins. The
person you suspected is one of the most recent murder victims. You
couldn't be more lost."

"I've learned my lesson," I objected. "I'll go through everything
we have from the beginning."

"Perhaps it would be best to bring in a fresh pair of eyes. Perhaps you two can't see clearly enough. This is a very complicated
case. You are running this investigation by the book, but you're not
getting any results. You must have done something very wrong for
both of you to be at funerals yesterday. I'm sorry to be so frank."

"Don't you realize that's what he wants? He wants you to take
us off the case," I said, controlling my impulse to shout. "That's
why he's made it personal."

"What do you mean by that?"

"It's obvious the murderer is keeping a close watch on us. He
wanted to give us this coup de grâce precisely because it would

push us away from the case. That means we were getting close—he knows we're on to something and can catch him."

"If only that were true, if only I could believe what you're telling me," she said, slipping back into a more professional tone. "This time the killer chose Calle Dato, in the Ensanche area, which means he is now in the nineteenth century. I can't imagine where he will leave his next victims, because that period covers almost the entire city—and that has Superintendent Medina very worried. I can give you one more week. If by then there are no results, I'll have to take you off the case."

When she dropped us off at headquarters, we were both despondent. Neither of us was in the mood to talk.

"We have to go through all the statements again and interview the witnesses we haven't had time to talk to," Estíbaliz said when DSU Salvatierra had left us.

"I agree, but I'm also going to dig into the twins' past. The key must be in front of us; we just can't see it."

"What are you planning to do now?"

"I'm going back to Santa Isabel Cemetery. I'd like you to come with me."

She agreed, and a short while later we entered the silent city of the dead.

"What are you looking for?" my colleague wanted to know.

"The only living person here. Come on, he told me he has a toolshed at the back of the cemetery."

We walked rather uneasily between the tombs. Maybe it hadn't been such a good idea to start here. Both Estí and I were haunted by funerals. In fact, this was the last place I wanted to be.

Just then I caught a glimpse of the caretaker, on a ladder as he pruned the wayward branches of a stout cypress.

"My, it's you again! It seems you like the graveyard."

"Could you come down a moment? I didn't introduce myself the other day: I'm Inspector Ayala, and this is my partner, Inspector Gauna. I'd like to continue the discussion we began a while ago."

He looked me up and down for a couple of seconds, then nodded obediently.

"Of course, I'll be right with you."

Once he had reached the ground, he greeted Estíbaliz politely and looked at me expectantly.

"You were telling me you witnessed an incident involving the Ortiz de Zárate twins the day their mother was buried. Could you tell us precisely what happened?"

"Yes, of course. You don't forget things like that, even after all these years."

"It was 1989, if my information is correct," I said.

"That's right, a long time ago. A lot of people came to her funeral, important people and journalists, just like the one a week or so back. Then, after everyone else was gone, her sons stayed with their girlfriends—at least, they were holding hands. The sons were identical and wore suits with black armbands. I couldn't tell one from the other."

"So what happened that was so memorable?"

"After the four of them had been on their own for a while, a young man of about their age appeared. He must have been under twenty. He was dressed the way we villagers used to dress for special occasions: a pair of jeans and a white shirt. He was quite plump and had bright red hair. He looked unkempt, almost like a beggar. Look, I have no idea what he said to them, but whatever it was, he didn't deserve what they did to him."

"What did they do to him?" Estíbaliz asked.

"They beat him up, right there, in front of the Unzueta family vault, in front of the angel. Come with me and you'll understand better," he said, the pruning saw still in his only hand.

We followed him along the avenues lined with cement graves and flowers, until we reached the famous angel.

Uneasy, I moved to one side, took Estí by the shoulders, and held her tight.

"Do you see that grave on the other side? Back then it was empty. It had been a common grave with six coffins in it, and the city council told me to empty it because the time limit had elapsed. I was crouching down behind those headstones, and I saw everything. I didn't know if I should run away and call the police."

"That's what you should have done," said Estíbaliz.

"I was afraid to leave the kid—I was sure they were going to kill him. They kept punching him, and then, when he fell to the ground, one of the twins started to kick him while the other one egged him on. Look, I don't know what happened between them, but when the kid stopped moving, they filled his mouth with earth and tossed him into the empty grave. They shouted something like: 'And don't ever come back to Vitoria, you lousy bumpkin,' although I'm not sure he could even hear them."

"You're telling me that the twins killed a boy on this very spot?"

"No, they didn't kill him. After staring at him and talking among themselves for a while, they went away. They left him for dead."

"So did you finally call the police, an ambulance, somebody? Do you know if there's an official record of the incident?" Estíbaliz insisted.

"What record, young lady?" he asked with a sad smile. "As soon as the group left, I ran to see if the kid was alive or dead. I found him with a mouth full of dirt, badly beaten, his face smashed. He looked at me . . . as if he was expecting me to thrash him as well, as if he didn't expect anything else from anyone. I can't imagine what it was like for him in that grave, battered and almost choking, with the Unzueta angel staring down at him. I removed the dirt from his mouth as best I could; with only one hand, I couldn't help him as much as I would have liked. I brought him water from the hosepipe and washed out his mouth, cleaned off all the mud and blood so that he could breathe properly. I wanted to call an ambulance to take him to the hospital, but he wouldn't let me. He went crazy, saying nobody could find out what had happened, that it would only make things worse for him."

"So you just left him there?" I asked.

"No, sir. I had the impression he had nowhere to spend the night, so I said he could stay in my hut. He accepted and, in the end, spent several days hidden there. I took him food every day—garlic soup and potatoes with sausages, to help him recover. The boy was very well behaved: a little clumsy, but he didn't give me any problems."

"Can you give us a name, tell us what he was called?"

"I couldn't get it out of him. He just said, 'Please don't ask me.' I think he was afraid the twins might come back to the cemetery asking about him, and either I would tell them willingly or they would force me to tell them what I knew."

"Do you remember any other details, anything that might help us locate him?"

"He was constantly repeating that they had thrown him out, or that's how he felt. He said lots of strange things that I couldn't understand, that his family had thrown him out, that he had spent his life looking for them, and that now they were throwing him out of Vitoria. The strangest thing of all is that it wasn't the beating that hurt him the most; he didn't complain about the pain in his back or his face. It was what those rich kids had said to him that drove him crazy."

"Could you describe the girls?" asked Estíbaliz.

"One of them was striking. She was slightly plump, with long, straight blond hair. She was a real looker; I could tell that from where I was hiding. I don't remember what the other one was like. I was finding it hard enough to avoid panicking and having a heart attack."

"Do you know what became of the boy after he left your hut? Do you know where he went?"

"He said he was going to go to Pamplona and never wanted to come back to Vitoria. But one morning he went to the bus station on Calle Francia. . . . Do you remember when it was on Calle Francia, before they tore that lovely building down? . . . When he came back, he hid the ticket and . . . well, you get bored in here, the dead don't provide much entertainment, so I searched around and saw he'd bought a ticket for a village. I don't remember which one, but the ticket was for the Burundesa line, the one that goes to Amurrio. So I knew he was lying, but I think it was because he was scared the others would come back and ask me about him. I played along, and when he left, I wished him good luck in Pamplona."

Estíbaliz pulled up a map of northeast Ávala on her cell phone and showed it to him.

The gravedigger took a pair of half-moon glasses out of the pocket of his coveralls, put them on, and peered at the screen.

"Try to remember: Apodaca, Letona, Murguía, Lezama?" I queried.

The old man's brow furrowed, until finally he pointed his fat thumb at the screen.

"Izarra! That's it! The boy bought a ticket to Izarra," he said triumphantly.

I looked at Estíbaliz. She knew that region better than I did. Izarra had, at most, five hundred inhabitants; Vitoria was its police headquarters. But it was going to be impossible to track down this individual without a name.

We said good-bye to the gravedigger and almost ran out of the cemetery, anxious to leave the tombstones and burials behind.

"Now what?" said Estíbaliz. "His story doesn't give us much to go on."

"I know it will be complicated getting Ignacio to admit that he nearly beat a stranger to death twenty-seven years ago, especially if there's no record of it and his attorney is standing beside him. But I think I can get something out of his old girlfriend. Since Ignacio has fallen out of favor, she seems much more willing to talk about his shortcomings. I'll see if I can talk to her today. And I'll try to contact Tasio, even though he's due back in prison in two days. We have no time to lose now that we only have a week. Besides, there's something troubling me. I don't know if you've noticed, but ever since he got out of Zaballa, Tasio hasn't updated his Twitter account or sent me any tweets."

"That's probably normal, with everything that's happening to him. Everyone on social media thinks he's guilty: for once everybody agrees on something."

"But that happened before. After the other murders, public opinion turned against him, but that didn't stop him from sending several tweets a day," I said with a shrug.

"The only thing we know is that after he got out, he shut himself up in his apartment on Calle Dato. But to tell you the truth, Unai, if I'd been in prison for twenty years and was allowed out for the first time, even just for five days, I wouldn't bother with Twitter or social media. I'd just want to live."

Yet, we never do, I thought. I was not the best person to give lessons on how to live.

The social-media break had also given me some respite. I was still receiving condolences from all over the world on the death of my sister-in-law. People had grown accustomed to using #Kraken to get in touch with me, as if I were a public service open twenty-four hours a day. At least they were no longer calling me useless, although they continued to insist we should arrest Tasio before he could go on killing.

I sent *I want to see you, Tasio* to the *Fromjail* address. I knew MatuSalem would be checking it and pass it on to Tasio. After spending the past twenty years behind bars, Tasio would have no idea what it meant to carry a cell phone linked to the Internet in his pocket.

It didn't take long for MatuSalem to respond:

> Kraken, I'm worried. Tasio has not contacted me since he got out of prison. That wasn't the plan. I don't know how to explain this, but something bad has happened to him.

37

THE DUENDE UNDERPASS

THURSDAY, AUGUST 11

I was about to dial Alba, but she beat me to it.

"Unai, I'd like to talk to you. In private."

"I have something to say to you as well, ma'am," I said, unsure whether to address her as a lover or a police inspector. "Where?"

"I shouldn't be seen at your place. Do you know somewhere out in the open that not many people go, even in broad daylight?"

"The Duende Underpass," I said quickly. "It's one of the city's black spots—it has the highest number of thefts and attacks on women. Everyone avoids going there. For you and me, it's the safest place in the world."

"Where is it?"

"It's a tunnel under the railway lines, at the end of Calle Rioja. On the far side, it joins Paseo de la Universidad; you can't miss it."

"See you there in twenty minutes," she said, and hung up.

Not long after, we met in the dark tunnel. As a precaution I entered it from the opposite end, in Calle Ferrocarril. Alba was waiting for me, staring at graffiti of a girl with blue eyes and green hair blowing bubbles.

It was eleven o'clock on August 11, and there was absolutely nobody using the underpass. Calle Rioja looked dead, and the asphalt was already burning hot.

"What is it, Alba?" I asked as I walked up to her.

"I can't stop thinking about what happened the night of the lantern procession," she said softly, still staring at the graffiti. "Do you think anybody saw us on your roof?"

"I've been thinking about that as well." I sighed. "At that time of night, the Plaza de la Virgen Blanca was dark, and everybody was watching the procession. But maybe the murderer was close to the crime scene, observing people's reactions. It's possible that he saw us. I can't rule that out. In fact, I thought the Eguzkilore might have seen us. He could have learned where I live from his sister, and we know he was prowling around when the sheet was discovered. He was one of the people who took photos of the bodies. But I was wrong. Bitter experience has taught me that a series of coincidences doesn't necessarily lead to the truth."

"Why is the killer attacking your family and friends now? That's what I can't figure out. What have you done to make this personal? What changed?" she insisted. "You're the profiling expert. You said before that this killer turns his victims into objects, that they are simply individuals who are the right age and have the right names, but with these last murders he wanted to hurt you and Estíbaliz, really hurt you."

And he succeeded, Alba. You can't even imagine how terrible I feel for what he did to Martina.

"I told you," I replied, keeping my voice steady. "We touched a nerve, although we don't know which one. We've discovered something, and he knows that if we can follow it through, we'll get to him. The easiest way to get us out of the way was to bring our families into it, so that you would take us off the case."

"No, Unai," she said, "that's not the easiest way to get you out of the way. That's why I called."

"What are you talking about?" I said, leaning against the tunnel wall, keeping a sharp lookout.

"Unai, I'm terrified," she said slowly, without looking at me. "I want to get you away from this. When do you turn forty?"

So that was it.

"If you're asking, it's because you already know."

"It's tomorrow, the day of the Perseid shower, isn't it? Is that why you invited me, so that I would spend your birthday with you?"

"I know you can't come. I only need to be rejected once."

"Stop trying to avoid the subject. I want to protect you. Aren't you afraid the killer will come after you this time?"

"Oh, you don't know how much I would love that bastard to come for me!" I said without thinking. I was getting angry, and that wasn't good, especially in the middle of the street, however deserted it might be. "At least then I'd finally know who he is."

"And it might be your last memory. Your birthday is tomorrow, and then you'll be on the list of the condemned."

"So what should I do, emigrate? Hide under a rock? You said it yourself, if a murderer has decided to kill me, he'll find a way to get to me, especially in this case. I'm ready for it, Alba, and I'm going to pretend I'm not insulted that you don't trust me."

She glared at me. "I don't understand what goes on inside your head. Any other man would be flattered that I'm so concerned, but you choose to be insulted."

"I'll be flattered the day you leave your husband and choose me!" I exploded. "I don't want to be just your summer fuck!"

"Do you think I'd risk my job and my reputation for a sad summer fling?"

"Sad, you say? Maybe you're not the person I've been with these past few days, because that was anything but sad."

"It was just an expression. It's impossible to talk to you when you're angry like this, Kraken. I swear I'll never forgive you if you end up dead," she said, then turned on her heel and strode off.

Back home, I went out for a run without giving it much thought, despite the heat and the danger of becoming dehydrated. I needed to clear my head, to stop thinking for a while. I was on the verge of going crazy.

Crazy with guilt for Martina's death.

Crazy with jealousy of Señor X, Alba's invisible husband.

Crazy with feeling so powerless over a mystery that grew more intricate with each new crime.

The murderer was talking to me in an incomprehensible language, as if I belonged to an inferior, less evolved species.

I felt like an idiot.

There were pieces missing.

I needed more facts.

After a half-hour run that left me exhausted, I called Aitana, Ignacio's former girlfriend. She was astonished to hear from me again but agreed to meet at Zabalgana Park.

When I arrived, she was smoking again, but this time she didn't have the baby carriage. Her gravid stomach was bulging under a black dress that was too tight for her.

"How are things, Aitana?"

"I'm pleased at the progress I made by telling you my story. For the first time I feel strong. I no longer feel guilty for what they did to me."

"I'm glad, really glad to hear it. But I'm afraid I'm going to have to ask you to dig into your past again."

"Whatever you want. What is it?" She lit another cigarette.

"We have witnesses who say they saw you with the twins the day their mother was buried. Doña Blanca Díaz de Antoñana, that is."

Her face tensed, but she said nothing, just kept walking beside me, staring in front of her.

"That day, when everyone else had left, and there were only the four of you outside the Unzueta family vault, the twins beat up a young man. You were there and heard what they said. What happened? Why did they beat him up and throw him into a common grave?"

"I don't know anything, inspector," she said softly, then dropped the cigarette and ground it out.

"You won't be considered an accomplice. The boy didn't make a complaint; besides, it was twenty-seven years ago. You can't be accused of anything now, if that's what's worrying you."

"I don't know anything."

I stepped in front of her. "Aitana, I know when you're lying. You have a tic: you stub out your cigarette, even if you haven't finished it, and light another one. You did it repeatedly during our first talk when you told me that Ignacio was good."

"That may be, but I don't want to talk about it. I have that right."

"Not if you're obstructing a criminal investigation. What if I promise that you won't appear in any report? That you'll remain anonymous? That this conversation never took place? Look, this is the only line of inquiry we have. You want this to end, whether the murderer is Tasio, Ignacio, or someone else entirely. You've been silent for twenty years about what they did to you. Don't you think it's time to face the past? It could also mean an end to the impunity the twins used to enjoy—wasn't that what you hated? Isn't that what ruined your life?"

She closed her eyes, and I could tell she had given in.

"It's very hot," she said, fanning herself with her hand. "I'm really tired; let's sit on a bench. If you're not careful, you'll make me go into labor."

"I wouldn't want to do that!"

I accompanied her to a bench in the shade and waited patiently.

I knew she had made up her mind, but she needed time to process memories she had probably tried to suppress for decades.

"I don't know why you're asking me about that incident. It was very strange, almost surreal. Once the burial was over, a young boy about our age approached us. He was filthy, dressed in charity-shop clothes: we thought he was going to ask for money—he certainly looked like a beggar, the poor kid. But he approached Tasio and said he had to talk to them, that he was also their mother's son. He swore his mother had told him that he was the product of her relationship with another man. Tasio and Ignacio attacked him to shut him up. They wouldn't allow him to insult their mother in front of her freshly dug grave. They had always been proud of being their father's sons, even of being descendants of Unzueta the slave trader."

"So they beat him up just for that?"

"You don't understand—it was ridiculous. He didn't just say they were brothers: he said they were triplets. Just think: Tasio and Ignacio, so smart and elegant, and that fat kid with carrot-colored hair, claiming they were triplets. I don't think he could have insulted them more. He touched what was sacred to them, got involved where he shouldn't have. They have always seen themselves as different, as the chosen ones, because they're monozygotic twins. And that ragamuffin said he was one of them. It was a crazy story, and he was a swindler, a vulture. It was obvious he was after the twins' inheritance, but it was all done so crudely that it was ridiculous they even pretended to believe him. And he showed up at a bad moment; they had just buried their mother, whom they adored. I don't want you to think I'm condoning the beating they gave him; in fact, I was amazed to see how violent they could be. I'd never seen them get into fights in all the years I'd known them. They'd always been intelligent enough to avoid them. That kid pressed the wrong button on the wrong day."

"I need details, Aitana. I have to find that boy. Can you tell me anything that would help me identify him?"

"He said his name was Venancio, though he didn't mention a last name. The twins laughed because no eighteen-year-old in Vitoria was called Venancio, but it's my grandfather's name, so I said nothing. I don't think I can tell you anything else, except that he was about the same age as we were, so he must have been born around 1971, like the twins. I don't know if that will be enough to identify him."

Finally, I had a name and a starting date I could pursue.

All right, that gives me something to work with.

That gives me something to work with.

38

TRES CRUCES

FRIDAY, AUGUST 12

All my hopes were dashed when Estíbaliz and I started to search for the elusive Venancio.

We scoured the civil register on our database but could only find one Venancio Martínez, a native of Izarra, born in 1972, died aged twelve in a traffic accident.

We widened our search to include the entire province of Álava. Nothing.

"Maybe the red-haired phantom just said the first name that came into his head," said Estíbaliz, who was sitting across from me.

"It's possible. But this is the only solid lead we've had," I replied wistfully.

"I'll go crazy if I have to stay cooped up in here much longer, Kraken. It's worse than death by a thousand cuts."

"Don't worry." I leaned back in my chair. "As of tomorrow, I suspect we'll be out looking for Tasio."

"What makes you so sure he won't show up at the prison tomorrow? You've changed your tune."

"I trust my source, and he is worried. Either something has happened to Tasio, or you've been right all along, and he planned this whole thing—he killed your brother and Martina to taunt us, and now he's vanished."

I stood up and gazed through the bulletproof glass in Estíba-liz's office, trying to conceal my despair. "It infuriates me that Sal-vatierra won't let us go after him until tomorrow. We're wasting precious time."

Alba hadn't set great store in the info from MatuSalem. A quick check showed Tasio's ankle tag emitting a signal from his apartment on Calle Dato, where he had been staying since his release. As long as that was the case, we couldn't intervene. She had also been in touch with the squad monitoring the entrance to his building, and no one matching Tasio's description had left the premises, which meant he was still inside.

I insisted we contact Tasio in person, but Alba refused, arguing that she didn't want another media circus, and she didn't want to give Tasio the chance to accuse us of harassment.

Maybe she was right. Maybe Tasio wanted to spend a few days alone in his apartment, disconnected from social media, trying to forget that he would soon become a media hostage again.

"There's nothing we can do today, Kraken, you said so yourself. But if Tasio doesn't show up tomorrow, then, my friend, the hunt is on! I can't wait to go after that bastard, to get him on his own—"

"Careful, Estí. This isn't a personal crusade. Our bosses will be watching us like hawks, you know."

My partner stood up, came over to me, and leaned her head against my arm.

"I know." She sighed.

I realized she was as frustrated as I was.

After a while, we both sat down and resumed our search.

I hated wasted days—clues that led nowhere, useless witnesses, going in circles, coming up against a brick wall and knowing that, even if I jumped over it, I would find nothing on the other side.

And so it was back to square one. Office work, cross-checking facts, names, timelines. No matches.

Who could have known that the key to the mystery was in my own house, kept for decades by my own flesh and blood?

It was my fortieth birthday, and it was a Friday. At any other time, I would have thrown a huge party, but none of my friends who called to wish me a happy birthday asked if we were going out. We were all still devastated by Martina's death. The truth was I didn't feel like seeing anyone.

As soon as I finished work, I pointed my Outlander in the direction of Villaverde. I knew Alba wouldn't be joining me on my rooftop to watch the Perseids streak across the sky, and I'm not the type to wait too long for anybody. That's the trouble with bruised egos: they're very sensitive.

And so I headed for the village, to spend my birthday with Grandfather and Germán. I had taken precautions in case the killer decided to follow me and turned up at my raucous birthday party. I was armed with my HK service revolver, and I didn't plan on letting it out of my sight.

It was still light when I arrived, and I whistled as I mounted the steps. I was surprised not to find Grandfather downstairs, and I continued to the loft, where he was contemplating the old photographs from the case twenty years ago, which I had spread out on the Ping-Pong table.

"Is something wrong, Grandpa?"

"No, son, nothing. I just wish I could help you, but I don't know how."

You can help me by staying alive, Grandpa, I thought, but didn't say it.

"Let's go up to Tres Cruces," I said, clapping his back, which was as hard as oak. "The San Lorenzo meteor shower is due tonight."

"All right, let's go." He rose from the small wicker chair and took one of the boxwood canes he used for walking in the hills.

"Shouldn't we wait for Germán?" I asked.

"Your brother called; he isn't coming. Something to do with work. If he keeps barricading himself in that office day and night, I'll go to Vitoria myself and drag him out, by his feet if necessary."

Anyone hearing my grandfather would think he was exaggerating. I was the only one with enough experience to know that he meant what he said.

Germán had responded to Martina's death by burying himself beneath a mound of pending cases. I planned to give him a few days. After that, I'd have to intervene; that is, if Grandfather didn't beat me to it. He was more persuasive.

"Let's go, then," I said, rather halfheartedly.

We went via the garden shed, where Grandfather grabbed a couple of empty sacks. They smelled like mud and potatoes but were good for lying on.

We walked up the Tres Cruces path, which led straight from the village into the hills before branching out toward the three other cardinal points.

At that time of evening, the tractors had gone home. All around us were fields of harvested wheat, and a few fallow ones waiting to be sown the following year. We stopped where the four paths met and spread our sacks on the ground. We lay on them, surrounded only by the drone of crickets.

"Keep still, Unai, don't make a sound," the old man whispered suddenly.

Rousing myself, I did as he said, and watched him straighten up, reaching gingerly for his cane.

"A snake, do you see? There, coiled on the path." He pointed.

"It's not moving, Grandpa. I think it's dead."

"Dead? Nonsense! The snake is the smartest creature on the mountain," he said, striking the ground with his cane.

The snake uncoiled quick as a flash and, before we knew it, disappeared into the long grass beside the path.

"I doubt it'll come near us again. As it gets dark, and the temperature drops, the snake will take shelter beneath a rock."

I wasn't so confident and remained alert to any shadows moving nearby for a while, until, a few hours later, I forgot about the snake and relaxed.

We could see a few constellations: Orion, Cassiopeia, the Herdsman, the Big Bear, which Grandfather insisted on calling "the Cart." Much later, at about three in the morning, the meteor shower began.

They went by, sometimes one at a time, sometimes in threes, so fast we couldn't count them all. We really had to focus because if we blinked, we missed them. Maybe the same principle applied to the good things in life. Like being there with Grandfather, lying on the earth that would one day clasp us to its bosom.

"I made you a gift, son. I thought, he spends so much time looking at it, he might as well carry it with him." His husky voice broke the enveloping silence.

He handed me a small wooden object. I felt it in the darkness, but I couldn't work out what it was.

"Thank you, Grandpa. What is it?"

"It's a view of the peaks from Villaverde. El Toro Pass to San Tirso. I carved it out of boxwood, so it should be resilient."

I searched for a distant glow from the few streetlights in Villaverde and held up the tiny carving to study its outline.

Grandfather had always been a good carpenter. Now, due to his failing eyesight, he made spoons and carving forks, so I knew that this tiny, intricate piece must have been a labor of love.

"I made a small hole there." He pointed, trying to conceal the pride in his voice. "In case you wanted to use it as a keychain. But you don't have to, if you don't want to."

I was deeply moved. I fished my keys out of my pants pocket, brushing the loaded gun at my side, and attached my miniature sierra to the ring. No one, no matter how well they knew me, would ever give me a better birthday present. No one.

The next morning, I awoke to the smell of fresh bread from Bernedo that Grandfather was grilling on the wood-fired stove. We had a few jars of homemade brambleberry jam left over from the previous fall, and we ate our breakfast in silence, polishing off a whole loaf between us without even realizing it, each immersed in his own labyrinth of thoughts.

"Son, there's something I want you to see. I think it might help you."

"With what, Grandpa?"

"With your job. What else?"

I looked into his eyes, clouded with the milky gray of old age, and realized that this case was affecting him, too. That he was as shocked as anyone by Martina's death. That he was concerned about me, afraid I might be the next victim.

"Grandpa, you mustn't worry about all this. We're dealing with it. I'm dealing with it; nothing is going to happen to me."

"Come with me," he said brusquely, rising from the kitchen chair.

"Where are we going?"

"To the loft, there's a photo I want to show you."

I followed him, somewhat confused, and he led me into the loft and over to the table.

He plucked a picture of a woman standing next to an enormous car from among the old images and press cuttings.

The photo was part of a short piece in the society pages about the twins' mother, Blanca Díaz de Antoñana. I read the caption, but I didn't see how this brief report on a vintage car exhibition in Vitoria in 1985 could provide me with any valuable information.

"Take a look at that monster of a car."

"Yes, it's very big. You know more than I do about cars. What make is it?"

"It's a 1925 Isotta Fraschini. My commanding officer used to drive one when I was stationed at the Ciudad Universitaria in Madrid in '36. This is its twin, and it came here to Villaverde, and so did that woman."

"What did you say?" I asked, bewildered.

"Simply that many years ago, she came to Villaverde in that car. It's not something you forget in a hurry; it was almost too wide to get down Cuesta de Fermín. She had to leave it parked outside the grain store on the main road, when she asked about your great-aunt and went to talk with her. People asked your great-aunt about her elegant visitor, but she gave nothing away. Still, it was the talk of the village for weeks."

"With my great-aunt? I had no idea they knew each other."

"Nobody did, but you might want to ask her about it now."

You bet I do.

"Will you come with me to see her? You've always had a way with your sister-in-law."

"Of course," he said, adjusting his beret, pleased to be able to help me. "Let's see how her head is today. She'll be in her vegetable garden picking peppers."

"Do you think she'll remember? It was a long time ago," I said anxiously.

"Like me, she has an old person's memory. She can't tell you what she had for breakfast yesterday, but she remembers that on the day the bishop of Vitoria came to visit the schoolchildren, and took pictures of everyone in the village, I was involved in the black market in Laguardia. She hasn't forgotten that. I think that was in

1947. Your grandmother kept pestering me to take her to see that film *Gilda*. Afterward, people having a lunchtime aperitif after Sunday Mass in the bars in Vitoria and Logroño asked for a *gilda*. A *gilda* was a cocktail stick spiked with a hot pepper, an olive, and an anchovy, and apparently, it got its name because it was spicy like the film. Not that I've ever had a *gilda*."

I watched open-mouthed as he descended the stairs. He hadn't spoken that much all year. My grandfather only ever exceeded his habitual seven words when he was extraordinarily happy or excited about something.

We went down Calle San Andrés, the longest street in the village, until we reached the lane to the cemetery. To the right was a small path and a vegetable garden, which you entered through a rickety wooden door.

The door was ajar, so we went in, walking along a narrow beaten-earth track, taking care not to step on the rows of zucchini and lettuce.

Saucers of milk had been strategically placed in the sunniest corners of the garden. My great-aunt still believed that milk attracted snakes, so she poisoned it and put it out for them to drink.

We found her stooped over her tiny hoe turning over a mound of earth.

"Do you want some green peppers?" she asked in her high-pitched, girlish voice, sensing our approach. "I'll have to throw most of them away this year. I don't have the energy to grill and preserve them all. I won't plant any next season."

My great-aunt Felisa had no intention of dying, despite being a hundred and two years old. Her notion of time was completely different from the rest of ours.

I remember when her husband, Great-Uncle Sexto, died at eighty-nine. During the wake she kept staring at his coffin in disbelief and saying, "But he was so young. . . ." She had clothes in her wardrobe that were brand-new. "I'm keeping them for when I'm old," she would say.

"Felisa," Grandfather began, "Unai wants to ask you a few questions. You'll have to think back a bit."

"Of course, son," she said offhandedly, continuing her hoeing.

"Auntie, did you know Blanca Díaz de Antoñana, the wife of the industrialist Javier Ortiz de Zárate?"

She paused for a moment, pushed up the glasses that concealed her droopy eye, which was the result of who knew what injury, then went on furiously pulling weeds.

"Why do you want to know?" she said, her back to us.

"Actually, this is about her sons, Ignacio and Tasio Ortiz de Zárate. But I gather she came looking for you once, here in Villaverde, and that you met with her. Can you tell me what she wanted?" I coaxed.

"That was a long time ago. I'd almost forgotten about it."

"What had you forgotten, Auntie? Can you be more specific?" I insisted, realizing that I was coming up against another brick wall.

Extracting information from old folk in the villages was an almost-impossible task. They had lived through a civil war and nearly forty years of dictatorship. They were accustomed to keeping quiet and being evasive. It was in their genes.

"Unai, do me a favor and pop up to the cemetery, would you?" the old man interrupted me. "That southerly wind we had last Monday must have dried out your grandmother's flowers. Could you throw them away?"

I looked at him, and he gave his beret a twist.

I walked along the lane and looked through the iron grille into our tiny cemetery. It was little more than a wall containing twenty or so recent niches surrounded by sacred ground, which no one in their right mind in Villaverde would dare walk on. It was earth that contained the bones of our ancestors, heaped on top of one another when space ran out and they decided to build the concrete niches. Only a few years later, the niches were also filling up.

Grandmother gazed at me from her framed photograph, silently imploring me, as always, to take care of Grandfather. Only this time I noticed a change in her expression—this time she was imploring me to take care of myself.

Dejected, I walked back down to my great-aunt's vegetable garden.

I never did find out what Grandfather said or how he convinced Felisa to talk to me; whenever I tried asking him, he shrugged.

But the fact is, I returned to find Felisa sitting in an old deck chair, her hoe set aside, ready to talk.

"She's remembered," Grandfather whispered in my ear, as I unfolded another shaky deck chair and sat down next to her.

"Auntie, why did Blanca Díaz de Antoñana come here to speak to you?"

"She wanted to find the child. Her husband had just died, so she was safe."

"Safe from what?"

My aunt sighed and looked out toward the hills.

"Doña Blanca's husband was a brute. She was terrified of him."

"You mean she was a victim of domestic abuse?" I asked.

She screwed up her good eye.

"Did he beat the living daylights out of her, Felisa?" Grandfather clarified.

"You can say that again. He was the lord and master of Vitoria. Back then he could do whatever he wanted, and no one dared cross him."

"You say she came here looking for a child. What child? If she came to Villaverde just after her husband died, that must have been around 1989."

"Don't ask me what year it was, son. I get them all jumbled

up. Best you let me do the talking first," she replied, smoothing out the creases in her skirt.

"All right, Auntie. Tell me everything you remember about her visit."

"I was Doctor Urbina's nurse, and he was Doña Blanca's gynecologist. I also took care of Javier Ortiz de Zárate's first wife at the Vitoria Clinic. Blanca came to see me in Villaverde because she'd been diagnosed with cancer, poor woman, and she wanted to put her affairs in order before leaving this world."

"What did she want from you?" I interjected when she paused for breath. I was trying to focus the most informal interrogation I had ever conducted.

"She wanted the family's name so that she could find the boy."

"What boy?"

"An old affair concerning an adoption." She glanced at Grandfather.

He folded his arms over his chest and gestured to her to continue.

"I suppose it's all right to talk about it after all this time," she muttered.

"Yes, please do, Auntie. I think I'm getting a better idea of the situation. Tell me, did Doña Blanca have triplets and give the redhead up for adoption?"

She started when she heard my outlandish theory, the same one the red-haired youth had tried to explain to the twins at their mother's graveside.

"How do you know about this? The only people present at the delivery are either dead or here in this garden."

"Auntie, I'm a detective. I'm investigating this matter, and it's important, very important. Can you give me a date so I can look for the paperwork?"

"There isn't any paperwork. Doctor Urbina and I were trying

to save her and her children from that animal of a husband, but that was the last time I ever saw Doctor Urbina. The poor man had no idea who he was dealing with."

"What do you mean, exactly? Why would Doctor Urbina have been involved in an illegal adoption? Was it about money? Did you sell the child?"

"Money never came into it. We were risking our necks."

"I don't understand."

"Well, it couldn't be more obvious." My aunt sighed, a little irritated.

"Unai, your aunt is trying to tell you that Doña Blanca had an affair with Doctor Urbina and that he was the father of the triplets, not her wretch of a husband," Grandfather said in a patient voice, as if he were explaining the birds and the bees to me.

My God, I thought. *So the twins are neither Ortiz de Zárates nor Unzuetas. What eighteen-year-old who stood to inherit a fortune would want to hear that?*

"Who did you give the baby to, Auntie?"

"To a couple in Izarra."

At last, a connection, a sign that my great-aunt wasn't senile, that what she remembered was true.

"Do you know their last name?" I asked, drawing closer and clasping her hand.

"Lopidana, the bee people."

"The bee people?"

"Yes, they sold honey at local markets. They were good people, son. Good people who were desperate for a child. Doctor Urbina's predecessor, Doctor Medina, put them on his waiting list out of friendship. They were his neighbors. Doctor Medina occasionally gave unwanted babies to infertile couples. As for me: I see, hear, and keep quiet. Some people's lives were helped, others destroyed."

"Do you know if they called the boy Venancio?"

"Truth be told, I have no idea. I left a tiny red-haired baby at a farmhouse, hoping to offer him a better life than if he had stayed in Vitoria. He wouldn't have survived for long there, I can assure you. He looked too much like Doctor Urbina and his two other sons. The whole of Vitoria would have discovered the deception. Back then everybody knew everybody else, not like now. When I go to the clinic in El Pilar, I don't know anyone." She gave a wistful sigh. "Are you sure you don't want any green peppers? Sexto doesn't like them; he says I fry them in too much oil."

My aunt had returned to the present, where for her everything was more nebulous. Her chin was trembling slightly, and I was worried I had forced her to think too hard. Grandfather also gestured to me to stop as soon as she started talking about her deceased husband.

"Go on, then, give me a couple of bagfuls. I'll share them among my *cuadrilla,* who will thank me for it," I said, rising to my feet.

Half an hour later, we set off for home laden with lettuce, squash, green peppers, onions, and several pounds of plums, a fruit I'd always detested. At that time of year, the plum trees in Villaverde were creaking beneath the weight of insane quantities of ripe fruit, and everywhere you went people offered you their plums, or begged you to take them.

"Was that helpful, son?" Grandfather asked as soon as we returned to the kitchen and tried, unsuccessfully, to fit all the vegetables into the fridge.

"Absolutely, Grandpa. I have what I need to keep investigating."

"That's what you have to do, keep investigating. Try to catch that fox so we can all sleep soundly in our beds. And I'll keep trying to help you by looking through the photographs and the other stuff you've saved, if you'll let me," he said, avoiding my gaze as he pretended to rinse dirt off a squash.

"Of course, Grandpa. I'd be delighted for you to keep helping me," I said, swallowing hard. Grandfather didn't go in for displays of affection and would have been embarrassed to see his grandson choked with emotion.

I drove back to Vitoria in a better mood than I had been in for a long time. I felt exhilarated and couldn't wait to get back to police headquarters to share my news with Estíbaliz.

I arrived well before midday to find my partner waiting for me expectantly in my office.

"How was your birthday, Unai? I didn't say anything to you yesterday, I didn't want to—"

"Give me your condolences on turning forty and making it on to that damned list, I know. My birthday was as quiet as I wanted it to be. I went to see Grandpa in Villaverde. It was perfect. Why so nervous?" I asked. She couldn't stop fidgeting.

"It runs out in less than thirty minutes."

"What does?"

"The time limit on Tasio's parole. The Spanish media, not to mention the foreign press, is posted outside Zaballa. It's live on Twitter."

"Any new hashtags?" I asked.

"Oh, plenty! #TasioEnters, #TasioUnmasked, #TasioMissing . . . people are curious to see if they can get a glimpse of what he looks like now."

"They're not missing anything, I can assure you."

"This is morbid fascination at its best. Show some respect." She winked, and I nodded, grinning. Things between us felt almost normal. With any luck, both Estí and I would bounce back from this. Possibly.

"Well, I've made huge progress, thanks to a most unlikely

witness. Hold on to your hat, you're in for a few surprises," I said.

"Let's hear it."

"You know I have a hundred-year-old great-aunt."

"The one who never gets sick?"

"That's right. Great-Aunt Felisa. My grandmother's sister, Grandfather's sister-in-law. She was a nurse before she retired; she worked at the Vitoria Clinic for years."

"Okay, I'm with you so far."

"What if I told you that the story about the redhead the twins beat up was true?"

"The one about the twins having a poor triplet?"

"Uh-huh."

She tied and untied her ponytail several times. "You'll need to draw a diagram. I'm a little lost."

"Okay, in the early seventies, when the twins were born, Great-Aunt Felisa worked for a Doctor Urbina. Felisa claims that her boss had an affair with Blanca Díaz de Antoñana, the twins' mother, and that Blanca's husband, the industrialist Javier Ortiz de Zárate, was a dangerous man who beat his wife. Felisa assisted at the birth of the twins. As far as I can tell from the press clippings, they took after their mother. However, a third baby was born, and he had red hair just like Doctor Urbina. Aunt Felisa claims that, at the request of both Doña Blanca and Doctor Urbina, she gave the baby to a couple in Izarra."

"She said Izarra?"

"Yes, and now we have the same village mentioned by two different sources. I know we shouldn't rely on simple coincidence—it's a lesson I've learned recently," I said, trying not to let the words burn my mouth. "But that's not the only one. Grandfather told me that, shortly after her husband died, Blanca Díaz de Antoñana came to Villaverde asking for Felisa. She was no longer afraid of the story coming out and wanted to know what had become of her third son. My aunt told her the name of the couple to whom she had given the boy. They were on a waiting list for illegal adoptions that Doctor Urbina's predecessor, Doctor Medina, had started."

"I can believe that. A couple of years ago, when the national press started to expose cases of stolen children and illegal adoptions, several allegations were made against the Vitoria Clinic, among others."

"I know, but I didn't mention it to my aunt. I doubt she heard about the allegations at the time. She hasn't followed the news in years. She told me that the couple in Izarra, the Lopidanas, were friends of Doctor Medina and that they produced honey. We need to look them up on the database right now."

"Another interesting connection with the case," said Estí.

"From now on, we're going to be wary of connections like this. Still, we not only have the honey and Izarra; we also have a narrative, Estí. And, more important, we have a motive."

"You mean, the redhead, this Venancio fellow."

"Yes, and it's a strong motive. Not only was he disinherited, but his own brothers beat him half to death and hounded him out of Vitoria. That's a strong enough motive to hate them and want to destroy their lives." I was thinking aloud.

"Why don't we tell the DSU about this? I'd love to give her a result for once, instead of feeling like we're a couple of losers," she said, rising from her chair.

"Yes, I agree. We need to inform her."

When we entered Alba's office, we found her speaking on her cell phone yet again.

"I'll be home in time for dinner, don't worry," she said in a hushed voice, her back to us.

It was obvious from her tone that she was talking to her husband.

Was he controlling? Was he affectionate? Was he demanding she come home early from work? Was this a usual exchange between them?

I realized I hadn't wanted to form an image of him: it hurt less when he was ethereal, invisible. To me, he had no body and no shape; he didn't occupy a space measuring between five and six feet. I knew that if I started to wonder about what kind of relationship they had, I was in danger of obsessing over it and making myself suffer.

Estíbaliz cleared her throat to get Alba's attention, who ended the call and turned around.

"I'm glad to see you two concentrating on work again. Do you have any news?"

"It would appear so," I began. "We're following a fresh line of inquiry. We told you that we wanted to take a closer look at the twins' past, at their background. That's because if neither one is the killer, then the culprit has to be someone with a powerful enough motive to want to implicate them in serial murders."

"So far, it makes sense. Please, sit down."

Estíbaliz and I did as we were asked.

"We have reason to believe that the twins had a—"

Just then, someone called Alba's phone again. She had changed her ringtone to "Lau teilatu," and the fact that she would do that knocked me sideways.

I looked straight at her, and her face turned bright pink.

"DSU Salvatierra," she replied in a professional tone, checking the number on the screen.

Alba listened to the woman, who was speaking quickly, and waited for her to finish.

"All right," she said after some time, "we'll set the relevant procedures in motion. Meanwhile, I'll send officers to search the premises, and I'll call you back as soon as there's any news. Please don't talk to the press until we know what the situation is. Tell them the investigation is ongoing and you aren't at liberty to discuss it."

After she hung up, she sat down in her chair, frowning as she made a series of rapid decisions.

"Tasio didn't return to prison when he was supposed to, and the electronic tag is still giving his location as the apartment on Calle Dato. I want you to get there as quickly as you can to see if he's still there, if anything's happened to him, or if he's given us the slip."

39

DOÑA LOLA'S YEW TREE

IZARRA
MARCH 1989

Blanca Díaz de Antoñana knew that the road to Izarra would be treacherous after the recent snowfall, but she couldn't afford to wait until it was cleared. Since her last appointment with the doctor, she felt as if the world was spinning too fast and she was moving too slowly. There weren't enough hours in the day for the thousand and one arrangements she had to make. She managed the pain by increasing the dose prescribed by her oncologist.

She had just sacked Ulysses. He was close to retirement age, and she could have waited, but Javier was dead, and this was one legacy she had no wish to inherit from her husband. She had handed the driver several million pesetas that she had taken from one of the safes Javier had kept at the mansion. Although she acted as if it were a gesture of gratitude, they both knew that this was her way of saying, *Get out of my house. I don't want you anywhere near me now that Javier isn't here.* The old driver was happy to accept it. He packed his belongings into a small suitcase and left the same day, with his limping gait and crooked shoulders.

In the end, how easy it had been to rid herself of the shadow that had followed her every move for years, under instructions from her husband. How lighthearted she had felt strolling down Calle Dato and Calle General Álava without that bent-backed crow on her heels.

She had kept her aunt's apartment, although she had hardly used it for fear Javier might suspect her of having a lover.

She climbed behind the wheel of his car. She felt safe in the Isotta Fraschini; it was robust, and the engine had never given her any problems. She headed north out of Vitoria, toward the Altube Pass. Izarra was less than fifteen miles away, so it wouldn't take her long to get there. The twins had gone to San Sebastián for the day with their *cuadrilla*. Now that they both had their licenses, they were never at home, and being alone suited her fine. After all those years in that gilded cage, it suited her just fine.

She inquired about the Lopidana family at the train station. It was an effort: she had taken her medication several hours earlier, but the pain was coming back and beginning to cloud her mind.

"They live west of the river, in the old part of town. Their farmhouse is next to Doña Lola's yew tree, between the two streams. I'm not sure Señor Lopidana will be at home, though, it's market day today," the thickset woman at the ticket office told her, after looking her up and down from behind the glass partition and ogling the sable collar on her coat.

"Do you know if they have a son?" Blanca ventured to ask. The station was deserted, so no one could hear them.

"They have two five-year-olds, a girl and a boy. Little darlings, they are, mischievous as anything," said the employee, happy to have someone with whom to make conversation.

"Don't they have a son around eighteen, a red-haired boy?" Blanca insisted. Perhaps there were two families in Izarra with the same name, or the Lopidanas had moved to another village.

"Ah, Nancho! They raised him, but he isn't their son. He's the farmhand; he looks after the hives."

"But doesn't he live with them?"

"Oh, yes, in the cellar, I think." The woman nodded, delighted. Now she would have some interesting gossip when she went home for her midday meal. A rich lady asking after Nancho, if that wasn't something to speculate about . . .

When she realized the woman didn't have much more to tell her, Blanca said good-bye, started the car, and drove toward the bridge.

She came to a run-down farmhouse set apart from the other dwellings in the village. It didn't look as if the owners were well-off. Although the place looked almost neat under the mantle of snow, the stench of filth was noticeable from the road. The building was substantial, but on closer inspection one side of the long, gabled roof had practically caved in. The main door, protected by a dried *eguzkilore*, was missing several panels. The once-red tiles that peeped through the snow were covered in grime, and the paint was peeling around the window frames and at the edges of the house, which desperately needed a whitewash. Some of the windowpanes were cracked or had been replaced with bits of board.

Blanca stepped out of the car, hitching up her white fur coat so it wouldn't trail in the mud left by the melted snow.

She leaned over the rickety fence but couldn't see anyone.

She took the plunge. "Is anybody at home?"

No one answered, and Blanca paused for a moment, ears pricked.

"Who's there?" a young man's surly voice eventually replied.

"I'm looking for the Lopidanas. Are they at home?"

When she saw him, she almost forgot to breathe. *It's him, it's him. Keep calm, Blanca. Keep calm,* she told herself.

A rather short, plump young lad in a pair of grease-stained blue overalls came to the battered front door. His ginger hair was cut in an old-fashioned style, as if he were stuck in the seventies. One long lock fell over his eye, as if in a halfhearted attempt to hide his chubby, acne-scarred face.

Yet what Blanca saw was the calm gait and shy gestures of

Álvaro Urbina. It was if she were looking at a teenage version of the man she had loved so much.

Overwhelmed, she raised a hand to her mouth.

"Are you all right, señora?" The lad approached, concerned. "Aita and Ama are in Bilbao selling honey at the market, but they'll be home this evening. Do you want me to give them a message?"

"So you are the Lopidanas' son?"

Nancho gritted his teeth and looked away. It vexed him not to be able to answer that question.

"What do you want, señora? Perhaps I can be of some help?" he replied, evasively.

"You're Nancho, aren't you? My name is Blanca Díaz de Anto-ñana, and what I'm about to tell you will sound very strange, but I don't have time to beat about the bush. I'm searching for a red-haired boy who was given to the Lopidanas eighteen years ago by a woman called Felisa. I believe you are that boy, but if I'm mistaken, please tell me and I'll continue my search for my son."

Instinctively, Nancho drew back. This lady in white was searching for him? He raised his eyes, almost afraid to look at her. He could see none of himself in her: She was on the thin side, with an oval face. She had lines around her mouth, but she smelled like money the moment she leaned over the fence. What possible relationship could he have to this stranger?

"Señora, I know what people in the village say about me, and that's hard enough to bear without you coming here to mock me as well—"

"No, son!" Blanca broke in, horrified. "I'm not here to mock you, on the contrary. I need you to confirm that you are the child she brought here, because I'm the mother who allowed it to happen. I came to look for you because I want to put my affairs in order before I go. May I come in?"

"We'd better walk along the path. This place is too smelly for you, and you might get your coat dirty. Let's walk up to the yew tree. I go there when Aita has no work for me," said the boy, flushing. He had never spoken to such an elegant lady, and he wasn't quite sure how to address her.

Blanca gazed at the youth with a mixture of pride and unease. Had he spent his whole life in this hovel?

They walked along the muddy track in silence. Blanca staring at him intently, Nancho's head lowered, as they skirted the mounds of snow.

"Here we are," he said, when they were a few yards from the huge yew. "I come to this tree to think. Did you know that our ancestors worshipped it?"

"Are you a good student? Do you like history? Your brother Tasio loves it, he wants to be an archaeologist, and with his brains, no one doubts he'll be one of the best."

"My brother?"

"Yes, you have twin brothers. They look like me, while you're the spitting image of your father."

"My father?" he ventured, swallowing hard. "Do you mean my real father?"

I have a father, another father who isn't Aita? Maybe he won't treat me the way Aita does.

"Yes, your real father's name was Álvaro Urbina. He was my doctor at the Vitoria Clinic. He disappeared soon after I gave birth. I've always suspected my husband was responsible for his disappearance, but I have no way of proving it. I've never spoken to anyone about these things, but I don't want to hide anything from you now. We gave you away because you looked too much like your father. My husband was a very powerful man in Vitoria; he wouldn't have let you live."

"Wait, wait. Are you telling me I was given to this family because of my red hair, and that you brought up my twin brothers?"

There it is again, he thought. *My red hair.*

How he hated it, how he hated being different. The village boys called him "Ginger Nut" when they felt like amusing themselves at his expense. And now here was this woman saying they had gotten rid of him as a newborn because of his hair. He'd spent his life wondering what he had done to make his parents abandon him, and all this time it was his accursed hair.

Blanca blushed, ashamed of herself. Her son had every reason in the world to be angry.

"What I did to you was a crime, and I'm probably also responsible for the crime your real father committed. Perhaps I have too many crimes weighing on my conscience, and I am no longer able to bear it. I came here to take you away, to give you the part of my estate you are entitled to. I've been diagnosed with an extremely aggressive form of cancer, and I don't have much time left. I'll come back next week with my lawyer. Until then, say nothing to your parents. I'll speak to your father when I come to pick you up. From now on, I want you to live with me and your brothers at our house on Paseo de la Senda in Vitoria, as is your right. As soon as I register you as my legitimate child, you will inherit your share of the estate. But I'll need your identity card to set things in motion."

"I don't have an identity card. Aita didn't want to get me one. That's why I can't drive outside Izarra, because I can't take the test, either, even though I've been driving since I was ten," he said, pointing to the Renault 4 parked on the slope next to the road.

Blanca stared at him in astonishment. "How can you not have an identity card? Did you go to school?"

"I wanted to, but they wouldn't let me. Aita and Ama have always left me in charge of the hives. I taught myself to read by looking at the magazines old Hermógenes brought—the woman who does Amaxto's hair. I have a friend," he said proudly. "The schoolteacher's son. He gives me his old textbooks. I hide them under the stones next to the hives so that Aita won't see them. He doesn't approve of books; he says they brainwash you and make you crazy."

"Have you ever been to Vitoria?"

"Only to buy garlic on El Día de Santiago and during las Fiestas de las Blusas, to take my"—he was about to say *brother and sister*, but even they didn't like Nancho calling them that—"to take Aita and Ama's children, Andoni and Idoia, to the fairground. I'm not allowed out in the evenings; they say that's for drunkards."

"Well, I'm taking you with me to live in Vitoria, if you want to leave here. You have to meet your real brothers, Ignacio and Tasio. But first I must talk to them, tell them about you. They don't even know you exist."

"Señora—" He interrupted her, his thoughts in turmoil. "What about Aita and Ama? How are they going to react?"

"Tell me, Nancho, do your parents treat you well?"

"They let me eat with them, and I have *somewhere* to sleep," he said, embarrassed. He shrugged dismissively.

"Son, do they treat you well?" Blanca repeated, cupping his face in her hands and studying it.

She noticed a couple of old bruises around his eye that were strategically covered by his hair. They pained her more than if they had been hers.

What kind of life have you had, my son?

"That's between Aita and me, señora. I won't say a bad word about him," replied Nancho, brushing her hand away from his face.

"I was told in the village they don't treat you like a son, but that you're a farmhand, a beast of burden."

Nancho flushed to the roots of his hair. That's the way things had been since *they* were born, out of the blue—his brother and sister. Before that, his parents had brought him up as their own son, they had let him call them Aita and Ama. But his life changed the day Amatxo returned from the doctor's saying she was pregnant.

"Is that why you came here, to mock me, to rub my face in it?" the boy snapped, fighting off the painful memories. "Señora, I have enough troubles as it is, and now I'm late with the deliveries. If my father finds out that I haven't taken the honey to the store in Aurora, he'll beat the living daylights out of me."

Blanca also snapped. What had those wretches done to her son? She drew close to the boy, who was a few inches shorter, and grabbed his chin, forcing him to look into her eyes.

"Son, I've been through it myself, since before you were born, and if you have to remember me for anything, let it be this: When somebody hits you, it's never your fault. Never. Do you hear me? He will insist that it is, because he needs you to stay so that he can keep doing it to you, but it's not your fault."

"It's not my fault," Nancho repeated.

"Let me put my arms around you, son."

"What did you say?" Nancho was bewildered.

"Let me put my arms around you; I've been wanting to do this for eighteen years." Blanca didn't wait for the startled youth to give his permission. She embraced him with every bit of strength she had been saving for the encounter, and Nancho surrendered to the warmth of that white coat and the woman who was wearing it.

After the embrace slackened and Blanca pulled away, she placed her pale hand tenderly on the boy's burning cheek. Nancho closed his eyes—this was almost as good as being in heaven. And he knew this gesture would stay with him forever. His first caress. The first caress from someone who truly loved him.

"Tell me, do your parents have enough money?" Blanca said at last, trying not to lose her composure.

"It's rude to talk about cash. They taught me that," he said, with a flash of pride.

Blanca turned and looked at the hovel in the distance.

Let's see if I can pay these people to let you leave. Somehow, I doubt they'd raise many objections.

Ever since she learned she was dying, she realized how little she cared about what people thought of her. The priest at San Antonio's, Andresa Apaolaza, the mayor's wife, and the entire heavenly host of the Círculo Vitoriano could go to hell.

They could all go to hell.

It was Sunday, and the Lopidana family was dressed for ten o'clock Mass at San José Church.

Nancho sat down at the back of the men's pews, as Aita had always ordered him to do. He hadn't been baptized or made his First Communion, so he couldn't take the Host.

All week, he'd been waiting anxiously for Blanca Díaz de Antoñana to return to the farmhouse. But the days had gone by, and the elegant car had never come back. Maybe she'd changed her mind after meeting him; perhaps she had meant well but thought better of it when she saw that he was just . . . well, just him.

He was wearing the only decent clothes he possessed: a pair of jeans, a nearly new, white T-shirt he had won at a Coca-Cola raffle, one of Aita's cast-off jackets, and some white sneakers he had cleaned up with some of Amaxto's shoe polish. He had pressed his clothes first thing that morning, eager to look his best in case today was the day Blanca and her lawyer came to fetch him, although he had hesitated over whether to iron a crease in his jeans.

After Mass, Aita and Ama and the children went to the bar in the square for olives and beer. He followed them, looking around for Blanca's car.

He approached the counter idly and started to leaf through *El Diario Alavés*. Then he saw the news and stood motionless, gasping for air.

At first, he thought the whole thing was a bad joke.

Once he calmed down, once he convinced himself it was real, he concentrated on reading the full-page obituary of Blanca Díaz de Antoñana, born in Vitoria, died in Vitoria on Saturday, March 18, 1989, widow of Javier Ortiz de Zárate, mother of the grieving Ignacio and Anastasio.

In a panic, he saw that the funeral was at twelve today. He looked at the wall clock above the bar. It was eleven thirty.

He approached the table where Aita and Ama were chatting and drinking beers. There were several banknotes and some loose change for the bill on a triangular metal dish on the table. Nancho moved closer and seized the opportunity to pocket four hundred pesetas when Aita stood up to greet an acquaintance. That would be enough.

Just then, his father turned around and Nancho made a dash for the station, his stomach churning out of fear of the consequences of his departure, and from the shock of discovering that this woman, this white angel who'd come down to Earth to save him, was now dead.

He bought a one-way ticket from the lady at the office, who stared at him, wide-eyed, as he ran onto the platform. Minutes later, the train arrived. It would take half an hour to get to Vitoria, hardly long enough to get his thoughts in order.

He wasn't sure what to do next; he just knew that he had to arrive in time for Blanca's funeral, and he had to talk to his brothers. They would speak with the lawyer. The man must be aware of his mother's intentions.

He sat down on one of the threadbare crimson seats and examined his clothes, relieved that for once he was properly dressed.

The train soon arrived in Vitoria. Nancho hurried along the platform and into the red marble hall. He ran over to a map of Vitoria, searching for the name of the cemetery he remembered from the obituary.

Exasperated, he read through the street names but found nothing like what he was looking for.

"Are you lost, my boy?" inquired an elderly lady sitting on a nearby bench.

"I'm looking for Santa Isabel Cemetery. Is it very far?"

"Well, it's halfway across town, but easy enough to find. Go down Calle Dato," she said, motioning with her stick toward the exit, "cross the Plaza de la Virgen Blanca, and walk right to the end of Calle Zapa. When you get to Fuente de los Patos, go straight down Portal de Arriaga until you reach the cemetery."

Nancho memorized the street names so he could ask along the way.

"How long will it take?" He looked at the clock below the three huge windows. It was half past twelve already.

"Half an hour, if you walk fast. I think they've cleared all the snow from the streets."

"Bless you, señora," he heard himself say, as he sprinted down Calle Dato, where families were crowding into the local tapas bars to get warm.

In his haste he fell twice, most humiliatingly in the Plaza de la Virgen Blanca, where he landed with a crash in front of a group of giggling girls his age. Once again, he cursed his clumsiness and looked ruefully at his white T-shirt, now soiled from the dirty snow.

He resumed his sprint through the Old Quarter, and half an hour later, he finally reached the cemetery.

He knew he had not missed the entire service from all the shiny cars double-parked outside the entrance.

He caught up with the elegant crowd and waited patiently until the funeral was over and these strangers went back to the warmth of their centrally heated houses.

It didn't bother him. He was immune to the cold and the damp after all those years sleeping in the farmhouse cellar.

Finally, when the last black overcoat had departed, he saw his brothers. His real brothers, his flesh and blood.

They were holding hands with two beautiful girls, as elegantly dressed as they were.

He gazed at them in disbelief, finding it hard to contain his emotions.

He hadn't arrived too late. He could still change his life. He could have a family who truly loved him, who didn't beat the living daylights out of him.

He went up to them, controlling his nerves, and introduced himself.

40

NUMBER 1 CALLE DATO

SATURDAY, AUGUST 13

Judge Olano issued a warrant to search Tasio's home as soon as he received DSU Salvatierra's call. Estí and I grabbed a thirty-pound battering ram, just in case we had to break down any doors, jumped into a patrol car, and headed straight for Calle Dato, where a few journalists and a lot of onlookers were already gathered.

The swarming crowd made our job more difficult. Before we got out of the car, Estíbaliz pulled on a balaclava and handed one to me. I didn't want to wear the damned thing—I knew my height would give me away anyway—but I gave in.

The entrance was flanked by a Barbour store and a French soap shop. The green-and-gold metal front door had glass panels that gave only a dim view of the interior. We rang the apartment's doorbell, a shiny gold button worn from years of use, although we knew no one would answer.

"EFE News Agency. Inspector, do you think Tasio Ortiz de Zárate has absconded?" one of the reporters asked, thrusting his microphone under my chin.

I pushed him aside and pushed the button a second time.

More passersby joined the crowd. They were grinning excitedly and filming us on their phones, as if this was a spectacle they would show to people later—at home, in the bar, at work.

"Kraken, has Tasio outwitted you? Do you believe he murdered your sister-in-law?" asked one tiny female journalist, holding up her microphone with outstretched arms.

This is noise, I forced myself to think. *Just noise.*

"Will you let us do our job!" Estíbaliz finally shouted, losing her temper. "If no one comes out," she whispered, "we'll radio for a couple of patrol cars to cordon off the area so we can work in peace. This is impossible."

Suddenly, the heavens, or rather the door, opened for us. A venerable old lady stood in the entryway. Her hair was pulled back in a bun, and she was using a walking stick.

When she saw us in balaclavas and me holding a battering ram, she recoiled but then seemed to grasp the situation.

"May we come in, señora?" I asked, pulling up my balaclava. The reporters seized the opportunity to blind me with their flashes.

"By all means, come in, come in," she said, in an unexpectedly gravelly voice.

Perfect, we wouldn't need to break down the door in front of all the media. The old lady ushered us into the hallway, and after she had stepped outside to smile and wave to the crowd, she closed the door behind her, and all at once the clamor in the street ceased. Blissful silence.

We took the elevator to the fourth floor, and again we tried the bell outside the apartment on the left.

"Tasio!" I shouted, pounding on the door. "Open up! Are you in there?"

There was no reply, and so Estíbaliz, who had run out of patience, seized the rear handle of the battering ram. On the count of three, we swung it at the reinforced door.

I felt my teeth vibrate, but the door didn't budge. It finally gave way after several attempts, and we found ourselves in Tasio's apartment.

We checked it, room by room. There was no mistaking the quality of the furnishings and the purchasing power of their owner, but everything was twenty years out of date.

When I saw the photographs of Tasio and Ignacio in the living room, always side by side, or arm in arm, identically dressed from the time they were born, I didn't know what to think. I took several pictures on my phone of all the photos that featured their parents. They might be helpful later.

We searched the closets and drawers in the bedroom. No one had taken away the suits that Tasio had worn before his arrest. Given how neat and tidy the rest of the apartment was, I was struck by the fact that the bed was unmade. In the kitchen, we found the remains of a takeout meal in the garbage. I imagined Tasio's frustration at the fact that, after twenty years of wishing he could go out and enjoy the city, he had ended up isolated in his apartment, unable even to go downstairs to a bar on Calle Dato and have a few tapas.

The famous study, in which the bag of yew leaves had been found years ago, looked as if it had been used recently. The clay *eguzkilore* had been thrown in the trash. There wasn't a speck of dust on the desk, where books on Alavese archaeology were stacked. They had clearly been consulted in the last few days.

"It looks like he's been cooped up in here all this time, just like the technicians monitoring his tag have been saying," Estíbaliz observed. "Christ, Kraken! The tag. We have to look for it. According to them, it should be here."

"According to them, it should be here, and Tasio should be wearing it," I replied uneasily. "I hope we aren't going to find out he's been bricked up, or something."

"Don't be morbid," hissed Estíbaliz.

But just to make sure, she went into one of the bathrooms and pulled back the shower curtain.

"Wait a minute," she said suddenly. "I'm going to check something."

I followed her down the hallway to the bedroom.

Estíbaliz lifted the rumpled sheet and we found it: the electronic ankle tag, its black transmitter shaped like a cigarette case.

"Call the monitoring unit, Kraken. Our bird has flown the nest," she said, arms akimbo.

"Or he's been pushed out, Estí. Take a closer look at this."

I turned on the bedside lamp so we could see better, pulled on a latex glove, and beckoned her over to the tag. It looked like a black plastic digital watch, but the strap had been slashed with a box cutter or some other sharp instrument.

"These look like bloodstains to me. Call forensics, they need to process the scene. They have Tasio's DNA from twenty years ago, from the semen they found in the girl's body. We can also ask Ignacio for a sample, to see if there's a match with a family member. But the blood is on the inside of the strap, so chances are whoever took it off him cut through it from the outside."

"He could have removed it himself," protested Estí.

"Wouldn't you be more careful not to cut yourself, if you were wearing a tight band around your ankle? You'd have to be pretty clumsy to injure yourself with a box cutter, and Tasio doesn't strike me as clumsy."

"Okay, let's make those calls and inform the DSU. The warden at Zaballa is also waiting to hear from us. There's nothing more we can do here."

"Too true," I murmured, preoccupied.

I pulled the goddamned balaclava over my head again, aware of how scary I looked in it. After putting crime-scene tape across the broken door, we took the stairs down to the first floor.

"Regardless of what went on in the apartment, how the hell could Tasio have left the building, whether on foot or feetfirst, without the patrol car in Calle Dato seeing him?" I asked.

"What if he left through the entrance to Number One? You've given me an idea. Let me check something on Google Maps." Estíbaliz pulled out her phone and began to type rapidly.

Her phone gave us an aerial view of the apartment building that we were in. It was a rectangular structure flanked by Calle General Álava and Calle Postas, with the Plaza de los Fueros at the back. But what interested us were the innards of the building, the network of internal yards invisible from the street. We discovered an interior arcade that ran from Calle Postas, opposite the post office, to General Álava, next to the old glass Treasury building.

"Sonofabitch!" exclaimed Estíbaliz. "He got out through Galerías Ítaca."

Galerías Ítaca was a small row of properties and shops on the first floor of the building. It seemed feasible, and yet I wasn't entirely convinced.

We searched the hallway until we found a hidden door in the wood paneling behind the staircase.

Estíbaliz gave it a few hefty shoves, and we found ourselves in an internal yard. In one corner was a glass door, covered with brown wrapping paper. The door was ajar. I pushed it open with my shoulder, and we went inside. It was the back of an empty store. Not much light filtered in, but it seemed to be a shop that had suddenly gone out of business. There was a white melamine counter with broken drawers, several empty wicker baskets strewn around the floor, a few posters of flowers, and some bouquets pinned to the textured yellow walls with thumbtacks.

"This was a florist, wasn't it?" I asked Estíbaliz, though I wasn't completely sure.

"We'll need to dust all the handles for fingerprints," she said, approaching the main door.

Although the door was chained and padlocked, as I leaned against it, it gave way. The chain slid to the marble floor with a clank and lay there like a coiled snake. "It looks like you were right.

We need to inform the owner. Someone cut the chain, possibly with a pair of shears," I said, closing the door. "And we should notify the residents' association at Number One. Anybody can get into their building right now."

"I'm tempted to go out through the arcade to avoid all those journalists," Estíbaliz said with a grin.

"Hmm, that sounds like a plan. But if they don't see us leave the way we came in, we'll be advertising the fact that we've found another exit. Also, if Tasio, or whoever took him, is watching us, we would be giving him a useful advantage. And I don't want to give the slightest advantage to whoever's responsible for all this."

"What a shame." She sighed.

We retraced our steps and put our balaclavas back on, then left dutifully through the main entrance to Number 1 Calle Dato, where the press was waiting for us.

"Can you confirm that Tasio isn't in his apartment?" the journalists shouted, almost in unison.

We lowered our heads, elbowing our way through a group of photographers who were refusing to budge.

"Has the prisoner escaped? Can you tell us that?" some insisted, still hoping we might give them an answer.

We slammed the door of the patrol car in their faces and headed back to police headquarters, where Salvatierra was waiting for us with her arms folded, pacing around her office like a caged lioness.

"So Tasio isn't in his apartment," she said as we entered.

"We found his ankle tag, probably removed with a box cutter or something similar, and what looked like a bloodstain. Right now, the forensics team is processing the scene for fingerprints or other organic traces," I reluctantly admitted.

"First impressions?"

"Mine are that he's been abducted, or else he left the blood smear to make us think that," I replied, sitting down.

"I've persuaded the judge to issue an APB. We'll step up sur-
veillance at the airport and at the train and bus terminals. And
we'll keep tabs on the car-rental agencies. We've already alerted
the border authorities in France, Portugal, and Melilla," said Alba.
"Here's a copy of the press statement we've drafted. It's very concise.
No doubt Tasio, or whoever has spirited him away, will read it. But
there's something else bothering me. It may already have occurred
to you—Tasio is forty-five, isn't he?"

"What are you suggesting, ma'am? That Tasio could be one of
the killer's future victims?"

Alba gave me a sidelong glare, a look like molten steel. "If he
is, first you have to prevent a possible crime against two forty-year-
olds. This is getting messier."

But there was more. There was more.

An hour later, I received a call from the last person I would
have expected to hear from that day.

It was Garrido-Stoker, Ignacio Ortiz de Zárate's attorney.

"Inspector Ayala?"

"Yes, what is it?"

"I'm afraid I have bad news. My client, Don Ignacio Ortiz de
Zárate, has been missing for twenty-four hours."

"What?" I exclaimed. "How the hell did that happen? I
thought he was being monitored by the CCTV at your residence."

"I'm as puzzled as you are, more so since we've spent the past
few days working together on several possible lines of defense.
Which is why I've decided to report him missing at the San Sebastián police headquarters. Judging from the footage I've been able
to retrieve, he appears to have left the premises of his own accord,
but his actions don't make sense. My impression is that something
serious has happened to him. He hasn't been in touch to explain
himself, and he isn't picking up my calls or replying to my e-mails.
Look, maybe he tricked me—anyone is capable of that, even our

nearest and dearest. And I can assure you that in my profession, I'm not in the habit of sticking my neck out for people, but if you want my opinion, both as Ignacio's lawyer and as his friend, he would only leave the house because something he wasn't expecting happened."

Okay, so now it's Ignacio, I thought, attempting to digest the news.

"What exactly does the footage show?" I asked, forcing myself to concentrate.

"Yesterday morning we said good-bye after breakfast, as usual, and I went to my office. He spent about forty-five minutes downstairs in the gym training on the exercise bike and lifting weights—again, just as he always did. When he finished, he took a shower and got dressed. Then he must have received a call or a text message, because he went over to look at his cell phone. As we told you from day one, Ignacio came to my house because he wanted some privacy. All I can tell you is that he picked up the phone and looked at it at length, but the resolution of the security cameras isn't sharp enough to show any details. Then he raised the phone to his ear and had a brief conversation. Judging from his body language, I assume the exchange made him anxious, because he walked from one side of the bed to the other clutching his head with his free hand. After he ended the call, he opened the drawer in the bedside table, took out his wallet and passport, walked out of the chalet door, crossed the garden, and left the premises. The exterior cameras show him heading toward the center of San Sebastián. I'll send you the tapes right away."

"What's your first impression?"

"I think there are two possibilities: either he received a text message from someone he doesn't know who then called him, or someone he knows called him unexpectedly."

And I doubt Tasio had a cell phone twenty years ago, so he couldn't have made the call, I thought.

"Can I rely on your discretion vis-à-vis the press, Señor Garrido-Stoker? Regardless of what may have happened to your client, you know that the media is going to milk this for all it's worth, and the public isn't exactly on Ignacio's side after those photographs were published. If you could keep Ignacio's disappearance quiet, it would really help us. And besides, this is all speculation. Nothing has been confirmed officially. We'd have a lot more room to maneuver if the press didn't get wind of this."

"I agree with you one hundred percent, inspector."

"Then I'll let you go. If there are any further developments, or if Ignacio contacts you, please let us know immediately. Speed will be of the essence if we're going to respond adequately."

"I understand. Then that's settled," the lawyer replied before hanging up.

I made my way to Estíbaliz's office, where she was staring at her computer screen.

She raised her head when she saw me. From the way she frowned, the news must have been written all over my face.

"What's new, Kraken? You look as though you've just returned from the wars."

"I'm afraid that from now on this is open warfare, Estí," I replied, still absorbing what Garrido-Stoker had just told me.

"Come on, Kraken. The suspense is killing me."

"Ignacio has also absconded—from his hideout in San Sebastián. Yesterday morning he received a call or a text and took off on his own, with no explanation. His lawyer is bewildered. So now we have forty-five-year-old twins who are missing. It's possible Tasio lured his brother away with a phone call and killed him. Or Ignacio could have received a message from his brother asking to see him, sent by the person who removed Tasio's electronic tag and abducted him," I said, thinking aloud.

"The question is what do we have here, Kraken?" said Estíbaliz. "Two suspects, two victims, or one murderer and one victim?"

41

THE AIURDIN PASS

IZARRA
MARCH 1989

Three days had gone by. It was Wednesday now, and the bus was jolting along the road through the Aiurdin Pass, avoiding the snowdrifts that still lingered on some stretches.

Nancho was gazing anxiously out the window. His rib cage hurt whenever he sat down, but he realized the journey would be impossible standing up—the driver would yell at him, and the other passengers would shout at him to sit down. So he remained in his seat and put up with it, despite the pain.

He was tired of putting up with things, but what else could he do?

He arrived back at the farm midafternoon. His brother and sister would already be home from school, and unless they had work to do, Aita and Ama would also be there. He regretted disappearing like that. He knew they would be worried sick.

That first night, after the beating, when he stayed in the one-armed man's hut in the cemetery, he lay awake for hours, convinced that Aita would have alerted the police and they would be looking for him. He had invented a few excuses, which he realized weren't very convincing.

He didn't want to go back to Vitoria; he wanted nothing to do with that rich family who had made him dream and then thrown him into a grave. They could rot in hell. He had nothing in common with them—he belonged to the family who had cared for him since he was born. He was going to try his best to be a good son, to take more care with the honeycombs, to spend time with Idoia and Andoni, to look after them whenever Ama or Aita asked.

Opening the gate into the yard, he found the two children playing with their toys.

"Hello, Idoia! Your brother's back, don't you want to give me a hug?"

The little girl sneered at him in disgust and carried on playing with her brother as if she hadn't seen him. She often ignored him. Nancho had always blamed this on the fact that he wasn't very good with women, even less so with little girls, although, to be honest, he wasn't Andoni's favorite person, either. The boy never went to bed when Nancho told him to and had the infuriating habit of kicking his shins whenever they were alone together. Ama did spoil him and always made excuses for him, saying that it was just that his nails needed cutting when he scratched Nancho's face.

He could hear voices coming from the floor above, and so he went upstairs. He knocked on the door to his parents' bedroom. They seemed to be quarreling, as usual.

"Aita, may I come in?" he asked, lowering his voice so as not to annoy them.

"I've told you a thousand times: I'm not your aita!" his father yelled, getting up from the bed. He had taken off his shirt and was wearing trousers and an old undershirt. "You've got some nerve coming back here after you robbed us last Sunday and disappeared! What's the matter, have you come back for more?"

"No, Ai—Venancio," he said, lowering his head. He could feel his face flush bright red with shame. "I can explain. I'll pay you back the four hundred pesetas, I—"

"Where have you been, out drinking and carousing, is that it?

What's the matter, doesn't the little gentleman like working with the hives?"

Venancio moved toward him, wrapping his belt around his fist.

Nancho looked at him out of the corner of his eye and swallowed hard. He hated the belt: the metal buckle left marks on his back. For weeks he would have to cover himself so people in the village didn't see the bruises and laugh at him.

Venancio wasn't a very big man, and yet it had never occurred to Nancho that he was now tall and strong enough to defend himself. He didn't do so this time, either, and as he fell to the floor, he stared at his ama, sitting on the edge of the bed staring blankly out of the tiny window. He knew she wasn't going to intervene. She never did, and he always forgave her because she received a beating herself from time to time. She stood up without a word, walked past him, and made her way silently downstairs, perhaps to see to the children's dinner, knowing he would be in no fit state to prepare it.

But then, as he cast about for a pleasant image to help him escape the pain, he remembered the words of his real mother, his white angel: "It's not your fault."

"It's not my fault," he reflected.

And for the first time in his life, he didn't care about anything, and he started to laugh. He laughed out loud. He felt liberated.

He felt so good.

Puzzled, Venancio interrupted the beating. "What the hell? Are you stupid or what! You dare to come into this house drunk?" he yelled.

Now Nancho had really made him furious. Venancio beat him, viciously this time, the way he thrashed the mules when they refused to walk along a stony track.

Nancho stopped laughing, knowing that this brute wouldn't stop beating him until he fell silent, and yet for the first time in his life, he felt strong. Strong enough to change his life. He had never imagined he would have the strength to do that.

He let his body go limp, to see if that scared Venancio. And, after a while, when he realized that Nancho wasn't moving, Venancio paused. Perhaps the lad wasn't as resilient as he thought. He had always found him slightly repellent, and so, instead of bending down, he prodded Nancho with his foot. When that nurse suggested they take the boy in, his wife had insisted he would eventually be useful around the farmhouse, but he wasn't even that anymore.

Not quite sure what to do, Venancio left him sprawled at the foot of the bed and went downstairs to have dinner. Later, he would think of a way of punishing the boy that would make him think twice before he stole again or went out carousing.

Nancho stared at the once-white ceiling. For the second time, he felt like he was being banished. From his family in Izarra, and from his other one in Vitoria. From all sides. Like Adam and Eve, as Don Tiburcio had explained, punished for committing that shameful sin.

He waited until the clatter of spoons against plates had stopped. Now, in the dark, he was able to smile. Because he wanted to, because he had decided to smile and there was no one to stop him. How good it made him feel.

And for once, he allowed himself to revel in the dark thoughts he had every time that skinflint Venancio insulted him, every time Venancio's lazy wife ordered him to make dinner or to run a thousand errands, every time those spoiled brats refused to answer him.

And he felt envy, envy toward those twins. He wanted to be like them, handsome, stinking rich, and with appetizing young girls on his arm. He resolved to be like them: someone who wouldn't think twice about leaving a person for dead, because he knew that nothing would happen to him.

Nancho wanted that, the power to make and break people without being held accountable.

After a while, he heard weary footsteps creaking on the stairs he had mended countless times. He tensed automatically before realizing it was his ama.

She entered the darkened room and leaned over him where he lay on the floor.

Maybe she's worried about me, after all, he thought, lamenting the plan he was hatching.

"Nancho, I have one of my migraines, go downstairs and put the kids to bed, will you?" she said, without turning on the light. "Now, get out of my room at once, I want to get undressed. Venancio and I have decided that you'll work to pay us back the four hundred pesetas, so we're sending you to mend roofs with Jose Mari, the road-mender."

"Yes, Ama," he replied. But for the first time it was different, now he was smiling in the darkness, and he enjoyed the fact that she couldn't even see him.

"Don't call me Ama, I'm not your mother," she said, just as she always did.

"Don't worry, Ama, I'll never call you that again, I promise," he replied, stifling a laugh as he dragged himself to his feet and left the room.

I'll be back, he thought.

And for the next hour, the last one he would spend at the farmhouse before he wiped it off the map, he brushed Idoia's and Andoni's teeth as they protested the nasty taste of the toothpaste, dressed them in the pajamas he would soon pull off them, and agreed that they could sleep in the same bed because they had been frightened by the story of Sacamantecas at school.

When the house finally fell silent, he went to the beehives to retrieve his hidden textbooks, which he had decided to reread until he knew every word by heart. No one would ever call him a yokel again.

He would travel to a city; he would imitate them, become them.

Then he opened the red cookie tin where his father kept the rolls of five-thousand-peseta notes that he didn't want to put in the bank, and, after packing his belongings into the big backpack he had to carry whenever the family visited the cross on Monte Gorbea, he went into the shed, picked up the cans of diesel oil, and made his way slowly toward the hives.

42

MURGUÍA

SATURDAY, AUGUST 13

A Twitter storm erupted as the rumor that Tasio had broken his parole started to spread. A few jokers made light of it, and the hashtag #IveseenTasio was trending that morning. People in the most unlikely places claimed to have spotted him. Some uploaded blurry photos, or crudely Photoshopped images. A few of them were amusing, others sinister.

#IveSeenTasio in El Zaramaga neighborhood, #IveSeenTasio having tapas in Calle del Laurel in Logroño, #IveSeenTasio with Elvis at Loch Ness.

A big joke.

The twins were missing. The national police were patrolling the country's borders. Our entire force was deployed in Álava and Guipúzcoa.

The worst part was feeling as though there was nothing else I could do. I'd lost the two main characters in the story. They may not have known it, but they were probably the key to the crimes.

Estíbaliz was more practical. She couldn't sit still twiddling her thumbs, so she spent the entire morning, without coming up for air, immersed in the civil registries for all the outlying villages.

"I've found a Venancio Lopidana, born in Llodio in 1944, died in Izarra in 1989. Interestingly, he was married to Regina Muñoz, a native of Izarra, born and died the same year as her husband—aged forty-five. If they died on the same day, then it had to be an accidental death," she declared triumphantly, poking her red head through my office door.

"So we have an eighteen-year-old Venancio who isn't listed in any registry, and a Venancio Lopidana old enough to be his father who died, with his wife, right around the time Blanca Díaz de Antoñana went looking for her son, and the twins beat up a red-headed boy claiming to be their brother."

"Assuming your great-aunt's story is correct—"

"Great-Aunt Felisa, the gravedigger, and Aitana Garmendia. We have three separate statements that corroborate one another in terms of the events they describe and when they happened. Whether they're connected to the crimes is another matter. It's quite possible the twins had a brother, a triplet, who was illegally adopted, and when he demanded his share of the inheritance, they beat him up. The kid got the fright of his life and has been hiding out ever since, undocumented, herding sheep on Monte Gorbea. End of story."

"Do you really think it's possible that Venancio Junior had no official ID?"

"It would explain why we can't trace him. The adoption was unofficial, so no documents would have been exchanged. A baby was given to a childless couple. They probably didn't know how to legalize the situation and decided to raise the kid without any papers."

"What animals. We could search the newspaper archives for any reports of fatal traffic accidents in Izarra to see if we can find a cause of death for the Lopidanas," Estíbaliz suggested.

"Yes, we could. But why not go to Izarra and ask the neighbors? It's a tiny village. If there was an accident, people must know about it, and we're bound to find someone willing to talk to us."

We strolled around Izarra for a while to get a sense of the place. A single train track divided the village. The section on the right looked relatively modern, with low apartment buildings and new stores.

Crossing the tracks, we found ourselves on the more rural side of town, full of charming, freshly whitewashed farmhouses with red-painted roofs. We set off in search of the church and immediately came to a square, where the villagers congregated to look after their grandchildren and pass the afternoon in the shade.

"Good afternoon, are you from around here?" Estíbaliz asked a woman in her sixties who was holding a bun in her hand and chasing after a child on a tricycle.

"Yes, I'm from here. Are you lost?" she asked, pausing to catch her breath.

"Not exactly. We're looking for anyone from the Lopidana family."

"I'm afraid I don't know. I left here as a girl to go to college in Vitoria, and now that I'm retired, I've returned to the village. But my father might be able to help you. His name is Casto." She gestured toward one of the two elderly men dozing on a bench.

"Don Casto?" I said, as we approached them.

"Casto will do, I'm not the mayor," he said, guffawing. He had a receding chin that gave him a Hapsburgian air.

"Are you by any chance a native of Izarra?"

"Born and bred. I've never left the village, except when my generation was called up to fight at the Battle of Villarreal."

"Then maybe you belong to my grandfather's generation." I sat down next to him on the bench when I saw him shuffle over to make room for me. "Tell me, did you know the Lopidanas?"

"The bee people?"

"Yes, that's them. Venancio Lopidana and his wife."

"Heavens! You've come here asking about them after all these years! Why, they've been pushing up daisies for goodness knows how long."

"Do any of their relatives still live here?"

"No, all four of them died in that fire."

Estíbaliz and I exchanged a quick glance.

"All four of them?"

"Yes, Regina, that brute Venancio, and the two kids they had late in life. A little boy and a little girl."

"I had no idea there was a fire. Where did it happen?"

"Right there, at the farmhouse." He turned his upper body and pointed behind him. "It was gutted. It stood like that for years until they built Hotel Doña Lola. They named it after Doña Lola's yew tree, which has been there forever and is now a protected site. People come here from all over the world to take photographs of it, and then they go somewhere else to take more photographs. They barely stop in the village."

"Do you remember a young lad who lived with them, a redhead?"

"Nancho, who worked with the hives?"

"Yes, that's him."

"He mowed my field once. I gave him a pair of trousers, although he was a plump young lad and they were a bit tight on him. Venancio never bought him any clothes, you see. I believe he left shortly before the fire. Venancio was furious and went around telling everyone in the village. Of course, he was mad—he used to send the lad to work for anyone who needed him, and then he kept the boy's earnings for himself."

"Do you remember if the fire was investigated? If anyone thought it was arson, or if the police came to the village?"

He shrugged. "Oh, they came here all right. They questioned

everyone, and then they left. Everyone here said a spark caused it—
that Venancio was too miserly to get the wiring fixed. You see, his
cheapness cost him dearly in the end."

"Well, thanks, Casto. I've enjoyed our little chat."

"I'll be seeing you," he said, laughing at his own joke, aware
that at his age every encounter could be his last.

That same afternoon we requested access to the old report on the
1989 Izarra fire. By then, Izarra was under Vitoria's jurisdiction,
and the province's old case files had been moved to the basement
at headquarters.

When we received the file in Estíbaliz's office, we opened it
with the enthusiasm of junkies, like we had been brought back
from death's door.

The prosecutor had opened an investigation based on the Murguía fire chief's report. He had found some evidence that suggested
arson.

Police forensics went to the scene and took photographs of the
farmhouse and victims.

According to the report, the partially charred remains of a man
and a woman aged forty-five were discovered on a bed on the upper
floor of the building. They were identified as Venancio Lopidana
and Regina Muñoz.

On the floor below, in another bedroom, they found the bodies
of two five-year-olds. The children's bodies were in worse shape due
to their proximity to the fire's origin, but they could still determine
that the bodies were the couple's children, Idoia and Andoni.

Two possible scenarios were considered.

First: Venancio Lopidana started the fire to kill his family and
afterward took his own life.

According to the testimony of various neighbors, Venancio had a history of domestic violence, although his wife never reported him. He had been known to fly into a rage over land disputes with his neighbors, or over debts he had accrued at the village bar. Nobody liked having to deal with him, although they agreed that he produced excellent honey.

This unconfirmed theory posited that Venancio had killed his family because he was in debt to various creditors.

The second line of inquiry pointed to an electrical fire caused by a spark from some old wiring. The blaze was determined to have started on the first floor, close to the oil tank, which could have acted as an accelerant. According to this theory, the victims inhaled the fumes as they slept, lost consciousness, and were burned to death.

Postmortem examinations were conducted at the Basque Institute of Forensic Medicine, but the bodies were too badly damaged due to the extreme temperature of the fire.

No relative came forward to claim them, and the case was closed.

I took a deep breath before examining the photographs. I found the images of the charred bodies particularly grueling. But for once the ordeal was worth it; when I saw the remains of Venancio and his wife, I knew we were heading in the right direction.

Forward, for a change.

"Look, Estí." I pointed to the blackened hands. "This could be our serial killer's first murder."

There it was again, that famous gesture—the hand touching the other's cheek. Venancio and his wife had both died in that position. I closed my eyes and tried to conjure up a different image, the beech forest on the winding road to Bajauri, anything to erase what I had just seen, so that Venancio's charred remains wouldn't haunt my sleep.

"See if you can find any headshots of the children," Estíbaliz told me, holding her breath.

I didn't want to look at the photographs of the boy and the girl. I had hoped I might be able to avoid it. Childish of me, I know, but sometimes I'm like that.

Steeling myself as best I could, I spread out the cache of photos.

There it was again: the children, sleeping side by side, were caressing each other's cheeks with their opposite hands.

"Maybe it started here," I thought aloud. "Maybe this was his first crime. Then over the years, he refined his approach until he ended up with the ritual we know today. But the basic elements are already there: the naked couples making that comforting gesture with their hands, the bees, the yew tree. I wonder whether young Nancho killed them by placing bees in their mouths, or if he poisoned them with yew leaves. . . . The bodies were too badly burned for any of that to have shown up in the autopsies."

"Maybe he didn't need to. Maybe starting a fire downstairs with a powerful accelerant was enough. But then, afterward, he spent years thinking about his first crime and began to incorporate the elements he was familiar with: the yew poison and the bees," said Estíbaliz.

"Have their ages struck you?"

"What about them?"

"The two children weren't twins, but they were both five years old when they died. Venancio and his wife were also the same age: they both died when they were forty-five. Doesn't that coincidence in ages remind you of something?"

"Sonofabitch," said Estíbaliz under her breath.

"I'd like to talk to some of the eyewitnesses to the fire," I told her.

I picked up the report again and looked for the name of the fire chief who dealt with the blaze at the farmhouse: María Jesús Letona.

"That's unusual—a female fire chief twenty-seven years ago," observed Estíbaliz.

"This woman wrote a report because she saw signs of criminal activity. And yet forensics showed no real interest in clearing up the case. I think it would be interesting to speak to her, assuming she's still alive and we can locate her."

"Let's see what we have in the database."

Estíbaliz leaped from her chair and began a search. She was as relieved as I was to get away from the macabre array of photographs on the desk.

"Bingo! She's sixty years old and lives near Murguía. Her profession is listed here: children's book illustrator. That's a big career change," she observed. "How about I call her, and we pay her a visit?"

María Jesús's stone farmhouse stood outside the village, next to the river Ugala, on the road to Gorbea Nature Reserve. Clearly, it had once been a watermill. You could still see the gigantic wooden axle and its round millstone, which must have weighed several tons. It would have turned ceaselessly, day and night, driven by the force of a current that was now a trickle.

María Jesús was waiting for us next to a huge oak tree at the entrance to the property, beside a charming vegetable garden, which was as orderly as its owner.

She was middle-aged, with fine white hair cut short in a typical country style. She had the tranquil smile of someone who takes life at a leisurely pace and isn't glued to her phone. Her eyeglasses were antireflective, and made by a luxury brand, which told me that she made a good living as an illustrator.

"Good afternoon, María Jesús. Thank you for seeing us on such short notice," said Estíbaliz, smiling and extending her hand. "My name is Inspector Gauna, and this is my colleague Inspector Ayala."

"Please, call me Txusa. Would you like some mountain tea? I

nearly killed myself gathering it, so you can't possibly refuse," she said with a laugh.

"It'll be a pleasure," I said, smiling.

We didn't even enter the farmhouse. Her backyard was pleasant, and there was a cool breeze rustling the leaves of the oak trees, so we were content to sit around the green wrought-iron table.

Txusa served us a golden liquid with such an overpowering aroma it was as though we were nibbling herbs at the top of the mountain.

"So what brings you here, all these years later, inspector?" she said, addressing Estíbaliz. "You said on the phone that you wanted to talk to me about the fire at Venancio Lopidana's house in '89, isn't that right?"

"Yes, and I must say, I was surprised to find a woman's name on that report."

She set her tea down on the table, a little vexed. "More people curious to know why a woman would want to be in charge of a fire brigade?"

"On the contrary, Txusa," Estíbaliz explained hastily. "As soon as I read the report, I felt you deserved my admiration. You must have had a lot of guts to lead a team of men twenty-seven years ago."

She shrugged. "I liked the work, and I wanted to help fight the spate of wildfires. Back then, the summers were a nightmare. Fires were constantly being reported. But after the sleepers' murder, everyone thought I was crazy, and I lost the respect of the town council. Some of the men disobeyed my orders during subsequent fires, placing us all at risk. I felt powerless, so I gave up. I decided to quit and leave it all behind. Now I illustrate children's books. It's a much quieter life."

"Excuse me, did you say, 'the sleepers' murder'?"

"Yes, that's what I used to call them. From the moment we

arrived to douse the last flames, I was convinced it was a crime. The fire spread very fast, because the oil in the tank acted as an accelerant. But I noticed so many unusual details that I wrote a report to Vitoria suggesting they send in a forensics team. Forensics disagreed with me, and in the end, I got tired of being ignored. The other firefighters were worse. They told me I was crazy and eventually forced me to quit my job. Some people blamed faulty wiring; others maintained that Venancio Lopidana had killed himself and taken his family with him. But there were several things that didn't add up: it had been snowing, and yet the entire family's pajamas were found outside the house, directly beneath the windows, as if someone had thrown them out of the bedroom windows. The police said the place was a filthy hovel, and this was a pile of discarded clothes, but I believe someone stripped them—who in their right mind sleeps naked in Izarra in winter?"

"We didn't see any pajamas in the photographs accompanying the report."

"When forensics arrived, I insisted they photograph them as evidence, but they told me to stop interfering and let them do their job. They thought it was just a pile of dirty clothes. But the pile was directly below what had been the windows of the two bedrooms. Look, I don't pretend to be a detective, but for a man to start a fire by emptying a tank of oil, then go upstairs, undress his sleeping children, throw their pajamas out of the window, place their hands in that bizarre position, and then go up to the second floor, take off his wife's nightdress, throw that out the window, and then take off his own clothes and lie down in that same position waiting to die. . . . Well, it's the most bizarre suicide I've ever encountered."

"Yes, *bizarre* is the word," I replied.

"Venancio was a brute and a simpleton. People like that usually only have enough imagination to pick up a shotgun, kill their family, place both barrels in their own mouth, and blow their brains out. Why go to the trouble of staging a fire if you're accompanying your family to the next world?"

"Tell me something, Txusa: Did you know Nancho, the red-headed boy who lived at the farmhouse with them?"

She shrugged. "No, I met Venancio because he sold his honey at the market in Murguía on Thursdays, but he came alone or with his wife. I knew nothing else about him. I had no idea where in Izarra he lived, or even that he had two small children. He was a honey producer, that's all. Why, is it important?"

"We don't know yet," said Estíbaliz, rising to her feet. "We need to continue with the investigation, but thank you for telling us what you remember. If you think of any other important details, you have my number, right?"

We really didn't want to leave that green oasis behind, but we took a few pouches of mountain tea with us, and its fragrance perfumed our journey back to Vitoria.

"Txusa seems convinced," Estíbaliz reflected as she drove. "Neither a suicide nor an accidental fire."

"Which brings us back to Nancho Lopidana, who doesn't exist on paper."

"I've run every search I can think of. So how do we find an undocumented phantom?"

Maybe, I thought, *just maybe it's time to call in the cavalry.*

43

THE BATTLE OF VITORIA MONUMENT

TUESDAY, AUGUST 16

I got up at the usual time. I think I dreamed that the buzzer downstairs woke me and Alba came up to my apartment to sleep. It must have been a waking dream, though, because I lay very still, waiting for someone to ring the bell on the third floor, but it didn't happen.

What are you doing, Unai? I thought.

Like all the important things in life, it didn't make much sense. I switched on my phone and sent her a text.

> **Are you running?**

Yes.

> **Paseo del Batán, by the stream,**
> **in twenty minutes.**

See you there.

When I arrived, Alba was down by the tiny brook, near a row of poplars. The riverbank was still cloaked in darkness, so I couldn't see her expression.

I spoke first. "We need to talk, don't we?" I was standing right next to her, leaning against the back of a bench.

"Yes. I don't see how we can go on like this, Unai. Encounters at dawn, searching for out-of-the-way places where we can meet, like a couple of teenagers. Your apartment isn't an option: It's too central. We could easily be discovered if someone were to see me enter your building. And we're investigating a high-profile case. If anyone found out a DSU was having an affair with an inspector, we'd both be destroyed"—she lowered her head—"not to mention the personal cost, and the impact on my marriage."

"Yes, your marriage. Tell me, Alba, are you happy in your marriage?"

"Relatively, yes."

"Relatively?"

"Yes, I'm as happy as I am unhappy. Like everyone else."

Okay, I thought. From the way she spoke, I didn't sense she had any real desire to leave her husband.

"I don't want this, either," I said. "I don't want to hide. I don't want us to sneak around like thieves in the night. I don't want to be the third person in your relationship. If you want to continue seeing me, it has to be because your marriage is over. Regardless of what is, or could be, between us, neither of us deserves for this to become something we have to lie about to our friends and family. That's not who I am—I don't want that."

"Nor do I, Unai."

I straightened up. It would be light soon, and the day ahead promised to be difficult. "I suppose this is good-bye. We'll keep working together as if nothing ever happened, and I'll change my running routes to avoid bumping into you, okay?"

Alba nodded, her eyes fixed on the trunk of a poplar. "All right, but . . ."

"But what?"

"Don't give me those smoldering looks at work."

Don't look at you, touch you, inhale your pheromones when we're in the same room, I thought. *Okay.*

"I won't, ma'am," I replied, looking down at my sneakers.

I watched her leave in the opposite direction, her braid swinging from side to side. When she had grown so small that I could no longer see her, I let off steam by hurling stones into the water until I ended up pulling a muscle in my shoulder.

Several days had passed since Estí and I had made the discovery about the fire, and I was still brooding over how to find a reliable trace of Nancho Lopidana. I hesitated for a long time, and then reluctantly called my old friend Golden Girl. I had already asked several favors of her during the investigation, and sooner or later she would start calling them in—something dubious about her pension, her apartment, her inheritance. Something that would doubtless put my job on the line. However, the red-haired phantom's ability to give us the slip whenever we came close to picking up his trail was making me desperate.

It's the price you have to pay, Unai, I tried to tell myself. *Nothing is free.*

"Golden, I need you to track down any information you can on a Nancho or Venancio Lopidana born around '71. He doesn't appear on the civil register. He was illegally adopted as a child, and was probably undocumented, at least until the age of eighteen. Focus your attention on Pamplona and Navarra. We've already checked the church and school registers in Álava, and there's no trace of him."

"I'll use my imagination, Kraken. Leave it to me. Is it urgent?"

"I needed it yesterday."

"You won't make old bones, my friend."

That isn't my priority, I thought.

"Who are you talking to?" interrupted Estíbaliz, poking her head around my office door.

"My brother," I lied.

"Say hello for me, and tell him I'll stop by his office sometime."

"Germán, Estí says hello. I'll let you go now."

Golden laughed on the other end of the line and hung up.

"What is it, Estí? Anything new?"

"You bet. Lutxo gave me access to the archive at *El Diario Alavés*, and it's a veritable gold mine. Take a look at what I found on the family history of the Ortiz de Zárate twins."

She laid a bundle of photographs on my desk, like a hustler dealing cards.

"In 1970, Javier Ortiz de Zárate was admitted to the Vitoria Clinic after ingesting a toxic substance. That was a year before the twins were born. The paper gave it no more than a few lines on the inside pages, but it isn't the only strange report involving the love triangle of Javier, Blanca, and Doctor Urbina. Look at this," she said, pointing to a photocopy of an article dated March 1971, a few weeks after the twins' birth.

Exactly as my great-aunt had said, Doctor Urbina had vanished, and his wife had reported him missing.

"You see, Aunt Felisa's memory is reliable. Now we have concrete evidence that this happened. Urbina left of his own accord, or someone bumped him off, and his disappearance coincided with the birth of the twins, or rather the triplets."

Estí sat down and continued to pore over the array of old articles.

"Kraken, what if Doctor Urbina is the one taking revenge and killing all these people? What if he disappeared on purpose?"

"That would mean he would have had to create a new identity. Imagine trying to find him after all these years; it would be a nightmare. Besides, Felisa implied that Blanca's husband was behind his disappearance."

"Okay, just imagine the possibility for a moment," she insisted. "Where would that idea lead you?"

I thought about it briefly, but I wasn't convinced. "In my opinion, the theory doesn't hold water. If Urbina is the killer, why would he allow Tasio, one of his own sons, to shoulder the burden of guilt for more than twenty years?"

"Tasio is his son, yes, but the twins were brought up to adore the man they thought was their father, and don't forget that Doctor Urbina might have tried to poison Javier. Also bear in mind that the twins beat Nancho half to death when he told him who their real father was. He could be taking revenge for his son."

Yes, it was possible, but it didn't add up.

"Estí, either Doctor Urbina is dead and buried, courtesy of Javier Ortiz de Zárate, or he flew the coop forty-five years ago and has a new identity. He would be about seventy-five or eighty by now. He'd have to be exceptionally fit to kill two people every few days."

Estíbaliz examined the old clippings for a while but finally gave in.

"It's a bit far-fetched, I know. But we're still groping in the dark. How about you, anything new?" she asked, almost as an afterthought.

"I left a few lines of inquiry open early on in the investigation, when things were still fresh. Do you remember the director of the independent TV channel, the so-called Stone Lady Ignacio mentioned when we went to his apartment after the Slow Food Show?"

Another unsolved line of inquiry was the embarrassing matter of who had sent the photographs of the fifteen-year-old girl and the twins to Lutxo. But I planned to look into that calmly later on, because I knew the best way to approach my good friend. For now, I would concentrate on the Stone Lady.

"Yes, Inés Ochoa. Were you able to speak to her?"

"I haven't had the pleasure. I'll look up her contact details right now and get in touch. She's another person who worked with both twins around the time of the murders. I expect she'll have an interesting take on the matter."

I began searching on my computer and found her immediately. Phone number, date of birth, ID card number, address. I did a double take when I saw where she lived: Inés Ochoa's apartment was in the Plaza Nueva, on the fourth floor of the building next to the sports bar, which meant that her windows overlooked the Plaza de la Virgen Blanca directly across from my house.

I didn't mention anything to Estí. What would I have said?

She might have seen me on the roof about to have sex with our DSU, but don't worry, that has no bearing on the case or on the fact that my sister-in-law and your brother were the killer's next victims.

"Did you find her? Do you want to go together?" she asked.

"We could, except I'm going to meet up with Germán afterward—he seems very low. You don't mind, do you?"

"Of course not, don't worry, I'll have lunch by myself."

I left the office feeling more like a rotten, despicable partner than ever. I dialed the Stone Lady's number, found her at home, and gave her no choice but to meet me there. I wanted to check out what she could see from her picture windows.

I arrived at the entrance, rang the doorbell, and took the stairs to the fourth floor. On my way up, I bumped into a strange creature who looked like a bad-tempered ogre.

He made no attempt to move aside when our paths crossed near the top of the staircase. Instead he looked at me with a vaguely hostile expression and replied to my greeting with a grunt. He was built like a weightlifter: four hundred pounds, a bull neck, and a small, rather flat head.

"Don't mind him." Inés Ochoa's voice rang out from the door to her apartment, a few feet above my head. "He's the proverbial gentle giant."

"And he is . . . ?"

"My brother. I've always taken care of him. He isn't exactly Einstein, but he'll do anything I ask."

"I see," I whispered, taking note.

"Come on up, inspector. I was on my way out, but it sounded as if you were in a hurry to see me."

I couldn't help glancing around the apartment as I entered. Apparently, the Stone Lady was something of a film buff. Her entire apartment was a tribute to old black-and-white movies. There were posters the length of the hallway, and mannequins dressed in reproductions of costumes worn by Lauren Bacall or Veronica Lake.

"I see you're a movie fan."

"*Noir, très noir,*" she replied casually, lighting a cigarette. "How about we get straight to the point?"

Inés Ochoa was sixty-something and wore her dyed ash-blonde hair in a pageboy. There was a brusqueness to her gestures—the way she flicked her wrist when she smoked—that suggested someone who liked quick solutions.

"I'd like you to tell me about both Tasio and Ignacio when you first met them," I said. I ignored her invitation to sit down on the blood-red sofa, and instead paced around the living room, surreptitiously trying to get close to the windows.

Inés launched into a monologue. Every other sentence contained the word *ratings*. She began by describing the contract she had signed with Tasio and the clauses he had breached when he switched to the national channel after viewer ratings increased.

She saw everything through the lens of her profession. She didn't give me a single detail that wasn't directly related to the performance of her TV channel.

"Do you think Tasio was the dominant twin?" I cut in, forcing her to talk about something more subjective, potentially personal.

"Yes, undoubtedly. Tasio was the alpha male. Ignacio played the beta role when they were together. He was the organizer. Tasio made the plans, and Ignacio executed them."

"One was the brain, the other the hand?"

"Yes, very much so. There was a strange complicity between them; they were excessively dependent on each other."

"And yet the public admired the way Ignacio sacrificed his brother," I added, testing how far I could draw out the conversation.

"Make no mistake, it gave them both a kind of sick pleasure to see Ignacio on TV after what happened. He looked exactly like Tasio."

"You were also accused of exploiting them."

"I knew the press would hang Ignacio out to dry, which, incidentally, was the main reason he resisted signing a contract to do a show on my channel."

"And you knew the controversy would attract viewers."

"But I couldn't have done it if he hadn't agreed. He wanted to change careers; he had money, but he needed to occupy his brain. I made sure he kept busy during those first few years, which were the most difficult for him."

"Why did he want to change his career? I thought he decided to join the police as a vocation," I said, puzzled.

"It probably was to begin with, but the first time we met after his brother had been sent to prison, Ignacio told me he wanted to leave the force. He was deeply disturbed by recent events and wanted no part of more homicides and arrests. I think he was suffering from post-traumatic stress, although he kept it from the doctors, so it went untreated. He was the kind of man who thought that a diagnosis would make him seem weak. He used to wake up at night in a cold sweat, screaming Tasio's name, curled up in a ball, trembling, as if he thought he was going to be beaten. I've never seen anyone as terrified as he was back then."

"You've just confessed that you and Ignacio were lovers."

She paused, her cigarette in midair. "I said no such thing."

"Perhaps not consciously, but you gave a pretty detailed description of what it's like to live with someone who has post-traumatic stress disorder."

"That has to stay within these four walls." For the first time, she sounded rattled. "You don't have my permission to use that."

"Now that we're talking about more personal things, tell me: Did you sleep with Tasio as well? Is that what happened? He was your biggest star, and when he left you for another station, you replaced him with his double?"

Is there any woman in Vitoria these guys haven't slept with? I thought.

"Of course. I killed all those children to increase my ratings, and when Tasio abandoned me, I incriminated him and took his twin to bed. Is that what you're thinking?"

"Is this a confession?" I stepped up the pressure.

"Should I call my lawyer?"

"Not yet," I said, knowing she would reach for her phone the minute I left.

"You're barking up the wrong tree."

She went over to look out of the window at the Plaza de la Virgen Blanca.

Where have I heard that before? I can't remember.

"What do you mean?" I said, taking the opportunity to move closer and peer over her shoulder.

I felt a shiver run down my spine. Straight ahead, approximately twenty yards away, were I could see the orange tiles on my roof. Assuming she was awake and staring out of her window at six o'clock in the morning, it wouldn't have been difficult for her to notice two hooded runners slipping through the doorway into my building.

"The murders were all over the news," she continued, "but perhaps you should be focusing on other types of media, not just me and my TV channel."

"I still don't follow."

"I'm talking about the two newspapers in this city and the rivalry between their editors; those thieving magpies haven't been outside their offices in decades. They manipulated public opinion time and time again during the investigation. The people of Vitoria believed whatever they wanted them to believe. If they mentioned a suspect, then the public said that person was guilty. In my opinion, a newspaper editor has the power to turn sinners into saints or destroy the reputation of the most honorable person in the world. And the editors of our two venerable papers are no exception."

Inés Ochoa was no novice at putting up smoke screens and throwing people under the bus—she was a skilled manipulator, and right then she felt cornered. All the same, I left her apartment mulling over a couple of things I had chosen to ignore previously. And while I wasn't exactly thinking about those two dinosaurs at the helms of Vitoria's daily papers, I was dwelling on someone much closer to me.

I was thinking about Lutxo again, for the second time that Tuesday.

Perhaps I needed to talk to my journalist friend, in person this time, so I could pin him down.

After all, Lutxo had put me on the Eguzkilore's track—he made me suspect Estí's brother right from the start. He also knew where my sister-in-law lived, and she would have trusted him. Lutxo was a skilled manipulator, and as a journalist, he could approach young people under the pretext of interviewing them. Maybe he lured them into a press vehicle to drive them to the newspaper's head office on Calle General Álava, which everybody knew. Maybe Lutxo knew about Rohypnol and how to administer it. Estí's brother might even have supplied him with it. And as a reporter, Lutxo must have used his press card on numerous occasions to gain access to the Old Cathedral, the Casa del Cordón, and the balcony in San Miguel Arcángel Church.

I walked back out onto the Plaza de la Virgen Blanca and was approaching the entrance to my building when Golden called me.

I looked at the screen, puzzled. "Already?" I exclaimed.

"You said you wanted it yesterday, so I'm sixteen hours late."

"Golden, you must come work for us someday."

"Dream on."

"So you found the guy?" I said, sitting down on one of the slatted wooden benches that surround the monument to the Battle of Vitoria.

A little stone girl with pigtails who was missing her nose and her mother looked sternly down at me from the monument.

"There's a Nancho Lopidana who took night classes at an academy in Pamplona and passed his school certification there in the early nineties. After that, I lost track of him. It's strange, because I searched all the Ministry of Education databases and that's the only place he shows up. The academy was run by the state. He got good grades, and yet he didn't go on to get a degree or go into vocational training, which is usually what adults who attend night school do."

"Do you know if that academy still exists?"

"It has reinvented itself as a center that helps prepare people to take the public-service entrance exam. But with the way things are at the moment, I doubt they have many students."

"Do you have an address?"

"It's in the old part of town, near Calle Estafeta."

Golden gave me the details, and after a brief Google search, I discovered that the Hemingway College was open during the summer for students who needed to retake the exam.

I dialed Estíbaliz's number. I had to share the good news with her. We both needed it.

"Estí, we're going to Pamplona right now. Finally, we have a solid lead on Nancho Lopidana."

44

HEMINGWAY COLLEGE

Tuesday, August 16

The college was on the first floor of a house in the historic center of Pamplona. It had a certain old-world charm—wooden school desks from the 1950s, their lids tilted at thirty-degree angles with a hole where the inkwells used to go.

As we walked in, an elderly woman put a finger to her lips to tell us to be quiet. A couple of bored students pretended to be writing on their mock public-service exams. At the back, a boy who looked about twelve was playing Minecraft in silent mode on his cell phone. Either the old lady hadn't noticed, or she was pretending not to see.

"Come into my office," she whispered. "We don't want to distract the students."

Estíbaliz and I exchanged a quick glance and then followed the diminutive woman, who swerved around the desks with the agility of someone who had been doing it all her life.

The office was home to an assortment of folders, from old yellowing ones to modern white plastic ones. The evolution of half a century of office supplies seemed to be staring at me from the shelves behind the old lady.

"Do you wish to enroll your child? It's a little late, as the summer is nearly over, but I'm sure we can do something. There's always a way to help these children. Most of them simply need to acquire good study habits," she said reassuringly, sitting down in a capacious chair that left her feet dangling several inches above the floor.

Embarrassed, Estí and I glanced at each other, and she hastened to clear up the misunderstanding.

"Goodness, no, we aren't—I mean, we didn't come here to enroll our child or anything like that. We're investigating a case in Vitoria, and one of the leads brought us here. My name is Inspector Ruiz de Gauna."

"Well, I certainly wasn't expecting this. Is one of my students in trouble?"

"Actually, we're looking for a student you had many years ago, in the late eighties, early nineties. We believe he passed his school certification here. This was an adult-education center back then, wasn't it?"

"Yes, and now we prepare high school students to sit for their exams, because there are hardly any civil servants these days." She rose from the enormous chair. "Can you give me any more precise details about this student?"

"His name is Nancho or Venancio Lopidana," Estíbaliz said. "I doubt you remember him, but if you could possibly look through the registration forms."

"Nancho Lopidana . . . of course, I remember him. A charming boy, and a gifted student. He made me so proud, and he raised our ratings with his exam results," she said, gazing wistfully at the certificates on the wall. "I'll have a look in the archives for his file. It might take a while; I'll need to go through them year by year."

The old teacher stared at the wall of files and plucked out one at eye level.

"Now, let's see. . . ."

She put on the pair of bifocals that hung from a silver chain around her neck and began to leaf through each page meticulously, wetting the tips of her fingers and shaking her head each time she came to a new student.

Craning my neck, I could see that the registration forms were filled in by hand and that they all had a passport-size photograph attached.

"Would you like us to help you?" suggested Estí.

"Oh, no, that wouldn't do at all. These papers contain confidential information about our students. I wouldn't want to break the rules," she murmured.

I shot a glance at Estí, wondering if I ought to step in, but she shook her head. No need to ruffle the old lady's feathers when she was being so cooperative.

An hour and a half later, when the yellow light from the streetlights was already seeping through the college's frosted-glass windows, and my brain was threatening to shut down from enforced inactivity, the old lady's quivering forefinger stood poised at a point on the page as if it were the center of a bull's-eye.

"Nancho Lopidana, here he is!" she declared, triumphantly.

"May we see his photograph?" I asked, waking from my stupor.

"Well, there isn't one," said the woman, somewhat bemused.

"Why not? What about his ID card? Can you give us the number?"

The woman held up the file, and her face flushed.

"So, you can confirm that he passed his school certification here and that he was an excellent pupil, yet you have no photograph or record of his ID number, how is that possible?" I pressed her.

"Look, I'm usually a stickler for the rules, but when someone touches your heart, you have to be human and bend a little, don't you think?" she said uneasily.

I knew exactly what she meant, and why she had misgivings.

"We're not here to make problems for you; we're just trying to obtain information that's vital to an ongoing investigation. I can assure you that my partner and I have no intention whatsoever of reporting you to the Ministry of Education or any other authority because of whatever paperwork you may have overlooked twenty years ago."

Besides, the statute of limitations on falsifying documents expired long ago, I thought.

"Will you give me your word? The college is registered in my son's name; although, as you can see, he doesn't come here very often, and I continue to do most of the . . ."

Despite having reached retirement age long ago.

"I wouldn't want to risk being shut down. This is my son's only source of income."

"We won't report the irregularity. However, we will need you to explain why someone who respects the regulations the way you do permitted a student to enroll without being able to provide proof of identity."

"Because the poor boy had no identity card; he was undocumented. I had never come across anything like it before—a young man of nearly twenty, born not far from here, who had no papers. He wouldn't talk about his family history, but you only had to look at him when he first arrived to see that he had a troubled background. The boy only wanted the education no one had given him, and you see, I didn't want to be the evil witch who denied him that. I suspect he had tried all the other schools in Pamplona before he came to Hemingway College, and they had all asked for his ID papers. I didn't have the heart to turn him away, and I don't regret it." She swallowed hard, lowering her eyes, like a child caught with her fingers in the cookie jar.

"Could you give us a physical description of Nancho Lopidana, so we can be sure we're talking about the same person?"

"He was very heavy when he first arrived, but over the year he slimmed down drastically. That boosted his confidence, and he became a little more sociable. He wasn't very tall, maybe five feet seven or eight, the same height as my son. Shorter than you, but taller than her, if you see what I mean. With ginger hair, like your partner here. He used the local vernacular a lot, but I weaned him off that while he was here. Let's just say I did my best to help him appear less provincial. We also worked a lot on his handwriting, which was big and clumsy, like a five-year-old's. But he was an avid reader. I once told him a story about my grandfather's friendship with Ernest Hemingway, so he started to read all Hemingway's works. He would go to Café Iruña. . . . I can picture him now walking around with a copy of *For Whom the Bell Tolls* tucked under his arm. He used to say he wanted to be an editor, to correct what authors did badly because they were in too much of a hurry. I've never forgotten that, because it struck me as unusual. He was like a mature, sensible overgrown child. You couldn't help liking him."

"Can you give us any other information about Nancho? Where he lived while he was studying at the college?"

"At the student hostel on Calle Amaya, a few streets over."

She handed us the file so that we could write down the address of the hostel, which was listed as his main residence.

"Do you know what he did after he left? What his plans were?" I asked.

"His plans? He wanted to continue his education, of course. He planned to take the university entrance exam and get a degree in the humanities. He was very keen on history. And yet he didn't enroll to sit the exam here. I never understood why, after all that I did for him . . . you know, regarding his identity card. Sometimes you grow attached to a student, and to be honest, I was hurt when he didn't get in touch again. He might have enrolled at another college here in Pamplona, or maybe he changed his mind and didn't go to the university."

The woman looked at her watch and stood up to dismiss the three remaining students. Before we left, we helped her secure the rusty bolt on the metal shutter. I couldn't help wondering how a woman weighing all of seventy pounds had managed to open and close something so heavy day-in, day-out for all these years.

"Listen, if you find Nancho, send him my regards from Hemingway College. I hope he finished his studies and made something of himself. If anyone deserved to, he did."

Estíbaliz and I glanced at each other awkwardly and took our leave of the old lady.

"It's dark already; we should head back to Vitoria," said Estí as we strolled along the cobbled streets in the Old Quarter.

"You can drive back if you want. Since we're here, I'd like to visit the student hostel."

"In that case, I'll go with you."

"Estí, I might spend the night at the hostel, assuming they have rooms available now. It'll do me good to get some distance, to take a break from Vitoria. You have someone waiting for you at home, so don't be silly. I'll catch a bus first thing tomorrow morning."

"Now that we know this Nancho character exists, I want to stay on his trail. So it's decided—we're staying. Where did she say that hostel was?" Estí was already checking Google Maps on her phone.

"Calle Amaya, next to the market," I said, rolling my eyes.

The hostel occupied several floors of a neoclassical building in the city center. A narrow hallway led to a steep staircase; inside, the walls were adorned with black-and-white photographs of Hemingway imitators. Some of the city's traditions weren't easy to escape. At the reception desk, a glum-faced girl with cropped bangs greeted us with a forced smile.

"American, Australian?" she ventured.

"We're from Vitoria, actually," replied Estí. "Could we speak to the landlord or landlady?"

"That's my father. He'll be here first thing tomorrow morning. May I help you?"

"Do you have two single rooms for tonight?" I asked.

"The only room available is February Second."

"Is that the name of the room?"

"Yes, years ago we had more single rooms, but after the renovations we only have seven. Most of our guests are from abroad, backpackers or people coming from San Sebastián, Bilbao, and Vitoria for the San Fermín fiesta. The rooms are all named after the lyrics of the song that is played during the fiesta: January first, February second, March second, April fourth."

"How many beds does February Second have?" asked Estí.

"It's a double, the smallest we have. There's an extra-long bunk bed, so your friend should be okay. It's the room we usually give to the Norwegians and Swedes. Otherwise they can't sleep and start drinking, which is bad for everyone, believe me."

I moved away from the counter and drew Estíbaliz to one side. "Estí, are you sure you want to share a room? We don't have to, if it makes you feel uncomfortable. We can look somewhere else," I whispered.

"Unai, sometimes you seem ready to take on the world, and other times, like now, you're a big baby. Don't be such a prude. May we have the key, please?" she said, turning to the girl.

"Sure, if you could give me your ID cards and fill out this form. We take a night's payment in advance, if you don't mind, and then I'll show you upstairs."

Once we had finished the paperwork, Saioa, the receptionist, took us up to the third floor. We followed her down a narrow hallway covered in posters that were unnerving to say the least: BEWARE OF THE GHOST STUDENT.

Saioa came to a halt outside one of the doors, which bore a painted inscription that read: THE GHOST STUDENT LIVES HERE.

"What exactly is the ghost student?" I asked.

"It's a tasteless joke that has become an indelible part of the place." She made a face to show how fed up she was with having to explain it. "You're not scared of supernatural phenomena, are you?"

"That depends on how real they are. Why do you ask?" said Estíbaliz.

"It's an urban legend. We mentioned it in a tourist guide once, and it's haunted us ever since, if you'll forgive the pun. I'm tired of repeating the same story. I'll tell you about it in the morning, if that's okay with you. I have to go and lock up the register now."

"Of course," I said. "Could you let us know when your father arrives tomorrow? We'd like a word with him."

Saioa left us on our own in a small room with a pine bunk bed. The upper bunk was covered with a green mosquito net, which doubled as a canopy. It was very basic, a typical student residence. I smiled—it felt like being back at the university.

"Come on, I'll take you to dinner," I said, to break the ice.

"Done. I wasn't sure how to tell you, but I'm famished."

"We're pals, Estí."

We ordered grilled rib eye at a steakhouse on Calle Estafeta and a tray of mixed vegetables to help us digest all that protein. No minimalist cuisine or delicacies for the fainthearted. We feasted.

A couple of hours later, we undressed in silence in the darkness of the ghost student's room. Despite the air-conditioning, the room was stuffy. I assumed Estí slept in her underwear, while I stripped down to my boxers.

I said good night to the mattress above me and closed my eyes.

"I know the two of you are together." A voice rang out in the dark.

"What did you say?" I managed to reply, groggy with sleep and slightly confused.

"I know that you and DSU Salvatierra are seeing each other, Unai."

"Estí, I don't know what you saw or thought you saw, but I can assure you that—"

"Stop it! Don't you dare lie to me. I'm offended enough that you didn't think you could tell me, so don't make things worse by trying to lie."

Okay, how do I wriggle out of this without hurting Alba?

"I only kept it from you because Alba is married, and she's my superior officer. I'm sure you can understand that the fewer people who know the better."

"Yes, but you could have told *me*, Kraken," she said, raising her voice.

"Is it that obvious?" I asked anxiously.

"When you're together at headquarters, you exude some kind of hormone that makes it impossible to breathe. It's a chemical thing, very physical. It's actually pretty repulsive."

Was she serious, or half-joking?

"Well, we stopped seeing each other. Do you think anyone else at work or in Vitoria knows about it? This is important, Estí, think hard."

"You and I are close, and we spend a lot of time together, both as friends and as colleagues, whereas Alba Díaz de Salvatierra is new to Vitoria, so I doubt anyone would notice if she were behaving oddly. Look, Unai, I'm sure no one else knows, but I can't prove it to you. And stop changing the subject. I'm upset that you didn't tell me about the first fling you've had since you became a widower. Is that any way to treat a friend?"

"I thought about telling you, but then your brother was killed, and I thought our friendship was over. Even now, I don't know where we are, Estí. I really don't."

"Where we are is that I want you to be my best friend again—my brother, my family, my confidant, my everything."

"Then we're more or less on the same page. But I also need you to tell me about your personal life, Estí. For example, what's going on between you and Iker? You haven't mentioned him for ages or talked about the plans you're making together. How are the wedding preparations going? You never tell me anything and, to be honest, I feel left out sometimes, too. Now that your brother is gone and your father is sick, I'd love to be the one who walks you down the aisle."

"Iker and I split up. The wedding is off. I hate weddings, anyway. Frankly, it's a blessing."

I could scarcely believe what Estí was telling me. She and Iker had been together forever. They were inseparable when I first met them and had been ever since.

"What?" I said, inanely.

"We've split up, Unai. I should never have agreed to get married. Flowers, veils, and priests aren't my thing. Plus, long dresses make me look like a dwarf."

"Okay, but you can explain all that to Iker and he'd understand. You two really broke up? How long have you been together? It feels like it's been since the death of Francoism."

She remained silent for a while. A very long while. So long I thought she had fallen asleep. I prodded her mattress to make sure she was still alive.

"When my brother died, I realized that Iker was unable to console me. Being with him didn't calm me down, cheer me up, or make my day better. And that was that. I'm better off on my own, Unai. After all this time, Iker has become like a cousin. Occasionally we have mechanical sex, out of a sense of duty and to persuade ourselves we're still attracted to each other. I don't want to spend the rest of my life with a friend with benefits. I don't want to negotiate my side of the closet, or the shopping cart, or which bars we go to on weekends. With Eneko gone, the relationship feels like an uphill battle. I don't need Iker anymore. For years I've been living like a zombie, going along with things out of habit. The funny thing is, he felt the same, except that it never occurred to him that he could change anything—he thought it was okay to live a mediocre life. This has been liberating for both of us. He's going to Pakistan in September to climb Nanga Parbat, the Killer Mountain. The idea used to terrify me, and I always talked him out of it, but now there's no one to stop him. It's strange the ways we inhibited each other."

"So you're not suffering? You don't need to cry on my shoulder? I don't have to console you?"

"Quite the opposite, I need a new drinking buddy."

"Consider it done. As soon as we get back to Vitoria and this investigation is finished, we'll paint the town red."

"That's assuming it doesn't finish us first," she said.

"Touché," I replied, my eyelids drooping. "It's late, Estí, and I'm beat. Let's get some sleep now, and we'll talk more tomorrow."

"Wait, Kraken. Don't go to sleep yet, this might be the only opportunity I have to discuss this with you."

"Discuss what?"

"Listen, I have a present for you. I wanted to give it to you on your birthday, but we've been so . . . Well, it didn't seem like the right time."

"A present? Thanks, Estí. What is it?"

"Okay, here goes—it's a drug I asked Eneko to make for you. Drug dealers end up with quite a bit of chemistry knowledge."

"Anyone who watched *Breaking Bad* knows that," I commented, a little nervously. "Where are you going with this? Because so far I don't like what I've heard."

"It's a beta-blocker, made from the extract of mandrake root and other substances."

"Mandrake root? Isn't that poisonous?"

"As with everything, it depends on how you use it."

"Says the narcotics expert." The conversation had taken a sur-real turn, and it was starting to annoy me.

"Let me finish, you owe me that. The compound he made stops the body from absorbing other psychotropic drugs, like Rohypnol."

"*Other* psychotropic drugs? Meaning this is also a psychotropic drug."

"I didn't mean that. I don't know . . . I don't know what the side effects are. Eneko insisted there aren't any, and that it is used to prevent the uptake of Rohypnol. He told me it was one of the best-kept secrets of the nineties, and that even the police didn't know about it."

"And you want me to take this stuff?"

"We don't know who the killer is, but he knows exactly who you are. If he goes a step further and comes after you, your martial arts classes won't help you. And neither will your strength or your height. Remember the Viking, the Casa del Cordón victim. He had the same build as you, and he was twenty-five. But he didn't stand a chance, and neither will you."

I didn't want to hear this. I didn't want to think about it.

"Is that why you went to your brother's store?"

"Yes, I was picking it up when I bumped into you. What do you say? Will you take it?"

"I'm not sure, Estí. I've never taken drugs in my life, and I don't want to start now. And no offense, but I'm especially not interested in something your brother cooked up."

"All right, then ask someone you trust to prepare it for you. Your pharmacist friend, Asier, for example. He could have it ready in a couple of days."

"You're not listening to me. I have no intention of taking a psychotropic drug, adulterated or otherwise. Plus, are you saying I'd have to take it for a whole year, since the killer would be interested in me until I turn forty-one?"

"I hate to be the one telling you this, but I'm afraid you don't have that much time. The killer will strike again during the next big festival in Vitoria."

"You're trying to turn me into an addict. I won't do it, and that's final. Go to sleep, Estíbaliz. This conversation is over, and tomorrow we'll pretend it never happened."

The next morning, the tinkle of a telephone woke me. I sat up with a start, but the solid pinewood boards halted my trajectory and I fell back, my forehead aching from the blow.

"I was going to say, watch your head. Did you hurt yourself?" Estí said, peering over the edge of her bunk.

"A little, it's nothing," I replied as I made a lunge for the telephone on the table. "Hello?"

"Reception here. You asked me to tell you when my father arrived. He's in a bit of a hurry, so do you mind coming down now?"

"Fine, give us five minutes."

We descended the steep stairs without taking a shower or even looking in the mirror. A man with a generous paunch and a gray goatee was waiting for us in reception. He stood wedged behind the counter, wiping the sweat from his face every so often with a blue-and-white-checked handkerchief.

"Good morning, I'm Inspector Ruiz de Gauna, and this is my partner, Inspector López de Ayala. We're investigating a young man who lived here in 1989. Did you work at the hostel then?"

"Yes, with my father. I was just starting to take over the business. Why are you interested in something that happened so long ago?"

"It's part of an ongoing investigation, and I'm afraid we aren't at liberty to talk about it. The person we're looking for was a young man, about nineteen years old, named Nancho Lopidana."

"Nancho Lopidana?" said Saioa, turning pale. "Of course he was here. In fact, he died in the room you just slept in. He's the ghost student."

45

ARRIAGA PARK

WEDNESDAY, AUGUST 17

A re you telling me Nancho Lopidana is dead?" I said in disbelief. That was impossible.

Impossible.

Yet another brick wall.

"Yes, he lived here for the better part of a year, in the room we now call February Second. He shared it with a fellow student," Saioa's father replied with a frown, as if he didn't relish having to explain it to us. "One night he was alone in the room, and he fell asleep reading by the light of an old lamp. Apparently, the wiring was faulty; it sparked and set fire to the sheets and the mattress. My father was on duty at the time. He was elderly by then and must have nodded off. Some boys came running downstairs to tell him that smoke was coming out from under the door to the room. My father called the fire department, and they managed to prevent the fire from spreading to the rest of the hostel, but the poor lad was burned to a crisp in his own bed."

He looked rather uncomfortable, as if he would rather not answer our questions and was eager to get away from us.

"Did the police come here?" asked Estíbaliz.

"Yes, of course, the regional police. They asked my father and some of the lodgers a lot of questions but concluded that the fire was caused by Nancho's negligence, and that the hostel management wasn't responsible. We had to close for nearly three weeks because it was impossible to sleep here with the stench of smoke. We took the opportunity to renovate the place—we made alterations in some of the rooms, repainted the hallways and the stairwells. That's when all this nonsense about the ghost student started. The people who stay at the hostel are young, they come here to enjoy themselves, and they aren't what you'd call squeamish. An accident like that at a hotel would have frightened off the clientele. But here, everybody was fascinated by the story of the student who'd died in a fire in one of the rooms. Some people claimed to have seen Nancho's ghost come out of the room and walk down the stairs. The reports of sightings increased, no doubt fueled by whatever many of our guests had taken. Then my father mentioned the ghost student to a friend who was writing a tourist guide about Pamplona. And the story stuck."

"Could you give us the name of his roommate?"

He would be a valuable witness, I thought. Someone who lived with the elusive Nancho.

"Listen, it was such a long time ago, I don't remember all the details," he replied wearily. "It was unpleasant enough at the time, without having to rake over it again. I don't remember his roommate's name."

"But Grandpa might," Saioa interrupted him.

"We don't want to bother Grandpa; besides, he's senile."

"Not entirely," I thought I heard the girl murmur.

"Look, my father's very elderly and he won't remember anything. We cooperated fully with the local police and forensics at the time. I don't see how you can expect us to give you any fresh information all these years later."

All right, time to withdraw, I thought.

We returned to our room to shower.

I went first, still annoyed about the previous night's conversation. Estíbaliz went out into the hallway, and after a while she knocked on the bathroom door.

"Here, have a coffee." She handed me a scalding plastic cup. It was so strong I almost didn't drink it.

"Let's visit the Pamplona police headquarters, Kraken. I want to see the report on that fire," said Estíbaliz, finishing off her milky coffee.

"I'm with you on that." I nodded. "There are too many fires in Nancho's life."

And so we left the hostel without speaking to the owner again. We headed for Calle Fuente de Teja, where the regional police headquarters was located.

"Good morning," I said as we walked in. "My name is Inspector López de Ayala, and I'm with the Vitoria police. This is my colleague Inspector Ruiz de Gauna. We're hoping to locate a file on the death of Nancho Lopidana, which occurred in 1990 at the hostel on Calle Amaya."

"It'll take us a while to dig it out. In the meantime, if you could fill out these forms . . ." the duty officer said.

An hour later, we were able to access the report.

As before, the photographs were shocking. But this time, the body wasn't completely carbonized, only the areas around the face and hands were affected. Part of the clothing was intact—the pants, although they were slightly blackened.

"Do you see, Estí?" I asked, pointing to this detail.

"Yes. If we weren't looking at the accidental death of a student, I'd say this was the work of a hit man who didn't want the body identified. The face and fingertips are burned to a crisp."

"Who ID'd the body?" I asked, riffling through the papers in the file.

"The former owner of the hostel, the father of that friendly guy who was so forthcoming earlier. It says here that Nancho Lopidana had no relatives."

"What about his roommate? Or a friend, or acquaintance?"

"No other names are mentioned. This report is a bit—"

"On the short side, to put it mildly."

"I'd call it minuscule. We know that Nancho didn't have papers, and they mention that here. They couldn't find him anywhere in the system, realized he was undocumented, so they didn't follow it up. The guy has a death certificate but no birth certificate. Great. They concluded that the fire was caused by a spark from the faulty wiring in the bedside lamp. Case closed. There ends our triplet's tale. Poor guy, he had a sad life."

"And a gruesome death. You know what this means, don't you?" I said.

"If Nancho died in 1990, he can't be our serial killer—not twenty years ago and not now."

I wasn't so sure. I wasn't so sure at all.

"Who wrote the report?"

"Inspector Legarra."

"Then let's talk to him. He's probably retired, but with any luck he'll remember the case. People don't die in fires every day."

We signed the file back in with the uniformed officer who had helped us earlier.

"One more favor. Can you tell us where we might find Inspector Legarra? We'd like to talk to him about this case."

"Sadly, you're too late. Legarra retired last January, and three months later we went to his funeral. Pancreatic cancer, terminal. But he was a good cop, and his reports were extremely methodical. Believe me, if you didn't find anything, it's because there was nothing to find."

"Right," I said.

The man may have been a good detective at the end of his

career, but he certainly wasn't when he wrote that report. It was as leaky as an old bathtub.

Or maybe there was nothing more to it. A young man falls asleep reading, his lamp catches fire, and he ends up dead.

Period.

Estíbaliz took the highway back to Vitoria, and when we arrived at police headquarters, we went our separate ways.

Then I received a call from a number I didn't recognize. I sighed and picked up.

"Good morning, Inspector Ayala. Garrido-Stoker speaking, Ignacio Ortiz de Zárate's lawyer. I wonder if I could talk to you off the record," he said, without preamble. "Will you give me your word that this conversation won't appear in your reports?"

"We have eight dead bodies and missing twins. Believe me, right now, I don't give a damn whether it's on the record or not," I retorted.

"I knew we spoke the same language. I'm calling about something that might help locate my client. So far my computer . . . the technicians have drawn a blank. I was wondering whether, as a detective working for the Criminal Investigation Unit, you sometimes resort to using individuals who aren't on the official payroll."

"You know the answer, and I have the best. What's this about?"

"Ignacio was a detective for many years, and, as you've seen, he knows how to protect himself, in every sense. He owns a very exclusive, expensive brand of cell phone, which he told me he had fitted with a tracking device. We installed a signal receiver in one of my computers that shows the phone's location in real time to within six feet. The transmitter is a device the size of a battery that Ignacio carries around with him, usually in the pocket of his pants, similar to the GPS trackers used by the police, only smaller. That way, if the phone gets lost, or if it's taken from him after he's abducted, we can still trace him, provided they don't remove his clothing."

"I've heard about those devices. They aren't very common in Spain, at least that's what the statistics say."

"Ask one of your billionaire friends, they'll tell you," he retorted with lawyerish wit. "Here's the thing. Ignacio took his phone when he disappeared, but when I tried to trace him on my computer, the receiver showed that both his phone and the tracker had been switched off. That's why I became concerned and reported him missing. I find it very strange that Ignacio would want to prevent me from tracking him, which makes me think he's been abducted or murdered. These systems have a backdoor, so even when they are disconnected, it should be possible to locate him using the GPS signal. The program Ignacio bought can't be accessed by police computers, but I'm wondering if——"

"As I already told you, I have the right person for the job. I just don't know if they'll want to cooperate."

"I am sure Ignacio will offer a generous reward if they locate him."

"I don't think money is what pushes my technician's buttons, but I'll find out what does, and I'll be in touch. The way I see it, discretion is a two-way street, so this exchange stays between us, okay?"

"I never called you, and you never spoke to me. This phone can't be traced to me, so I will always call you from this number, and when this is over, I'll never use it again."

"One last thing, assuming my collaborator agrees, we'll need Ignacio's cell phone number, as well as access to your computer," I said.

"I was counting on that. I've wiped everything."

"Take my advice and wipe it again, thoroughly."

After hanging up, I sent an SOS to MatuSalem:

I think I know how to find Tasio, but I need your help. Now.

It took him took two seconds to reply. It seemed he was still monitoring me, and he hadn't forgotten about Tasio:

> Armory Museum, third floor. It's very old, there are no cameras, and it's deserted in August. When?

Now means now, I wrote back.

I ran out of my office toward Paseo de la Senda. The museum was on Paseo de Fray Francisco, next to the Palacio de Ajuria Enea, the official residence of the *lehendakari.*

On the third floor, I found a lad with a white hoodie concealing his face, next to a dummy with a musket and a helmet.

"I must be crazy," he said, turning his back to me as he quietly scanned the empty room. "Asking a cop to meet me in a room full of weapons next to the presidential palace."

"Don't worry, I'm not going to run you through with a fencing foil."

"What do you want from me, Kraken?" he said, eyes fixed on a cabinet displaying ancient firearms.

"I have a challenge you're going to love: a tracking system we don't use in this country that your mentor's brother paid more for than you or I could afford. The cell phone and GPS microtracker, which Ignacio had on him when he went missing, have been switched off. But I believe that you, and only you, can find a backdoor into the system. In fact, I know you can."

"And what do I get out of it?"

"Besides my respect and immunity from any cybercrime charges, you could help clear Tasio's name, and possibly save his life. . . . I don't know to what extent he protected you in prison. But just imagine if you went missing and he refused to find you. His brother's lawyer also mentioned an enticing sum of money, which would keep you from committing Internet fraud for a while. Come on, Maturana, join the good guys. Hackers like you don't make old bones, unless you go into the start-up business. You could retire on this. Aren't you fed up with having to wear a hoodie, looking over your shoulder all the time?"

"Okay, Kraken, that's enough already. I made up my mind half an hour ago. If you sweeten the pill anymore, I'll get a sugar high."

I suppressed a triumphant smile and watched him turn around, leaving behind the seventeenth century.

"Let me know what data you need!" I yelled as he descended to the exit. "And keep posting on Tasio's Twitter page, even if it's only advice for screenwriters, or else the two of you are going to lose all your followers."

I had been sitting still for a while, lulled by the peace of that place embalmed in time, when I heard the panting breath of someone hurrying up the stairs.

I looked curiously at the woman entering the room, but when I saw who it was, I froze. Literally. I felt a sudden chill in my hands and face, as if someone had turned the air-conditioning on full blast.

"I've been looking everywhere for you, Unai. Your colleague told me you were here," said my sister-in-law, Martina.

"What the hell?" I spluttered.

I could see it was my sister-in-law, but I couldn't believe my eyes.

"Wait, Unai." She restrained me with a gesture. "Let me explain, before you have a heart attack. I've already spoken to Germán. How on earth could you both give me up for dead? I was in Santander on August 9 at a conference on family mediation at the Palacio de la Magdalena. I told you, don't you remember?"

"What are you talking about, Martina? I saw your dead body in the autopsy room. I identified you."

"There's been a mixup, Unai. It was my sister. I can't believe

EVA GARCÍA SÁENZ

you thought I was dead—are you crazy, or what?" she said, drawing closer to me.

She was so close that I recognized her scent and her kiwi-colored eyes.

"Give me a hug, will you? I'm going to need your help calming down Germán; he's hallucinating in Technicolor."

She embraced me, clinging to me like a limpet, and I felt the warmth of her slight frame. After a few seconds of genuine shock, I stroked her black hair, which was just growing back in after chemo, and planted a kiss on the top of her head.

She's hallucinating, I thought.

And suddenly it dawned on me.

Damn it, Unai. You're the one who's hallucinating.

I pulled away from Martina, who looked at me, unsure whether to be annoyed by what had happened or relieved to see me back to my old self.

"You don't have any sisters, Martina," I said to my sister-in-law's ghost, or whatever she was.

"Of course, I have a sister. A twin sister."

I rubbed my eyes, hoping I could make the vision disappear. When I looked again, Martina remained stubbornly in front of me.

I had no experience coping with something like this, so I decided to resort to a therapy method I had read about for patients who suffer from visual or auditory hallucinations.

"Martina, I know you're not real, and I'm going to stop talking to you now. I don't care how many times you appear to me, I'm going to ignore you. I just want to . . ."

To hell with therapy.

"Since we seem to have a second chance to say good-bye, even though it's only in my damaged head, I just want to say thank you. Thank you for the life lesson you gave me. You're my family, Martina. I loved you like a sister."

The Martina in my head didn't appreciate my valediction one bit, but I walked straight past her and headed for the stairs.

As I did so, I couldn't help taking one last look at the room, but there was nobody there. Just helmets and pikes.

Damn you, Estíbaliz! I grabbed my cell phone so hard I almost crushed it, and punched in her number:

"Where are you, Estí?"

"In my office. Why?"

"I'll meet you outside in the parking lot. We need to talk. I'll be in my car."

I arrived in a rage, and found her waiting for me, a worried look on her face.

I parked as far away as possible and pushed open the passenger door. Estíbaliz came over and got in.

"What's wrong? You're as pale as a ghost."

"Am I really? Funnily enough, I've just seen one, and it almost gave me a heart attack! But not only did I see this ghost, I also spoke to her. To Martina's ghost, Estíbaliz."

"Pardon me?"

"Pardon me?" I repeated, my cheeks burning. "No, I won't pardon you. Not this time. You've lost your mind, your moral compass. You've overstepped the mark, my friend. Giving me a psychotropic drug during a crucial stage of an investigation, when I need to be more focused than ever, with my brain working at full capacity. Are you out of your mind? Did you spike my coffee this morning in Pamplona, is that it?"

Estíbaliz pursed her lips, folded her arms, and stared straight ahead.

"If you already know, stop asking rhetorical questions."

I heaved a sigh, waiting to see if my anger would subside, but it wasn't that easy.

"How long will this crap stay in my system?"

"The side effects will fade, I think, but so does your immunity to Rohypnol."

"How long?" I repeated, on the verge of losing my temper.

"Twelve hours . . . I think."

"You think?"

"Yes, your body should metabolize it by tonight; that's what Eneko told me."

I wasn't just angry; I was also sad.

This was good-bye. There was no coming back from here.

"Estí, after what you've done, I—I can't work with you anymore. I won't report you. I have no desire to ruin your career, but I can't trust you now. I won't be able to trust you whenever you offer me a coffee or something to eat. I'll talk to the DSU tomorrow. Either you leave the case or I will. And when it's over, we'll no longer be partners."

"I'll leave, Inspector Ayala. You shouldn't have to pay for my mistakes."

"It's too late, Inspector Gauna. I already have. Please get out of my car."

I sat there for a long time, unable to think straight, disturbed by the drug in my body.

I was through with everything. With Estí, Alba, everything.

If this case didn't destroy me and all my relationships first, I would take a break once it was over. Maybe with Germán, to get him away from Vitoria, to take care of him.

I was afraid this damned drug might stop my brain from working, so I resolved to stay active, to keep moving.

What haven't you done yet, Unai?

Lutxo, I needed to speak with Lutxo.

I dialed his number and hoped he wouldn't try to worm his way out of seeing me.

"Lutxo, I'd like to meet you. Do you have a moment? And for God's sake, don't give me any of your elaborate excuses."

Much to my surprise, he seemed willing to talk. I asked him to meet me in Arriaga Park, a neutral, out-of-the-way place where I could converse in relative peace with a guy who had been my friend since we were at San Viator together.

"It's been ages, Kraken!" he said, head down, as he clapped me on the back. "Actually, I guess it's only been a few weeks, but with everything that's been going on, it feels like a lifetime. How are you coping with what happened to your sister-in-law?"

My sister-in-law, I thought, gritting my teeth. *My sister-in-law came down from heaven to look out for me. Will you do as much, my friend?*

"Frankly, the best thing I can do for Martina is to find the bastard who killed her. And you're going to help me, aren't you? Lutxo, you and I have some talking to do."

"Spit it out, then, because you've lost me," he said, sitting down on a bench facing one of the ponds.

"When we last spoke, I asked you who sent you the photos of the twins with the fifteen-year-old victim, you refused to tell me who your source was. I'm beginning to see how influential the press has been in this case and in the one twenty years ago, and it looks like your priority hasn't always been merely to inform."

"Who are you accusing, exactly?"

"You, your newspaper editor . . ."

"Me? What are you talking about?"

"You were the one who planted doubts about the Eguzkilore in my head, you were the one who destroyed Ignacio Ortiz de Zárate's public image and made it impossible for Tasio to reintegrate into society. Maybe I should start asking about your movements on the dates of the murders."

"You can't be serious, Kraken?" He looked at me, in shock. "I can't believe that a friend like you doesn't trust me. How long have we known each other, since we were six?"

"You're changing the subject, Lutxo," I warned him. "And it doesn't make you look innocent."

"What is this?" he yelled, leaping up from the bench. "Are you really accusing me?"

I also rose to my feet. I didn't like people shouting at me from above.

"Then help me out, Lutxo! Make my life easier, because I could make yours extremely difficult if I charged you with obstruction of justice for refusing to tell me who your goddamned source is. Maybe if I had done that earlier, Martina and Eneko would still be alive. I don't know how you can look Germán in the eye."

Lutxo sat down again, stroking his white goatee over and over.

"My boss will kill me; he'll kill me for this . . ." he muttered to himself.

"Come on, Lutxo," I cajoled. "You know you're going to tell me, just get it over with."

"Okay. The newspaper's best-kept secret is that everything we publish in relation to this case is sent to us in an envelope with no return address. And it's been like that for the past twenty years."

What? I thought, flabbergasted. "In an envelope?"

"Yes, it was quite normal back then. There was no Internet, and press notices often arrived by mail or were delivered by hand. The paper received a lot of anonymous material. We took basic precautions to detect possible letter bombs, but unless a package was particularly bulky, we opened all the mail normally."

"What exactly did these envelopes contain?"

"The photographs we published, and complete articles that didn't even require editing. We got a whole lot of information that *El Correo Vitoriano* didn't have. The envelopes were addressed to me. I had just started working on the paper as a trainee, with a salary and contract to match. I was the new boy, a kid with dreams of conquering the world, who had come up against the reality of a journalistic hierarchy, and whose six-month contract was unlikely to be renewed. Not staying at the paper would have meant leaving Vitoria—there aren't many openings in this city for young journalists."

"And they were addressed to you? Why didn't you tell the police? They might have found fingerprints or DNA in the saliva on the seal."

"I just told you. Do I have to spell it out? I gave the first batch to my editor, without telling him where they came from. I don't think he was all that bothered. The guy was obsessed with the case and wanted to devote more and more pages to the story. We sold a record number of copies with that edition. When more envelopes arrived, I couldn't think straight. Each time, I spent the whole day with the editor in his office. I became his favorite reporter, and he offered me a permanent contract."

"Do you think the same person sent the last envelope you received, the one with the photographs of the twins with the girl?"

Lutxo thought for a moment, then looked at me sheepishly. "Well, yeah, I hadn't thought of that."

"You cretin!" I yelled, beside myself with rage. "This means that the same person has been doing this for the past twenty years. Are you even remotely aware of how significant that is? Don't you realize that whoever sent you those photographs and articles wasn't doing it to help you get job security, but to manipulate public opinion? This is someone who knows more than both of us put together, who is always one step ahead of us. It could very well be the killer, someone whose aim has always been to destroy Tasio and Ignacio. Because of you, an entire line of inquiry that should have been started twenty years ago has been suppressed. And as a result, sixteen people have died. Your job cost those people their lives."

"Shit, Kraken, don't be mad at me. I never thought of it that way."

"Yes, you did, Lutxo. You most definitely did, but you are incapable of seeing beyond your damned news desk. Send me those envelopes before I call the prosecutor and have your fucking newspaper shut down."

I turned away and walked out of the park. I was next to the shrine of San Juan de Arriaga, where, hundreds of years ago, the Hermandad de Arriaga had come together to defend their interests. Time hadn't done much to change our traditions—the people of Vitoria were still fighting one another, and the people of Álava were still killing one another.

46

THE OLD QUARTER

THURSDAY, AUGUST 18

Early the next morning I received an unexpected call before I'd even left the house.

"Hello?"

"Inspector Ayala, it's Saioa, from the hostel in Pamplona. I hope you remember me."

"Of course, I remember you, Saioa. Is there a problem with the credit card?"

"No. That's not why I'm calling. It's . . ." She paused for a moment. "You are Kraken, the guy investigating the Tasio Ortiz de Zárate case, right?"

I sighed—this was becoming an epidemic. "If you know who I am, then I don't need to introduce myself."

"Okay, so, yeah, I'm following the double murders in Vitoria on Twitter, but I didn't recognize you yesterday because you look smaller in the photos."

"Why are you calling me, Saioa?"

"Okay, as I'm sure you noticed, my dad doesn't like the cops much. They carry out a lot of drug searches at the hostel because of the kind of guests we attract. He gets frustrated, and, well, he's sick of you guys. Look, I don't know if what happened to Nancho Lopidana has anything to do with Tasio, it's just that you mentioned an old case yesterday, and—"

"You know I can't talk about that, Saioa. I'm listening, though."

"I just thought, if this helps solve the case, then I'll have done something, instead of looking the other way. My grandfather kept all the guest registers, dating back to when the hostel first opened. They're at his place. I spoke to him, and he's eager to talk to you. He says the police ignored him twenty-six years ago, and he's been wanting to talk to someone about it ever since. You have to come to Pamplona, though, because he's pretty much housebound. And it's best if my father doesn't find out."

"I'm on my way. Give me your grandfather's address and tell him I'll be with him in an hour and a half. And one more thing, Saioa—"

"Yes?"

"Thanks a million. If only everybody were as conscientious as you."

I ended the call, ran out to my car, and dialed Estíbaliz's number: "Estí, the conversation we had yesterday is on hold. Listen, I'm heading back to Pamplona to talk to the former landlord of the hostel in Calle Amaya. He has the guest registers from twenty-six years ago, and his granddaughter thinks he can give us some more information. But before that, I have to tell you what happened with Lutxo."

"Lutxo, our Lutxo?"

"Yes, our Lutxo."

I updated her on the anonymous envelopes, and after she let out a few expletives, we agreed she would drop by *El Diario Alavés*'s offices and make sure Lutxo handed over the envelopes as soon as possible so we could have them analyzed.

The address Saioa had given me was in Pamplona's Old Quarter. I pressed the buzzer and climbed the narrow staircase to the second floor, where a stout old man greeted me. He had a paunch like his son's, and his red nose was a maze of broken blood vessels. He walked with the help of a cane that seemed a little short. At his request, I sat down on an old, green fake-leather armchair. I politely refused the glass of sloe gin he poured for me, after which he tried offering me various things, until finally I accepted a pastry from a box he produced out of a quaint seventies-style cabinet.

"My granddaughter updated me. All these years, I've been hoping someone would reopen the Nancho Lopidana case."

"The case hasn't been reopened," I explained, my mouth full of sticky sponge cake, "but the name has come up in connection with another investigation."

"Well, they should reopen it. I wasn't at all happy about what happened."

"Can you tell me why that is?"

"Look, it wasn't just that Nancho died that night. His roommate left without paying, and I never heard from him again. I told the police about it, but they said that unless his relatives reported him missing, they weren't going to mount a search for him."

I remained speechless for a few seconds. I wasn't expecting this.

"Are you saying Nancho's roommate also disappeared? There's no mention of that in the report."

"What do you mean?" he replied angrily, jabbing the floor with the tip of his cane. "There must be! I gave the inspector enough grief about it."

"No, there isn't. So how did the police know it was Nancho and not his roommate who died in the fire that night?"

The old fellow spread his arms wide, as if to say it couldn't be more obvious.

"Because he was in Nancho's bed, and because, even though the clothes were partially burned, we could tell they were Nancho's."

The evidence was weak. A good detective would have kept looking, I thought.

"All right. Can you recall the name of Nancho's roommate?"

"Not offhand, but if you don't mind waiting, I can dig out his registration form. On second thought, it might be quicker if I showed you the photograph album. I used to write down the names of our student lodgers on the backs of the photos so I wouldn't forget them. There were so many."

"You have photographs of Nancho?" I swallowed hard.

Finally. Finally, I was going to find out if he had any connection to the twins.

"Of course, and of his roommate, too. We used to have parties at Christmas, and on other feast days, for the students who didn't go home to their families. Those two were inseparable. In fact, every day they looked more and more alike; they could have been brothers."

"Sorry?"

"Yes, look. If I show you the photos from that year, you'll see what I mean. When Nancho first arrived at the hostel, his clothes were awful and his hair was a mess, but when he started hanging around with the other lad, he smartened up, lost weight, and had his hair cut like the journalist at the same barbershop. Although Nancho was ginger-haired and his friend dark-haired, they ended up looking like Chip 'n' Dale. It was the funniest thing. If Nancho had dyed his hair, they would have looked identical. You can see for yourself. I'm not exaggerating."

"Sorry, did you just refer to Nancho's roommate as the journalist?"

"Yes, didn't I mention that before? The student who disappeared was in the first year of a degree in journalism. His parents were both dead, and he was an only child with no relatives. I think he came from Madrid, but they left him some money, and his father's dying wish had been that he would follow in his grandfather's footsteps and become a reporter, or something."

"May I see those photo albums, please?"

"Pass me the one for 1989, would you? With my shaky hands I'd probably drop them." He pointed to his antique cabinet.

I stood up and went through the albums year by year until I found one labeled 1989–1990. I sat down beside him, trying to contain my excitement. The old fellow began to turn the pages of the thick volume.

"Here!" he exclaimed, placing his finger over a face I couldn't make out.

"Could . . . Could you take your finger away so that I can see him?"

"Yes, of course. Look, there's Nancho Lopidana when he first arrived at the hostel. That was taken early on, but he and the journalist were already friends."

I studied the image more closely. The colors were typical of a photo from the nineties, and the shot looked like an Instagram filter had been applied to it.

I guessed that Nancho was the moon-faced boy with the button nose and close-set eyes. His features looked as if they were a size too small. He had straight hair with a rather straggly long lock swept up at the front. He wasn't looking straight at the camera but had his head lowered, like someone who is cripplingly shy. He appeared distant, almost scared amid the rest of the students, who were blowing paper party horns and throwing streamers.

"That's his roommate, look, the one on his left," declared the former landlord, pointing with his finger.

The other boy was handsome, slim with short dark hair, and he looked straight at the camera with a self-assured expression. He had his arm resting on Nancho's shoulder, as if he wanted to include him in the fun.

"Is his name on the back?"

The old man peeled away the plastic film protecting the photograph and turned it over.

"Ah, no, this one must have gotten past me," he said, frowning. "But don't worry, I have lots more."

We turned the pages, and he pointed out all the photos that had Nancho in them. He and his roommate were always together, side by side. Sometimes they appeared to be chatting, sharing secrets. At other times they were making rude signs at the camera with the brashness of teenage youths.

"You see?" He pointed again. "Nancho started chain-smoking, and his friend, the journalist, couldn't stand it, and wouldn't let Nancho light up in their room. On the night he died, Nancho was alone, so he had a cigarette. I reckon the poor kid fell asleep while he was smoking."

He was right. In the later photographs, Nancho always had a roll-up in his mouth. I counted seven photographs of the two friends, and, looking through them, the change in Nancho was evident.

"Do you mind if I take out all the photographs with Nancho in them? I promise to put them back in the right order."

"Go ahead, go ahead. We can sort them out afterward," he urged.

I pushed aside the bag of supermarket pastries and lined up the seven photographs on the coffee table.

The change in Nancho wasn't just obvious, it was creepy: In the space of a few months, he lost weight, cut his hair short, and was wearing a Levi's jean jacket with a sheepskin collar identical to his friend's. In the most recent images, he looked like a completely different person than the one in the earliest pictures. He was laughing with his peers, chatting up girls in miniskirts like a young Romeo, or drinking beer with his arm around his roommate, the perennial roll-up between his lips.

Christ, this guy's a chameleon. I felt a flash of fear.

Nancho wasn't simply adapting to his surroundings; there was a pathological aspect to his transformation. This wasn't just imitation; it was impersonation. He had chosen a body, an identity, and then . . . possibly replaced him, using his charred remains as a host.

I turned over all the photographs. Fortunately, some had several names scrawled on the back. I handed them to the old man.

"Now do you remember the journalism student's name?"

"Let me see," he said, putting on a pair of thick-lensed glasses. "Mario, that's right. Here he is: Mario Santos."

What?

"Sorry, did you say Mario Santos?" I repeated, incredulous. "Could you find his file for me, with all his details, including his ID card number?"

Mario Santos, the journalist at *El Correo Vitoriano?* That was impossible, it couldn't be that Mario. He was the nicest, most laid-back guy.

Exactly like Nancho, I thought.

Exactly like Nancho.

For a criminal profiler, this is the hallowed moment: when your theoretical profile melds with the real-life person, when the cloth you have cut in your head based on your observations of their behavior fits the suspect to perfection.

I had my moment of epiphany with those seven photographs spread before me on a seventies-style coffee table, the indigestible pastry still stuck in my throat.

Exactly like Nancho.

The old man had stored all the guest-registration cards on tiny ring binders, and we had to trawl through hundreds of them before we found the one for Mario. Mario Santos Espinosa, born April 16, 1971. The youthful photograph scarcely resembled the adult I knew as Mario Santos.

On the other hand, when I looked at the last photograph of the slim, short-haired Nancho taken at the hostel, my blood ran cold.

Because I realized that this was the grown-up Mario Santos I had met countless times over the years. A twenty-year-old Mario, who still had red hair. More boyish, with weaker shoulders, his features less well defined, and yet I recognized the straight eyebrows, the close-set brown eyes. . . .

This was the Mario I had always known. Nancho Lopidana had defied his brothers and returned to Vitoria with a different identity. For twenty years he had controlled one of Vitoria's leading newspapers from the shadows, while sending the most scabrous photographs to its rival.

As a journalist he had easy access to historic buildings; his mild manners and unthreatening appearance had enabled him to approach his victims.

My God! He had used me, too, slowly gaining my trust, never putting pressure on me.

"Do you know something?" I told the old man at last, feigning a composure I was far from feeling. "I think you were absolutely right about Mario Santos's disappearance being suspicious. I'm going to do what I can to correct this police error, but I'll need your permission to take these photographs and files as evidence. Do you agree?"

"Of course, son. Provided that in return, when the investigation is over, you call to tell me exactly what happened. It's been preying on my mind for many years."

"Consider it done." I squeezed his hand the way my grandfather did. "I give you my word."

I headed back to Vitoria with the stash of photographs, my head buzzing.

Mario?

Mario Santos?

I called Estíbaliz and told her what had happened.

"He's a chameleon, Estí. Nancho Lopidana has been posing

as Mario Santos for decades, but we had no way of knowing. He could have been anyone. Did you get the envelopes from *El Diario Alavés*?"

"Yes, and I've informed the DSU. We sent them to the lab in Bilbao to be tested for traces of saliva that might contain DNA. It'll take a few days, so fingers crossed. Right now, it would be very helpful to be able to link Mario Santos to the case."

"I know, Estí. I know. I want you to search the database to see if the number on this ID card matches that of our journalist friend. Write it down."

I read out the number on the yellowing registration card from the hostel and listened to my partner pounding on the keyboard. I was only twenty minutes away from Vitoria, but I wanted to go faster, to finish this thing for good.

"Shit! It's him all right, Kraken," said Estí. "It checks with the number on Mario Santos's ID card. But how did Nancho manage to substitute his fingerprint for the real Mario Santos's?"

"He could have bought a false ID card on the black market in Mario Santos's name, but with his own photo and fingerprint. Afterward, when he renewed it, it became legal," I replied.

Twenty years ago, few government offices were fully digitalized, and it wasn't unthinkable that, without an automatic system to detect the difference, the real Mario's old fingerprint could have been replaced by Nancho's new one. At a busy police station like the one in Pamplona, where they renewed lots of ID cards every day, they were unlikely to examine every fingerprint. To confirm a match, experts have to find at least twelve identical ridges—the famous minutiae—and police stations back then didn't have the staff or technology on hand to carry out that task.

"Even so, he was taking a risk," insisted Estí.

"Nancho had been undocumented his whole life. He couldn't deal with bureaucracy or exist legally like the rest of us. Usurping the real Mario Santos's identity was incredibly advantageous for him—he had a birth certificate, he could enroll at a university, he had bank accounts with Mario's money in them—an entire past complete with documents. That's why he stopped being Nancho Lopidana after he got his school certificate. That identity had helped him achieve a basic education, but he no longer needed it. And by taking on a new one, he wouldn't face the risk of being connected to the fire that wiped out the rest of the Lopidana family. And then there was another fire at the hostel. Too many fires connected with him where he ended up as the sole survivor, wouldn't you say?"

"Now I understand why the body at the hostel had no fingerprints and why the face was burned beyond recognition," said Estíbaliz. "If he can do that to a friend, imagine what he can do to people he doesn't even know."

"I'm afraid we've all seen what Nancho is capable of," I said, suppressing a wave of disgust as I imagined the Mario I knew stripping my sister-in-law and placing bees in her mouth. "Estí, call in a search operation. See if you can locate him at the offices of *El Correo Vitoriano,* or at his home address. Take an armed squad. I'll inform the DSU so that Judge Olano can issue a warrant. We need either a confession or physical evidence that links him to at least one of the murders. We could examine some of the cold cases in Izarra and Pamplona—I doubt he would have worn gloves back then or would have been as meticulous as he is now. I doubt we'll get a quick confession out of someone who has spent the last twenty-seven years wreaking vengeance. This guy must have prodigious amounts of self-control."

The beast's lair, I thought. *We need to find the beast's lair.*

The place where he took them, where he killed them, prepared them for his sinister staging. It had to be outside Vitoria. Mario must own other properties in the vicinity.

I checked the clock in the car: it was past noon. Alba would be at home having lunch, so I called her cell phone. I wanted to give her the details, and I also wanted to hear her voice. To tell her that this torment, this nightmare, this black cloud that had been hanging over us since we first met, was finally lifting.

"Alba, we've got him!" I exclaimed, unable to contain myself. "We know who the murderer is. We have photographs from Pamplona of Nancho Lopidana and proof that he changed his identity. He didn't die, Alba. And the envelopes he sent to *El Diario Alavés* could provide conclusive DNA that will link him to the case."

"Would you please calm down, Inspector Ayala? Right now, I'm at home with my family in the middle of lunch."

That word, *family,* burned like a mouthful of napalm. I knew she was warning me that she couldn't talk. But the intensity of my reaction made it hard to find the words for what I wanted to say.

"I understand, but this is urgent," I snapped.

Just then, I received another call. It was MatuSalem.

If only.

If only this was good news, and he had located Ignacio.

"I'll let you go. I have to take another call. I can explain everything to you later. I'll be in Vitoria in less than twenty minutes; hopefully by then you'll be back at headquarters, because we need to catch this killer."

47

TREVIÑO

Thursday, August 18

For once, MatuSalem sounded agitated.

"Kraken! I've found the signal. Both Ignacio's phone and the GPS tracker are transmitting from the same area. I've triangulated the zone, but it's probably too big to be of any use."

"At this stage, I'll take anything you can give me. How big?"

"Five square kilometers."

"Okay, that is big, especially if it's in a built-up area, but I can work with that. Tell me which zone it is, and then text me the coordinates."

"It's south of Vitoria, in Treviño."

"Treviño?"

"Yes, beyond the Puerto de Vitoria. There aren't many villages in that area. Uzquiano, Ajarte, Aguillo, Imiruri, San Vicentejo—"

"San Vicentejo?" I repeated.

The chapel. He's holding them at the San Vicentejo chapel.

It made sense. Only three or four old people remained in the village, and neither of the two houses they lived in had a view of the chapel. Mario could have easily driven his drugged victims there and carried them into the chapel. He probably still had a key from when he'd helped renovate the place as a youth. Once inside, he could have removed their clothing, administered the yew extract or introduced the bees into their mouths, all without any risk of being disturbed.

"Text me those coordinates, MatuSalem. I think you've just returned Tasio's favor."

I put my foot to the floor, ignoring common sense and traffic lights, and reached headquarters in record time.

I bounded up the stairs, hoping to find Alba already in her office.

I flung open the door without knocking.

"DSU Salvatierra, I know where . . ."

But I was talking to an empty office. Alba still wasn't in the building.

I stood outside in the hallway, wondering whether I should try her cell phone again.

Just then, I saw Pancorbo approach, and he stopped in front of me.

"Are you looking for the DSU? She's probably still at lunch. Her husband, Mario, came by to pick her up a couple of hours ago."

"Sorry, did you say Mario?"

"Yes, Mario Santos, the guy from *El Correo Vitoriano.* Didn't you know he was married to our DSU?"

"To Mario Santos?" I managed to repeat.

So you were the invisible man.

"Yes, she's very discreet about it, which is understandable. She doesn't want to be accused of favoritism when it comes to informing the media. I think it's a good idea; you know how people around here like to talk."

"So how come you knew about it?" I asked, propping myself against the wall and taking a deep breath.

"Mario and I go back a long way. He covered the double murders twenty years ago, and back then he was my contact at the newspaper. His articles were impeccable, and as a reporter he never crossed the line. Actually, I consider him a friend," said Pancorbo, alarmed at the grimace on my face. "Are you okay, Ayala?"

"A friend . . . So did I, Pancorbo. I also considered him a friend. And yet we have every reason to believe that Mario Santos is our killer."

He stared at me in disbelief.

"That's impossible, surely not . . ." he said, drawing back.

"You wouldn't think so, would you? Listen, we're wasting time. I'll keep trying to locate the DSU. You get on to Judge Olano, and ask for an arrest warrant for Mario Santos, and another to search his home. E-mail them to Inspector Ruiz de Gauna. She'll be waiting there with backup."

Pancorbo reacted more quickly than I expected. "Consider it done!" he said, hurrying down the stairs before I had finished speaking.

I grabbed my service revolver and a bulletproof vest from my office and sprinted out of the building.

I headed for the SUV in the parking lot and called Alba's number again.

"Come on, pick up. Don't do this to me . . ." I hissed at the cell phone, which continued to ring.

I drove south toward the Peñacerrada Highway. I ignored the right-of-way on several roundabouts and flew through the Puerto de Vitoria.

"Come on, Alba! You have to pick up."

But Alba's phone rang and rang until it went dead.

Is that you or Mario?

Who had switched off her phone?

Why on earth would Alba do that?

I pressed my right foot to the floor, and almost missed the sharp turnoff that descended toward San Vicentejo.

The car skidded on the gravel road, but I managed to stay in control of the heavy vehicle. If I'd been driving an ordinary passenger car, I would have probably wrapped myself around one of the trees on the far side of the road.

Calm down, Unai. Don't mess things up before you even get there, I told myself.

But I wasn't calm, or clearheaded. Far from it.

I parked next to the blue-and-yellow recycling bins at the side of the road, threw my bulletproof vest on, and jumped over a flimsy wooden fence, brandishing my revolver.

I knew it was foolhardy to go in alone. I knew I should have called it in and waited for Estíbaliz to arrive with backup.

I approached the heavy wooden door. It was decorated with thousand-year-old studs, doubtless nailed there by one of my ancestors' neighbors.

How on earth was I going to get inside?

I hadn't brought a battering ram, and even if I had, no prosecutor would issue a warrant to destroy a historic monument. I needed to ask someone for a key, possibly Don Tiburcio, although I had been in too much of a hurry to have thought of that earlier.

In a rage, I circled the building and noticed three narrow windows in the apse, eight feet or more above the ground. I was sure they would light up the tiny space enough for me to see if there was anyone inside.

I returned to the SUV and drove it up onto the tiny hillock where the chapel was perched. I parked parallel to the wall of the apse and climbed onto the roof of the vehicle.

Glancing up, I almost shuddered. Just above my head was a tiny bas-relief of the hermetic couple, the man and woman lying side by side, each with a consoling hand resting on the other's cheek.

This is where it had all started in Mario's mind, and this was where it was going to end.

And yet, when I managed to peer through the glass into the diaphanous interior of the temple at last, there was no one there.

I saw nothing more than four rows of ancient pews and a small stone altar.

I contorted myself to look through the other windows, even though I knew there was nothing to see. The chapel was empty.

If Ignacio's GPS was transmitting a signal in that area, where exactly was he being kept?

I climbed down from the roof and was clambering back into the car when I realized I wasn't alone.

"For heaven's sake, Grandpa! You made me jump! What are you doing here?"

Grandfather shrugged at me from the passenger seat and pointed at the Ochate church tower.

"Feliciano from Imiruri brought me. Son, I think I know where the fox's lair is."

48

OCHATE

THURSDAY, AUGUST 18

The fox's lair, I repeated to myself.

"Do you remember when the people in Imiruri saw lights at Ochate during the night?" asked Grandfather. His tranquil voice had an immediate calming effect on me. "I've been making inquiries, and they also saw lights twenty years ago, when the fox began his killing spree. UFOs, my eye, Unai. It was the headlights from that bastard's car, as it bumped along the track. He must have a shack in Ochate."

"I doubt it, Grandpa. The place was abandoned in 1934. Look at the church tower; there are no electrical towers for miles. I doubt the killer would choose a place without electricity or running water."

"There's plenty of water in the river Goveloste," he parried, "and many of the shacks around here have their own generators. Come on, let's drive over there. I know an old goat track we can take where the road ends."

"Grandpa, I'm in the middle of a complex operation. You shouldn't be here—it's dangerous."

"Son, I've seen more guns fired than you'll see in your lifetime. I'll go with you to Ochate, help you find him, and then I'll take the path back to Imiruri. You know I can find my way around these hills better than you can."

He was right. I hadn't been to the ghost village since I was a child, and I wasn't sure how to get there. I also knew my grandfather had more common sense than my entire team put together, so I agreed to let him ride shotgun and moved off in the direction his finger was pointing.

"Promise me you'll go straight back, Grandpa. Promise me."

"I don't make promises. You have my word. That's all you need."

He was right. Back in his day, agreements were made with a nod and a handshake, and he never broke them.

I looked straight ahead. Spreading before me were fields of scrub grass with hay bales stacked by the sides of the road. Every so often I hit a steep slope, but the SUV climbed them with ease. We drove another four hundred yards or so until we came to a barn where the road ended. On the right was a footpath and on the left was an overgrown track.

"We'll get there quicker if we take the footpath," the old man said.

I took his advice and parked the car out of sight behind a nearby clump of wild hazelnut trees. We got out and headed for Ochate, a bell tower with no bell; it was all that remained of the church of San Pedro de Chochat. Its walls were sprayed with tags, obscene graffiti, and a few satanic symbols. In front of the tower stood the ruined facades of what must have been two village houses. When I peered over the front walls into the interiors, all I could see were rows of tall nettles.

"There's nothing here, Grandpa," I said, turning back to look at him.

"How about beyond that slope?" he asked, pointing to the east. "I think I see a tin roof."

We approached silently. Hidden behind the crest of the hill was a ramshackle house surrounded by a low stone wall. One side of the corrugated-iron roof and the main building were in ruins, but the rest was big enough to accommodate several rooms. It had two stories, and although the windowpanes were missing, it had a brand-new steel door, which seemed incongruous in a village that had been uninhabited for more than eighty years.

"Get down, Grandpa. Is that a van over there?"

I wasn't sure, but I thought I glimpsed the outline of a white vehicle behind a line of poplars on the riverbank, toward Aguillo.

We crept over to the house, and when we were about forty feet from it, my grandfather let out a curse.

"Shh," I hissed, turning toward him.

"Dratted bee, she stung me," he whispered, clasping the palm of his hand.

"A bee?"

I looked and saw the sting buried in my grandfather's callused hand.

"It looks as though there are more of them, and they're angry," he said, swatting away several others circling above our heads.

Angry bees. I hope he isn't using them on Alba right now, I thought, praying to the goddess Mari, to Urtzi, and to the whole pantheon of Basque divinities.

"Grandpa, I think this is the house. It's time for you to leave. I'll see you in Villaverde."

"I will, don't worry. I think we've found the fox's lair. But remember, son: once you're inside, you have to be the smartest creature on the mountain. Do you understand?" His voice rang out behind me.

"What animal do you mean, Grandpa?" I said, turning around, baffled.

When I looked behind me, he wasn't there. I straightened up with a start and looked anxiously in every direction, but there was no sign of him.

How could it be? Grandfather had been walking in those mountains for nearly a hundred years and could move around almost silently, but it was impossible for him to have disappeared that quickly.

What if . . . What if that wasn't my grandfather? What if it was another trick my mind was playing on me, another hallucination caused by the Eguzkilore's potion? I cursed him and all his ancestors. If I couldn't trust what I was seeing or who I was speaking to, I had little chance of getting out of this alive.

At least I'm still immune to Rohypnol, I consoled myself.

Supposedly.

No, I couldn't rely on that, either.

The buzzing of another furious bee refocused my attention.

I drew my gun from the holster and edged closer, avoiding the front of the house.

As I circled the building, I looked up at the empty windows. I could try scaling the wall. The concrete that had once held the stones together had turned to dust, and the window frames were only a few feet above my head. However, if Mario was inside, and he looked out, I would be at his mercy. Peering down at the ground, I noticed a small skylight, like the ones they used to have in the cellars of the *txokos.* I crouched down. My body could fit through the narrow opening. I peered inside, saw no one, and lowered myself down, feetfirst.

When I looked around me, I almost passed out.

I had landed in a closed room containing a well-preserved antique wardrobe, a desk with a long row of folders on it, and what looked like a comfortable chair. Next to it was a large sack. I went over to it and saw several *eguzkilores*—six of them. Three for each double murder. So he planned on killing four more people. Two forty-year-olds and two forty-five-year-olds.

In the wardrobe, on hangers, I discovered the clothes of all his victims. They were carefully pressed, arranged according to size, from zero to XXL, just as if they were hanging in a boutique. I recognized Martina's festival outfit: jeans, white T-shirt, and a red neckerchief.

They still smelled like her.

Goddamnit.

Maybe these were the clothes he'd never had. Maybe he was making us all pay for his stepfather's avarice.

In the wardrobe I also found, lined up and switched off, cell phones from his eight most recent victims. Ignacio's expensive model was there as well. I suddenly remembered the twins. It was easy to be distracted by this abundance of evidence.

I went over to the desk and looked inside the folders. They contained information about the New Cathedral and Artium, the Museum of Modern Art on Calle Francia. Symbolic buildings from twentieth-century Vitoria. There were photographs of employees' uniforms, timetables, photocopies of name tags, and a couple of interviews with the director and staff members of the cathedral's Museum of Sacred Art for his newspaper.

So these were the places he intended to leave the bodies of his next victims. Probably mine among them.

In one folder, I found all the case material on Tasio Ortiz de Zárate. Mario had known for months that Tasio was due to leave prison on August 8, 2016.

I was well versed in the tendency of serial killers and psychopaths to create shrines, to keep trophies from their victims so that they could obsessively relive the moment of their crime, almost like masturbating. But I had never come across this level of organization.

A sound coming through the wall snapped me back to reality. Someone was banging a stone on the far side of the belly of the whale.

Clasping my gun in both hands, I pushed open the ramshackle door that would lead to that chamber of horrors. On the other side were the ruins of a small passageway leading to a rickety staircase. The stairs led up to ground level, but the noise I heard was coming from one of the rooms at the far end of the cellar. As I approached, I glimpsed through the gloom a wooden door with a thick chain and padlock across it. I passed other doorless rooms, which, as far as I could make out, contained only rusty farm implements: an overturned plow, discarded parts from threshing and baling machines, and a few millet brooms.

When I reached the padlocked door, I saw that it had a tiny hatch set into it. I lifted the metal flap carefully, and what greeted my eyes made my blood run cold. Inside was a filthy hay barn, strewn with untidily stacked bales. The intense heat coming from inside made me gasp for air.

I could see Tasio—or maybe Ignacio—sprawled on the floor. I wasn't sure which one—he didn't have his prison mustache and his hair was cropped short. He appeared to still be alive, but he was in a pitiful state—almost skin and bones, dressed only in his underwear. The clothes I'd last seen him in when he left prison— the famous Barbour jacket with the hood—lay in a heap along with a pair of pants, some shoes, and a blue shirt, which I assumed belonged to Ignacio.

The other twin continued to strike the wall with a stone, as if he hadn't noticed me yet.

"Shh," I called out to him softly. "Ignacio? Is that you?"

"Inspector Ayala!" he whispered, dropping the stone as if his strength had suddenly drained away.

"What's going on? What's wrong with Tasio?"

Ignacio came over to the hatch, grasping the bars with emaciated fingers.

"He's dehydrated and suffering from malnutrition," he said,

through cracked lips. "It's like a crematorium in here, and he's been locked up in this place since he was released from prison. That madman isn't ready to kill us yet. Just when I think my twin is about to die, he comes to give us a sip of water. Get them to send an ambulance—he won't last much longer, and neither will I."

"I'll call my partner. She's on her way with backup," I whispered, dialing her number.

"Estí, I'm in Ochate. I've found Tasio and Ignacio. Call an ambulance right away. They've had almost no food or water for over a week. We're in an abandoned house south of the tower near a line of poplars by the river. I haven't located Mario and DSU Salvatierra yet, but I think I saw a white van."

"What do you mean, DSU Salvatierra?" she said, puzzled.

"She's married to him, Estí. Mario is the DSU's husband. He must have overheard our conversation when I called to tell her we knew the killer's identity. Bring backup, but don't break down the main door. If he's in the house, he'll hear you and then both she and I will be in danger. I'm going to—"

"Unai, get out of there!" she interrupted. "Wait for us outside, we'll be twenty minutes."

"Alba could be dead by then. I haven't searched upstairs yet. I'm going to stay in the house and try to free the twins. We're in the basement—there's a hay barn at the end of the hallway. I found clothes belonging to the victims, police reports, *eguzkilores,* and other proof. I'm going now," I whispered, and ended the call.

"Do you have any water?" Ignacio hissed impatiently.

"No, but there's a river nearby. I'll try to unlock the door. If you can get outside, follow the row of poplars. Are you strong enough to drag your brother with you?"

"He's my twin. Do you think I'd leave him here to die? When he called me in San Sebastián, I knew what I was getting into. Tasio has already paid the price for a crime he didn't commit."

"Okay, I'm going to look for something to open this door with."

I went into the adjoining room and came out with a stout broom handle. I pushed it through a link in the chain and started to twist, praying it wouldn't snap. Ignacio watched from the other side of the door, sweat streaming from his brow.

"Do you know if he's here?" I asked. "The killer, I mean."

"He arrived about half an hour ago. I recognized the sound of his car engine. Tell me, has he murdered the two forty-year-olds yet?"

"No, why?"

"Because we're going to be the forty-five-year-olds," he said. And after that the killings will stop. After taking everything else from us—our freedom, our reputation in Vitoria—he is planning to take our lives, and then he will stop killing. He said he is going to spend the rest of his life in Vitoria, as if nothing had happened."

"It's Mario, isn't it?" I asked, dripping with sweat as I attempted to snap the chain.

"Yes, Mario Santos, the journalist. Who would have ever guessed?"

"He still hasn't told you who he really is?"

Ignacio looked at me, bewildered.

"I don't know what you mean."

"Damn it, Ignacio, he's your brother. All this happened because of you, and twenty years later, you still haven't figured it out." I flushed with rage, unable to contain myself. "What Nancho, or Venancio Lopidana, told you at your mother's funeral was true— you are triplets. Mario is the red-haired kid you banished from Vitoria after you beat him half to death."

"What do you mean? The redhead? You have no idea how terrible I felt about what we did to that poor kid that day. It haunted me for years. One of the reasons I joined the police force was to atone for my sin, to ensure I would never harm another person.

And now you're telling me that the poor boy we almost killed is our triplet?"

"Ignacio," I interrupted, "you need to act like a policeman. Put that out of your mind, and listen. Did you hear a woman's voice? I think Mario must have brought DSU Alba Díaz de Salvatierra here. She's his wife. I believe he intends to kill her, and—"

"Ayala, look out!" cried Ignacio, but it was too late.

I felt an icy coldness in my neck. The injection Mario had given me was excruciating. It felt like frost bursting through my veins.

"And you, my friend." I recognized Mario's calm voice behind me. "I'm going to kill both Alba and you. Come on, up you go. She's ready and waiting for you."

Still reeling from the pain of the injection, I felt for my revolver, but he had already removed it from the holster and was pressing the barrel against my neck.

"Up you go, Unai," he said again.

The icy drug felt like a torrent coursing through my body. I had no way of knowing whether the Eguzkilore's potion was still in my system or whether it could block the effects of the Rohypnol Mario had just given me. In any case, I thought it best to act as if it was working. What were the effects of Rohypnol again?

Feeling hot and cold.

I trembled. My clothes were too much but scorched me as well.

Dizziness.

I stumbled up the stairs. Mario held on to me like a good friend, concerned in case I fell.

Loss of will.

Although I obeyed as meekly as a lamb, I was oddly aware of everything. It was as if my mind was focused on a point in space, like the Aleph in Borges's short story. The entire universe was contained within a tiny sphere.

We came to a partially covered yard, and Mario led me over to an open area. He stood facing me, the gun still aimed at my head. He was wearing a white beekeeper's suit with gloves and overshoes.

I noticed several beehives in the yard, but there was still no sign of Alba.

Until Mario stepped aside.

A big piece of plastic sheeting was on the ground in the center of the patio, flattening the weeds that were growing there. On top of it were two body bags, and across them lay Alba, naked, her mouth taped. She wasn't moving and appeared to be either unconscious or dead.

Mario's approach was professional—not a single fingerprint, no contact with the ground. Up in these hills, Mario had managed to create an environment so antiseptic we would have never found a single trace of DNA linking him to his crimes.

"Take off your clothes," said Mario, his voice flat. "Didn't you want to be with Alba? Well, she's all yours. You've earned her."

I didn't want to obey, and yet some of my muscles, almost involuntarily, did as he said. I dutifully removed my bulletproof vest and began to unbutton my shirt and pants.

And I didn't care. I didn't care, because Alba's lifeless body lay at my feet, and I wanted to lie down next to her. I wanted to have bees in my mouth and place a consoling hand on her cheek. I wanted to wait for nightfall, to search for a trace of the Perseids. Or maybe wait for next August 12, for a birthday I knew I would never celebrate.

Then, for some reason, I remembered my grandfather's final riddle: *Be the smartest creature on the mountain.* And the memory of that snake came to me clear as day. The snake that played dead on the path at Tres Cruces. Yet I was somehow incapable of keeping still, of playing dead. All I could do was submit to Mario's voice.

Was there part of me the Rohypnol had not yet taken over?

Difficulty talking and moving.

I wanted to get undressed and end it all, but my limbs refused to obey. I could hardly take off my black boxer shorts to lie down naked next to Alba.

The walls were spinning slightly, but I must have retained a measure of common sense or survival instinct because, when Mario drew near, an Unai rose from my unconscious and tried to take his gun.

I think the weight of my body was enough to make him fall backward, but he shot me. He shot me, and then I thought I saw Estí's flame-red hair firing at him in turn from the broken window on the second floor.

It was terrifying to see such a normal, friendly, well-educated, thoroughly nice guy take aim at your head and shoot. He shot me the way he might draw breath or drink coffee, the way he must have made love to Alba. It was just another aspect of his serene, tranquil, relaxed nature. The same nature that had seduced the woman I loved, the woman who was dying beside me, watching a sky without falling stars.

I think I remember the gun going off.

Then everything in my wounded brain turned to darkness and silence.

49

SANT IAGO

Saturday, August 27

There were no screams, no applause, no hysteria.

A city that boasted thirteen civic centers and 245,000 inhabitants wasn't going to lose its nerve.

A rally was organized for me the day before they switched off my life support, and throughout the silence was audible.

The people of Vitoria held hands and formed a human chain that started at the Old Cathedral, continued down past the Casa del Cordón, up to the balcony of San Miguel Arcángel Church, across Calle Dato, past El Caminante, and ended at the entrance to my apartment building at Number 2 Plaza de la Virgen Blanca, where all week members of the public had been leaving candles and bouquets of flowers.

Several international news helicopters hovered in the indigo skies above Vitoria, filming the string of tiny candles that my neighbors lit in unison. How splendid it must have looked from above, although I wasn't there yet.

Far from it.

Someone close to me, probably Estíbaliz, had let it slip that my favorite song was "Abrazado a la tristeza" by Extrechinato u Tú, and the loudspeakers in my square began to play the first verse—those words I had sung a billion times:

Arm in arm with sorrow I went outside,
Sad and ashamed to see what everyone else ignored.

My grandfather became something of a city legend. He didn't leave my side, he didn't eat, he didn't sleep, he wouldn't even drink water. The doctors realized that this man had taken root in the intensive care ward, and the only way he would leave was feetfirst.

"Leave me be," he said, whenever the authorities at Hospital de Santiago tried and failed to reason with him.

He stayed awake all night, telling me the stories he had regaled me with a thousand times when I was a child. The one about the whoremongering priest who left his umbrella at a brothel in Logroño, or the cousins from Teruel who recognized each other's voices above the whistle of bullets from the enemy trenches during the civil war and who forbade my grandfather and the others in their respective platoons to fire on pain of death . . .

But I was treading a much darker path. I saw no white light to guide me. Blackness was everywhere, and only the anesthetic saved me from dying of pain. I didn't see my parents, although I would have liked to, to say good-bye, and so they could see me as an adult. But there was no one amid the nothingness of death. Only the terrifying loneliness, the knowledge that there was no going back.

But Grandfather wasn't so sure. He was no stranger to the Grim Reaper—they had rubbed shoulders for a hundred years, and he allowed himself to play one last trick on death.

The day Germán went to Villaverde to tell him, voice breaking, that I had been shot in the head, that a bullet was lodged in my brain, that I was in a coma, and that even if I regained consciousness, I'd be a vegetable for the rest of my life, my grandfather hurried down to his vegetable garden with a basket to pick apples.

They arrived at the Hospital de Santiago, and Germán had to employ all his skills as a lawyer to convince the staff to allow the old man to enter my room with the basket of apples, a knife, and some string.

When he was alone with me, he stripped me naked, sliced the apples into quarters, and rubbed them all over my body, leaving a lingering aroma of cider in the sterile room.

Afterward, he asked Estíbaliz to drive him to Villaverde. It was dark already, but the moonlight was enough. No need for a flashlight. He went back to his vegetable garden and dug a grave to fit the contours of my body.

Then he sat down and patiently tied the quartered apples back together with string until they formed whole apples once more. Finally, he placed them in my empty tomb and buried them.

He determined that they would take ten days to rot. The earth he had heaped on them was good and damp.

"And hurry up about it, my grandson doesn't have much time," he told them, as he climbed into Estí's car to return to the hospital.

Ten days later I saw a path at my feet, bordered by the apple trees from my grandfather's garden. I followed it. In a way, I had been happy in the void—calm, relaxed, free from pressure, at peace, I think—and yet, when the path appeared before me, I knew I had to go back.

50

LAGUARDIA

Sunday, August 28

I woke up to find my hand clenched between my grandfather's giant veiny paws. Germán was asleep, his head resting on the edge of my sheets. Estíbaliz was at the foot of the bed. I watched her pace around like a cat for a while, waiting for the images to steady, for the mist to clear from my eyes.

I think I'm alive, I tried to tell them, but the words wouldn't leave my mouth.

For some reason, my mouth refused to obey; it wouldn't open. I couldn't utter the words.

I felt a stab of panic—what else was wrong with me, what else wasn't working? I moved my legs, fearing I might be paralyzed. But no, they obeyed, they moved. I threw my head back, relieved.

I think I wept, softly, noiselessly. I think I wept, but I couldn't be sure; I still wasn't completely in control of my body. I moved my imprisoned hand, and this roused Grandfather from his stupor.

Realizing my eyes were open, he straightened up, adjusted his beret, and crushed my hand in his vise-like grip, unaware of his strength.

"You took your time coming back, you little fox cub" was all he said, swallowing hard. I looked into his near-century-old eyes and saw his relief and joy. "I brought the little mountain amulet, in case you wanted to keep it."

I nodded and clasped it in my hand. I squeezed it harder to test my strength despite the little jagged peaks digging into my flesh. I let go when the pain got to be too much, but I was thrilled to be able to feel even pain.

Germán also woke up, clambered onto the bed, and flung his arms around me.

"Don't ever do that to me again," he whispered in my ear, soaking it with his tears.

Estíbaliz rushed to the side of the bed and pressed a button above my head, setting off a noisy alarm.

"In the nick of time, Unai. They were going to disconnect you today."

That won't be necessary, I tried to say, but once again I was unable to get out even those few words. For a few seconds, I panicked. We looked at each other, and I think she understood.

"Take it easy, Unai. Don't exert yourself. The doctors weren't expecting you to come out of the coma; they said that if you did, your speech would be affected. The bullet was lodged in the Broca's area, but they managed to remove it. A long and tricky operation, and you have a long recuperation ahead of you, my friend."

I looked at her in astonishment. Grandfather and Germán both squeezed my hand; it was their way of telling me, not for the first time: *We'll get through this.*

"I brought you something," Estí said tenderly, handing me a tablet with the text app open. "Try to write down what you're thinking."

Gingerly, I took the tablet. What else up there was malfunctioning? Would I be capable of writing, or would I have to give that up, too?

Fortunately, the synaptic connections between my brain and hand were still intact.

What happened to Mario, the twins, Alba, everybody? I wrote and showed it to Estí.

"I shot Mario when I saw him fire at you. He died instantly. The DNA from the saliva on the envelopes from *El Diario Alavés* matched his genetic fingerprint. We also found traces of his DNA in the shrine he created with the victims' clothes in Ochate. The prosecutor has issued an order to reopen the investigations into the fires in Izarra and at the hostel in Pamplona, as well as the eight murders for which Tasio was sent to prison."

How is Tasio? I wrote.

"Not good, Kraken. Mario held him captive for ten days with almost no water. He's been on the brink of multiple-organ failure a couple of times. His brother flew over the world's top specialists, but he's still in critical condition. Ignacio has recovered and is out of danger."

I picked up the tablet again and looked at the keyboard. Only four letters, but I had enormous difficulty typing them. Perhaps I was too fragile to have my fears about Alba's death confirmed. Was that why Estíbaliz hadn't mentioned her?

"Son, I need something to eat. Do you mind if I leave you to it?" said Grandfather.

I shook my head. I hadn't realized how haggard he looked. Germán planted a kiss on my forehead—somewhat embarrassingly, I felt, seeing that other people were in the room—and left with Grandfather. I noticed that they had both lost several pounds.

God, what have I put them through? I thought, feeling guilty.

Then it was just Estíbaliz and me.

Come over here, I need a hug, I wrote.

"Of course." She sighed and climbed up onto the hospital bed, laid her tiny frame down beside me, and embraced me. This woman had saved my life, possibly in more ways than one.

What happened to Alba? I ventured to write sometime later.

"It's unbelievable, Unai. What happened to our boss is unbelievable."

I looked at her, eager to hear yet at a loss.

"Her bastard of a husband drove her to Ochate, injected her with Rohypnol, then put the bees in her mouth and taped it shut. That's when he heard noises down below. When he saw she wasn't moving, he left her for dead and went after you. But Alba had eaten the bees, Kraken. She ate them before the Rohypnol could take effect. They stung her on the tongue and the inside of her lips, but they were dead before they reached her throat, so she avoided being asphyxiated. When Mario returned with you, the DSU continued to play dead."

So you were the smartest creature on the mountain, I thought.

She was alive.

Alba was alive.

Estíbaliz sighed and sat upright. "She offered to resign pending an investigation, but both the prosecutor and the commissioner are satisfied that there is no evidence to suggest she colluded with her husband. They believe that Mario Santos, or rather Nancho Urbina, used her to be able to follow the investigation from the inside and to monitor our activity. She has been granted a leave of absence, and the last I heard she was back in Laguardia, although she isn't on active duty."

Did she come to see me? I wrote.

"I don't think so."

Okay, don't worry. It's for the best, I wrote, but it didn't feel that way.

"Give her time, Unai. Not only did she just lose her husband, she was also married to the country's most notorious serial killer, and he tried to murder her and you. She has a lot to process."

Estí was right.

We had a lot to process.

And so, when they discharged me from the hospital, I moved back to Villaverde with Grandfather and Germán, to allow time to sort out the disorder in my damaged brain.

SAN TIRSO

MONDAY, OCTOBER 24

I spent the late summer in a daze, sticking to the routines Grandfather devised for me in his vegetable garden, drifting along.

The Criminal Investigation Unit insisted I attend daily sessions with a speech therapist. They said I couldn't go back to work until I was able to speak again, only I wasn't so sure I wanted to keep chasing criminals, or even to talk again.

The truth is I was all out of desires.

I didn't want anything. Just, for once, I wanted to float.

When the fall arrived, I spent my days picking brambleberries and sloe berries at the edges of the fields where the tractors hadn't sprayed herbicides.

I made so much jelly and sloe gin that I considered changing my career and selling my artisanal products at gourmet stores. Germán, who was keen for me to put aside guns and crime scenes, even helped me draw up a somewhat optimistic business plan.

One Monday in October I climbed San Tirso in what had become my weekly ritual—I would sit propped against the massive rock and take a nap. Occasionally, despite the morning frost, I would spend the night there.

From that peak I could see three provinces: to the north, spread out beneath my feet, were Navarrete, Villafría, Villaverde, Bernedo,

Urtri, and the Izki Nature Reserve. To the east was the region of Navarra. And if I turned toward the south, I could make out the Rioja Alavesa, and some of the larger towns, such as Elciego, Cripán, Yécora, and Laguardia.

Laguardia, a mere eight miles or so from Villaverde as the crow flies.

How close and yet how far away that seemed to me then!

I felt fine in my mountain paradise and had no wish to return to reality. I didn't want my life to go forward in any direction.

It was a call from Saioa, the granddaughter of the former hostel owner in Pamplona, that reminded me I had failed to keep a promise. I felt terrible. I had shaken the old man's hand on it, and then forgotten about him. The man who gave me the key to solving the case.

I wasn't in the habit of taking calls: I didn't see the point in remaining mute on the other end of the line, unable to reply, but when I saw her name come up on the screen, I automatically pressed the green icon, without thinking about the fact that no sound would emerge from my lips.

I stood up and stepped away from the rock, gazing down at the beechwood below.

"Inspector Ayala, this is Saioa, I hope you remember me."

By way of reply I gave a rather gruff grunt, but she didn't let it put her off, and continued talking.

"I'm calling to say that my grandpa was able to read about what happened to Nancho Lopidana and Mario Santos in the papers, and it was a huge relief to him. Grandpa died yesterday, but he asked me to thank you for having listened to him. I . . . I know you can't speak because of your gunshot wound, so I won't keep you any longer. Thank you for answering my call," she said, and hung up.

Sometimes it's as simple as listening. A lot of people get caught up in the circumstances surrounding a crime, and they could tell the police a great deal, if we would listen. We think we're the experts, but we don't know the people. We don't know the perpetrators or their victims. Those around them do.

Sometimes all you need to do is listen, I thought.

Maybe she won't care that I'm mute. Maybe all I have to do is listen.

And so, I called her. It must have been on a day when the south wind, the *hego Haizea*—the wind that drives men crazy—was blowing, because I would never have called her if I was in my right mind. What was the point when I couldn't speak?

I dialed Alba's number, focusing my gaze on the south side of the mountain.

"Unai, is that you?" replied a rather bewildered voice. "Can you speak?"

I didn't open my mouth. I didn't even try, partly out of embarrassment, partly because of how it felt to hear her voice after so long.

"Unai?"

I ended the call but opened WhatsApp before my silence made her uncomfortable. I was reading her words, but it felt as though I could almost hear her voice. As if she were there with me.

I wrote,

> Alba, it's best we communicate this way.
> I want to see you, okay?

She wrote,

> Maybe that isn't a good idea.
> We have too much unfinished business.

> Exactly.

> This is as good a medium as any. You first.

> If you insist. I'm still angry at you, Alba.
> The day we talked about my birthday in the
> Duende Underpass, you should have told me
> you were forty, too, and that you were on

the condemned list, just like me. But you
chose to hide it from me.

I've always taken care of myself. As you see,
I dealt with the bees.

That's not the point. The point is, you didn't
trust me. We've never enjoyed the kind of
trust couples share.

That's because we were never a couple.
I was married, Unai.

And now you're a widow,
like me, a widower.

Do you know his mother was named Blanca?
Ironic, isn't it?

All the more reason never to pretend you're
someone else again. Now you know what
it feels like to be with a person who leads
a double life.

Maybe I was a bit too harsh, but I had a lot of pent-up rage,
the toxic kind that turns your insides black.

He dyed his hair. Mario dyed his hair brown,
and I call myself a detective. I lived with him,
and yet I couldn't see what was right in front
of my eyes. You say psychopaths have no
emotions but can manufacture them. I was
married to someone incapable of having
feelings. I was going to have a child with him.

I'm not Mario. With me, what you see is what
you get. I do have emotions, maybe too
many, and right now my feelings are raw.

But Alba wasn't having a conversation with me; this was a monologue, a confession, an outpouring.

> He studied my notes at night, all the material
> I brought home while I was in training and
> after my promotions. He read everything,
> familiarized himself with our methods, soaked
> up every conversation he and I had about
> my work. My bad days, when I let off steam,
> were a mine of information for him. He
> convinced me to ask for a transfer to Vitoria,
> because Tasio was due to be released, and
> he was planning on carrying out the second
> phase of his revenge. I gave up my life, my
> friends, my town, simply because a murderer
> wanted to start killing again. All these years,
> I've been living a lie.

I read her long message and had to stop myself from tossing the cell phone down the mountain.

> It wasn't all a lie. I don't accept that.
> What you and I had was genuine. It still is.

> Listen to us, Unai. Listen to what we're saying.
> We're still too damaged. Right now, I need
> to figure things out in my head, do you
> understand that?

> No, but I accept it.

> You don't understand?

> I saw you dead.

> And I saw you die. I saw my husband
> shoot you.

Haven't we been through enough, Alba?
What more do you need?

Time.

There's nothing to stop us, no husband, nothing. I know how it feels to die, and I see things differently now. I'm tired of waiting for the perfect moment. It doesn't exist. Just let me say one thing: Don't give up your career because of what happened. Don't give him that satisfaction, and don't do it just so you won't have to see me. If you want to live your life without me, go ahead, but we can meet at work without hurting each other. We'll get used to it.

What a crude ploy to have her near me again.
She wrote,

Right now, I need time.

I was afraid she was entering a loop we'd never get out of.

Are you going to come
back to Vitoria to work?

I don't know.

I insisted.

May I visit you in Laguardia?

I'm standing at the top of San Tirso, I can see your town from here. If I had the eyesight of the eagle circling above me, I'd be able to see you now.

Will you be able to speak again?

I bridled.

> Careful, Alba. That's a sensitive subject.

You didn't answer me.

I wrote, irritated,

> Why are you asking?

**Because we're both still recovering. I need to
heal my wounds by myself, and so do you.
I don't want us to be together because we
need each other. If I decide to be with you,
it will be when you are whole again, healed,
when you have overcome this by yourself.
I don't want you to need me, and I don't
want to need you. We're both strong people;
we'll come back from this.**

I decided to clutch at these straws, even though they made me despair.

> OK, when I'm completely
> recovered, I'll find you.

But the awful truth was that I couldn't. Fall came and went. I gathered hazelnuts and became an expert at making *garrapiñadas*. I waited anxiously for chestnut season so that I could roast them on the fire with Grandfather and Germán.

As for my brain, I was afraid of taxing it too much. It felt fragile, and I was constantly aware of the entry wound. I hated seeing it in the mirror, and let my hair grow to hide the scar, so that I didn't look like something out of a freak show.

How ironic that it would be the Ortiz de Zárate twins who would be responsible for remedying the situation.

KRAKEN'S CITY

THURSDAY, NOVEMBER 10

That afternoon it didn't rain. All week long it had been coming down in buckets, although I didn't mind. Rain didn't bother me, it was just clean water making my clothes wet. Still, I took advantage of the lull to work in the vegetable garden, next to the giant pear tree.

"There's someone here to see you," I heard Grandfather say behind me.

"Who is it?" I gestured with my head.

With Grandfather, I didn't need to write. He and I had developed a unique language that consisted of frowns and tilts of the head that only we could understand, and it worked like a charm.

"One of the two foxes. And in his mother's car," he added.

"I don't want to see anyone." I shook my head.

"And all of Álava knows that. But he refuses to leave. Should I fetch my shotgun?"

I shrugged. What did I care? As if that would deter him.

So I followed Grandfather up to the house and reluctantly climbed the steps. He was waiting for me in the old kitchen, warming his hands by the fire.

Amazing what three months as a free man can do, I wrote on the tablet, by way of greeting.

The Tasio in front of me looked identical to the Ignacio of recent years. He had gained weight, fixed his teeth, and was wearing a blue shirt that gave him a fresh, clean-cut look. The suit he had on beneath his Barbour jacket must have cost what I earned in a year. He had become an attractive man again, although Grandfather couldn't have been too impressed, because I could hear him loading the shotgun, just to be on the safe side.

"It's okay, Grandpa." I nodded.

"We did it, Kraken. We got him," Tasio declared triumphantly.

He was different. Tasio was a different man. Now he had a hearty laugh, relaxed gestures, and a frank expression. He had stopped being terrifying. In fact, if he had been a woman, the only thing on my mind right then would have been how to get him into bed. Repeatedly, if possible.

You were never a drug addict. You were just a chameleon, a brilliant masquerader, I wrote.

Tasio ignored my remark. It was as if he had well and truly left his twenty-year stint in jail behind.

"I'm going to LA, to get away for a while. HBO has commissioned a new screenplay. We're looking into the possibility of fictionalizing everything that took place here in Vitoria. Right from the beginning. My attorney, Garrido-Stoker, will be in touch with you to discuss the adaptation of your character. Don't worry, Kraken. I won't take any artistic license. I just want to tell the story."

What are you going to call it?

"The Silence of the White City."

How does it feel to know that the killer was your triplet?

"We destroyed his life, and he destroyed ours. There's a kind of justice to it. I've made my peace with him. Ignacio is struggling; he feels bad about what we did to him."

It'll do you good to get away, I wrote, showing him the screen.

"Yes, I still get strange reactions from people in Vitoria. Kids ask me for my autograph, but their mothers yell at them and snatch the paper away before I can finish. It's a little unnerving. They're still scared of me. A whole generation has grown up thinking I'm the Sacamantecas."

You never give up, do you?

"What do you mean?"

Trying to woo the people of Vitoria so they fall in love with you again.

"Everything will be as it was before, just you wait. I'll walk down Calle Dato and people will greet me with a smile."

I nodded, just to humor him.

He wanted his throne back. That had always been his chief motivation.

"But it won't happen overnight, and the sooner I leave, the sooner my exile will end. I came to say good-bye, Kraken."

What about your twin?

"He's coming with me, of course. Being apart for twenty years and five months felt totally unnatural. It won't happen again."

Of course. Have you settled your differences, then?

"Differences? He's my twin. There are no differences to settle. He's here with me, taking a stroll around the village. Do you want me to call him?"

Okay. I nodded.

A few minutes later, Ignacio appeared in the kitchen doorway.

"Look what the cat dragged in," I thought I heard Grandfather mutter behind me, still clasping his shotgun.

Ignacio embraced me warmly, oozing charm and smiles. The truth is that the two of them together were dazzling; you couldn't take your eyes off them.

For God's sake, you're identical, I wrote.

They laughed as one, like a double-headed hydra, enjoying their game of mirrors.

Suddenly, it dawned on me. I don't know why; clearly the profiler in my head was still switched on.

You tried to pull a fast one on me. You're Ignacio, and you, damn it, you're Tasio, I wrote.

They exchanged a flustered glance.

"You're the first one to . . ." Ignacio began.

". . . catch on since we left the hospital. Obviously we're out of practice. Well played, Kraken," said Tasio.

"By the way, we brought you an invitation from Vitoria City Hall . . ." Ignacio added.

". . . and there are others, from a bunch of other associations, among them the Brigada de la Brocha of old MatuSalem," Tasio concluded, winking at me.

I don't want any official ceremonies, I wrote, shaking my head.

"Tell us something we don't know. Come on, let people spoil you a bit. This city has been living in a state of fear for twenty years . . ." said Ignacio.

". . . what it needs now is a fiesta, to help people externalize that fear and accept that it's all over. Do it for your neighbors. They need to celebrate the fact that you're still alive," said Tasio.

I attended the ceremony reluctantly. I felt uncomfortable shaking hands with all those people without being able to talk or respond in a normal way. Grandfather had persuaded me, using only slightly less dramatic methods than his shotgun. He, Germán, and Estí accompanied me. We all felt a little alarmed when the city's top officials and their fake smiles surrounded us in the Plaza de la Virgen Blanca. Then they made us march all the way down Calle de la Correría, the old guild street behind my apartment building.

I knew we'd arrived at our destination when we reached the bottom of Cantón de la Soledad, the hill that, until a few months ago, I used to run up at dawn, in another life, when I still went jogging, hoping to meet . . . What did I care? What did I care?

A huge crowd was gathered there. Neighbors, my *cuadrilla,*

reporters, people I didn't know who greeted me as if they were my friends. I responded with a grin, slightly overwhelmed. The necktie Germán had bought me was too tight, and I didn't feel good about my hair. Maybe my scar was too visible.

"Turn around, Unai," said Estí. "The people of Vitoria want to honor you."

I turned and saw that the facade of the old building was painted with a mural I'd never seen before.

"They've called it *Kraken's City.*"

And it was true: a gigantic Kraken with tentacles that looped around everything—the Witch's Lair dolmen, the ancient settlement of La Hoya, the Valle Salado at Añana, Vitoria's medieval wall, the Old Cathedral, the Casa del Cordón, the balcony of La Virgen Blanca, El Caminante statue . . .

They had also written a few words, the final verse of "Abrazado a la tristeza":

> *I feel sad when people admire bravery in battle.*
> *It's a good thing they can't kill words with guns.*

I swiveled around, my body tingling with emotion, too overcome to handle all those people anticipating my response. It was then that I saw her.

I saw her.

In the crowd.

Alba's black braid.

Staring at me with her intense gaze, responding to the questions my eyes shot at her, she was there. She had kept her part of the bargain.

It's a good thing they can't kill words with guns, I told myself.

That day I decided it was time for me to start talking again.